ACROSS THE RIVER

Richard Snodgrass

Furnass — The Civil War Years

Pittsburgh

Published by Calling Crow Press
Pittsburgh, Pennsylvania

Book design by Book Design Templates, LLC
Cover Design by Jack Ritchie

Printed in the United States of America
ISBN 978-0-9997699-1-1
Library of Congress catalog control number: 2018907761

For Ron Hokanson, or maybe Lane;
and, as with all things,
for Marty

It occurred to me if I could invent a machine—a gun—which could by its ra-pidity of fire, enable one man to do as much battle duty as a hundred, that it would, to a great extent, supersede the necessity of large armies, and conse-quently, exposure to battle and disease be greatly diminished.

Richard Jordan Gatling

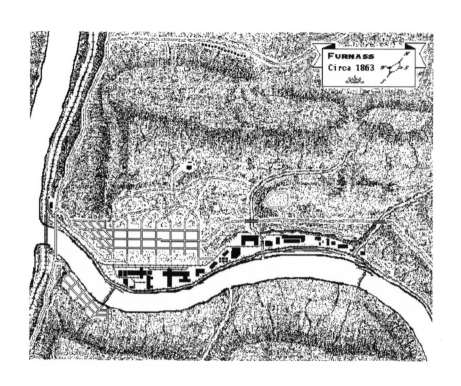

FURNASS

Circa 1863

ONE

In early summer of 1863, two riders—two Confederate horsemen, the one in the lead dressed in a Yankee cavalry officer's uniform, the one behind in a dark broadcloth suit and derby hat—made their way down the steep slope of a valley in enemy territory. Afternoon sunlight cracked through the branches overhead. The Western Pennsylvania hills were thick with trees, white oak and maple and hickory, a hundred shades of green, softening the contours of the valley, belying the abrupt shale cliffs and sandstone bluffs. Even in shade, the day was hot and dry. The two men were covered with dust, their clothes prickly; small insects circled them like auras. Through openings in the trees were glimpses of a town downstream on the other side of the valley. A massive ironworks, smoke roiling from the tall stacks, drifting over the river. Among the sounds of the horses breaking their way down through the brush, the twittering birds, was a distant rumbling, an undertone like cannonade, coming from the mill.

"I don't know where you think you're taking us," Reid said, following behind the other. "The town's back there. Why do you want to circle around and come at it from this direction? I say we're here, let's get on with it."

I say if you don't shut up and let me do my job I'm going to knock you one, Judson Walker thought. But he didn't say anything. He guided his horse between two red maples and continued to descend the face of the valley wall. The roan hunkered down, sliding at times on its rump down the steep sections of the slope. Walker gave over the reins, deciding the horse knew more what to do at this point than he did. Down through the brush and the trees.

Walker was a tall angular man, with a long face, deep-set eyes, a full black mustache; in his late thirties, a little old perhaps for this sort of mission. The left sleeve of his jacket hung limp, his arm inside the jacket pressed tight against his body. Despite the Yankee uniform, he was a captain of the Second Kentucky Cavalry, Confederate States of America. One of Morgan's raiders. A bullet had grazed his side under his left arm when they ran into a Yankee patrol near Wheeling the day before. The wound didn't seem serious, the bleeding had finally stopped, but it was starting to hurt more and his left side was tightening up again, the muscles pulling whenever he moved his arm, the arm itself as if crippled. He wanted to take a look at the wound, but he didn't have anything to change the dressing with; he'd have to wait until they got to the town. Near the base of the slope the roan took two last steps and leapt to a halt on the bank of the river. The jolt sent a wave of new pain through Walker. He patted, rubbed the horse's neck.

"It's okay, girl, you're okay, we made it, steady on now."

Behind him came the sound of Reid's horse crashing down through the brush, along with a groan. Walker turned in the saddle, still steadying the roan; the young man coming down the slope was hanging on to the pommel with both hands, his eyes wide. The big gray gelding slid to a stop beside Walker.

"Christ, Walker, you're going to get us both killed!"

"Just you, from the looks of it," Walker said. Turning around had pulled his side and he didn't smile.

Jonathan Reid was in his late twenties; he was slight in comparison to someone the height of Walker, and his close-cropped red hair and goatee might have seemed pixyish except for the coldness in his blue eyes and his tight-set mouth. As soon as Reid had caught his breath, Walker led them along an old Indian trail close to the river, among the willows and sycamores along the bank, to the mouth of a small stream. The branches of the willows slanted out over the shallow water, shielding the two men from anyone across the river. Walker dismounted slowly with the pain, stripped to his drawers and socks, and plopped himself down, sitting unceremoniously in a foot of water.

"Might as well wash these drawers while I'm at it. How about you? You getting undressed, or are you thinking of dunking your suit?"

Reid, watching with a kind of disgust, turned his horse and rode a little ways upstream behind some bushes; in a few minutes Walker heard him splashing in the water. The two men rested— out of sight of each other—until their clothes were dry and evening started to come on, then mounted up again. As they emerged from the willows along the river, Walker held up his hand.

"Just so we both know what we're doing. If anyone asks questions or says anything to us on the way going in, I do all the talking. They'd spot your Southern accent a mile off."

"And you think your'n is that much better?" the young man said, readjusting his derby hat.

Don't fight me, son, ain't nobody going to come out of this alive that way.

"We'll see Lyle at his house tonight," Walker went on wearily. "I want as few people around as possible the first time we talk to him. We don't know who else has contacted him, or what else is going on. We might be stepping into something we don't want any part of. And if he gets wind of who we really are, he may not take it too kindly. Some people get funny ideas when they're asked to become traitors to their country."

"Can we just get on with it?" Reid said, looking impatiently downriver toward the town.

"None of this is open for discussion. I'm in charge, and I'm telling you how it's going to be. It's my job to get you here safely and to keep you safe while you're here, and I'm going to do it the best way I see fit."

Reid looked at him with a little smile as if to say, We'll see about that.

Why do I even bother? Walker thought. Because that's what I was sent here to do.

"And if there's trouble, you get the hell out of there as fast as you can. Don't wait around for me. Just do what you did at Wheeling, turn tail and run, this time it's appropriate. We'll meet up back here. If I'm not here within a day, it means you're on your own."

"I'm sure I'll manage."

Walker cocked his head. "You know, don't you, that if you get caught, they'll hang you for a spy. Same as me."

"I'm not a spy. I'm an engineer."

"Somehow subtleties like that are lost on hangmen."

Downriver, a crow called raucously from a treetop, swaying up and down on a branch that was too thin for its weight. I know how you feel, bird, Walker said to himself. Still, it could be a good sign. He looked out over the shallow river, the trees on the other side, the glimpse of the road a little ways up the slope. When he was sure it was clear, he motioned them forward. "Slow, now. Just like regular folks."

The river was shallow at this time of year, only a few feet deep, even here backed up behind the falls. Dusk came early to the valley. The sun was beyond the hills; the valley was already in afterglow, though the sky remained an intense blue, a sense that beyond the ridge it was still light and sunny somewhere else. Free of the trees and the cover of the bank, Walker knew they were exposed, vulnerable, but there was no help for it. On the opposite bank he led them along the railroad tracks until they came to a dry creek bed the horses could manage up the steep slope. When they gained the main road, they continued on toward the town, two ordinary travelers, coming down the valley from the north. The way his family used to, to get supplies for their farm farther upriver, when Walker was a boy here.

In a few miles the forest gave way to hardscrabble farms, a house here and there among apple and cherry orchards. Then the shelf of land ended and the valley widened with the winding of the river. The town sat within the S-curve of the river, the Allehela, before the valley opened to the wider valley of the Ohio River, ten miles or so downstream from Pittsburgh. The main street of the town cut across the face of the hillside; the rest of the town was scattered about the lower half of the slope, clusters of buildings as if the townspeople couldn't decide where to build and hoped to fill in the blank spaces later. Walker thought of the names they had for Northerners back in Kentucky: pasty-faced mechanics, crop-eared Puritans. The town had changed, grown considerably in thirty years. He remembered a few cabins tucked away among the trees, a main street with only a half dozen buildings, an old iron furnace and a gristmill at the north end of town. Now the large brick buildings of the Buchanan Iron Works stretched for a mile along the river—blast furnaces, a rolling mill, foundries, a host of other shops—domineering the town, as if the town climbed the slopes in an attempt to get away from it, and couldn't. Thick black smoke plumed from dozens of smokestacks, one nearly a hundred feet tall; along the river, steam billowed from slag and hot coals dumped down the bank; the air was full of the smells of sulfur and burning ash and hot metal. There was the sound of machinery, a constant rumbling and throbbing accented by the ring of metal against metal. In the growing darkness, the mill flickered orange and red from the glow of the furnaces, the rows of coke ovens.

"The Keystone Steam Works is down there somewhere," Walker said, nodding toward the far end of town. "Closer to the falls, and the Ohio."

"It's beautiful," Reid said, awestruck at the mill. "It's almost as large as the Tredegar Works in Richmond. And this is only supposed to be one of their medium-sized mills. I hope I can get a look inside."

You've got a strange idea of beauty, son, Walker thought. The two men rode on. The lamps were lit along the streets; lamplight glowed in the windows of the houses. There were families on their front porches, strollers along the wooden sidewalks, everyday life going on. The war far away, or so they think, it occurred to Walker. In a backyard a pregnant woman gathered in her clothes from the line. For an instant, Walker thought of Mattie, wondered if she was all right, if she had had the baby. For an instant he wondered why Morgan chose him for this mission. To escort the young engineer to this particular valley. Walker was certain he never said anything about growing up here, he was too ashamed to have ever been a Yankee. Coincidence? The other possibility, that there was a good chance whoever came here wouldn't return, he brushed out of his thoughts.

There was a commotion at the corner ahead of them, the cry of a horse and somebody yelling; behind them men came running from between the buildings, rushing toward them in the dusk. Walker reached for his revolver but his horse reared before he could pull it from the holster; the men ran past them, on down the street. There was an accident on the hill, men struggled to untangle a couple of wagons and free a wagoner from under a load of iron. Walker had the gun in his hand.

"Put that away, Walker," Reid said. "Your anxiousness to shoot somebody just about got us found out."

Walker glared at him but decided to let it pass. "It's up there," he said brusquely and spurred his horse up the hill.

Jonathan Reid watched the other brush by him, Walker's horse nudging his own horse out of its way, on up the hill, the captain's figure blending quickly into the dusk. Reid took one more look at the fiery spectacle of the mills at the bottom of the hill, his heart as full of excitement and longing as schoolboy's, before following after the other horseman. Certainly, Captain Walker, you're in charge. For now.

He didn't like Walker, didn't trust him—not his loyalty, necessarily, but his intelligence, his rationality. There were times during their journey here when the captain acted reckless, even crazed. When they crossed the Ohio below Wheeling and happened upon a Yankee patrol in the midst of eating lunch, Reid fled, as any sane man would do, but Walker flew at the dismounted troopers, chasing the militiamen into the woods and scattering their horses—and in the process getting himself wounded. Such mindless heroics almost cost them the mission. Walker typified everything Reid hated and wanted to change about the South—the backwoods mentality, the backwater view of the world. Rustics could be little better than animals; it made them brave certainly—it could even send them screaming like banshees across battlefields such as Manassas and Shiloh to win short-lived glories—but it also made them foolish. Such homespun thinking would keep the South from assuming its rightful place among the other civilized nations of the world. Reid was very much aware that, if the Confederacy had any long-term hope of survival, it required men of quality and intelligence who understood all the changes that made up the modern world. Men like Jonathan Reid.

On the hillside above the town, the streets turned quickly into roads, then to little more than double-tracked paths, crisscrossing the face of the slope between the clusters of houses. Sycamore House sat isolated on a stretch of ground above the rest of the town, halfway up the hill. It was a large imposing structure with a number of peaked roofs and a long veranda across the front; the house appeared a jumble of additions and mismatched styles, Gothic Revival, Norman, and Romanesque, though the ivy that covered the front and sides obscured the details of the structure. There were no lights in the windows, and in the darkness, the closer they got, the more the ivy-covered house seemed to blend into the dark trees in the backyard, the dark woods on the hillside.

"We should have come earlier," Reid said.

"I doubt if they're asleep already," Walker said. "And if nobody's home now, chances are there was nobody home earlier."

Walker dismounted and tied his horse to the picket fence. Reid hurried to catch up as Walker went through the gate and started across the gentle slope of the lawn. When they reached the front steps of the house, a figure appeared from the shadows of the porch.

"Can I help you, Captain?"

Walker stopped, blocking Reid from going any farther. "We're looking for a Mr. Lyle. Colin Lyle."

"And what would a representative of the Federal Army want with him? Especially at his home, and at this hour of the night?"

"Allow me to introduce myself," Reid said, taking a step forward. "My name is Jonathan Reid. This is Captain Walker. We're here on some very important business." He added, "Government business."

"I don't know what we have to talk about. I don't have any government contracts right now."

Reid was overjoyed to hear it, but was careful not to let it show. "We're hoping to rectify that situation. We have a proposal to make to you that I think you'll find most interesting."

In the darkness and the shadows of the porch, all Reid could make out was the dim figure of a man in a waistcoat, the sleeves of his white shirt ghostly as if a pair of disembodied arms. Lyle seemed to find something amusing.

"Well, you must think it's important to come all the way up here in the dark."

"I assure you it's very important," Walker said.

Reid wanted Walker to stay out of it; Walker wouldn't know how to talk to a man of this caliber. "I think you'll be very interested in what we want to talk to you about. It involves a new way to use steam engines, a way they've never been used before. It will introduce a whole new era, it will change the way people think about machines. You're the only man I know of with the intelligence and foresight to understand a project of this magnitude."

Lyle laughed. "I hope your offer has more substance to it than your attempts at flattery. But now that you're here I might as well listen to what you have to say. Welcome, gentlemen."

Lyle extended his hand; Reid made sure that he was first up the steps to take it. Something stirred in the dark along the porch. There was a flash, and something caught fire: the glow of a lamp. In the circle of light, a woman in a black dress replaced the chimney of the lamp, got up from where she was sitting, and carried the lamp toward them. In her other hand was a Colt revolver but it wasn't pointed at them.

"My wife, Elizabeth," Lyle said. "As you can see, she's the cautious type."

"We saw you coming up the hill," the woman said, nodding to Walker and Reid in turn. "You can't be too careful these days, what with all the talk of spies and invasion."

"That's a good way to get yourself hurt, ma'am," Walker said. "If you're not sure how to use a gun like that."

"Thank you for your professional advice, Captain. But I know perfectly well how to use it. A woman is just as capable of pulling a trigger as a man."

"Libby can aim well too, Captain, as you just witnessed," Lyle said, bemused. "Let's go inside."

Lyle took the lamp from his wife and led the way, through the vestibule and down the front hall to his study. As they waited for Lyle to light a couple more lamps, Reid felt awkward; he stood in the center of the room, nervously touching his fingertips to his mouth, spreading his fingers repeatedly to smooth the hairs of his mustache along his lip. He didn't know quite what he expected of Lyle, but he felt somewhat disappointed now that they were here. Lyle was a tall man in his early fifties, bald except for a circle of hair like a tonsure, with full sideburns that swept down his cheeks and arced up under his nose. The room was comfortably furnished, not lavish—overstuffed chairs, gilt-framed paintings and shelves of books, Oriental carpets overlapping on the floor. Maybe that was part of Reid's uneasiness, somehow it seemed too comfortable, too ordinary. Somehow it didn't fit the image of a man of genius that Reid carried in his mind.

"Captain, you've been wounded," Libby said. "There's blood on your jacket."

Walker was embarrassed. "It's not serious. I just need to take a look at it, if I could. . . ."

"My apologies, Captain Walker," Lyle said. "I assumed your arm was the result of an old injury."

"How did it happen?" Libby said.

Walker and Reid looked at each other. Reid was at a loss, his mind gone blank.

"We ran into some trouble yesterday," Walker said. "Bushwhackers. Probably Rebel scouts."

"It doesn't surprise me," Lyle said. "The papers are full of Lee's invasion in the eastern part of the state. And there's talk that Morgan is headed for Ohio."

Reid wanted to ask for more information, but Walker spoke up quickly. "I think these men were just lost. We happened on them and took them by surprise."

"That doesn't change the fact that you're wounded and you need looked after," Lyle said.

"I don't want to be any trouble. . . ."

"Captain Walker, you need to realize that for my wife you're the answer to a prayer. She's felt terribly left out of the war and the other great events of our day. She's not the type to be content with knitting socks and tearing up old clothes for bandages with the other good ladies of our town. You're giving her the chance to have a real-live soldier to nurse, all for her very own. It's her dream come true."

"Come along, Captain Walker," Libby said, taking hold of the empty sleeve of his jacket. "As you can tell, Mr. Lyle takes great delight in mocking me. It's the only way he's found to deal with me. I've found the only way to deal with him is to ignore him. Which I'll continue to do." She towed Walker from the room by the dangling sleeve as if he were on a lead.

Lyle watched them fade into the shadows of the room and away along the dark hall; he picked absently at a spot on his bald head and become suddenly withdrawn. Reid couldn't contain himself any longer.

"Mr. Lyle, I've come to talk to you about the machine you call the road engine."

It took Lyle a moment to return from his thoughts. Then he smiled ironically and sat down in one of the horsehair-covered chairs, waiting for Reid to go on.

Yes. Now is my chance. Now.

There was a glow at the end of the dark hallway. In the darkness her skirts rustled busily, and Walker could smell her—he recognized lilacs. Libby led him into the kitchen where a mulatto woman sat at the table, darning a sock in the glow of a lamp.

"Sally, get us some water and some material for a bandage," Libby said.

For a moment Sally seemed unable to move. She stared at Walker as if she were witnessing an apparition.

"Go on, Sally," Libby said. "Do as you're told and get what I asked you to. And be quick."

As Walker sat down at the table, Sally got up and backed away, still holding the sock that she had been working on. Then she tucked the sock under her apron and disappeared into the shadows of the pantry.

"You seem to have made quite an impression on Sally," Libby said. "It will be interesting to see what she brings back, if she comes back at all."

Libby was a delicate, fine-boned woman in her mid- or late thirties, with deep circles under her eyes, dark enough to be dirtied or bruised, and a wide mouth that seemed on the verge of either laughing or crying. Her skin had the quality of china that you could see through if held to the light. Her sleek black hair was parted in the middle and pulled back; her paleness contrasted with her black dress buttoned high at the neck, cuffed tightly at the wrists. Here in the kitchen, when she spoke to either him or Sally, her voice seemed to carry a touch of a Southern accent;

Walker wondered if his ears were playing tricks on him, if he only imagined it from his exhaustion.

"I could use some whiskey too, if you have it," Walker said.

"This is a good Christian home, Captain Walker. Mr. Lyle's religion is very strict on the evils of spirits and tobacco, as well as a host of other things. He would be deeply grieved to hear that you thought we might keep such instruments of the devil in this house."

"I'm sorry, ma'am, I didn't mean to offend. . . ."

"However, you happen to be in luck," Libby said as she went over to a cupboard. "We do keep some brandy here in the kitchen, for emergencies only, of course."

"Miss Elizabeth," Sally said, returning with some clean cloths and a pan for water.

"Wonders never cease," Libby said to Walker. She brought the brandy and a glass to the table. "You needn't worry, Sally. I'm sure Captain Walker will help us keep our little kitchen secret."

"My lips are sealed," Walker said.

"Captain Walker is undoubtedly used to keeping a lot of secrets. Aren't you, Captain Walker?"

Walker tensed, wondering if she was trying to draw him out. She bustled around the kitchen, a faint smile on her face as she got a pair of scissors and a knife from a drawer. After Sally drew a pan of water from the pump outside and brought it to the table, she returned again to the shadows of the pantry. Libby reached across Walker to pour a glass of brandy; she seemed aware that he was watching her but was careful not to acknowledge him. Then she raised up abruptly and looked at him straight on.

"What? What are you staring at?"

Walker felt himself color. "Nothing. I mean, why did you say that about keeping secrets?"

"Oh that," she said and placed her hand to her breast. "Well, it's true, isn't it? We all have secrets about ourselves. And I would think that you probably have more secrets than most."

"Such as?"

"Such as why a captain in the Union cavalry would have a Southern accent."

She didn't seem to be challenging him, only curious; she cocked her head as she waited to hear what he had to say. But Walker was unnerved, he thought he'd been able to eliminate any trace of an accent. When he didn't respond right away, she prattled on as she arranged the things on the table close to him.

"It's not much of an accent, certainly, most people probably wouldn't notice it at all. I'm sure Mr. Lyle didn't, any more than he would recognize Mr. Reid's—Mr. Lyle tends to be oblivious to much of what goes on around him. But I have a good ear for accents—I'd say yours is from the border states. I'm sorry if I made you feel uncomfortable."

"I'm just surprised. I was about to ask you how a Yankee industrialist came to be married to a Southern belle."

She tipped her head as if to acknowledge a score. "Touché, Captain Walker. Very good. And thank you for the compliment, I don't think of myself as fitting into the 'belle' category at my age. But I asked you first."

"Kentucky," Walker said. He was thinking about the maid, Sally, and where she had gone; he was wondering if Libby had said something to her and she had gone for help; he was considering escape routes, how to get back to the horses. . . .

"South Carolina," Libby said, lapsing into a deep Southern drawl as she gave a small curtsy. "A planter's daughter, kind sir, if you-all must know." Then the accent was gone just as quickly. "If Mr. Lyle had his way, he'd probably have me speak in those sweet Southern tones all the time. I think they remind him of the days long ago when we first met. But that's neither here nor there. We need to have a look at your wound."

She started to unbutton his tunic but Walker pulled back.

"My, the captain is modest. I would think you'd like a woman fussing over you."

"Well, I don't. I can get it myself."

Walker's mind was racing. It was crazy to be here like this, getting undressed in an unfamiliar kitchen with this woman hovering over him. He had no way of knowing what was happening with Reid, no way of knowing that it wasn't a trap, Yankee soldiers could burst in on them at any moment. Still, he knew that he needed to change the dressing on the wound, and he couldn't see any alternatives without making more of a scene. He took a large swallow of brandy and removed his jacket.

He had torn up his shirt to use for the bandage; his braces cut across his bare skin. The bandage was stiff with dried blood. As he unwound the strips, the cloth stuck to the scab on his side and fresh blood seeped around the edges as he pulled the bandage loose. Libby gasped and her knees gave way.

Walker jumped up and grabbed her as she tried to steady herself against the back of a chair. Sally emerged from the shadows of the pantry and rushed to her side.

"Here, Miss Elizabeth," Sally said. "That's my job. You've got no business bothering yourself with things like this."

"Oh dear, I'm afraid I've made a fool of myself."

"Are you all right?" Walker said.

"Yes, yes, I'll be fine. Just let me rest a moment. . . ."

Walker supported her as he pulled out the chair so she could sit down. He hadn't realized before how slender she was; she felt small, almost fragile, in his hands, as if instead of her body within the layers of dark clothes, he could feel the framework of bones inside her skin. Libby sat ramrod straight, blinking, as if willing herself strong again.

"You sit back down there," Sally said to Walker. "If there's any nursing to be done around here, I'll do it."

She was Libby's age, with a broad, open face and full lips, liquid brown eyes and curls of soft brown hair framing her face. In the lamplight, her skin was the color of melted butter. She was wearing a brightly colored dress with large red and yellow and green vertical stripes and a lace collar at the neck. Her hoopskirt tilted against his legs, ballooning this way and that as she worked around him; Libby's black skirts hung straight, full from the layers of crinolines, but without the fashionable hoops inside.

The wound was clean and healing properly. Walker was relieved; at least that was one thing he didn't have to worry about. As Sally washed off the dried blood, she watched Walker's face, not for signs of pain but as if she were trying to read something from it. Before she wrapped a fresh bandage around the wound, Walker had another drink of brandy, then took the bottle and poured some over his side. It burned more than he expected; he tried not to let it show.

"I think I could use a little brandy myself about now," Libby said and poured some in the glass. She drank it down in two swallows. Sally stopped to watch her, then continued bandaging the wound. Libby held the empty glass in her lap as if it were a memento.

"You really should have that wound looked at by a doctor. We have a good friend, Dr. McArtle. . . ."

"No, this will be fine," Walker said.

"I feel I should do something for you. I'm certainly useless as a nurse. Thank you for helping him, Sally."

"I'm not helping him," Sally said. "I'm helping you. Besides, I don't want him dripping blood all over my nice clean floor."

After helping him get his good arm back into the sleeve of his jacket, Sally stepped back, searching his face again. For a brief instant Walker thought she looked like a madwoman, her eyes tormented, filled with rage. Then she moved out of the circle of the lamp again, back into the shadows.

Libby put the empty glass on the table and stood up quickly. "Well. I guess that takes care of that. Do you need anything else? Are you or Mr. Reid hungry?" Before he could reply, she leaned close to him, taking his good arm and speaking softly. "I have a favor to ask you. Please don't say anything to Mr. Lyle about my little fainting episode, will you? He would never let me hear the end of it. It will be another one of our secrets. Agreed?"

Then she was gone from the room, out the door and down the hallway. Walker stumbled after her in the darkness, his boot heels dragging on the runner, back toward the lights in the study. Reid glared at them for interrupting, but Lyle was obviously glad to see them, rising from his chair. Libby went over to her husband and hugged him around the waist, wrapping her arms around him as if he were a tree trunk, looking back at Walker.

"I was just saying to Captain Walker that we have plenty of room and would be delighted to have him and Mr. Reid stay here at Sycamore House. That way you gentlemen can talk to your hearts' content about your precious machinery."

"I was about to make the same invitation," Lyle said to Reid. "I think we need to continue this conversation tomorrow after you've had some time to rest from your journey. And I can take you down to the steamworks and show you the road engine in person."

"That's very kind," Reid said, looking at Walker, "but I believe Captain Walker—"

"Thank you for your hospitality," Walker said. "We'd be happy to accept."

"I'll have Sally get your things," Libby said. As she did so, Sally appeared in the doorway carrying the valises from Walker's and Reid's saddles.

"I thought you might be needing these. And I already told my George to take the horses out to the stable and feed them."

"Well then, it's settled," Lyle said. "You can't argue with the women in this house, gentlemen. I've learned that from experience. You just go along with whatever it is they say."

Reid was staring at Walker, bewildered.

"That's the most intelligent thing I've heard Mr. Lyle say in a long time, isn't it Sally?" Libby took one of the lamps and brushed between Walker and Reid on her way toward the front hall. "Perhaps you'll be here long enough to join our Tuesday Night Entertainments. We could certainly use some fresh voices and talent. Come along, I'll show you to your rooms."

Reid shook hands with Lyle—Walker only nodded, in deference to holding his arm—and they followed Libby, preceding them in a circle of light up the front staircase. Sally and their bags had disappeared. At the top of the stairs, Libby held a finger to her lips and pointed to doorways at one end of the hall.

"The childrens' rooms," she whispered, and led them down the hall in the opposite direction. She stopped in front of two doors at the far end of the house.

"I trust you'll both be very comfortable. And safe." She leaned close to them and spoke intensely as if to share a secret. "The only ambush anyone runs into in this house is in their dreams. Good night."

She gave the lamp to Walker and looked at him a moment, a trace of a smile on her lips, as if there were something else she wanted to say to him but didn't quite know what it was. Then she whirled around and faded out of the lamplight, back up the hallway, her stiff skirts rustling. She's drunk, Walker thought, or at least tipsy. He wondered if Lyle would notice, and what her husband would think.

"What the hell's going on?" Reid hissed.

Walker nodded for him to go on into the room. Reid's valise was sitting on the bed. Reid lit the lamp on the dresser and confronted Walker.

"You were the one who said you didn't want to stay here at the house. Then you turn around and accept their invitation. What's going on?"

"Keep your voice down. Things are working out differently than I expected. How are you getting along with Lyle?"

"Fine. Everything's going fine." Reid became animated, boyish. "I only told him a little bit of the overall idea, but he's interested. Very interested, I can tell. Tomorrow, if the road engines look like they can do the job, I'll talk to him about the structural modifications we need to make and try to get a commitment from him. I won't give him the full picture until the wagons get here. When do you think that will be?"

"Two, three days. Unless they run into trouble."

"I can't believe that a great man like him is wasting his time here in this little town. Every general in the North—Abraham Lincoln himself—should be beating a path to his door, there should be crowds on the front lawn waiting to listen to him. This man has ideas that are twenty years, fifty years ahead of his time." Reid's eyes narrowed with intensity, his fingers curled as if he grasped a ball of air in front of him. "And I know how to use his ideas in ways that even he hasn't thought of. You'll see, Walker. Everybody will."

Reid caught himself, as if afraid he had said too much. "So, what about yourself? What will you do while I'm with Lyle down at the steamworks?"

In other words, Walker thought, he doesn't want me along with him. Earlier he would have had to make an issue of it, but now there were other considerations.

"I want to stay close to the house. I want to keep an eye on things here."

"Do you think Mrs. Lyle or that maid suspects something?"

"I don't know. They both acted strange at times. I don't want to take any chances. And if things don't work out with you and Lyle, or if he starts to suspect something and tries to contact the authorities, there's still the possibility that we'll have to take the women hostage."

Such talk, even the idea of having to do such a thing, made him weary. All he wanted to do right now was to lie down, rest. He said good night to Reid and went next door.

As he closed the door to his room he heard a man's voice coming from outside. He extinguished the lamp and hurried to the open window. A black man was leading Walker's and Reid's horses toward the stable, complaining to them good-naturedly that they were going to mean more work for him and at this time of night too. Walker sighed heavily. Among the dark branches of the sycamores in the backyard, there was a red smudge in the sky defining the ridgeline at the top of the hill. He thought at first it was the remains of the sunset, but realized it must be from coke or brick ovens in the next valley. There was the sound of crickets, the occasional clop of the horses' hooves on the wood floor of the stable, the man's voice murmuring about something. Holding his arm close to his side against the wound, his hand in a limp fist against his navel, Walker felt his way in the dark back to the bed.

He lit the lamp again so he could find his bootjack in his valise and take off his boots. On the side of the jacket of the Yankee uniform was a stiff patch of dried blood and the tear from the bullet that Libby had noticed; he'd have to do something about it tomorrow before he could go anywhere. For a moment he thought of Libby, the way she clung to her husband's waist as they talked in the study; he wondered if she did it because she was tipsy, somehow it didn't seem a natural gesture between them, Lyle looked genuinely surprised. He thought of Mattie, the way she and her sisters hung out the upstairs window that first day when he and Morgan rode up to the house: Wait till you meet these young ladies, Colonel, they are the true flower of the South; he thought of the way she would fly down the stairs, her hair flying, when she was younger and knew that Walker was there to see her; he shook his head to put such thoughts out of his mind. Was he a bit tipsy himself? He draped the jacket on the back of the chair along with his gun belt and stretched out on the sleigh bed, on the diagonal so he would fit, to rest a moment before he finished getting ready for sleep.

He thought of Lyle and his wife, these unassuming, gentle people, and what they would think if they knew they had two Southern infiltrators in their house. If they knew they were harboring one of Morgan's raiders. It made him smile, though he was mindful that it could be dangerous for the Lyles later on. He thought about the early days of the war in Kentucky, how exciting it had been, a kind of fun, a dozen or so of them going deep into the woods at night, armed with shotguns to stalk pickets behind enemy lines; he remembered the night that he and Morgan got separated from the others by a body of cavalry; they lay side by side in a thicket by the edge of the road, afraid to move as 120 men passed only a few feet away. Then the two of them crawled on through the brush until they were close enough to smell the wood smoke of the Union campfires, lying under the pines as they listened for the number of long rolls on the drums that called the troops into position so they would know the strength of the enemy, before they scurried back through the brush to their horses and rode away, laughing together like schoolboys at their caper, Morgan calling to him as he waved his hat in the air, We got 'em that time, Walker! We got 'em! Aren't you glad you joined up with me now? . . . but Walker was already asleep.

Two

It grabbed him by the leg and would not let go, pulled him awake, pulled him upright in bed and then with a howl pulled him to his feet, the pain in his calf excruciating as he put his full weight down on the aching leg to ease the cramp. For a moment Walker stood blinking in the bright dappled sunlight from outside the bedroom window.

I'm like a goddamn old man. He took a few halting steps, his good arm flapping for balance, trying to work the cramp out.

Then he remembered where he was, and why. Shit. He rubbed his hand through his hair, trying to gather his thoughts. Now that the pain in his leg had let up, he realized how much his side was hurting—he must have twisted himself jumping out of bed. But these were the least of his concerns.

The Union cavalry jacket was gone. He looked around hoping he was mistaken—he hobbled over to check the wardrobe: empty—hoping that he only thought he remembered draping it over the back of the chair last night, but the jacket was not in the room. In its place on the chair were a brown tweed suit and waistcoat and a clean shirt. Walker approached them warily, as if the clothes might hide a snake; his gun belt and revolver were still hanging on the chairback, apparently undisturbed. Inside the suit coat was a label from a New York tailor saying the garment had been made expressly for Colin Lyle.

Walker held up the jacket and pants. Yes, they did seem to be about the right size; whoever left them had a good eye. But who left them? And what happened to the cavalry jacket? Maybe someone took it to clean it; maybe someone took it to show the authorities, to prove that he and Reid were guerrillas or spies. There was also a fresh pitcher of water on the stand and the slop jar had been removed. The idea that someone had been in the room and he hadn't heard them made him feel eerie; it was also dangerous, somebody could have gone through his valise. He was careful not to carry any papers, but there was always the chance he overlooked something; everything in the bag seemed to be the way he left it but he couldn't be sure. There were also the saddlebags out in the stable, he needed to make sure they didn't contain anything that could give them away. Lord knew what Reid might have in his bags. Walker considered himself a light sleeper, he must be weaker than he realized. He checked his watch in his pants pocket: it was a little after ten. Damn it!

He dressed quickly in the shirt and suit, strapped on his gun belt, and stepped into the hall. The house was quiet, too quiet for a household with children. He listened: nothing. The house was dark even in the daytime, the dark paneling soaking up the light; the only illumination came from the sunlight through the bedroom windows that spilled out the open doorways into the hall. Reid's room was deserted, all trace of him, even his valise, gone. Walker didn't like it. The wood floors creaked with his every step, telegraphing his movements. He eased down the hall past the staircase. The doors to the children's rooms were open, as were the doors to the other bedrooms at this end of the house—

Lyle and his wife appeared to have separate bedrooms—the beds were made, everything in order, but there was nobody here. Walker backtracked and headed downstairs.

His weight on each tread set off explosions of wood throughout the house, echoing in distant rooms, as if his presence were enough to unsettle the entire structure. The downstairs was darker than the second floor; heavy drapes covered the windows in most of the rooms; the air was muffled and close. In the dining room, motes of dust marched in legions through a slanting bar of sunlight; a crystal pendent on the chandelier caught the sunlight and splattered it in broken rainbows against the walls. A grandfather clock in the hall tocked profoundly. From the back of the house came a different glow than had been there the night before.

Walker poked his head into the kitchen. The room was full of greenish light from the leaves of the sycamores in the backyard, the azalea bushes and the ivy at the open windows. A breeze stirred from the open back door beyond the pantry; he caught a glimpse of the stable at the end of the yard, the woods on the hillside. A calico cat sat in the doorway, back leg aimed at the sky, washing itself. Sally was at the sink, snapping beans.

"You have two arms this morning," she said without looking at him.

"What? Oh yes." Walker lifted his left arm a few inches to demonstrate that it was better, but she kept her back to him and he felt a little foolish. Was she alone in the house? From the way she acted toward him last night, he half expected her to run screaming from the kitchen the moment he entered, but she seemed to be ignoring him. She was wearing an elegant morning dress of green satin, ballooned out with stiff hoops underneath. After fussing at the sink for several more minutes, she turned around to look at him, her hands rolled into her apron.

"Are you the rider on the red horse, or the gray?"

Walker didn't understand.

"My George said that one of your horses was red, and the other was light gray. Is yours the red one?"

"The roan," Walker nodded. "I guess you could call it red."

"I thought so." Her head was at an angle and turned slightly away from him, not as if she were being coy but as if she were peeking at him from around a self-imposed corner. Her large brown eyes were moist, dreamy. Why was she so concerned about which horse was his? Was she setting him up for something? Maybe that was the reason there was no one else in the house, they had already captured Reid and she was left alone with him to set the trap, no wonder she seemed distant. He started for the back door.

"My Miss Elizabeth told me to ask you what you want for breakfast. So I'm asking you. What do you want for breakfast?"

Walker stopped halfway to the pantry. "Where is Miss Elizabeth? Where is everybody?"

"Mr. Colin and your Mr. Reid left early to go down to the steamworks. They were babbling on about something, but Mr. Colin, he's always babbling on about something, so I didn't pay it no attention. And my Miss Elizabeth, she took the children and went to the cemetery."

"Did somebody die?"

"Somebody always dies."

"I mean, was there a funeral?"

Sally looked at him as if he were stupid beyond belief. "I went ahead and made you some cornbread. I figured where you come from everybody likes cornbread."

"Where do you think I'm from?"

"From where everybody likes cornbread. Are you going to tell me what you want for breakfast or am I just going to fix you some eggs and bacon and gravy to go with your cornbread? You, you just sit down there. You."

Her hands still rolled in her apron, she motioned with her head for him to sit down at the table where he sat the night before. There were a number of things he knew he should do right now—have a look around the yard, check the saddlebags in the stable, find out where Libby and the children had gone—but at the mention of food his knees gave way and his stomach gaped, he hadn't had a decent meal in days, weeks. He sat at the table and did what he was told.

She hummed as she worked around the kitchen, swaying back and forth to set her hoopskirt twirling about herself. He tried to make small talk, but she ignored him as if he weren't there. When he started to eat she watched for a few minutes from the pantry, her hands rolled into her apron again, then she disappeared out the back door and didn't return. That and her talk about where he was from made him uneasy all over again; he pulled his holster around on his lap to have it close at hand, just in case. After he sopped up the last bit of gravy with the last piece of cornbread, he went back through the silent house and out the front door.

He felt exposed, naked, in the bright morning sunlight, dressed in the strange clothes. Below in the valley, there was the clatter and bustle from the mills along the river, the smoke rising in columns from the smokestacks of the ironworks, signs of activity in the streets of the town. As he crossed the gentle slope of the front lawn, he wondered if army patrols ever came through the town, if the presence of two strangers staying with the Lyles would cause any talk. There was a cloud of dust on the road coming up the valley from the Ohio; he watched it for a moment but it was only some freight wagons heading for the brickyard. With the field glasses the day before, he had seen a cemetery in the hills at the north end of town. He thought of taking his horse but was afraid it would call more attention to himself. With the remnant of the cramp still pulling at his leg, the wound under his arm still pulling at his side—I'm a wreck, I'm getting too old for this—he struck off across the face of the hillside, following the pathways across the fields and through the woods.

The cemetery was laid out near the crest of a smaller hill within the valley. Paths looped around upon themselves; from the size of the cemetery, the town expected to grow—and die—considerably, but for the time being the graves were scattered here and there along the slopes. Libby was at the far end, standing a little distance from a knot of people gathered around an open grave. She was dressed in black again today—a black walking dress with a row of tiny buttons from neck to hemline, the skirt belled out behind and flowing but without a hoop, black gloves, and a bonnet with a veil tied up into a large black bow. Resting on her shoulder was a black parasol. She was alone, the children weren't with her. Walker stayed back, close to some bushes so she wouldn't see him. When the ceremony was over, Libby remained where she was, removed from the mourners who comforted each other as they slowly drifted away, back down the slope to their buggies. Besides herself, the only ones left were the two gravediggers; the sound of the first shovelfuls of dirt drumming against the lid of the pine box carried over the grass. She watched until the last mourners were in their buggies and headed back along the twisting road toward town, until the dirt being thrown into the grave was only a whisper. Then she turned and looked in Walker's direction, looked right at him as he stood near the bushes, as if she had known he was there all along.

"Are you spying on me, Captain Walker?" she called to him. She waited until he stepped from the bushes and climbed the hill toward her. The parasol tilted behind her like the rising of a black moon. "Oh dear, I'm afraid I've embarrassed you again. I suppose that was an unfortunate choice of words, given the situation of the country right now. Well, no matter, and I won't even ask you why. It's very pleasant to have you here with me now, no matter what the reason. You're looking much better than you did last evening, much more rested. I trust you slept well? Come, let's walk. You're just in time to escort me home."

Walker was taken off guard. She talked as if continuing a conversation they had started the night before, as if continuing a friendship started a long time ago. It made him slow-witted; he was prepared for something else, though exactly what he wasn't sure. She started down the slope through the gravestones, then stopped and looked back at him, as if to say Aren't you coming? She smiled as he came along after her.

"The suit looks good on you. I thought it would. It's English— well, it's an English cut and English cloth, I had it made for Mr. Lyle in New York but he never wears it. He doesn't feel comfortable in it, he says it makes him feel like a Surrey Country Gentleman. You'd have to know Mr. Lyle to know what an anathema that would be to him. Mr. Lyle would prefer to see himself as an American Industrialist. Or probably not even that. He would probably see himself as an American Workman. The egalitarian tendency is very strong in Mr. Lyle. But oh my goodness, you're limping. Don't tell me you have another wound."

"My leg's just a little stiff, that's all. A cramp last night. . . ."

"Undoubtedly from having to sleep all scrunched up on that bed. The man who made it said it was a double bed but I swear it's shorter than it's supposed to be, I forgot all about that when I put you in there. . . ."

"It'll be fine, Mrs. Lyle. I'm just not used to having a comfortable bed to sleep on, that's all."

"That's probably too true. And please don't call me Mrs. Lyle. It's Libby. Well, the least I can do is slow down a little, can't I? I should have thought of that because of your wound too. You're probably still weak, and after you walked all the way up here after me. Here I am chugging along like a steam engine. Sometimes I think if I had half a brain I'd be dangerous. Mr. Lyle is probably right, what he thinks about me."

In the spring sunlight crescented by the edge of her bonnet, her skin seemed all the more porcelain-like—he could see the course of blue veins beneath the surface—her eyes all the more sunken; as she talked her broad mouth sliced across her face like a series of repeated cuts. But most of the time he couldn't see her face; she was on the downward side of him so that he saw only the top of the parasol, the bottom of her dress sweeping along the dust and grass, and the toes of her boots kicking out as she walked along, slower now. They had reached the dirt road leading back toward town. Walker looked around, looked back up the hill at the grave site.

"What about your children?"

Libby peeked out from under the edge of the parasol. "What about my children?"

"Sally said you were taking them to the cemetery with you. I was afraid you were leaving them behind."

"I can assure you, Captain Walker, that if my children were with me, I wouldn't walk off and leave them."

"I didn't mean. . . ."

"Sally is a little turned around in the sequence of events. Which is not surprising, if you knew Sally. I'm afraid she is often lost in her own little world. My children—they have names, incidentally: Malcolm and Anna—were with me when I left the house, but I took them to a neighbor's for a few days. I decided it would be best with guests in the house. One thing I'm sure you don't need right now is to have a seven- and a ten-year-old running around. We'll all appreciate the peace and quiet."

Why had she taken the precaution of removing the children from the house? Was she expecting trouble? What did she know or suspect about what was going on? Walker couldn't lose the feeling that he and Reid were walking into a trap. Still, she seemed friendly enough, even too friendly, as if she were trying too hard. Maybe it was his imagination. He hadn't walked with a woman since he was with Mattie, he was out of practice—what to say, how to keep a conversation going; it was certainly different than talking to the men in camp, the only contact he'd had in the last few years—after the things he had seen during the war, how could he tell what was ordinary human behavior and what wasn't? She had slowed her pace, but she sashayed along, twisting her body from side to side, as if to maintain the same level of energy. Walker wondered if he should be seen with her, but decided it would be less suspicious than if he were alone, a friend of the family. He walked with his hands folded behind his back, his head inclined toward her to hear every word.

"I thought it was a good turnout at the funeral, didn't you? But I guess you wouldn't know, would you, you haven't been to any of the others. Silly me."

"Was it somebody in your family. . . ?"

"Who, the dead boy? Heavens no. I didn't even know him. He was from town, killed in your war. Jerome Taylor. I think somebody said that he was only eighteen."

"It's not really my war, exclusively."

"No, but you fight it," she said without rancor, simply as a statement of fact. She glanced at him from under the black edge, then was gone again. "Tell me, Captain Walker, what is war like?"

"Why would you want to know about that?"

"Or battle, if you will. One reads so much about them in the newspapers—Shiloh, Antietam, Bull Run—the names are etched into our minds, but I don't feel that I know what really goes on. I thought maybe you could tell me."

"I haven't been in many of the kinds of battles you're talking about. Mostly they've been smaller skirmishes. But I was at Shiloh, and I can tell you that nobody really knows what is going on in a fight like that, even while you're there. Mainly, it's a lot of confusion, and a lot of waiting. There are things happening all around you, but you don't really know what they are. You only know there's a lot of smoke and dust and there's men yelling and screaming, and the horses are scared and of course there's the noise of the guns. You rarely see the enemy. It goes on like that for hours. You're excited and terrified and bewildered, all at the same time. Then suddenly you're in the middle of something, things start happening right in front of you, you're running some-where or charging on your horse or firing your gun and then maybe for a couple of minutes there are men in front of you and the only reason you know they're the enemy is that they're trying to kill you so you try to kill them first, maybe even go hand to hand with some of them in the midst of all the smoke. Then everything shifts again, you're either moving forward or back with everybody else and you don't know what you're supposed to do next. Later somebody tells you if you won or lost."

"Thank you," she said intensely, as if he had just given her a gift. She had shifted the parasol to her other shoulder so she could see him. Walker was angry at himself. What had gotten into him, to go on like that? He had never told anybody what he had just told her, he felt that he had told her too much. It made him want to hurt her in some way, as if to get back at her for hurting him.

"I still don't see why you waste your time going to funerals for boys you don't even know. It sounds a little ghoulish."

"That's why I was pleased to see so many people at this one today. A lot of times there's not much of a family so there's hardly anyone there. Nobody else from town comes unless they knew the soldier very well. I feel I represent everyone else, all the people who would come if they thought about it or had the time."

I'm sure the dead soldiers appreciate it, Walker thought sar-castically. But he kept it to himself.

"Some of the caskets they ship home are very strange," Libby went on. "I even saw an ad in the paper for metal caskets. And you can sign up with one company that will go to the battlefield after the fighting is over and collect the body of the customer if he's been killed and ship him home. It's a whole new business, brought about by the war. I guess it would at least make sure that the body was returned. Sometimes the caskets are so light, I've wondered if there was anything in them at all."

"Sometimes they can't find all of a person afterwards. Sometimes there's only a few parts left."

She slowed, as if that was something she had never thought of before.

"I'm sorry," Walker said. "I shouldn't have said that."

"No, no, I'm glad you did. I need to be aware of such things, I want to be able to hold up under the worst of what the world has to offer." She thought about something for a moment. "You don't like me much, do you, Captain Walker?"

"What?" He felt his face color. "I didn't mean to—"

"That's quite all right, you needn't apologize. I'm the one who should apologize to you. I'm sure I got off on the wrong foot with my little fainting escapade last night when I tried to help you. You'll never see another exhibition like that from me again. How is your wound today? I meant to ask you earlier."

"It's feeling better." He raised his arm to show her—and wished he hadn't, he pulled it more than he meant to. He tried to apologize again for giving her the impression that he didn't like her—he wondered if she was right—but she raised her gloved hand to cut him off.

"I blame myself for it entirely. I'm sure I misled you in telling you that I'm a planter's daughter. People from the North, they think all Southerners are the same. They couldn't know the difference in class structure between someone from the border states, such as yourself, and someone from the Deep South. Whether such antagonisms should exist or not, I think we both know they do."

"I think you do me an injustice, Mrs. Lyle."

"Mrs. Lyle again. Always the gallant, Captain Walker. At least we share that about the South, don't we? The appreciation of chivalry and manners. Northerners simply have no idea how ingrained they are in our society. But I insist you call me Libby. If it helps you, I'll tell you a little secret: you probably think it's short for Elizabeth, don't you? Well, it could be, I suppose, but Mr. Lyle was actually the first person to ever call me Libby, and he never did so until after we were married. To his mind it's short for 'Liberty,' which I'm sure he thinks I have too much of. It's another one of Mr. Lyle's little jokes. So you must call me Libby too."

"All right. Libby."

She smiled, as if she had won an important point, and moved behind her parasol again.

"What I failed to tell you last night was that I'm the daughter of an unsuccessful planter, or at least only marginally successful. It's a sad story in a way, and probably rather typical of things that happened in my father's life. He knew in his heart that keeping slaves was morally indefensible. But rather than make the leap in his ideas, he tried to sidestep the issue by investing in machinery to do the plantation work instead of people. It wasn't a bad idea, I suppose, only limited. Somehow or other he heard of Mr. Lyle and his steam engines, and my father invited him down to our plantation to explain what his steam engines could do. Of course, as an impressionable young woman, I saw Mr. Lyle as the epitome of Yankee ingenuity and intelligence and yes, power. And he did cut quite a striking figure in those days, as I think he still does. It was typical of my father that he set out to save his plantation, and ended up losing his daughter."

"Didn't your father see what was happening when Mr. Lyle started to court you?"

"Actually, Mr. Lyle barely paid any attention to me the whole time he was there. Perhaps that's what helped to spur me on.

Perhaps if he had tried to court me, there wouldn't have been any mystery or challenge. And I probably misled you again when I called myself an impressionable young woman. I was twenty-five at the time, and was used to getting around on my own—and used to getting my own way, I might add. At any rate, Mr. Lyle ignored me, or pretended to. I've always suspected that he knew the way to win me was to pretend to ignore me, because he knew that was the one thing I wouldn't be able to tolerate from him, or anyone for that matter, to be ignored. At least I've always held to that idea about Mr. Lyle. And as for my father noticing what was going on between Mr. Lyle and myself, my father paid little attention to anything that went on with his family. The only love he really ever had was his love for the land."

They had come to an open spot on the hillside, a small promontory overlooking the valley and the winding river and the town. She stopped as if to take in the view, but her eyes looked far away.

"Regardless, a few months after Mr. Lyle left—without having sold my father on the idea of a steam engine, I might add—I packed my trunks and told my parents that I was going to New York on one of my shopping trips. I took the train, which was considered very risqué in my set in South Carolina; when the other women I knew made such trips, they usually took their own carriages complete with outriders and attendants, and maybe even a second carriage to carry all the packages home again, an entire retinue. I always made my trips with just Sally and myself, except this time I changed trains in Baltimore and came here to Furnass. I took rooms at the Colonel Berry Hotel and presented myself to Mr. Lyle—I never told him I was coming, I was never even in contact with him once he left. A foolish thing, perhaps, but I thought it was my one chance at passion and romance in my life. I knew I would always regret it if I didn't take the chance once it presented itself to me. What attracted me even more once

I got here was that Mr. Lyle didn't seem particularly surprised to see me, he took it more or less as a matter of course. That's what I saw at the beginning in Mr. Lyle: his strength. He was strong enough to put up with me. We were married within a month. Later on I learned that very little actually surprises Mr. Lyle. He's not surprised, because most of the time he's preoccupied with his machines. What's going on around him never registers."

"What did your family say when they found out you were here and going to be married?"

"My father disowned me, of course. As I fully expected he would do. After all, a Yankee." She glanced at him, almost coy.

"Do you ever see them or correspond?"

She reached down and gently brushed away a small grasshopper that was clinging to her black skirt. The insect arced into the air and dropped among the tall grass. "I hear from my sister once in a while. Never from my father. And I don't expect to. They're all in Charleston now, to get away from the Yankees in the area. Daddy's very ill. It doesn't surprise me. Leaving his land, even though there was hardly anything left of the plantation, would probably kill him."

Why is she telling me all this? What is she getting at? What does she think she knows about me? She didn't seem sad or bothered by what she told him, only matter-of-fact; she smiled at him, tight-lipped, as if to say So, what do you make of that? Walker didn't know what to make of it. She closed her eyes and tilted the parasol behind her, lifting her face to the sunlight.

"Isn't it glorious? I love it up here in the hills. You get such a beautiful view of everything. Of course, this is my home now. I suppose I had better love it, hadn't I?"

Walker looked at the view. Along the river, the smokestacks of the mills sent up columns of smoke and steam like signal fires. The town was busy, a market day; the roads in and out of the valley were crowded with wagons, with farmers bringing their produce to sell and people coming in to do their monthly shopping. The way his family had come here when he was a child. He supposed it was his home too, in a manner of speaking, but he felt no compunction to love it. He only felt strange that it was the enemy now, or that he was: there were people in the town below who, if they knew who he was and why he was here, would see him in jail, would see him dead. Hanged, or shot like a dog. It might look peaceful, but that was only if you belonged. For him it was dangerous.

He decided Libby was dangerous as well. He couldn't get a bead on her; he was glad that he came after her this morning and that they were having this little talk, but exactly what he was learning about her he couldn't say. She seemed to be up to something, she seemed to know more about what was going on than she would readily admit. He'd have to keep a closer watch on her than he thought. He'd also have to watch his step around her, she was a clever lady, tricky.

"But here, I've prattled on enough about me, too much in fact," she said. "Now I want to hear all about Captain Walker."

Her voice sounded sincere enough, but he noticed her eyes had a faraway look to them, as if she were watching something come over a distant hill.

She was getting a headache. The warm sunlight felt good on her face but it hurt her eyes and made her squint. She could hardly wait to get home, to lie down in a dark room with a damp washcloth over her eyes. When she closed her eyes now, she saw a troop of phantom cavalry riding along the top of the valley's hills, in the clouds above the hills, monster figures, gods, the guidons snapping in the wind, bugles blowing, sabers at the ready as they wheeled in formation and then suddenly charged down the sky toward her, above the treetops, froth flying from the mouths of the horses, their eyes wild—oh beautiful, beautiful—a sword glinting in the sunlight as it slashed down at her, the pain above her eyes like a blade piercing her temple, a swirl about her of dust and screams and horses' hooves. She opened her eyes. Captain Walker was watching her, a puzzled expression on his face.

"What?" she said, adjusting the parasol to block the sunlight again.

"I said, there's not very much to tell about me."

"I don't believe that for a moment. For instance, you say you're a soldier, but you don't talk very much like a soldier."

"Why do you say that?"

He seemed a little surprised that she would notice such a thing. Libby smiled to herself, pleased to find a soft spot. That she could get such a reaction from him made him not quite so imposing.

"You seem too intelligent for a soldier, for one thing. I suppose generals have to be intelligent, but you're not a general."

Walker laughed. "No, I'm certainly not a general. But I was a lawyer before I joined the army. Maybe that's what you hear. And I served for a while on the Senate staff in Washington."

"Perhaps." She turned away from the view and started walking again, along the road across the face of the hillside. "From up here, it's all so very picturesque, idyllic. I remember when I first came to Furnass, I thought I had stepped into a picture of a town. That's the real beauty of being up here in the hills. One doesn't have to deal with the people who live here. All the LBLs and the SNNs."

"Who are they?"

"That's my name for them. The Low-Bred Loafers and the Snooty-Nosed Nobodies. Mr. Lyle gets upset when I call them that. He's known these people all his life, so I guess he's used to them. But I can't help the way I feel. These people have shown no love for me, on the whole. And I have no love for them."

"Then why do you go to these funerals?"

"I've wondered myself. I've wondered if the reason I go is to show the LBLs and the SNNs what they should be doing. Maybe it's only a way to show them up and put them in their place. But the truth is, I don't really know why I go. All I know is that I think less of myself when I stay away."

It was getting hot; the many layers of clothes were beginning to weigh on her, she was sticky all over, she felt as if she had rolled on the ground. But she never would have dreamt of letting him know she was uncomfortable. She strode along, the hem of her black skirt sweeping a trail of ridges in the loose dust.

"So. You were a lawyer. I suppose that explains some of what I hear in your speech. But of course it raises more questions. Such as why an educated man, an attorney and in government too, would give up his career to join the army. The cavalry at that."

"I believed. I believed it was a just cause."

"'A just cause.' And what cause would that be, Captain?"

Walker didn't answer for a few moments, thinking carefully what he wanted to say. It was strange to see this strange man in her husband's clothes. Walker filled them well; in fact he looked better in the suit than Mr. Lyle had the few times he wore it, though Walker obviously lacked the grace and bearing that she had always admired in her husband. It was disappointing; she wanted the captain to be as dashing and romantic as the cavalrymen she read about, even in these civilian clothes. Walker scuffed along, kicking up little clouds of dust with his boots. One hand clasped the other behind his back, a gesture that in some men would have appeared learned and thoughtful, but in Walker seemed more cautionary, as if he were holding on to his hands back there so they wouldn't do things that they weren't supposed to, his own prisoner. It made Libby want to prod him all the more, to see what other soft spots she could discover.

"Come now, Captain Walker, it can't be that difficult to give the reasons why you decided to risk life and limb in the service of your country. I would think your reasons would be very much on your mind."

"I believed that people have the right to determine the way they're going to be governed."

"That almost sounds secessionist. I thought you were a Northern man."

"You said yourself that Kentucky's a border state. Things there aren't so cut-and-dried as they are in South Carolina. Or Pennsylvania."

"Why do I get the feeling that you're holding something back, Counselor? Why do I sense some equivocation, some lawyer's twist with words?"

"I don't know," he said, not looking at her.

Libby didn't think he was holding back at all, but the statement evidently had its desired effect, she seemed to have touched another nerve. He was not the type of man she considered handsome, though she supposed he might be attractive after a fashion, in a rugged—if she wasn't trying to be polite she would have said homely—sort of way; his skin was leathery from being outdoors, the worry lines etched around his eyes, his mustache allowed to go wild, his hair like a thicket. Without a hat, there was a line across the middle of his forehead, the skin decidedly lighter above, as if, if she had the right key, she could lift off the top of his head and peer inside. She remembered her vision of the phantom cavalry and wondered if the trooper who sabered her was Captain Walker. Nonsense. Her own head was throbbing and she was growing weary of the day and of his company; but she decided to goad him a little further, on the off chance that she might learn something interesting.

"I wonder if there was a woman involved in your decision."

Bull's-eye. Though masked by his weathered complexion, Walker appeared to blush. Well, well. Presented with the opening, Libby pursued it.

"I can't believe that it was a wife, pressing you to join for the sake of some local glory. I know there are such stories, of men who don't really want to go to war but are pressed into it by their wives."

"No, there was no wife pressing me. I'm not married. Never have been."

"But there was a woman, wasn't there?"

Walker looked away, watching a red-tailed hawk ride an unseen current close to the ridgeline. "She was impressed at first when I decided to join. She thought she was the reason I did it, that I was trying to impress her. But that wasn't the reason I joined up, and I told her so."

"You should have let her go on thinking that way, even if it wasn't true. Women like to think they have the power to influence men."

"I suppose you're right. But I thought it was more important for her to know the truth. The fact that I didn't join the army to impress her didn't mean that I loved her any less."

"But she didn't know that."

"No, evidently she didn't know that."

"So what happened?"

"She married another man. Another soldier."

"Did he become a soldier to impress her?"

"No, he did it for the same reason I did. Because it was something he believed in. But now that they're married he's started to do things to impress her. At least it seems that way. He's an officer, and he lets her influence his decisions, or he lets his feelings for her influence them. Getting married changed him, and not for the better."

In her mind's eye, Libby saw herself for a moment as the woman, standing on the front porch of a trim frame house in Kentucky, the house isolated on a tabletop of endless rolling grass-covered hills, the way she envisioned the Kentucky land-scape to be, as a young general in the Union Army, resplendent in gold braid and epaulets—a man who looks uncannily like the drawings she has seen of Jeb Stuart, only in a blue uniform, not gray—rides up to her front gate on a prancing white charger, dismounts and comes up the walk, his silk-lined cape flapping about him like wings, his hat decorated with an ostrich plume, and goes down on one knee in front of her to present his sword, while on a distant hilltop Captain Walker watches what is going on, turns on his horse and rides away. And for a moment she felt the woman's anger, the hopelessness and loss and frustration that Walker gave up so easily, that she was left with this gaudy figure offering trinkets when the man she really wanted turned his back on her, wouldn't stay and try to win her. She was called back to the present by Walker leaning toward her.

"Are you all right?"

"I'm fine, Captain Walker. Just fine."

"You looked as if you were in pain. . . ."

She shook her head, smiled briefly, and moved the parasol again, as much to shade her face from him as from the sun; be-yond the edge of the black circle, he became only a pair of lanky legs, a pair of clasped hands behind a back. Across the cleared fields on the hillside, she could see a corner of Sycamore House poking out from among the trees; it wasn't too much farther now. Her headache was growing, it would be with her for days if she let it. But she wouldn't take anything for it until tomorrow, she could bear it until then. It would be too complicated otherwise with strangers to entertain in the house, tomorrow things will have settled into a routine; besides, she needed to ask the doctor for more of her medicine. She knew she was being witchy to this nice man—and after he had been a perfect gentleman to not mention a word about her display of weakness the night before—but she couldn't help it.

"So tell me, Captain, would you still have joined the forces of the Union if you had known that President Lincoln was going to make it a war to abolish slavery? Were you an abolitionist before the war?"

"That was never an issue with me. I never owned any slaves in Kentucky."

"But that's not the question. Would you own slaves? Would you allow others to have slaves, while you just turn your back? Do you think that would put you in the right while others committed a wrong?"

Walker thought for a moment before he said anything. "I think slavery started as a principle of economics. And irrespective of any questions of moral right and wrong, I think that the changes in economics would have freed them anyway."

"So you think it's tolerable to keep a person in bondage, as long as the economic or social factors support it."

"I didn't say that."

"And yet you would keep a person in bondage, if you had the chance."

Walker was obviously being careful not to say the wrong thing, so he said nothing at all. Libby smiled to herself. What she considered to be a battle of wits had brightened her spirits momentarily. She spun the handle of her parasol like a top.

"You said as much yourself, Captain. You as much as told me that you would have married that woman back in Kentucky, if you had had the chance. And that would have put her in bondage to you."

"Oh, you're only talking about love." Walker was noticeably relieved.

"Only about love. Only about a woman. Silly me, why would I presume to think that a woman could be as important as a slave?"

"I hardly think you can compare the keeping of slaves to marriage—"

"The lions have written the books."

"I don't understand. . . ."

Libby smiled sadly. "It's from a book by Mrs. Elizabeth Oakes Smith entitled *Woman and Her Needs.* Of course you wouldn't think that marriage is slavery. You're one of the lions, one of the masters as ordained by our society. Such a comparison would only occur to you if you happened to be one of the ones in bondage. Make no mistake, Captain Walker, a woman in marriage is a slave to her husband. That is, if she allows her husband to exert the authority that convention gives to him. Everything in our society is directed to make a woman subservient, from the confining nature of the fashionable clothes we're supposed to wear to the fact that we can't even vote. When a woman marries, she gives up her name, her right of self-determination, her control over her own finances. We become dependents, minions to our lords, called upon to keep a sunny disposition and serve our liege in every way. For a woman, a marriage vow is an oath of allegiance, a self-imposed contract that gives another person control over her life. Women are not equals in this society."

"You seem very independent. And very much an equal."

"That's because I've made myself independent. And I fight to be an equal. But don't be fooled, Captain. I haven't done away with the leash, I've only lengthened the lead. Society would never permit me to throw it off completely. I would be branded a fallen woman, condemned before I could say a word in my defense. Tell me: you fight to free the slaves even though you don't necessarily believe in the cause. Would you also fight to free women even though you don't believe in our cause either?"

Walker didn't say anything; he slouched along, studying the ground in front of him, his head resting progressively lower on his chest. Libby was furious with herself; she had allowed herself to get carried away, she had said much too much. They had reached the front gate of Sycamore House. Libby stopped and turned to him, a different woman now, all smiles and flutter.

"Just listen to me, how I do prattle on. You're a dear man for listening to all my foolishness. And thank you for escorting me home, kind sir. You are a perfect Southern gentleman, even if your present situation requires you to wear a Yankee uniform. I just want you to know how glad I am that you are here with us. It means so much to Mr. Lyle, to have somebody finally taking an interest in his ideas. He's a genius, Captain Walker, he truly is. I've seen him neglected so much, and I know it hurts him even though he'll never say anything. It's about time the world started to appreciate him, and I'm delighted that you're the one who's come to reveal his light from under the bushel. You, and Mr. Reid, of course. Oh, and before I forget, we're having a little dinner party tonight in honor of you and Mr. Reid. Now, don't fret, it's really no trouble at all, and I won't take no for an answer. It's really not much of a party, the only other guest I've invited is our good friend Dr. McArtle. I know you said you didn't want to see a doctor about your wound, but I thought he could take a look at it as long as he's here. Well then, it's all settled."

And before Walker could protest or say anything at all, Libby turned and headed up the walk toward the house, making her skirts and petticoats flounce the way she used to as a girl when she left a suitor standing at the gate. Sally waited among the shadows inside the open front door, watching her approach.

"You all right, Miss Elizabeth?"

"I've got a headache, if you must know," Libby said, crossing the porch. "Why are you wearing my good green satin morning dress?"

"You never minded me wearing your clothes before."

"It doesn't quite seem appropriate, that's all."

"Judging by the look on Captain Walker's face, you told him what's appropriate too."

"That will be enough, Sally," Libby said, brushing past her in the vestibule. The darkness inside the house was cool and welcoming.

"You just go and rest, Miss Elizabeth. I'll get you a nice damp washcloth for your eyes."

Was Sally mocking her? Probably, but she wasn't able to deal with it now. She swept on through the front hall and up the steps to her bedroom. She went at once to the window overlooking the front yard, but Walker wasn't there. Well, what did she expect? That the man would still be hanging around, dumbfounded by her ramblings? She smiled to herself; it was a possibility, the way she had carried on. She told herself that she had to be more careful when she was with him, there was too much at stake otherwise.

This deal was so very important to Mr. Lyle. He hadn't said anything specific—he never did—but after his talk with Reid the night before, she could tell he was excited about the prospects. He had had so many setbacks, so many failures. So many fallen dreams and crushed hopes. She wanted to do everything she could to make sure this deal worked out for him. She would show her husband that she could be the perfect hostess, she would make him proud of her; for once she would play the role of the dutiful wife.

She rested her forehead against the glass; curious: the glass was both warm and cooling at the same time. With the bottom half of the window open, she looked at close range through double layers of imperfections in the panes; a slight tilt of her head sent ripples cascading every which way through her view of the front lawn, the town on the hillside below, and the hills across the river. She was glad at least that she liked this Captain Walker. A strange, sad man. Not at all the way she thought a dashing cavalry officer would be. What did he mean when he said only about love? She'd have to ask him more about that. She'd also have to be nicer to him, no matter how much fun it was to spar with him. Turning away from the window, she sat in the high-backed rocking chair close to her vanity. But oh, the good captain did get the most perplexed expression on his face at times! The breeze from the open window stirred the gauze curtains, played across her face. She took the pins from her hair, letting it fall loose around her shoulders. Leaning her head against the padded rest, she closed her eyes as she slowly rocked back and forth, back and forth.

THREE

Through the open doors, framed by the dark interior of the stable, Walker could see the sycamores in the backyard, the gardens, and the rear of the ivy-covered house, the open back door where Sally worked in the kitchen, the windows to his and Reid's bedrooms. It was a relief to be inside again, away from where someone might happen to see him, hidden away; his sense of tactics also took comfort in a place that would be easy to defend. Their saddles and tack had been placed on railings to air and dry out. Walker went through both his and Reid's saddlebags, but everything seemed to be in order, if there was anything incriminating someone else had already found it. Why in hell is Reid carrying around a two-week-old piece of fried chicken? Some kind of keepsake? He hated to leave his carbine in the saddle scabbard out here in the stable, but it seemed improper to take it in the house. The horses were well taken care of, fed and watered; their stalls were already cleaned out this morning. In the other stalls were the family's matched pair of bays, a couple of saddle horses, a carriage, and a wagon. Walker took off the suit coat and vest and hung them on a nail, keeping an eye on the open door.

He loved the smells of the stable; the smells of the hay and oats, old leather and dried wood, the horses. He relaxed a little in spite of himself. From his saddlebags he took a curry comb and began to groom the horses, first Reid's—the gray with a white blaze down its nose and white forelocks—then his roan. They had acquired the horses shortly after they left Cincinnati, leaving their blown horses in exchange, the way they always acquired fresh horses when Morgan was on a raid; the owner had cleared out when he heard the Confederates were coming and had left the horses unguarded in a field. At the time he hated to abandon his good Kentucky saddle horse to the North, it offended his sense of loyalty; besides, there weren't that many good horses left in Kentucky, they had been used up in the war. But the roan was a real beauty, as fine a horse as he had ever had, and he was attached to her already. Stick with me, girl. After this damn fool war is over, we'll take nice leisurely rides together to my office and do a tour around the park on Sundays. What do you think of that? For a moment he became lost in thought, remembering his home in Lexington, riding through the wild rye and bluegrass, the parklike forests of ash and bur oak; he stared into the intermingling of red and white hairs in the horse's coat, working the comb repeatedly down the croup and thigh. The horse finally grew impatient and shifted its position. You're right. First I have to get us out of this damn mess in one piece. Walker took his farrier's knife and began cleaning the hooves of both horses.

What did Mrs. Lyle mean when she said that his present situation required him to wear a Yankee uniform? What was she referring to, what did she suspect? The danger surrounding her statement was pushed aside momentarily by the memory of how Morgan referred to it in the early days whenever they disguised themselves as Yankees. "Come on, boys, it's time to go play

Union." And he remembered parts of a poem someone had written about one of Morgan's raids, about a Northern woman trying to calm her child's crying as she hears the clatter of hoofbeats coming down the street:

Why, surely, 'tis the Morgan,
Him whom I would not greet,
For there's that in his glances
That makes my heart-strings thrill,
So darling, hush thy wailing,
And be for mother still.

It made it all seem so glamorous, with only make-believe dangers. But Walker had learned early on that there was nothing glamorous about what they were doing. Nothing at all.

. . . there was the time that Morgan led a dozen of them dressed in Yankee overcoats into Nashville, where Buell had his headquarters for the sixty-five-thousand-man Army of the Cumberland. They made their way through the city to the waterfront, a few hundred yards from the Yankee batteries around the state capitol; they could see the Union flag flying from the dome. While the others stood on the dock and watched, Walker and Sergeant Grady and another volunteer stole a skiff and rowed five hundred yards upriver to set fire to the steamboat Minnetonka, *anchored among some trees in a backwater. The plan was to cut the flaming boat loose and float it downstream into Buell's fleet of gunboats and troop transports and supply vessels, but the* Minnetonka *was secured with chains and burned at her moorings. A crowd of several thousand gathered on the dock to watch the blaze. When Walker and the men returned, he expected Morgan to be disappointed that they hadn't accomplished their original goal and destroyed the river fleet. But Morgan was ecstatic. As they stood*

among the crowd, Morgan grabbed Walker by the elbow and pulled him close.

"I love it, Walker, just love it!" he hissed in Walker's ear. "Do you hear what everybody's saying? They're saying that Morgan did it. They know we're here somewhere, but they don't know where. Did you read what they said about us in the paper? 'If a strange man in a cogitating mood walks down the street, a white hat cocked at an angle, and enters a house, it is John Morgan; if a strange man in a cogitating mood walks down the street, a white hat cocked at an angle, and does not enter a house, it is John Morgan; if an elegantly dressed man enters a hotel, it is John Morgan; if a drably dressed man leans against a lamppost, it is John Morgan.' They think we're everywhere, Walker. They think we're like gods."

Morgan pulled back to look at Walker, grinning with delight. He was nearly as tall as Walker, six foot, with a dark well-trimmed mustache and imperial beard, a perfect set of white teeth, and dark auburn hair. His gray-blue eyes narrowed, as if to display his cunning, but Walker noticed that Morgan was blushing like a schoolgirl. Walker had known Morgan since the time Walker's family moved to Lexington; they were the same age though never good friends while they were growing up. Walker's family struggled to make ends meet; Morgan's family had the pretensions of plantation owners, though everyone in town knew that Morgan's father was only more or less a hired hand, an overseer for his rich father-in-law. Walker knew Morgan as a wiseacre kid who rode through town too fast and liked to stand around on Main Street and swear at passersby; he knew him as a young man at the local college who was so bashful he couldn't speak in class, but who found his voice during the Mexican War and led a detachment of Kentucky cavalry against Santa Anna in the Battle of Buena Vista; he knew him as a local gambler, a man-about-town and ladies' man, a manufacturer of hemp and woolen goods whose social position came from dealing in slaves and racehorses. Walker knew that Morgan changed when he was confronted with battle, that Morgan grew as focused as a Minié ball, but he didn't recognize the changes that were starting to come over him lately.

"Buell's going to send us to the devil if he catches us here," Walker told him.

"The point is," Morgan said, gazing at the people around them, "Buell won't catch us. He can't. Nobody can catch Morgan."

"On my way back here I passed a large detachment of cavalry who sure looked like they wanted a crack at it."

Morgan grinned boyishly, as if he had just been flattered. "Very well, Walker. Send the rest of the men away if it'll make you feel better. Me, I'm going for a little walk. You coming?"

Walker ordered the rest of the men to head back to their pre-arranged meeting place outside of town. When Walker caught up to him, Morgan was sauntering along the docks watching the fire on the Minnetonka and the crews of Buell's riverboats scurrying around on deck.

"You see that, Walker? They're scattering like flies. They're afraid Morgan's still around. If Buell only knew we were here having a pleasant stroll along his waterfront, he'd shit himself."

Walker was afraid that he would be the one to shit himself if they stayed much longer, there were Yankee uniforms—with real Yankee soldiers wearing them—everywhere. It was another half hour before Morgan finally tired of the game. When they got to the rendezvous, the others were ready to go back into town to look for them. They were hiding in a clump of cedar trees, in sight of a tollbooth on the highway. The others were anxious to head back to camp, but Morgan was restless.

"You boys wait here," Morgan said, mounting up again on his horse, Black Bess. "I do believe some of the citizens down there on that road need to have their passes checked. Watch this."

Still wearing the Union officer's coat, Morgan rode down the hill and began to check the papers of anyone who came along. At one point when the road was clear and no one was about, Morgan faced his men watching from the hillside, took off his hat, and made a low sweeping bow. The men applauded. It was Sergeant Grady who saw the glint of bayonets from a company of soldiers just over the rise. Walker raced down the hill to warn Morgan, thinking, You crazy bastard, your fooling around is going to get us all killed. . . .

A shadow passed in front of the doorway; the light dimmed where Walker worked on the roan's shoe. A figure stood in the doorway of the stable, backlit from outside, a silhouette only. Walker froze, calculating how fast he could draw his revolver, how far it was to reach the carbine. The figure took a few tentative steps forward. There was something in his hand the size of a short-barreled shotgun. Before Walker could move, the intruder said, "Captain Walker? I was told I'd find you out here."

Walker slowly lowered the hoof. He thought he could probably get a shot off as he spun away and dropped to the floor but was afraid that one of the horses might get hit.

"Libby said you've got yourself a wound that I should take a look at. My name's Dr. McArtle."

As the figure came closer, deeper into the shadows of the stable away from the door, his features became more distinct. He was a big man, slightly pudgy, in his late thirties, with thin blondish hair that covered his head like flax beaten down by the rain. His face had a little-boy quality, broad and button-nosed, expanded on a head grown slightly oversized for the body, as if the child had been reluctant to leave the adult he had become;

tufts of sideburns projected straight out from either cheek as if in compensation. The vest of his black suit swelled with the effort to keep him contained. In his hand he carried a long narrow medicine case.

"I don't know why Libby . . . Mrs. Lyle bothered you with this. It's only a scratch and it's doing just fine."

"Why does Libby . . . Mrs. Lyle do any of the things that she does?" Dr. McArtle twitched his nostrils, then scratched his nose with a knuckle, revolving the tip rapidly as if it were a knob. "Your guess is as good as mine. Maybe it has something to do with women's intuition. Maybe she did it because she knew you didn't want her to. Most likely, she asked me to have a look at you because she took it into her head to do so. I've found that with Libby you have to be ready for a lot of variables."

"I still don't think it's necessary for you—"

"But whatever her reasons, she got me over here, so we might as well go through with it. I've also found it's easier in the long run to just go along with her."

With the toe of his shoe, McArtle dragged a stool over to the light from the doorway; he motioned with his head for Walker to come and sit down. Reluctantly, Walker went over and took off his shirt. The doctor unwound the old bandage, poked at the wound a couple times, grunted, and prepared a fresh bandage.

"Libby was a little vague as to how you got this."

"I was a little vague telling her about it."

"Do you want to tell me?"

"Not especially."

"Forgive me for prying." McArtle stopped and rubbed his nose again. "We're a little jumpy, what with this talk of invasions and all. We're not used to such things around here."

"It's nothing you want to get used to." Walker thought of Kentucky where they lived with the threat of invasion since the war started. He thought of his parents whose farm had been burned, not by Northern soldiers but by fellow Kentuckians, people they knew, who backed the North. "You folks have been lucky up to now."

"Yes, well. Let's hope we stay lucky. You were right, your wound seems to be doing fine. It's liable to be stiff and sore for a while, but you probably know that for yourself. The truth is, I don't see many gunshot wounds. You're probably more experienced in this than I am."

Walker didn't reply. When the doctor was finished bandaging his side again, Walker stood up and put his shirt back on.

"So," McArtle said, closing up his medicine case. "Libby said you're here on some special government project."

Walker went over and lifted the roan's troublesome hoof again. When Walker didn't offer any response, the doctor went on. "Heh heh. Obviously you don't want to talk about it. I don't blame you, it's best to keep those government projects secret. Heh heh. Excuse me for prying again, I guess I'm just naturally curious. This is a small town and people get interested in what goes on with everybody else. I'll do what I can to put people's minds at rest about the strangers visiting the Lyles.'"

Walker busied himself with the loose horseshoe. McArtle was smiling and jovial, but it was apparent that he was fishing for information. Walker's concern was why. The doctor stood close by, his medicine case tucked under his arm, his thumbs hooked in the pockets of his waistcoat; it looked like a pose he had copied from somewhere, the image of what he thought a doctor should be.

"Fortunately, for the sake of your secret mission, people in this town are used to Colin Lyle being mixed up with things that are out of the ordinary. I doubt if there's much he could do at this point that would surprise folks around here."

How about if he was working for the Confederacy? Walker thought. The horseshoe had a broken nail. He got his tools from his saddlebags to replace it.

"Colin is something of a local character, if you must know the truth. An eccentric. His father, Malcolm Lyle, was one of the founders of the town, so folks tolerate quite a bit. Malcolm erected the first mill here, around the turn of the century, a sawmill, then later on he and a man named Buchanan built the first blast furnace and iron forge. Then when Colin came along and took over the business, he sold his interest in the ironworks to start the Keystone Steam Works. That just about killed old Malcolm. The old man moved up into the hills and hardly spoke to Colin till the day he died."

There was enough of the nailhead left to catch hold of with his pliers. "The steamworks looks like it's doing okay for itself," Walker said.

"Oh sure. The steamworks is doing okay. They do the boilers for the boatyard across the river at Jacktown, they do a fair amount of steam engines and boilers for mills and factories. But they don't do half the business they could. Colin can never settle down to one thing. As soon as one part of the business starts doing well, instead of concentrating on that—say, steam engines for mills—he'll take whatever capital he's built up and sink it into something entirely different. Crazy new ideas. Railroads without rails, things like that. Heh heh." McArtle looked smug. "But I'm sure you know what I'm talking about."

Walker glanced up at him as he worked on the shoe. "No, I don't. But the gentleman I'm traveling with probably does."

"Oh yes. Libby did say there were two of you." The doctor looked around, as if he expected to see Reid sitting in the corner of the stable. "Where is your companion?"

"He's down at the steamworks with Mr. Lyle."

"Then don't expect to see very much of him. When Colin's working on a project or has an idea for something, he'll stay down there for days at a time. He even has a bed in his office." McArtle clucked his tongue. "He leaves Libby here all by herself. I mean, she has her maid and the hired man to watch out for her, it's not as if she's unprotected. But I'll be damned if I'd leave a fine woman like that all by herself so I could go tinker on some engine."

The doctor seemed to be considering something, lost in thought momentarily. Then he rubbed viciously at his nose again, snuffled air in and out of his nostrils several times.

"It's certainly dusty in here."

"Stables usually are," Walker said.

"Hmm. Yes." McArtle made a face. "Not the best-smelling places either." His sideburns sticking out from his cheeks had collected particles of chaff from the air. He peered at what Walker was doing. "You know we've got a pretty good smithy in town, if you've got a problem."

"I can take care of it myself. I've got a couple extra shoes if I need them."

"That's certainly resourceful. I didn't know the government equipped our cavalry so well. I thought it was only the Southern boys who were always prepared for emergencies."

Was McArtle a Southern sympathizer, a copperhead? Was he trying to let Walker know that he was on his side? Heaven forbid. Walker hated copperheads as much as Morgan did, two-faced do-gooders who only used the war for their own purposes. He certainly didn't want one hanging around, giving him secret handshakes and getting in the way. Before either one could say anything, Libby appeared in the doorway.

"Here you are, Doctor. Sally said you'd arrived."

McArtle spun around on his heel to face her, startled.

"Ah Libby," he laughed uneasily, as if he had been caught doing something he shouldn't. Then just as quickly he recovered his composure; he was once again the image of the prominent doctor. "I don't know what you were so worried about. This man's wound is fine. You got me over here on a wild-goose chase."

"I feel better knowing that you looked at it," Libby said, coming inside. "Besides, you know as well as I do that you like any excuse to come over here for dinner."

"I thought I was invited to dinner anyway." McArtle pretended to puff himself up with indignation, a degree of seriousness apparent in his kidding. "I didn't know my dinner invitation was in exchange for my services."

"It's about time you did something in exchange for all the free meals we give you," Libby said, coming right back at him. McArtle was embarrassed and colored noticeably. Libby turned to Walker, as sweet as could be. "I hope you found everything all right. And I hope you're not too angry with me for getting the doctor over here. For all his bluster, he's really quite good."

McArtle sputtered. Libby brushed past him and headed for the door. "Come along, Doctor. Let's leave this poor man alone. He has enough trouble without you trying to tell him how to do everything."

Libby waited for him at the door, half in and half out of the sunlight. When McArtle joined her, she reached up and flicked the bits of chaff from his sideburns, then continued across the backyard. McArtle, flustered and furious, glanced at Walker before hurrying after her. Motes of dust swirled in the space where he had stood.

He could hear the water rising from deep in the earth, feel the change of pressure in the workings of the primitive machine as the water was pulled from the underground spring toward the surface, before the water rushed from the spout. Colin Lyle gave the handle two additional pumps, then washed his hands in the chill clear water, bent down and let the water splash over his face and neck.

Washing at the pump behind the house each evening was a nightly ritual for Colin in the summertime. It started early in their marriage, just after he had this house built for his new bride; the first night he arrived home from work, when he tried to walk in the front door still grimy from the steamworks, Libby flew at him, drove him out the front door and around to the back, saying that she wouldn't let him bring all that dirt into her beautiful new house, that he'd have to wash at the pump first. Colin smiled at the memory, though at the time he wondered what kind of woman he had married. At the steamworks, Colin liked to take off his jacket and roll up his sleeves and go out on the floor of the shops and work along with his men; by the end of the day the lines of his face were etched with iron filings and grease and oil were ground into the ridges of his hands. In winter, he washed before he left the steamworks, but in summer he wore the dirt on his face and hands proudly as he walked up through the town— proud of the marks of his trade, as if he were a workman no different from anyone else—then washed out here in the open air, in the shadows of the house and the sycamores. But as to the question of what kind of woman he married, after ten years he still didn't know the answer.

The water ran from his shoulders and chest as he straightened up. His skin was smooth, as white as quicklime. He had remained trim for his age and in good shape, there was little extraneous about him; his arms were sinewy and thin—the muscles were like lumps caught in a tube—and trafficked with blue veins. On his face, the sideburns that cut down his cheeks and met under his nose were the shape of twin scythes. As he dried himself with the coarse towel that had been set out for him, Colin looked around the backyard, at the trees, the kitchen garden, the boundary where the civility of the yard became the wildness of the hillside forest. When he planned the house he envisioned himself sitting out here in the evenings under a tree reading Emerson, but he never got around to it. The truth was he liked the idea of Nature more than he liked to sit in it; he preferred a forged rod to the branch of a tree, the feel of wrought iron to the rich loam of a garden. It was a failing he recognized in himself, one more thing he wished he could change about himself. But he supposed it was too late now. As Emerson said, Nature abhors the old, and old age seems the only disease.

Colin put on his shirt and waistcoat again, tied his bow tie. In the kitchen window, Libby and Dr. McArtle were laughing about something. Colin looked away, feeling that he was intruding. He walked around the side of the house. On the front porch, Captain Walker was sitting in one of the wicker chairs reading the newspaper. Colin didn't especially care for the man—he didn't know that much about him, but Colin disliked the military mind—but it was his nature to be gracious. He was also aware that he needed to be friendly to the captain. It was the hardest thing about business for him, always had been: talking to people to whom he otherwise had nothing to say, being friendly to people just so they would do something for him. In this case, he couldn't get a line on who had the final say in this deal, Walker or Reid. So far he had talked only to Reid, but Reid seemed awfully young and . . . flighty for that kind of responsibility. It was possible that Reid was only the front man, that the real authority lay with Walker. Colin took a deep breath and went to talk to him.

At the sound of Colin on the front steps, Walker jumped, pulling the newspaper down from his face to see who it was.

"My apologies, Captain Walker. I didn't mean to startle you."

"No . . . that's all right. I guess my thoughts were miles away. It's so peaceful here, I wasn't expecting. . . . "

"Yes, my wife and I love this porch, in the summer we sit out here a lot. Are you reading about the invasion?"

"Yes." Walker hesitated, then looked at the paper again. "It says Longstreet is in a place called Gettysburg. They think he's probably headed toward Harrisburg or Carlisle. Where are they from here?"

"A couple hundred miles or so, in the central part of the state." Colin looked out over the front lawn. Two robins stood opposite each other on the grass, motionless, their chests puffed out, eyeing each other, their shadows stretched out of proportion in the lowering sunlight. "The newspapers have been full of the invasion for days. People can't talk about anything else. The thing is, they're so excited about it, you'd think Christmas was coming instead of Lee. Sometimes I think people just like to work themselves up, scare themselves. They don't seem to realize how terrible a thing like this invasion could be."

"I don't expect people can imagine how terrible it could be unless they've seen it for themselves."

"You're probably right. I tend to always expect too much of people. And then am disappointed." Colin smiled sadly at his failing. "But here, that's enough of this kind of talk. Dinner's about ready, let's go in. I see my wife has fixed you up with one of my suits."

"Yes . . . I hope that's all right. . . ."

"Of course, of course. You look better in it than I ever did." As Walker got up from the chair and collected himself, Colin stood with his arms wide, a model of graciousness, then led the way into the house. The activity on the porch sent the two robins winging off together across the lawn.

In the vestibule, Colin took his suit coat from a peg on the hall stand and put it on again before proceeding on into the house. Reid came down the stairs from the second floor and joined them. Libby and Dr. McArtle were waiting for them in the dining room, talking animatedly about something.

Colin took his place at the head of the table; Libby was at the opposite end, with the doctor facing Walker and Reid. It was Libby's favorite room in the house, one that Colin had designed specially to please her, and he was happy for her that she had the chance to show it off to strangers. The drapes were pulled back and the windows were full of the green light from the sycamores in the yard. High on the wall on either side of the fireplace were two small leaded glass windows, each depicting the setting sun; the colored glass glowed with the evening sunlight and in turn added more color to the room. Situated in places of honor on opposite sides of the room were two large sea chests; the chests were tall and undecorated—Colin respected their age and history, but couldn't help thinking they were ugly—mortised at the corners for strength and with the top and sides flat as planks, made by a carpenter (as opposed to a cabinetmaker) for a sea voyage, to fit between the beams of a ship. They had been in Libby's family since the family arrived from Barbados by way of Massachusetts, or vice versa, in the 1680s; Libby brought them with her—stole them, actually, had them packed and carried away before the family knew she was taking them—from her father's plantation when she came to Furnass. It was for occasions such as this—dinner parties, gatherings of friends or business associates—that she had wanted the chests featured in the room, a possible subject of conversation, and Libby was radiant as everyone got settled at the table. Seeing her this happy, Colin wished there had been more opportunities over the years for her to show off her house.

When everyone was seated, Libby asked Dr. McArtle if he would give the blessing. McArtle smiled at something, cleared his throat, looked around the table to make sure everyone was listening, then inclined his head.

"We give thanks for this humble meal
From our Father up on high,
Before the bullets start to whistle,
And the cannonballs to fly. Amen."

"Doctor!" Libby said.

"I call it 'A Soldier's Blessing' in honor of our guests. I thought you might ask me to say the blessing this evening, so I composed it earlier today," the doctor said, pleased with himself. He leaned toward Walker and Reid across the table as if sharing a secret. "Colin won't say the blessing because he doesn't believe."

"Yours was close to sacrilege," Libby laughed.

"Actually, I thought it was rather good," McArtle said. "I seem to have this knack for making up verse on any topic whenever—"

"Come now, Doctor, no stories about yourself." She motioned to Sally in the doorway of the kitchen to begin serving. "I'm sure these gentlemen can think of more interesting topics of conversation."

McArtle puffed, his bushy sideburns flapping, pretending to be offended; he was obviously embarrassed at the way Libby had cut him short. Colin considered McArtle a handsome man, in a boyish way, the kind who was appealing to women even though, or perhaps because, he was a bachelor; the doctor's voice was deep and melodious, which gave import to anything he said, though Colin had noted there was a back draft to it, as if whenever he spoke, part of the words were drawn inward. Colin smiled to himself: leave it to Libby to put people in their place. He felt very proud of her, proud that she was his wife.

There was a ham and fried chicken, boiled potatoes and squash, snap beans, peas, and fresh bread. For a while everyone was occupied serving themselves from the plates and bowls Sally brought from the kitchen. McArtle and Reid attacked the food like children in an eating contest. Walker was more restrained though he ate hungrily; he appeared pale and tired, and his wound seemed to be bothering him, several times he placed his hand under his arm, as if to hold in the pain. Colin was never hungry; he picked at a small piece of ham and some beans. Sally reappeared from the kitchen to see what else was needed.

"Sally always takes care of me," McArtle said as she leaned close to him to retrieve a dish.

"Sally always takes care of everybody," Sally said.

"I should tell you," McArtle said to Walker and Reid, "that even though Sally always takes care of me, she doesn't like me very much."

"But that never stops you any, does it?" Sally said and headed back toward the kitchen.

McArtle laughed; he dabbed at the corners of his mouth with his napkin and went back to dissecting a chicken breast. In Reid's enthusiasm to reach for the bread, he inadvertently kicked Libby under the table. There was a moment's distraction while they apologized to each other.

When things settled down again, McArtle said, "So, Captain Walker. What do you make of all this invasion talk?"

Walker looked at him for a moment, as if trying to get the measure of him, before responding. "From what I read in the paper it sounds like more than just talk."

"What did the paper say?" Reid said quickly.

Walker shook his head. "I'll tell you later. I'm sure these good people don't want to listen to us discuss the war."

"Thank you, Captain," Libby said. "I'm afraid I already wore you out on the subject earlier today."

Walker bumped the table leg with his knee, setting the glassware and silver to tinkling and starting waves in the water glasses. He seemed too large to fit at the table, though he and

Colin were about the same size; Walker was big-boned, and in profile his face seemed massive to Colin, heavy browed, with eyes like gun ports. Colin wondered when Libby had had the chance to talk to Walker. He told himself that she undoubtedly would have told him about it later, that he had barely seen her since he was home.

"As a matter of fact, Captain, I'd be very interested to hear you discuss the war," McArtle said. "You're a professional, the same as I am. I'm sure you could enlighten us quite a bit about what this invasion means."

"No disrespect intended to Captain Walker," Colin said, "but I'm sure he's weary of the subject if he tried to explain the war to Libby. My wife is many things, but she never allows facts to interfere with her notions of reality, even the realities of war."

"No disrespect to Captain Walker?" The doctor laughed. "What about disrespect to poor Libby?"

"I'm sure Libby knows how I meant it."

"I'm sure Libby does," Libby said.

She looked a little hurt and Colin couldn't understand why. He had sounded more patronizing than he meant to, but he genuinely thought she would understand that it was only an observation.

"Besides, the papers have probably given us all the enlightenment we need about what this invasion could mean," Colin went on. "If it continues, it will undoubtedly bring an end to our way of life. You can expect riots in the streets, people scrambling over one another for food and safety, the total breakdown of order. Our country will become as chaotic as Mexico."

Reid appeared about to say something, but a look from Walker shut him up.

McArtle rubbed vigorously at the tip of his button-like nose. "Say what you will, I think it's wonderful the way the newspapers keep us informed of what's going on. You can read reports of battles that happened only a day or so earlier—it's amazing. This is the first time in history that an entire country can keep up to the minute with its war. It makes fascinating reading—I can't get enough. The telegraph is the only one of these modern inventions that's worth its salt."

"You don't like progress?" Reid said. The intense young man in the carefully trimmed red hair and beard looked at the doctor as if he were viewing a strange life-form.

"I'm a cynic, I don't like much of anything." McArtle pulled his head back into his neck and smiled, flat lipped. Colin recognized the doctor's self-mockery, or perhaps mockery of self-mockery, but he wondered how it appeared to these two men who didn't know him.

Colin shifted in his chair, leaning on the arm and resting his weight more to one side than the other. "I'm sure the battle reports make fascinating reading for those who believe that God is measuring the amount of blood spilled in the war, and that the war will end when He decides enough has been let."

"No need to be sarcastic, Colin. We both know that you and I feel very differently about the subject." As McArtle waited for Libby to pass the bread, he clasped his hands off-center against his stomach as if he were a child ready to recite. "I tend to believe this war is meant to purify our society. I believe the very moral character of this nation is being transformed by the flow of blood of our brave army." He nodded to Captain Walker. Walker looked blank.

"Yet you would be the first to say that, North or South, we are all Americans," Colin said.

"Of course," the doctor said. "That's what the Revolution established: a sacred and inviolate Union. That's what we're fighting to maintain."

"Then how do you account for guerrillas who can terrorize and plunder entire communities of their so-called fellow Americans?

People here are terrified that Rebels will come and burn the town and carry off the women and children. I heard the story of a man in Ohio who was so afraid Morgan was coming that he hid his son in a dry-goods box for a week. How do you account for people who can create such terror among their own supposed countrymen?"

McArtle smiled smugly. "It's the Southern part of our society that mainly needs purged."

"I might remind you," Libby said, nodding in the direction of Captain Walker, "that at least one person at this table comes from a state that you would denigrate as 'Southern.'"

Libby was right, in the heat of the discussion Colin had forgotten that she had told him Walker was from Kentucky. Colin was disconcerted, but Walker seemed bemused.

"I've heard those stories too," Walker said, resting his fork upright on its tines in the middle of his plate, a miniature standard without a flag. "What I've never understood is what people think Morgan would want with a bunch of women and children. From what I know of Morgan, he always travels light, that's one of the advantages of being a guerrilla. And it's hard enough to feed people in the South these days without importing any more."

"I agree with you, Captain," Colin said. "I think these stories of Morgan are greatly exaggerated. It's another by-product of the way newspapers report the war. The papers spread the same stories over and over throughout the country. And people grow hungrier and hungrier for stories about exciting characters. It makes heroes out of the merely notorious. Women especially idolize anyone they've read about in the newspapers because the papers make that person seem important. We've never had this kind of hero worship before in America."

"Thank you for singling out women," Libby said. She sat with her elbows resting on the chair arms, her fingers interlocked before her mouth in a kind of cage.

"It's not just women, it's everybody, but women seem the worst offenders," Colin said. "A case in point. Libby's sister in Charleston sent her a copy of a book called *Raids and Romance of Morgan and His Men*. It's a popular novel in the South, portraying Morgan and his raiders as chivalrous knights in shining armor. It's the worst kind of drivel you can imagine, the kind that's usually written for women. But the book is selling as fast as they can print it, the South is wasting its precious paper supply on it. They may even reprint it here in the North. It's beyond reason."

"I must admit the book is overdrawn at times," Libby said as if apologizing in turn to Walker and Reid, speaking through her finger cage. "But I did enjoy reading about Morgan's exploits. It was very stirring."

"My point exactly," Colin said, shifting his weight again, trying to get comfortable. He was unused to sitting very long in any one place, much less in his home; he was used to getting up, pacing around, doing something with his hands. And this entire conversation made him uneasy. He had an inkling that what really bothered him wasn't the foolishness of women in general throwing themselves at false heroes, it was his concern that Libby might become too distracted by this tall, dark, mysterious cavalry officer sitting at her dinner table. He tried to drive such thoughts out of his mind. "You even find this mindless adulation spilling over onto men of real quality. Somebody like Stonewall Jackson. I read that he thought it was frightful the way the press and people seem to lean upon certain individuals. I'm sure he was talking about himself."

"You're an admirer of Stonewall Jackson?" Reid said, his fork poised halfway to his mouth. He seemed to vibrate, the effect of his leg bouncing under the table, like an engine left idling.

"As a representative of the United States government, are you surprised that I have admiration and respect for the late great general of the Confederacy?"

"I'm not sure I understand why," Reid said, returning his fork to his plate. "Many people consider Jackson the flower of the Southern generals, even more so than Lee."

"I'm surprised," McArtle said. "And I thought I knew you fairly well. I should remind you, old friend, seeing as how you're so concerned about the terribleness of war, that it was Stonewall Jackson who advocated shooting prisoners so he wouldn't have to be bothered with them. That's not what I'd call a basic concern for the well-being of humanity."

"I admire Jackson's sincerity and intensity," Colin said. "His aggressiveness. He was a man who got the job done, whatever the job, and at whatever price. He was the most Yankee of the Southern generals. He was the kind of man that makes you proud of America, regardless what his political ideas were."

"He was the kind of man who wanted to destroy your idea of America," Reid said, his blue eyes narrowing. "And he probably would have, if he had lived."

"That's going pretty far," Walker smiled politely. "But I think it's safe to say that he certainly would have tried." For a second, Walker and Reid eyed each other, until Reid turned away.

"The one I like is Sherman," McArtle said, happily chasing peas around on his plate with his fork. "I don't know anything about this man Meade. And McClellan was too tired, he didn't seem to know that modern war has to be total. Sherman, he seems a little gone in the head, but I enjoy reading about him. His motto is burn, sink, or destroy. That's sincerity and effectiveness for you."

"I have great faith in the individual's ability to direct the course of history," Colin said. "That's the definition of a great man."

"You've been reading Carlyle again," the doctor said, smacking his lips.

"I think it's important that a person can make a difference in the course of events. Emerson says—"

"Ah, you and your Emerson," McArtle laughed.

"He says that there is no such thing as history, only biography."

"Emerson also says every hero becomes a bore," McArtle said. "Be careful, Colin, that you don't become a hero."

"I think Mr. Lyle would like to see himself as someone like Jackson or Sherman," Libby said to Walker and Reid, lowering her hands from in front of her mouth and smoothing the wrinkles in the tablecloth from either side of her plate. The wrinkles spread away from her as if she dropped pebbles in a pond. "But the truth is that he's too good-hearted. And as for Emerson, Mr. Lyle's never forgiven him for being unable to resolve the difference between self-reliance and self-responsibility."

McArtle roared with laughter, almost choking on a bite of food. "She's got you there, Colin. The woman understands Emerson better than you do."

The others laughed politely and small talk continued around the table as Libby made sure that everyone was getting enough to eat. But Colin withdrew inside himself, picking absently at a rough spot on his receding hairline. Why did she do things like that? Why did she always try to lessen him in front of other people? It made him sad to think she still felt compelled to do so after all their years together. He watched her as she talked to the others around the table, chitchatting about this and that, filling in the blank spaces and leading the conversation forward when it began to falter; she was in her element, the pivot point of three attractive, attentive men. Libby had aged since he first met her, of course, the years of child-rearing and exile—and disappointment in her husband?—had drained her; it showed in her eyes, which had become increasingly sunken and surrounded by dark circles as if from makeup. But she was still an attractive woman, dainty and feminine, ethereal in some way, her skin luminous against the black dresses she favored now. She had a pretty mouth, her large blue eyes were still bright, and her long graceful hands worked the air as she talked. Colin loved her very much.

He fell in love with her the moment he first saw her—it was as if he were clipped from behind at the knees. When her father invited him to come to South Carolina to demonstrate the uses of his steam engines, Colin thought his luck was changing. It had been five years since he started the Keystone Steam Works, and so far it had been slow going. He had been unable to find the right market for his product; for that matter, he had been unable to find the right product. A number of companies in and around Pittsburgh manufactured steam engines, and Colin had been unable to land any of the major long-term contracts. As a result, the Keystone Steam Works built a little bit of everything. They built engines for riverboats; they built engines for factories and mills; they even built the donkey engines for the Buchanan Iron Works. But where some companies prospered from their diversity, the Keystone Steam Works suffered from the lack of recognition with any particular type of engine. The trip to South Carolina promised to change that. There was the prospect of specializing in the manufacture of farm machinery, not just for this gentleman by the name of Hayes who had summoned him to the South, but, as Hayes said, for all the planters in the area who would see firsthand the marvels of a Keystone Steam Engine. Colin even dreamt of finally developing a project he had been working on for years—a steam engine on wheels, something like a locomotive but without rails, that would be ideal for use on farms and plantations. So far, there were still hundreds of problems to work out, but Colin had seen enough articles in British journals to know that such farm engines were possible.

But South Carolina, or at least the Hayes plantation, turned out to be a disappointment—another one. The plantation, called Willow, was barely able to support expenses; the buildings were in disrepair, the lawns grown over, and the fields poorly cared for. Rather than a respected planter, Hayes was considered a poor businessman and an even worse farmer. His idea of using machines instead of man power, meaning slave power, only confirmed what the other planters in the area already thought: Clinton Hayes was either crazy or a fool. Or both. After a week Colin decided that Hayes was neither, he was simply unlucky. It was a melancholy conclusion. On one hand it confirmed Colin's belief in Emerson's notions about the role of Fate in human activity; on the other hand, Hayes' continual misfortune in everything he tried—if Hayes invested in a project it invariably went under; if weevils attacked one field in the area it was sure to be his; if it was possible to buy bad material or seed, Hayes bought it—reminded Colin uncomfortably of himself. Colin did not like to think that, no matter how hard he tried, his possibilities of success with the steamworks were left to the luck of the draw. He had the Yankee conviction that he could fix things, or make them to his liking. But in Hayes' case it became apparent that steam engines were not the answer to his problems; it also became apparent that he couldn't have paid for them even if they were.

Clinton Hayes was a short square man with a hammered face and threadbare swallowtail coats. The day after Colin arrived, he accompanied Hayes on a tour of the barns and outbuldings. The gin was an old dilapidated building with spaces in the walls where the edges of the vertical planks had rotted away and holes in the floor large enough to fall through. Under the floorboards, half a dozen black children played in the shadows; they gazed up through the holes with unblinking eyes at Colin whenever he passed. On the upper level several black men pushed and prodded the clouds of cotton down an old splintered chute, while on the lower level two young black women, in short gingham dresses and their hair tied up in bandanas, treadled barefoot at the cotton gin, pulling the cotton into the hopper with long rakes. Dust and wisps of cotton filled the air, drifting in blizzards through the cracks of sunlight. Within a few moments Colin's eyes were burning; in the close hot air the cotton fibers stuck to his sweaty skin, covering his face like sudden whiskers. He turned to leave before Hayes had finished showing him the mill: coming toward him through the clouds of dust, weaving a path through the stacks of baskets and curls of rope, down an aisle between the slanting bars of sunlight, was a young woman. She was wearing a dress made from layers of white gossamer, as though all the fibers floating in the air inside the gin had collected in one place and made a garment; the dress was cut along the same lines as those worn by the slave women and was as short—almost to the knees—but she wore white high-buttoned shoes and her legs were covered with white stockings.

"This is my daughter Elizabeth, Mr. Lyle," Hayes said, mopping his forehead with a handkerchief.

"You're staring, Mr. Lyle," Elizabeth said. She gave a little curtsy, more in playfulness than politeness, and smiled, looking him straight in the eyes.

"Ah . . . it's your dress. I mean. . . . "

"I decided the women who work here have the right idea. A dress like this is much cooler than traipsing around in corsets and hoopskirts. Of course, it upsets my father when I dress this way. If it were up to him, he would keep me as wrapped up as a chrysalis in a cocoon. My feeling is, if you're going to be a butterfly, then be a butterfly."

"I should warn you, Lyle," Hayes said, putting his arm around his daughter and giving her a squeeze. "This one likes to lead men on a merry chase."

Elizabeth rolled her shoulders to dislodge his hand and took a step out of squeezing range. "My father doesn't understand. Just because a woman wants to be treated like an equal doesn't mean that she's being difficult for its own sake. Would you agree, Mr. Lyle?"

"I don't think it's my place to comment one way or the other," Colin said.

Elizabeth looked at him steadily with her large blue eyes. "I must say I'm disappointed. You don't look like a man who would be afraid to speak his mind."

"I'm not. But I'm also aware that to speak one's mind can be offensive. Particularly when one is a guest in an unfamiliar part of the country."

"Don't hold back on account of ceremony, Lyle," Hayes said, holding his handkerchief in front of him like a white flag. "If you've got something to say about the subject, I'd be interested to hear it."

"Yes, I would too," Elizabeth said. "Perhaps you can convince me that I was wrong about you."

"My problem is that I couldn't discuss the problem of your equality without considering the rights of those women over there working at the gin."

Elizabeth clapped her hands once and laughed, delighted as a child.

"I understand your concern, Lyle," Hayes said. "Particularly because you do come from another part of the country and may not understand all the issues involved—"

"I understand enough to know that I didn't want to say any-thing—"

Hayes held up his hand to stop him, waving the handkerchief back and forth as if to erase something in the air. "Just let me say that one of the reasons I'm interested in your steam engines is so I can do away with the need to use slaves entirely."

"Then Daddy will have to decide what to do with all these people who have lived here all their lives. They won't have anything to do or anyplace to go and he'll end up having to feed them anyway." Elizabeth smiled prettily. "You see, it gets complicated. As the ancient Greeks knew, the problem with equality is that it has to go to equals and unequals alike. It takes a lot of strength to deal with people who want to be free, Mr. Lyle. My father knows as well as any man that equality can be a many-headed monster."

"You can call me Colin, if you wish. I'd like it."

"No," Elizabeth said, tilting her head as she studied him. "I think you'll always be Mr. Lyle."

Colin stayed at the plantation for the remainder of the week, but he didn't have another chance to talk to her. At meals, the conversation was dominated by her father talking about financial matters and questioning Colin as to how steam engines worked; though Colin would find Elizabeth watching him, she rarely said anything other than to make polite small talk. The rest of the time she was a figure on the periphery of whatever he and her father were doing. When he and Hayes toured the fields, Colin would see her riding on the distant hills; when they toured the mills, he would see her in the shadows at the ends of the aisles; when they sat on the front portico in the late afternoons, Elizabeth walked alone down the long avenue of weeping willows. Then on his last day there, he was strolling at dusk through the apple orchard when she appeared between the rows in front of him. She was dressed in white, as she had been throughout his visit, but for the first time she was wearing a long dress, encircled with tiers of ruffles, the full skirt belled out with hoops and the top cut low to expose her shoulders. Her hair, rather than divided in the middle and pulled back into her usual bun, was swept up high on her head and tied with red and white ribbons. His first thought was that she must be going to a ball. (That wasn't

exactly true: his first thought was that she was the loveliest creature he had ever seen.) His second thought was that maybe she
was celebrating because he was leaving the next day. In the half-
light of dusk among the rows of gnarled trees, she looked like a
vision.

"I love this old orchard at this time of evening," she said. She
didn't really look at him, she watched her hands as she played
with a leaf from one of the trees.

"They're fine old trees," Colin said.

"They're too old to have fruit now, at least most of them."
She lifted her head to look at the trees then looked at Colin briefly
and looked at her hands again. "Once in a while you find a branch
with a couple shriveled-up apples on it, but most of them seem
to have given up. That's sad about apple trees, isn't it?"

"Not really. Things get old and wear out. Like engines."

"'Like engines,'" she smiled. "Most people would try to make
the comparison the other direction, the machines to trees, rather
than trees to machines. You have a unique point of view, Mr.
Lyle."

"I guess machines are the only thing I really know anything
about."

"You seem to know something about people too. More than
you think you do." She held up the leaf in her fingers for him to
see: she had carefully torn the blade from the veins so only the
skeleton remained. She twirled it back and forth until the pattern
of veins was just a blur. Then she smiled and looked at him. "So.
What do you think of our Willow now that you've been here a
while?"

They fell into walking together, back through the rows of old
trees toward the house. "It's a fine place," Colin said to be polite.
"But I'm afraid there's nothing much I can do to help your
father."

"I didn't expect there would be. The kind of help my father needs won't come from machinery. But isn't it beautiful here?"

"Oh yes. I can see why you love it. I can see why anybody would."

Beyond the orchard, the house sat on a slight rise ahead of them. Fireflies lifted in the dark bushes near the house, the windows of the downstairs glowed with lamplight. From the slave quarters came the sound of a fiddle, people laughing and talking loud. There was the smell of wood smoke and honeysuckle on the night air; and the smell of lilacs, which he realized came from Elizabeth. Her shoulders were too slight for such a low-cut dress, they were thin and to a degree turned in upon themselves, but the glimpse of the top of her breasts excited him—he whose idea of excitement through much of his life had involved well-turned piston rods or perfectly formed castings. Her stiff skirt swished through the grass.

As they crunched across the front drive, she said, "And what about you, Mr. Lyle? Do you love it here? Can you ever see yourself living in a place like Willow?"

"No, I'm afraid not. I think I belong in a different kind of life. I think I'm a different kind of person."

"I think you are too," she said as they mounted the front steps. "Well, maybe I'll just have to come and see you in your kind of life. You said you live in a town called Furnass, didn't you, in Pennsylvania?"

In the light of the lamps beside the front door, her eyes looked gray rather than blue. She smiled, cocked her head and raised her eyebrows, as if to say You might be surprised, and handed him the leaf skeleton before she went on into the house. He didn't think much of what she said at the time—not that he thought she was fooling him, but that he was afraid he might be fooling himself—but he carried the veiny skeleton with him on the train heading back north, taking it out of his pocket and smelling the last bit of apple leaf from it until he had worn it to pulp.

And forgot about her. Or tried to. Tried to put her out of his mind. Then within half a year here she was, complete with Sally and George and her sea trunks, staying at the Colonel Berry Hotel and waiting for him to make the next move. How could he fail to marry her? He understood from the first that she had come here, not so much to be with him, but to get away from something in her life; he didn't know what it was that drove her north, and he didn't care. That she was here at all was enough. But as he watched her now talking to the others at the table, as she smiled at Walker with the smile that he knew could lift a man's heart, it occurred to him that he had spent a good deal of their time together wondering if she would eventually pack up her sea trunks and go again just as quickly.

The dinner was breaking up; Walker and Reid were thanking Libby for the meal as they pushed their chairs back and stood. McArtle rose and went over beside Libby, as if to receive the compliments with her. Colin folded his napkin and got heavily to his feet.

"You're back among the living," Libby said to him.

"I must have gone away with my thoughts," Colin said, embarrassed that it was noticed.

"You see what I have to live with, Doctor? I never know if he's present or not."

"The way he disappeared on us," McArtle said, "I thought he might be out there in the cosmos having a chat with the Oversoul."

"It's nothing as illustrious as that," Libby said. She smiled again to Walker and Reid as they bowed to her and left the room. "In his mind he's down there at the steamworks tinkering with his machines."

"You're a good woman to put up with such a quirky old man," Colin said.

"What am I ever going to do with a man like him, Doctor?" Libby said, shaking her head.

Colin went around the table and kissed her on the forehead. "Love him," he said.

Libby blushed. "Oh go on with you," she said, pushing at him gently and then busying herself collecting the napkins. "You're an impossible man." She wouldn't look at either one of them, but she was obviously pleased in spite of herself. McArtle looked as though he didn't know what to do with his hands.

Walker stepped out the front door and sucked in a lungful of air. Thank God to be out of there! As Reid went on down the steps and headed around the house to the privy, Walker stayed on the front porch, stretching his legs, shaking each one in turn, trying to work the kinks out of them from having been tucked under the table through dinner. It was evening below in the valley, though a streak of murky crimson traced the line of hills to the west. In the darkness toward the river, the lamps along the streets cast small circles of pale yellow light, though occasionally the town and the hills across the river were bathed in a bright orangish-yellow glow as a furnace flared at the ironworks. On the river, a skiff with a lantern on the prow maneuvered for a landing at the dock at the lower end of town. A string of lanterns defined the bridge across the end of the valley. Across the expanse of lawn, fireflies winked from the dark grass like a miniature bombardment.

Though he didn't like to think it, the dinner had confirmed his worst suspicions. What the people in the South said about the people in the North was true: they really were a race of crop-eared Puritans and pasty-faced mechanics—even when they were well-to-do, as he had just witnessed. It made them clever, certainly, but to Walker's mind they lacked culture; they seemed humorless, graceless, unable to think of anything or anybody but themselves and their immediate gain. Dr. McArtle. The perfect example. The evening also made him wonder if what he had heard was true about their immorality. Southerners said that Northerners were basically wicked, that Northern women believed in free love and gave themselves willingly to anybody. What he had seen with Mrs. Lyle and Dr. McArtle certainly got him thinking. He had never believed it before, after all by some definitions he was a Northerner himself. He remembered the way they looked at each other this afternoon in the stable, the way they acted toward each other this evening at the table. There was certainly something going on between them. Maybe Libby had lived here so long that she had become infected by these modern ideas. It made him wonder about Lyle as well. What kind of man would let such things go on with his wife? What is it with these people? It disappointed him, on many scores.

As Walker stood among the shadows on the porch, Lyle and McArtle came out the front door, exchanging pleasantries as the doctor took his leave. Walker remained motionless, hoping they wouldn't notice him, having had enough Northern pleasantries for one evening. As McArtle crossed the lawn in the darkness, Lyle watched him go, calling one last "Good night," and waved as the buggy pulled away. Then he turned to Walker.

"He's an insufferable man at times, without question. But he provides the only stimulating conversation I can find in this town. I think he's the only man I know around here who has even heard of Emerson, much less read him. And a couple of times he's been a real friend. I hope you won't judge him too harshly."

Walker was taken aback. "No . . . of course not . . . I. . . ."

"And I hope you won't judge me too harshly either. I apologize for drifting away like that at dinner. My wife was quite right to call attention to it. It was very rude, and I assure you it had nothing to do with either your or Reid's company. We're delighted to have you here."

"You needn't apologize," Walker said. "I figured you were just a man with a lot on his mind. I don't usually say much at table myself. Reid is the talker of the two of us."

"Yes, he certainly gets excited, doesn't he? Which reminds me. I hope you'll come down to the steamworks soon to see the road engines for yourself."

"I was planning to come down tomorrow."

"Excellent. I intend to fire up one of the engines in the morning to give Reid a working demonstration. It will be good for you to see it too." Then he fell silent, staring out over the front steps at the darkness. For several moments he was as distant and remote as he had become at dinner, thinking about something. Finally he said without looking at Walker, "What would summer be without fireflies?"

"Yes."

"I read somewhere that scientists now think that fireflies glow the way they do to attract a mate. I don't know how they could know a thing like that. The thing that bothers me about it is, if you pull the tail out of the bug, it keeps on glowing. I'm afraid of what that might say about people and their desires."

"I suppose a lot depends if you believe another thing scientists say nowadays, that we're all somehow evolved from the same forms of life."

"Hmm." Lyle glanced in Walker's direction. "Maybe that's why I find machines easier to deal with than people. When a machine doesn't do what you want it to, you simply make a new gear or whatever. Maybe someday we'll be able to make one for the human heart."

Why is he telling me all this? I barely know this man. What is he getting at? Lyle continued to stare out into the darkness as if there were something else he wanted to say. Then he turned abruptly.

"Good night, Captain Walker. I hope to see you in the morning," Lyle said, and ducked back into the house.

Walker was uneasy. Lyle seemed to be telling him something, or trying to. What was on his mind? Did he suspect something? That they were Rebels? Or was he trying to warn him about something? Walker looked out into the night. Sycamore House no longer seemed a peaceful, restful place. Troopers could be in the dark forms of the bushes at the end of the yard waiting to attack, waiting to pick them off or storm the house after they were asleep and bayonet them in their beds. Walker moved quietly off the porch. He had left his revolver in his room before dinner to be polite, but it was too risky without it; from now on he was going to keep it with him. Staying close to the house he moved around to the side yard. A figure stepped out of the bushes at the end of the porch. If Walker had had his gun he would have shot Reid.

"What the hell are you doing, sneaking up on me like that!" Walker hissed at him.

"A little jumpy, aren't you?"

Reid tried to suppress his smile. It was a little game he played with himself, played against Walker, on the long ride here; he liked to startle the captain, give him little surprises, jerk him around a bit, Walker took himself so seriously, in his supposed role as Reid's protector, as the supposed leader of this mission. Look at him, glowering at me in the dark. He thinks I answer to him. We'll see, Captain Walker, we'll see. . . .

"Come on, let's get away from the house," Walker said, looking around. "We need to talk."

"Sure," Reid drawled. He motioned: After you.

Walker led the way across the backyard toward the outhouse. He checked to make sure no one was inside, then they stood a little ways away, out of range of the smell.

"What was Lyle going on about?" Reid said. "I only heard a little bit."

"Something about fireflies and making new hearts. I'm not quite sure. How's the deal going? You said you'd have a commitment from him today."

"I don't have it yet, but it's only a matter of time. He just needs to think about it, that's all. What did the paper have to say?"

"Lee is in the central part of the state."

"If I can make the deal with Lyle tomorrow—and I'm sure I will—and if I can get started on the modifications right away, the engines should be ready by the end of the week. That means we should be able to join Lee in four or five days after that, especially if he swings west. What about Morgan?"

"Keep your voice down," Walker said, scanning the dark bushes around the property, the dark trees on the hillside behind them. After a moment he said, "I haven't heard anything."

Reid thought a moment. Walker's face was blackish in the darkness, his expression lost among the crags of his face, but something in his bearing, his demeanor, told Reid it was no time for games. It occurred to him that something had changed, or was changing, in Walker, and not knowing what it was made Reid uneasy. It was bad enough having to deal with primitives, Morgan and all his crew, partisans in Reid's mind being little more than outlaws, but Walker was a mystery to him, when it came down to it, an unknown entity, either smarter than the others or baser, with more animal cunning, he couldn't decide which. Regardless, Reid was going to need Walker, or if not the man himself, at least his men, if his plan was going to work. *I'm so close, so close. . . .*

He looked closely at Walker. "And if you don't hear any-thing?"

"My job was to get you and your material here safely and to wait to meet up with Morgan. My orders said nothing about stay-ing on if Morgan doesn't make it, or if I thought my men were in danger once I got you here."

"Your men aren't in any danger. . . ."

"We don't know that because most of them aren't here yet."

"Look, Walker, you can't think about pulling out now. . . ."

"This whole idea is crazy, crazy. . . ."

"Just wait till you see the road engines. That will convince you." Reid grew excited, trying to catch up Walker in his enthu-siasm, being boyish and he thought appealing, the way he'd learn to sway others to his ideas, the technique that had got him this far. "The Yankees have never seen anything like what we have in store for them, nobody has. We're making history here, Walker. This is going to change the idea of how wars are fought forever. You'll see. Come down to the steamworks tomorrow."

Walker nodded. "I intend to. After Mrs. Lyle goes to church."

Reid let a smile spread across his face as he continued to look closely at Walker. "What did you think of all that inane conver-sation at dinner?"

Walker shrugged, noncommittal.

"I must admit I was surprised at Lyle. By some of the things he said. He shouldn't let himself be distracted by fools like that doctor, he should be concentrating on his work, on his engines. He shouldn't have time for such nonsense. And the way he lets the doctor carry on with his wife. I guess he won't care if you follow her around too. He doesn't seem to mind what anyone does with her."

"You know why I'm staying close to her," Walker snapped.

"Easy, Walker. Take it easy. I didn't mean anything by it." Reid looked away and then back. "I'll see you tomorrow at the steamworks. You'll see for yourself why what we're doing here is so important."

Reid patted Walker's upper arm, the way he had seen other men touch their comrades, and headed back toward the house. Pleased with himself, with the way he handled the situation, the man. Thinking, I can take care of the good captain, when the time comes, I don't need to be concerned. . . .

Walker watched as Reid headed back toward the lights of the house, humming a song to himself as he disappeared into the darkness. I'm going to hit him, I swear before this whole shebang is over I'm going to hit him. He had thought much the same things of Libby and her husband, but hearing Reid say them out loud infuriated him. They made Libby sound cheap and tawdry. Whatever else she was or believed, Libby was a lady, a fine lady. In his mind's eye, Walker could see her on a Southern plantation, decked out in everyday finery, a long flowing dress all ruffles and lace, the picture of a Southern belle, leading a gracious life of parties and visits. It wasn't a way of life he had known, of course, but it was part of the Southern way of life, part of the graciousness of Southern culture which the North lacked.

He remembered at dinner, when the talk had grown strong against the South, Libby had defended his feelings by reminding her husband that Walker was from Kentucky. He remembered that her husband on other occasions during the meal attacked her or patronized her, and that she sat mute much of the time. Somehow it all didn't seem right.

A cat came toward him, picking its way through the dark grass. A calico cat, the same one he had seen this morning washing itself on the back porch.

"Hello, missy," Walker said softly. "What are you up to?"

Across the River

The calico cat meowed and gave a sharp uplift of its tail. As it rubbed against his pants leg, Walker squatted down on his haunches to scratch its ears. The cat rolled on its side and stretched, working its claws through the grass, wanting its back scratched as well.

He thought of the talk at dinner about the book on Morgan's exploits; it had been all he could do not to say something. He and Morgan and the others had read the book that spring; it was at the same time that Reid had sought Morgan out to interest him in his grand idea. The book had done a lot to lift the spirits of the men after a hard winter; it helped them forget, for a while at least, the shame that Grierson's Yankee cavalry had ridden virtually unopposed on a raid through the heart of the South, while Morgan had never been able to get close to the North. Though the events of the book didn't jibe with the way everyone remembered them, for a while they believed again that they were the bold cavaliers that some people said they were, descendants of Rob Roy and Waverly. Everyone believed again, especially Morgan, whom the book compared to Richard the Lion-Hearted. It had to be true, it was there in print. Walker could remember a time when he believed it too.

. . . You crazy bastard, your fooling around is going to get us all killed, he thought as he ran down the hillside from the woods. Morgan stood in the middle of the road in his stolen Union officer's coat, his hands clasped behind his back, watching with a bemused expression on his face as Walker ran toward him.

"If I had known you could run like that back in Lexington," Morgan said as Walker came up to him, "I would have raced you instead of my horses."

"I never had a company of Yankees coming down the road after me in Lexington," Walker said, bending over to brace his

hands on his knees as he caught his breath. "They're just over that rise. Come on, we got to get out of here."

Walker turned to start back up the hill, but Morgan grabbed his arm.

"Hold on, hold on." Morgan looked up the road to where the Yankees would be coming from. And Walker recognized the look on Morgan's face, the look he got before a battle, the intenseness in his eyes, the deadly little smile playing on his lips.

"Call up the hill, get the men and the horses."

"But we don't have time," Walker said. "The Yankees will hear me, and they're bound to see us now. . . . "

"That's the idea, Walker." Morgan stroked his imperial beard. "That's the idea. We'll make a guerrilla out of you yet."

Walker called up to the rest of the men hiding in the woods at the top of the hill. The dozen riders broke from the cover of the trees and galloped toward them just as the company of Union infantry came over the rise in the road.

Morgan and Walker mounted up quickly, but Morgan held up his hand.

"Not yet, not yet. Give 'em a chance to think they're going to get something. . . ." The Union soldiers spotted them and the first ranks ran forward, kneeling down to get ready to fire. Morgan waited . . . waited . . . then dropped his hand and yelled, "Go!" seconds before the Yankees fired. The volley sailed past harmlessly where the Rebels had just been.

They rode hard until they were beyond rifle range, then Morgan slowed them again, moving at little more than a walk out of sight of their pursuers. They continued for a mile or so until they came to a spot where the forest was once again close to the road. Morgan sent the men into the thickets on one side of the road, while he and Walker stayed on the other. The two men tied their horses to trees and crept forward to a place where they could see the road as it approached. It wasn't long before the company of Yankees appeared again, marching at the double-quick.

"Just as I thought," Morgan whispered to Walker. "All the pretty soldiers, all in a row."

He signaled to the men on the other side of the road to get ready, then he and Walker waited. But when the Yankees were forty yards or so away, the mounted officer called them to a halt.

"The bastards, the dirty bastards," Morgan hissed. "How dare they."

The officer on horseback conferred with a sergeant and several others; it was obvious they suspected something. Then the officer slowly rode forward, standing in his stirrups for a closer look. Morgan, still in the Union coat, walked out into the middle of the road.

"Good day, Captain," he yelled. "Looking for something?"

"Have you seen some Rebels headed this way?" he called back, still wary.

Morgan mumbled something that even Walker in the brush couldn't make out.

"What did you say?" the Union officer said, coming a little closer.

"I said, if you're looking for Morgan, sir, I'm sorry to say that you've found him." With that Morgan took out his pistol and shot him in the face.

The Yankees quickly fired off a volley as Morgan dove for cover, the bullets crashing through the trees and snapping off leaves and branches. The Rebels answered with several volleys of their own before mounting up and heading off through the brush, waiting to return to the road until they were out of range. Morgan was in high spirits.

"Did you see the look on that poor bastard's face? He thought he had found help, and instead he found Morgan."

"He found his reward in heaven for messing with Morgan,"
one of the men said.

"Yankees don't go to heaven," another one said.

"What's the matter, Walker?" Morgan said as they rode along.
"You look like something's bothering you."

"Walker's bothered because you lured that officer into a trap
and shot him in cold blood, right, Walker?" said Jeff Sterritt, one
of the men who along with Walker had been with Morgan since
the beginning in the Green River days.

Morgan laughed. "You tell me the difference between shooting
a man that way, and shotgunning pickets in the middle of the
night."

"Maybe that's what's bothering me," Walker said. "There is
no difference."

"Your problem, sweet Judson," Morgan said, "is that you
think too much. The fact is there's a big difference and I'll tell
you what it is: Jeb Stuart would never have the guts to stand up
by himself and shoot a man like I just did. Hah!"

Morgan's excitement set his horse, Black Bess, to prancing.
The members of the Second Kentucky Cavalry gave the Rebel yell,
and as they broke into a gallop heading back to camp, a few of
the men started to sing:

> *Georgia girls are handsome,*
> *And Tennessee girls are sweet*
> *But a girl in old Kentucky*
> *Is the one I want to meet. . . .*

In the grass, the calico cat lolled on its side, stretching,
stretching its claws as Walker absently scratched its back, the
cat turning its head to look at him. Was it possible for a cat to
look seductive? It almost seemed so, the way the cat gazed up at
him, blinking slowly. Walker, old son, you've been away too long.

The cat rolled over on its back, wanting its tummy scratched as well.

"You might as well make the most of it, huh missy?" he said to the cat.

As if in response, the cat stretched even further, rubbing its shoulders back and forth in the grass at the same time as Walker rubbed its stomach. Then the cat suddenly curled around Walker's hand and grabbed on to him with its front claws, biting at him as it dug at his wrist with its back legs.

"Whoa cat!" Walker said as he pulled his hand away. As leathery and calloused as his hand was, the cat had still broken the skin in a couple places. The cat jumped to its feet and arched its back, said "Brrt!" and bounded off sideways into the darkness. Walker looked to see where it had gone, and found Sally and her husband George standing on the path midway between the house and the stable, watching him.

"Strange cat," Walker said, feeling as if he were caught red-handed at something.

"Not really," Sally said. "She just has her own thinks."

His feelings of awkwardness were just beginning. After years of camp life, he was accustomed to squatting on his haunches for hours at a time, a necessity to keep from sitting in the damp or snow. But now, perhaps because of his overall weariness or because he was still weak from his wound, he found he couldn't stand up, or at least not with any semblance of dignity. To keep from embarrassing himself further, he remained squatting. For several moments, Walker and the couple stared at each other. Finally, George mumbled to his wife and they discussed something quietly.

"My George thinks you've shrunk yourself down to that size," Sally said to Walker. "He thinks you're a demon."

"No, I've got legs like everybody else," Walker said and tried to smile. Now that he had attempted to move and found he couldn't, his knees ached and he felt the cramp he had in his calf this morning starting to return. "I just feel like taking it easy for a while, that's all."

"I told him you weren't no demon," Sally said. "My George isn't always too smart. I told him you can't be a demon, because you're the Rider on the Red Horse. But he's still not convinced. You ain't helping matters none with your hovering down there on the ground."

"I'll be getting up here pretty soon."

The couple waited another moment, then Sally took her husband by the hand. "Come along, he don't want us watching whatever it is he's going to do." They continued on to the stable, hand in hand. George tried to look back once, but Sally slapped at him, warning him to keep his eyes forward. "You don't want to know what that Rider on the Red Horse is going to do, neither."

When they were gone, Walker tipped forward onto his knees, stretching first one leg behind him and then the other to loosen them up, then, bracing himself on his good arm to get started, pulled himself slowly to his feet. *What's happening to me, I'm as stiff as an old woman.* He looked around, slipping his hand inside the suit coat and pressing it against his wound. As it grew later, the evening became quieter, there were fewer sounds coming from the mills and factories along the river. Walker was aware of the crickets in the grass, the buzz of insects in the dark woods behind him; overhead, a nighthawk whistled repeatedly. Against the pulsing glow coming from the lights of the valley, the house seemed to dance, to jump toward him and away. *I've got to get some rest.*

Where was Morgan? The last word Walker had on Morgan's whereabouts was while he and Reid were in Cincinnati; at that time, Morgan was still in McMinnville, he hadn't even left Tennessee. What was holding him back? Walker was afraid he knew all too well what that could be. If Morgan was on the move, the papers would be full of it, but the only stories were about rumors and false sightings, outlaws mistaken for guerrillas. As soon as the rest of his men got here—if they got here—he'd have Sparky their telegraph operator find out what he could on the wire. Until then there wasn't much he could do except wait. If Morgan didn't come, if he and his men were left stranded here with Reid and his crazy scheme . . . He wouldn't think of that now. He started for the house.

There were lights in the downstairs windows; on the second floor, at the far end of the house from where he was, a lamp glowed in Reid's room. And as he watched, another lamp appeared on the second floor in a room closer to him, faint at first, then growing stronger, filling the room for a moment then moving on—faint again, then stronger—to the room beside it. Through the window, he saw Libby standing in the middle of the room, holding the lamp, apparently just looking around. Those are the children's rooms, she is looking in their rooms even though her children aren't there, even though she took them away, she must miss them. He was touched, and felt sheepish for witnessing something private.

He continued on toward the house when Libby moved to the window and stood there, looking out, bathed in the glow of the lamp, looking in his direction. For a second he wondered if it could be a signal to someone. He looked around expecting soldiers, betrayal, but the hillside was quiet, nothing moved. She was still at the window, the light shining up on her face, luminous, almost ghostly. Doesn't she know I'm out here, doesn't she know that I can see her? Or is that the reason? Maybe she's standing there looking for me. Or standing there so I can see her. After another moment, she turned from the window and the lamp grew fainter until the window was dark again. Son, you've got to get ahold of yourself. He went around to the front of the house.

On his way upstairs, he noticed Lyle was reading in his study. The only sign of Libby was the rectangle of light haloed around her door.

FOUR

Was it a dream? At this point, Walker wasn't sure; he was having trouble deciphering when he was awake and when he wasn't. In his half-waking stupor, he heard voices and movement in the house around him; there was the sound of Reid in the room next door, and then Reid and Lyle talking about something as they went downstairs. Walker knew he should get up and go with them, but having thought that, he promptly went back to sleep again. Or at least he thought he was asleep. He dreamt that he was awake, lying in bed in a strange house in a Yankee mill town in Western Pennsylvania. The only way he decided later that he had actually been asleep was that the next time he looked at the window, the sun was different in the leaves of the sycamores outside.

Earlier, the window was gray. A light fog drifted through the trees, filtering the sunlight and turning the window to pearl, the leaves as murky as gray-green memories of leaves. Now the fog had either lifted or been burned away; morning sunlight edged the leaves with shadow, intensifying the green and making each leaf distinct, calling attention to the collection of individual leaves rather than to the mass of the tree. As he lay there, he heard Libby go downstairs. He dozed again, waking a short time later when she returned. This lazying around had gone on long enough; he got up, washed and shaved with the bowl of water left on the washstand, and dressed. His wound was feeling better; there was only a tightness in the skin, it only hurt if he lifted his arm too far, and he felt stronger after the long night's sleep. All this trouble from one little scratch in my side, what the hell would I do if I was really hurt? Don't think about it. He was ready to leave the room when he remembered: he went back and strapped on the holster with his Colt Army revolver, checking in the mirror to make sure that the long suit coat covered it. He also remembered his hat. It was U.S. Army regulation—it looked pretty much like any other black slouch hat, though the gold and black braided cord was a giveaway; he reminded himself that he *was* supposed to be a Union officer—none the worse for wear after the roan stepped on it during their melee outside of Wheeling. He checked himself once more in the mirror. He looked okay. I shouldn't care. He was ready.

In the hall he could hear Libby behind the door of her room, singing to herself as she moved about. Without trying to be particularly quiet—he wanted her to know that he was there, and that he was getting ready to leave—he went on downstairs. There was no one around, but in the kitchen was a pan of cornbread on the table and a pot of coffee warming on the stove. With Sally not there, he wondered if Libby herself had left them for him. After a cup of coffee and a handful of cornbread, he left the house and crossed the front lawn, following the lane down the hill a little ways until he ducked into some bushes. He relieved his bladder, then remained hidden where he could see the house and waited.

The morning was sunny and bright, the air still cool from the night before. In the valley, a curtain of fog rose from the river, following the curves of the river as it wound through the hills, blanking out the other side of the valley but leaving untouched the town on the slope below him; the top of the fog disappeared in wisps into a sky the color of the light blue pants of a Yankee uniform. In the town a church bell was ringing, the sound of the solitary bell floating up through the valley. Something wasn't right; he looked about the hillside. Finches and meadowlarks twittered in the bushes around him; a crow and two jays were squabbling in a nearby tree; insects chirred in the grass. It occurred to him that the mills and factories along the river were quiet for the Sabbath; this was the first time he was outdoors since he had been here that there wasn't an undercurrent of noise, the steady thumping and rumble of machinery in the background, a sound part of every other sound. I've been here too long already, I'm getting used to all the noise just like a goddamn Yankee, next thing you know I'll be missing the soot and the stink too. Walker pulled the tassel from a stock of spike-grass and put the end in his mouth, chewing the moist stem flat.

He thought she might have George hitch up the team of bays and take her to church. But a short time later Libby appeared by herself on the front porch, opened her parasol, and came down the lane toward him. When she was past, Walker fell in a safe distance behind her, following the solitary figure in black as she made her way down the trails and crisscross paths of the hillside. A number of church bells were ringing now, scaring a flock of pigeons that wheeled in the sky above the main street; the birds would start to come to rest on a rooftop, but then another set of bells would start to peal and the birds would be off and flying again. Along the board sidewalks were clusters of people dressed in their Sunday finery.

Libby walked alone toward a small unadorned white frame church at the upper end of town. A few people stood talking in front of the church, but she moved through them as if they weren't there. As she mounted the steps she stopped to close her parasol; then she turned and looked back at Walker standing a little ways down the street. She smiled at him and inclined her head, as if to acknowledge his presence and thank him for the escort, as if it were a game to her. She knew I was here, she knew the whole time, but she didn't seem to mind. What does she think I'm up to? What is she up to? Son, I told you, you've got to be careful here. Very careful. Walker tipped his hat to her in return and backtracked toward the main part of town.

There were only a few people left on the sidewalks, stragglers hurrying to one church or another, an occasional family in a four-wheeler drawn by high-stepping horses. Gradually the town grew hushed as the church bells stopped ringing; the stores were closed, the streets were empty. Below the main street, down the side streets toward the river, there were a few boardinghouses and residence hotels, a few shacks and workers' cottages and saloons, but the hillside was mainly bare until the flatland along the floor of the valley. Walker headed down the slope, keeping his left arm pressed to his side against his wound. The silence of the mills seemed ominous, unnatural. Overhead, the rows of smokestacks disappeared into the fog that was just beginning to lift; as he got closer, the buildings of the Keystone Steam Works loomed above him, blocking his view of the wooded bluffs across the river. Then as he crossed the spur-line tracks, he heard a distant chugging and hissing, a sound he couldn't identify yet carried all the familiarity of a dream. He passed through the wrought iron gate and down a narrow passageway between the buildings, his boot heels sounding on the cobblestones.

The passageway led to a large central compound, surrounded on three sides by the buildings of the steamworks, the fourth side open to the river. The steamworks was an assortment of long three- and four-story buildings—pattern and carpentry shops, machine shops, a rolling mill and foundry, blacksmith shops, dormitories for the workers, an administration building and storage sheds—constructed variously of wood and stone and brick. A few men were hanging out the windows of the dormitories to watch what was going on in the yard, otherwise the buildings seemed deserted. The sound he heard was coming from the far end of the compound. In front of the doors to one of the shops was a steam engine mounted on wheels, the like of which Walker had never seen before. Black smoke poured from the stack, and, as the machine sat idling, the chugging and hissing were accented by the ring of metal hitting metal from slack in the drive train, chiming like a dull bell. Reid and Lyle were clambering over the engine, checking something as they yelled back and forth to each other over the noise. When he saw Walker, Reid waved and jumped down to greet him. His red hair and beard carried particles of soot and a large grease smudge covered one cheek. He seemed genuinely pleased to see Walker.

"Behold the future," Reid said. He made a grand, sweeping gesture toward the machine.

"The future's very noisy," Walker said, raising his voice to be heard.

Reid ignored the comment. "Come on, let me give you a ride. It will be an education."

"I'm not sure I want to be that educated. What about the deal with Lyle?"

Reid's face broke into a grin. "He agreed this morning. See, I told you he would." Reid glanced over his shoulder at Lyle working on the engine, then back at Walker. "He's got two road engines already built, this one and another one just like it. We can have them both. They're the same ones he used at the trials for the U.S. government last fall, so I know what they can do. And he's agreed to whatever modifications I want on them. For a price, of course. I told him we'd have the money for him as soon as the wagons get here. I'm assuming that they're going to get here."

"They'll get here," Walker said, wishing he believed it.

"I'll go over the drawings with him this afternoon and get everything lined out so work can get started the first thing tomorrow. He's got his own reasons why he wants this project to be a success, and he'll give us as many men and as much of his facilities as we need to get the engines ready. We'll probably be working around the clock, so I'll stay down here from now on. I want to be around if any problems come up. There's plenty of room in the dormitories. Why don't you stay here too?"

"No, I think I'll stay on up at the house."

"Why? Lyle's agreed to everything we wanted. He bought the story of a secret government mission completely. And even if he didn't, I'm convinced he'd go along with us regardless. This is his ticket to solvency, we're the answer to his prayers. We're going to put his company and this little town on the map."

"Don't forget it's still a Yankee map. Even if these engines do everything you want them to, the Keystone Steam Works is a long way from the Confederate States of America."

"If my engines are a success—no, not if, when—we'll own this town, and this state for that matter. When Lee sees what these engines can mean to the Confederacy, he'll march here and make sure this town can turn out as many engines as we need. Or say that for some reason we lose this town. With these two engines as prototypes, we can make others like them in the South. And after Lyle has a taste of success, I wouldn't be surprised if he wanted to direct their manufacture there. After all, he married a Southern belle, he can't be completely against the Southern cause."

"Let's keep Libby out of this," Walker said, and immediately regretted it.

Reid arched his eyebrows, feigning surprise. "So it's 'Libby' now, is it? Is that why you want to stay up at the house? You're not getting sweet on the lady, are you Walker?"

Walker didn't say anything. His wound didn't hurt but the bandage itched from his sweat and the skin seemed to be pulling tighter as the day wore on.

"Okay, okay," Reid grinned. He went to slap Walker good-naturedly on the arm but caught himself in time. "What you do is your business. I've got my own work cut out for me." He turned away and gazed at the road engine proprietorially. "Isn't it the most beautiful thing you've ever seen in your life?"

No, not exactly. The road engine bore a slight resemblance to a small locomotive—a horizontal boiler with a smokestack in front, the whole affair perhaps fifteen feet long—but there the similarity ended. Two small wheels were in front, and two six-foot-diameter wheels were in the rear; a fifth wheel, a large fly-wheel, was mounted high on the left side of the boiler. On top of the boiler were two piston cylinders, connected to the driving wheels by a series of chains and gears, and the steam dome; the two balls of the governor were spinning like a weathervane gone crazy. Behind the boiler was a deck with enough room for three or four men, and a tender to carry coal and water. Black smoke and cinders billowed from the stack, steam hissed from the safety valves, and hot water dribbled from a pipe beneath its belly.

"Come on," Reid said. "Let me take you for a ride."

Lyle was at the controls on the rear platform. He released one lever and pulled on another; with a great puff of smoke the road engine lurched forward a few feet. Walker jumped back. Reid looked at him and grinned.

"Don't worry, Captain, it won't bite."

"I'm not worried about being bit, I'm worried about being run over."

"I didn't think the brave Captain Walker was afraid of anything."

"There's a difference between being afraid of something and just not liking it."

Lyle released a cloud of steam from the boiler. The cloud jetted down into the dust and then spiraled skyward like a cyclone, enshrouding the engine in a ghostly mist.

"You're right, Captain, the entire modern world could run you over if you're not careful," Reid shouted over the noise. As Lyle set the engine rolling again, Reid hurried to catch up, scrambling onto the platform on his hands and knees.

"Or run away with you," Walker called, but Reid didn't hear him.

Spewing clouds of smoke and steam, the road engine lumbered forward. Walker expected the men in the dormitory windows to cheer, but they watched impassively, evidently having seen it all before. The compound was several city blocks square, and Lyle circled the area, threading the machine between stockpiles of coal and coke and stacks of iron plate as he instructed Reid on the controls. There were the smells of sulfur and oil and ash; once when the wind shifted, Walker was engulfed in a damp dark cloud, the oily mist pinpricking his face. After several times around the yard, Lyle turned the controls over to Reid and swung down from the platform as they passed Walker. Reid let loose several shrieks from the whistle and waved as he chugged on.

"He's like a child with a new toy," Lyle said as he came over to Walker.

A dangerous child, Walker thought, but didn't say anything.

Lyle rolled down his shirtsleeves and buttoned his waistcoat. "So, what do you think of the road engine? Is this the first time you've seen one?"

"I'm surprised it can go that fast. . . ."

"It can go faster than that, if I let it. I don't want Reid to wreck the machine before it's paid for." He looked at Walker with a sly smile.

"I've solved the problem of weight, Captain Walker," Lyle went on. "That and a number of other things, including the ratio of the size of the boiler to the amount of pressure it can develop. The English are generally ahead of us in developing road and farm engines, but I've come up with solutions they haven't thought of. On this type of engine you need to keep the boiler relatively short, so the water inside stays level as you're going up and down hills. On the other hand, you need a boiler that's large enough to develop enough steam. What I've developed is an internal system that keeps the water level so you can't swamp the boiler or burn the firebox on a grade. And there are twin cylinders instead of just one so the engines develop a full ten horsepower; the wheels are wrought iron instead of cast iron so they'll wear longer; and the engines steer from the rear platform instead of the front so one man can operate it. What you're looking at is an engine that can pull six fully loaded wagons, each one carrying five to six tons, and maintain a steady ten miles an hour up and down hills. . . ."

He was interrupted by the road engine rumbling by again, Reid busily at work at the controls. Lyle looked sheepish.

"Forgive me for going on like that," he said when the engine had passed. "I guess your Mr. Reid isn't the only one who gets carried away when he talks about road engines."

"It's quite all right," Walker said. "I'm interested to know what these engines can do."

Lyle smiled ruefully. "In business it's imperative that a prospective buyer knows what he's getting. But to me it always seems immodest to go on about one's achievements. I'm sure I do get overly excited when I start to talk about the engines. I truly believe my engines can revolutionize the transportation of goods and people, not just for the army but for the country as a whole."

"Is that what Reid told you they'd be used for? To haul supplies and troops?"

"They are essentially trains without rails. They can go anywhere there's a road, and even without a road. By using road engines, the army will be able to extend its supply lines almost indefinitely. Can you imagine what that means? One road engine can replace hundreds of horses and do away with all the problems that go along with keeping that many animals fed and healthy. A road engine can go hundreds of miles at a stretch, for days on end, and then turn around and head back. . . ."

"Have you ever thought about their use in battle?" Walker interrupted him.

Lyle looked at him a moment. "I've thought about it, of course. But it would be impractical. If you tried to mount a cannon on an engine, the recoil would knock the whole thing over the first time you fired it. No, Captain, don't waste your time trying to think up uses that are unsuited for the road engines. My engines will benefit the army the same way they will benefit mankind as a whole, as transportation . . . Excuse me. . . ."

As Reid brought the engine around again, Lyle evidently saw something that bothered him. He drifted over toward the engine and swung up on board as it passed, taking over the controls again. Unconcerned, Reid blew the whistle again, the shrieks careening off the factory walls. Looking back at Walker, he danced a little jig.

From the bottom of the hill close to the river, breaking the stillness of the Sunday morning, came the repeated screech of a steam whistle. That has to be Colin, Eugene McArtle said to himself as he sat in his buggy down the street from the First Congregational

Presbyterian Church. Colin playing with his engines again. He probably thinks it's a big joke. The fool. In his mind's eye he could see Colin firing up one of his boilers for no other reason than to blow the whistle on a quiet Sunday morning. He could see the glee in Colin's face with every toot. Hypocrites, this will show them a thing or two. Ring their church bells at me, will they? Well, I can blow my whistle right back at them. This will give them something to think about Colin Lyle. He does things like that just to upset people. Just to get back at them. Then he wonders why the town is against him. The fool. Dr. McArtle, sitting hunched forward holding the reins, slowly shook his head.

Jack, the horse, shifted his weight from one haunch to the other, flicked his tail.

"Steady, Jack," McArtle said. "You know the routine."

The buggy was parked down the street from the church under the shade of the trees, half a block away from the other buggies and carriages that were waiting for the service to let out. Jack shook his head to brush away some flies and shifted his weight back again.

"Sorry, Jack, but my experience is that there'll always be waiting. And flies." And fools.

The thing was, there was a part of him that admired Colin for blowing the whistle back at the town. For taking the town's opinion of him and throwing it in their faces. Especially the dour faces of the good church folk of Furnass. If witches and heretics were still burned at the stake, the doctor was sure that Colin would have been roasted to a crisp long ago. In the same way that, if he thought he could get away with it, Colin would have burned every church in Furnass to the ground, simply on intellectual principle. It was one of the principles they shared, one of the reasons McArtle valued his friendship. Without Colin he would have no one to talk to at all. Except Libby, of course. But that had grown to something more than just talk.

McArtle smiled to himself. He knew the dull clink of the Congregationalists' bell particularly drove Colin to distraction. Colin always said the first thing he was going to do when the steamworks was out of debt was to buy a decent set of bells for the church. It would be the ultimate affront. That way, Colin said, if he was going to be assailed by bells, he would at least have the satisfaction of knowing they were his bells. Colin had been an elder in the church, his family had been one of the founders of the church in town. But he left the church ten years earlier, when one Sunday the entire church body had censured him for planning to marry a non-Congregationalist. The fact that Libby was a Southerner, fifteen years younger than Colin, traveled around the country by herself, and had plopped herself down unannounced on Colin's doorstep—and worse, had taken rooms for herself in the Colonel Berry Hotel—didn't help the congregation's appraisal of her.

The week after Colin stopped going to the church, Libby started. At first McArtle assumed that Libby attended the church to force her detractors to swallow—and hopefully choke on—their own bile, something that she was certainly quite capable of doing. But as time went on he wondered if she didn't do it as much to aggravate Colin as well. She and Colin played complicated strategies. There was certainly nothing in her background, at least that McArtle was aware of, that gave her an affinity with a Scottish sect that sang only unaccompanied psalms and considered any musical instrument not mentioned in the Bible a tool of the devil. But whatever her reasons, she attended faithfully every Sunday, rain, snow, or shine. And every Sunday for more years than he cared to remember, the doctor made sure he was in the neighborhood when church let out so he could drive her home.

Jack shifted his haunches again, lifted his tail, and released a cascade of shit. Good, Jack. Just what I need. Another opinion. The doctor moved the horse ahead several feet so he didn't feel quite so much that he was sitting in it.

It was close to one o'clock. McArtle had been waiting for more than an hour when the dull clink of the bell finally started—he listened for the whistle down at the steamworks in reply, but Colin must have been busy with something else. As usual, Libby was one of the last to leave. He watched as she threaded her way down the steps without speaking to anyone, opened her black parasol, and came in his direction. When she was past the line of waiting buggies and carriages, he flicked the reins and pulled up beside her. Without saying anything, she climbed in.

"Hiyup Jack," McArtle said.

As they rolled past the church, a few of the people standing about turned to watch. McArtle tipped his hat in a general greeting, most of the people there being patients. Libby looked straight ahead, holding her purse and Bible on her lap.

"Sometimes I wonder who we think we're fooling," she said when they were on down the street. She relaxed a little, patting her hair into place beneath the brim of her small black feathered hat.

"Probably no one. But what is it that we're doing? I give you a ride home from church every Sunday. Doesn't sound like the height of decadence to me."

"I suppose not." She thought a moment. "As I said, who do we think we're fooling?"

Was she telling him that she didn't want him to pick her up anymore? For a moment he felt a wave of panic. But she said no more about it, she only looked at him briefly and smiled her enigmatic smile and went back to watching the town clop past. He had never been able to read her moods, though he had pretended otherwise, he had never understood half the things she said. Was that what fascinated him about her? He didn't think so.

Over the years of riding her home on Sundays he had devised a route to Sycamore House that made the trip last as long as possible. The route involved traveling through town almost to the end of the valley and then following a series of crisscross roads back and forth up the hillside. He had always planned to tell her, if she asked, that the reason he took the route was to save Jack from the steepest grades; it being Sunday, he thought his horse should have a day of rest too. But she never asked.

"I didn't want to mention it last evening at dinner because of our guests," she said after a while. They left behind the last store on the main street and rolled past a few workers' cottages clinging to the slope. "But I was surprised I didn't see you yesterday at the Taylor boy's funeral."

"Hmm," McArtle said, pulling Jack to the left to avoid some ruts in the road left by last week's rain.

"Which still doesn't answer why you weren't at his funeral."

She likes to pinion me. No, she likes to spread my colors out and stick me to a board like a specimen for her to look at. She does it I swear just to see me squirm, but why does she want to see me squirm? If I knew the answer to that one I probably wouldn't be here now or ever again.

"You know, Eugene, there's no reason for you to feel guilty."

"What makes you think I'd feel guilty about missing a funeral. . . ?"

"I didn't mean that. You should feel guilty about missing his funeral. It would have meant a lot to his mother. What I mean is, you needn't feel guilty about not joining the medical corps."

McArtle, sitting hunched over, his forearms resting on his thighs, the reins limp in his hands, looked over at her. She operates like I do. Without anesthetics.

"If you believe in something, then you should be willing to do what you can for it. And I do believe in the sanctity of the Union, and I do believe that slavery is wrong. But it is equally clear to me that I don't want to be in the army."

He looked over at her, to see if there was understanding in her face. How much do I tell her, how much do I dare? Not that, you don't. But all she seemed was tired.

"Look at it this way," he said. "I couldn't go to the army, because I couldn't stand to be away from you."

"You do have yourself in a quandary, don't you?" she said, tilting her head away again, as if it were too heavy to hold upright. "No wonder you hate Captain Walker."

McArtle felt himself color. He tried very hard to keep his voice even. "Who said I hate Captain Walker? Why would I hate him?"

"Why wouldn't you? A tall, handsome cavalry officer, who's not afraid to put his life on the line for what he believes. Who's already risked his life for his beliefs, at least once, and bears the wound to prove it. I think if I were in your shoes, he would be very hateful to me. Particularly if you were jealous of him on account of me to begin with."

I wonder how many times she has to see me wriggling to satisfy her, I wonder how many variations of species it will take before she grows tired of collecting them. I wonder which one of us will tire of the wriggling first. Probably her.

The buggy turned slowly into another of the crisscross paths and they doubled back upon themselves again, only higher this time, climbing gradually toward the lone house among the stand of sycamores. As they mounted higher on the hillside, the town below, the sweeping S-curve of the river between the hills, looked like a painting of a town and a river. The perfect sky was the color of the veins in his wrist.

"You did seem to be paying a lot of attention to him," he said after a while. "More than was probably necessary."

"Then you should also be jealous of Reid too, as long as you're about it," she smiled, apparently pleased with herself. "After all, Reid was the one who kicked me under the table. Perhaps he was trying to touch me with his foot and got carried away."

"Reid is just a puppy," McArtle said, and was surprised himself how much it sounded like a growl. "Walker's the one you need to worry about. He isn't one of your storybook soldiers, Libby. I think he's dangerous, and I think you should be careful of him."

She watched her hand on her thigh chase the wrinkles in the crinolines beneath the black silk of her dress. "I think I need to remind you that both gentlemen, Mr. Reid and Captain Walker, are our houseguests. It's my duty as a wife and as a citizen to be as gracious and as attentive to Mr. Lyle's guests as I possibly can—"

"Colin's a fool," McArtle blurted out. "Well, he is and you know it. He's a fanatic. He threw away his half of the ironworks so he could build steam engines, and now he's throwing away the steamworks to build these road engines or whatever he calls them. The town thinks he's crazy, and I can't blame them. I don't know how you've stayed with him all these years."

"If the town thinks anyone is crazy, it's me," Libby said calmly. "And on that subject the town can think what it wants."

Jack came to a stop on his own in front of the gate to the house. Libby was looking at the Bible in her lap.

"I don't know why I bother to carry this with me every Sunday. I never open it."

She didn't hear a word I said about Colin, she didn't get my meaning about her at all. She's just like Colin, she only hears what she wants to hear. Maybe the only reason she rides home with me is to aggravate Colin. Maybe I'm the one being taken for a ride.

For several moments they sat together without saying anything, Libby staring straight in front of her as if the buggy were still moving, the doctor staring at her. The afternoon was quiet. There was only the chirr of insects in the fields on the hillside, a finch sitting on a fence post whistling an intricate melody. Jack's tail flicked between the traces like a pendulum.

Finally she smiled and looked at him, called back from somewhere, or perhaps no place at all. "Well. Have you been practicing for our Tuesday Night Entertainments?"

McArtle nodded. She was trying to make small talk, as if everything were all right between them, as if this were nothing more than two friends having a chitchat about one thing or another, and he refused to make it easy for her.

"I was thinking of inviting Mr. Reid and Captain Walker."

"Certainly, why not," McArtle said and looked away.

Libby collected her things and stepped down from the buggy. He would have offered to help her but he knew from past experience she would refuse, she always did. She opened her parasol and waited, looking at him.

McArtle sighed and reached around behind the seat for his medical bag. He handed her a small brown bottle.

"Thank you," she said, and put the bottle into her purse. "I'm feeling my headaches more than ever lately."

"I don't know why you insist that I mix it for you. You could get the same thing at Slater's or any other pharmacy."

"Yes, and have the whole town talking about it. Besides, this way I know it's mixed properly. I know you would never do anything to hurt me, Eugene." She thought about something, then smiled coyly. "And it gives you something to do for me. I know you like that."

He wanted to take her in his arms, but he knew that was also among the things she wouldn't let him do. At the house, Sally stood in the shadows inside the front door, waiting for her. Libby started through the gate, then looked back at him with genuine affection.

"I know it hurts, Eugene. But please don't let it. There's nothing I can do about it."

He watched as she continued up the front walk and entered the house, until she was absorbed by the shadows inside the front door. There she goes, she just turns and walks away. It always seems so easy for her. Me, it's always like a stake through my heart. All these years and all these good-byes, you'd think I'd be used to them by now. I guess I better get used to them, it's all it's ever going to be. He flicked the reins.

"Hiyup Jack."

The horse turned around without having to be guided and headed back down the paths toward the town.

His own house was close to the main street, on what would someday be the street above the main street of town but was now only a few scattered houses along a road. It was a good-sized block of a house, the stucco lined to give it the look of sandstone, with a high-stooped entrance and elaborate Italianate ornaments; the tall, narrow, pointed-arched windows gave the facade an appearance of perpetual surprise. He tied Jack to the low cast-iron fence in front and went inside. Because it was Sunday his housekeeper wasn't there; McArtle had left early that morning on his rounds and the curtains were still closed, the house was dark and stuffy. He went to the windows now, but decided to leave the curtains as they were; it would be evening soon enough and he'd only have to close them again. He wandered through the downstairs for a while, through the rooms decorated and furnished as though for a family but lived in only by himself, through the waiting room and the rooms he used for his practice, but his desire finally got the better of him. Like a man condemned he slowly went upstairs.

In his bedroom, he went to the French doors and stepped out onto a small balcony. It was the only feature he had insisted upon when he had the house built, its inclusion at this particular level on this particular face of the house the only stipulation he made to the builder. The afternoon sun was already beyond the roof line; he stood in the brilliant sunshine that bathed the hillside. Above the valley rim, a red-tailed hawk circled on a current of air he couldn't feel. There were the myriad shades of green on the wooded slope. Fields of wildflowers and tall grass. Clouds white as gauze on a hopelessly blue sky. And in the center of his view, the house among the sycamores.

He wondered what she was doing now. Had she changed her clothes from church? Was she upstairs in her bedroom at this very moment, or was she somewhere else in the house? Reading? Or talking to Sally? Was she playing the piano, thinking about Tuesday night? Was she thinking of him? The way he always thought of her.

Maybe they're more alike than I ever gave them credit for, she and Colin. Maybe I'm a bigger fool than he is. And I don't care.

He had been standing there lost in reverie for—What? Minutes? A half hour?—when he became aware of the distant pounding, realized it came from his front door. He hurried downstairs, calling, "I'm coming, I'm coming." Thinking, Is it her? Could it be? Colin's hurt? The children? He opened the door to find a farmer in bib overalls.

"Doc, my name's Cleary. . . ."

"Yes, yes, I know who you are. What is it?"

"My boy, the wagon got him, run over both his legs. . . ."

"I'll come right now."

"I didn't know if I should bring him in or not. I didn't know if you'd come all the way out to our place. . . ."

"Of course I will, what did you think?" he snapped, then caught himself. "You did the right thing not to move him. Don't worry, I'm coming as soon as I find. . . ."

He looked around for his hat; he caught a glimpse of himself in the hall mirror and saw it was still on his head. Slamming the door behind him, he brushed past Cleary down the steps.

"I'm sorry to tangle up your Sunday and all," Cleary said, hurrying after him. "Me and my missus is very grateful . . ."

Jack raised his head, ready to go. McArtle knew already that gratefulness was about all he could expect from a poor dirt farmer like Cleary, that he probably wouldn't be paid for the trip unless he was willing to take a couple of chickens for his trouble. But he hurried to his buggy and climbed in, gathering the reins, lacing them through his fingers impatiently as Cleary pulled himself up to the seat beside him. No, Cleary, you're too dumb to know about such things. I'm the one who's grateful.

The passageway between the buildings narrowed around him. Were the walls this close earlier? Walker thought his mind must be playing tricks on him, he hadn't been bothered when he entered the compound; the passageway hadn't seemed so confining before. If there were Yankees waiting for him at the other end, he was trapped, he could never make it back to the open before they picked him off. He walked faster. Behind him, the road engine began to trundle around the yard again; Reid and Lyle must have finished another of their technical discussions. They probably hadn't noticed he was gone yet, it could be hours before they missed him. At the end of the dark passageway he kept close to the wall, his coattail pulled back and his hand on his revolver, looking out cautiously before he stepped from the shadows. The panorama of the valley opened up before him, the town on the wooded slope, the sweep of the hills. There were no soldiers, no ambush, nobody in sight.

You can't go getting crazy on me. You can't go letting your imagination run away with you, because you can't wear yourself out. You can't get tired thinking there's somebody out there trying to kill you because there is somebody out there trying to kill you, there's more than one person out there who wants to see you dead. The danger here is to start thinking there is no danger here. The day you stop looking for trouble is the day you'll end up stepping in it. And, son, you're already in more trouble here than you can ever imagine. . . .

Shadows patchworked across the hills, tracing every ripple, every nuance in the landscape, winking on and off as the clouds chased one another across the valley sky. High on the hillside overlooking the town was the Lyles' ivy-covered house, at this distance like a green lump in the shape of a house among the trees; he was going to have a long walk back when it was time. But instead of starting the climb up the hill, he turned left along the spur-line tracks until they joined the mainline beyond the steamworks, then continued on toward the end of the valley, walking along the ties, following the curve of the river. This close to the bank, the bluffs across the river towered above him, a wall of green and sandstone. Was it only two days ago that he and Reid were on the hillside, looking then to where he was now? What had happened between then and now to make it seem so distant? He didn't know. Across the slow-moving Allehela, circles occasionally broke the surface, catfish perhaps surfacing for insects. He had fished in this river as a boy, though that was upstream toward New Inverness where his family had their farm. Why did fishing for catfish here thirty years earlier seem closer to him, more real in his memory, than hiding in the hills across the river two days ago?

Tricks, my mind's playing more tricks. Be careful, Walker old son. They ain't going to get you, you're going to get yourself.

Your Honor, I present to you a man whose side, if it isn't exactly hurting, is certainly tight and tender to the extreme, a man who has lost a lot of blood in the last week but who can't find the time to build his strength back, a man who finds himself in a part of the country that is all too familiar and for that very reason seems all the more strange, a man who is on a dubious mission for a cause that is probably already lost and probably should be, a man whom a whole lot of people want to hunt down and kill because of a cause that he's not sure he believed in, in the first place. Your Honor, I submit the man is weary. My case rests, even if I don't.

I was a pretty good lawyer at one time, if I do say so myself.

You're a goddamned dead Rebel if you don't snap out of this playing around with yourself. Now.

Walker adjusted his hat to shade his eyes a little more and continued down the tracks, matching his stride to the spacing of the ties.

He passed under the bridges across the end of the valley, out to the point of land where the Allehela emptied into the Ohio River. The Ohio was low, only a foot or so deep; the runoff from the rain the week before had passed on downstream, there was no traffic on the river. It was a good thing, in one way; it meant they would have no trouble getting the horses across if they had to make a break for it south. But it also meant they couldn't use the river to transport the road engines; he had kept it in mind that, if a rendezvous with Lee became impossible, they could float the engines downstream to help lift the siege at Vicksburg. That made more sense to him from the beginning, though he had had nothing to say about it, the plans were made between Reid and Morgan. If Vicksburg was going to continue to be an option, however, it would have to rain in a hurry; according to the papers, the town couldn't hold out much longer. He wondered where Morgan was now, and the condition of the rivers there. Was that the reason he was delayed? The papers also talked about heavy storms around Louisville, the possibility of flooding farther down the Ohio. It would be welcome news for Walker at this point, it would explain why Morgan apparently hadn't left Kentucky. He picked up a flat stone and skated it out across the shallow water; the stone skipped once, twice, then edged over and dove beneath the surface and sank. Walker turned away, back toward the town.

The train station was wedged between the mainline along the Ohio River and the tracks heading up the Allehela Valley. At first, Walker wondered if it was closed for Sunday; there was no one on the platform, no one in the waiting room, the place seemed deserted. Inside, the station was cool and dark. Sunlight barely made it through the tall narrow windows; the benches, lined up like pews in a church, held only shadows. His boots thudded on the uneven wood floor. From behind the barred window came the click of the telegraph key. The operator sat at a table, his head cocked listening; when he saw Walker, he raised one finger to say he'd be with him in a moment. Walker hunched over his elbows on the counter and peered through the bars, taking in the details of the office, just in case.

When the key stopped clicking, the operator wrote something on a piece of paper and turned to Walker.

"Seems like a funny way to make a living, don't it?"

"How's that?" Walker said.

"Sitting here, listening to distant voices through the click of this little key. When I was first hired, I was only a baggage handler, I didn't have no idea what a telegraph even was. The operators used to tell me that they could recognize who was on the other end of the wire by the way whoever it was worked the key, but I thought they was just having me on. But ye know it's true. Ye can tell the different operators, ye get so's ye can recognize their styles, the length of the pauses and all. It's like each one has a different voice just like they do in person, I've got so's I can recognize them right off. But it sure does seem like an odd way to make a living sometimes. I wasn't raised with the idea that work could be fun or even interesting. It was supposed to be just work."

He was a pinched-faced young man in his early twenties with wire-rimmed glasses and dun-colored hair. His white shirt was homemade and several sizes too large for him; his neck was loose in the collar like a pestle in a mortar and his gartered sleeves draped in folds from his upper arms.

"So, what can I do for ye?"

"Have there been any messages for—"

"Hold on, let me give it a try." The operator studied him over the top of his glasses. "I'd say you're Captain Walker."

"How did you know that?"

"Part of the skill of my profession, Captain." He leaned across the table and closed one eye to show he was savvy. "I not only listen to the distant voices I listen to the ones close by too . . . out there in the waiting room, along the platform . . . ye know? I heard there was a Captain Walker and a Mr. Reid staying up at the Lyles' house. Ye look to me more like a Captain Walker than a Mr. Reid. In this business ye become sensitive to what names can tell ye about a person. I'm Cornelius Brown. Now, doesn't that tell you a lot about me?" He straightened up as if to be appraised.

"Are there any messages for me?"

"Nope. Nary a one. Ye don't have to worry, if there had been I would've sent it right up to the house or over to the steamworks, wherever ye were."

"You keep track of where everybody is in town?"

Brown laughed silently, sucking in gaspfuls of air. "No, but everybody else does. It's a small town, Captain. I'm sure if I went up to the main street and give a holler, somebody'd know where ye was at."

The question is, how much else do they know? And how much do they care? Walker straightened up, looked around. Bending over had pulled his side, his wound was beginning to throb. He worked his shoulders around inside his shirt and suit coat, trying to loosen himself up.

"I can see that makes ye a little uncomfortable, don't it, Captain? Well, I don't blame ye, this being a secret mission and all. But don't let it bother ye none, people aren't going to say anything to anybody and ruin yer secret, specially if it means hurting the chances for more work at Keystone. People may think Mr. Lyle is a little peculiar about one thing or another, but they know if the government buys the idea of these road engines of his, it could mean a lot of work for this town."

Christ, they know about the whole thing, I don't know what the hell I'm sneaking around for, I might as well be wearing a sign that says SHOOT ME.

"Let me tell ye something, Captain," Brown said, getting up from the desk and coming over to the window. His pinched face grew studious. "I think I'm in a position to know something about the modern world, what with my experience with the telegraph and all. I sort of think of myself as having my finger on the pulse of the times, if ye know what I mean." Brown winked at him cagily through his smudged glasses, then went on. "And I think Mr. Lyle's steam engines have a lot to recommend them."

"You do."

"Oh yes I do," Brown said, nodding.

"And you've seen Mr. Lyle's road engines?"

"Oh yes I have."

This must be the most well-known secret mission in history. Why don't I just sell tickets for the whole show, make some money out of it while I'm at it. Come have a look-see while the

Confederate spies get themselves hung. "Where have you seen the road engines?"

"Mr. Lyle brings them down the old canal path to try them out. Been doing it for four or five years now, as long as I've been working here at the station. I've seen them engines of his go through quite a few changes, let me tell ye. There was one of them, it gave him more trouble. . . ." Brown shook his head, remembering. Then he caught himself and grew serious again. "It's about time the government paid attention to what Mr. Lyle's been trying to tell ye about his road engines. There's a lot of folks in this town who don't think Mr. Lyle amounts to much compared to his daddy. But that's because people in this town don't appreciate machines and modern times. Mr. Lyle, he's a visionary, that's what he is. And I'll tell ye what, I heard my daddy talk about Mr. Lyle's daddy, and Mr. Lyle's daddy sounds to me like one mean son of a bitch. People around here make a lot out of ol' Malcolm Lyle being one of the founders of the town and all, but the way my daddy tells it, ol' Malcolm Lyle didn't care one whit about the town, the only thing he cared about was buying up as much land as possible around here before anybody else could get to it. Mr. Lyle now, he cares about people, I hear the men who work for him talking about how Mr. Lyle chimes in at the steamworks and gets himself dirty working just like everybody else. The man knows how to treat people, and he knows his machines. Ye should listen to him." Brown clucked his tongue twice, a sort of code.

"Well, that's what we're here to do," Walker said.

"Well, it's about time," Brown said right back at him.

Walker cocked his head to look at him. No, old son, the little weasel ain't worth it. And there's stuff to be learned here.

"What's the story with Lyle's friend, the doctor? What's his name . . . McArtle?"

"Ye've met the doc, eh?" Brown clucked again, more code. "He's a sly one, ain't he? Carryin' on that way with Mrs. Lyle right under her husband's nose. Maybe the three of them've made a sort of accommodation amongst themselves, that's what a lot of people around here think. But I'll tell ye what, that Mrs. Lyle, she's an unbridled woman. My guess is she's just too much for one man to handle, hee hee, but I'd sure like to sign up to try. Ye see, I have a theory about those skinny, frail-looking types. There sure ain't much to look at about Mrs. Lyle when you see her on the street and all. But I'll bet ye get her clothes off'n her and she'd turn out to be a raging torrent—hold it."

Brown held up one finger to silence Walker as the key started clicking. Brown smiled.

"It's Charlie up in Pittsburgh . . . wants to know if . . . we seen any . . . decent summer squash down this way. That Charlie . . . 'Scuse me there, Captain. The pulse of the nation is calling me. . . ."

Brown went back to the desk and began tapping out something on the key. Walker didn't wait for him to finish.

He headed back toward the town, along the bank of the Allehela, under the bridges for the railway and the road; behind him, the two structures closed off the end of the valley like twin walls. It made him sad and angry to hear someone like the weasely operator talk that way about Libby. It made him even angrier to think that he wasted any time considering it. He had been looking for information about the doctor, what kind of man he was and whether or not Walker should be worried about his snooping around, not the local gossip about Mrs. Lyle. What difference did it make to him what anybody in the town thought of her? Dumb crop-eared mechanics. Let them think what they liked. It had nothing to do with him. He had more pressing things to think about.

The ties no longer fit his stride; it was as if the spacing had shrunk or his legs had grown since he came down the tracks earlier. When he tried walking along the rail itself, his balance wasn't steady enough and he careened off. He moved off the tracks completely, scuffing down the old canal road. Sumac and prickly ash clotted the side of the pathway; in the sunlight dragonflies glinted on rainbow wings, feeding close to the water. His boots powdered little clouds of dust in front of him.

No word from Morgan. He had been hoping for a coded message, something to let him know if Morgan was still planning to come north. Now that Walker had seen the road engine for himself, he was more dubious than ever about Reid's idea, even if Morgan was able to join them. There was nothing to do but wait to see if his men arrived in a day or so with the wagons; despite his assurances to Reid, he was not at all sure the men would make it. If they didn't make it—it seemed almost impossible that they would, everybody in the North was on the lookout for infiltrators and guerrillas—if they ran into trouble and the Yankees found out who they were, there was every chance that the Yankees would come after him and Reid too. He would have to try to get Reid out of there and back to the South, even though Reid would be reluctant to abandon his great scheme. I'll take him out of here if I have to club him over the head and drape him over his saddle, which ain't such a bad idea no matter what happens. His wound was tightening up again; he walked with his arm pressed against his side, his fist balled and hanging by his thumb from his belt buckle.

And what the hell did women expect anyway, how else did they expect people to think of them, the way they threw themselves at men nowadays.

He thought again of the talk at dinner the night before, the talk of the book about Morgan and the way Libby's face brightened when she spoke of it. I truly enjoyed reading about Colonel

Morgan's brave exploits, he's very stirring. He thought of the early days of the war in Kentucky, the way the women would flock around Morgan whenever they rode into a town; Walker and the others had to protect Black Bess because the women carried scissors and tried to clip the horse's tail and mane, the crowds would have snatched the horse bald to have a keepsake of Morgan. He thought of the time just a year earlier when they returned to Lexington and the women all wore red and white ribbons on their bonnets; a river of red and white streamed around the horses as they tried to ride through, the crowds of women uuu-ing and squealing as they pressed to get closer, the way crowds pressed to get close to a famous actor or singer, the way crowds adored someone like Jenny Lind except that this was all for Morgan, the faces of the expectant, wide-eyed women gazing up at him as he rode past as if they could eat him alive, and Morgan loving every minute of it . . .

". . . Colonel Morgan! Oh Colonel Morgan, here!" she called from beside the road on the way out of the little town, where were they? he couldn't remember now, it was sometime early in the war though, they were still in Kentucky, before they had to take refuge in Tennessee, a little town with a tree-lined square in the middle of it and the people turned out along the sidewalks to wave handkerchiefs and cheer as they rode by, they were almost out of town—there was always a letdown after they rode through a town like that, after they left the cheering crowds behind, it always seemed to Walker that the cheers and the people clamoring to see them should make him want to go on all the more, should fill him with resolve and purpose because that was why the crowds were there, to cheer them on and send good wishes with them, when in fact all the cheering crowds did was make him want to go back to see more of the cheering crowds again—when there was this young girl, a young woman really, in her late teens or early

twenties, a beautiful girl with long dark brown hair cascading down to her shoulders and a full flowing white dress with a wide hoopskirt, the dress in layers of seven or eight flounces, the edge of each flounce tipped in red, and a large red sash tied in a bow under her breasts, her shoulders and arms bare as if she were going to a ball but she was only there to see Morgan, waving her handkerchief at him and calling to him from under the shade of the oak trees beside the road, and Morgan rode over to her and reined up in front of her and they talked for a few minutes, the girl patting Black Bess adoringly and feeding the horse some carrots that she had brought, Walker staying close by as he always did because though Morgan brushed aside the idea they were still in enemy territory, there were still many Kentuckians who supported the North and would like to have the fame and glory of having been the ones to kill the Marion of the South, you never knew who might be hiding behind a tree or some bush with a shotgun, Morgan having decided for himself that the risk of an ambush or an assassin was worth it to have the adulation of the crowds (and because he knew but would never say that he was aware that there were always men like Walker around him who took it upon themselves to watch out for him), and the girl said something to the effect that she was sure that Morgan and his brave men would be able to save the Confederate Cause and Morgan looked over at Walker and blushed as he usually did when people praised him, no matter how badly he wanted to hear it, a proud little smile on his face as the rest of the column came along and passed by, his men all watching him and the girl, then his eyes narrowing and his smile turning into more of a deadly grin, the look that came over Morgan when they were in battle when he knew that there was a course of action that he should take and that he was expected to take and that military theory said he had to take and yet he saw another, a new possibility, his own way to do it, a course of action that was bold and audacious and against convention and that excited him all the more because he knew he shouldn't do it and having once thought of it now couldn't not do it, caught up in something now that even he didn't understand but that was both outside of himself and from within the deepest regions of himself, as if every action he took, every bullet he fired and every command he made were preordained and couldn't go astray, couldn't go wrong, as if he were outside of himself watching himself except in a time lapse of either a fraction of a second or a millennium so that he knew already not having done anything yet that everything he was about to do was right for the moment, and he bent down and said something to the girl and she looked up into his face briefly as if she had just been addressed by a god and then squealed and clapped her hands and said, Yes, Oh Yes, and Morgan reached down with his gauntleted hands and she raised up to meet him and he lifted her, swung her in front of him onto Black Bess' neck, her hoopskirt ballooning up and for a moment engulfing girl and colonel and horse's head in a wave of white and red muslin until she beat it down into manageable shape again, the girl dissolving in giggles as Morgan clasped her around the waist with his left arm under her breasts and she held on to his arm with both hands and he turned Black Bess around and rode back down the length of the column with her, the men themselves now cheering as the crowds had cheered them before except this was something different, there was a different set of feelings and emotions to it than the hurrahs of the crowds as he continued with her back into the town again where the town was still cheering the passing of Morgan's raiders and people were still talking among themselves about the day they saw Morgan himself come through their town and then here he was back again, the cheers of his men approaching them like a wave coming back at them and their own cheers, a kind of echo only with a life of its own rolling toward them and over them as Morgan rode with the girl along the column and circled the town square with her, the town cheering too, wildly, all the more so but as though they didn't know why, Walker riding with Morgan and the girl, slightly behind them, as if part of what was going on and yet watching the crowds frantically, waiting for the gun barrel to appear, the shot to be fired, terrified more than ever that it could come at any second and not understanding why it didn't, and then thank heaven back along the column again and out of town, the cheers of the men rolling back again in a wave the other direction as Morgan passed again, the girl flushed and radiant and living the singular moment of her life, never aware for a second that she was being paraded like a prize, that for every man who saw her she might as well have been stripped naked and lashed to the horse's neck and taken there in full view of everyone the way Walker read the Cossacks did in Russia or the Huns in the Middle Ages, gathering up the prettiest women they found in the villages they conquered and raping them on horseback in every variation they could think of up and down the streets and squares and marketplaces of the villages while their husbands and sons and fathers watched before they slit the women's throats and spilled what was left of their lovely ravaged bodies on the ground, Morgan taking her back again to the spot where he found her and lifting her off and setting her back down again among a flurry of hoopskirt and crinoline and muslin, the girl bouncing on her toes as she settled her clothes around her again then gazing up at her benefactor, lord and master of desire, savior from the humdrum of everyday, and Morgan always the gallant took off his hat and made a low sweeping bow to her from the saddle and she clasped her hands and then curtsied in return and reached up and gave him her handkerchief, Morgan waving it delicately under his nose to smell her and then kissing it before he tucked it into his jacket over his heart and turned away, riding back toward the front of the column far ahead of him now, looking back at Walker as they rode on out of sight

*and earshot of the girl, grinning at Walker as he called to him,
"Let's see Jeb Stuart beat that . . ."*

*He tried to explain the change in Morgan now, to the one who
should recognize it most, to the one to whom it should matter
most.*

". . . he's different now," Walker told her.

*"That's because he's with me now," Mattie said, standing in
the doorway framed in candlelight. In the hallway behind her he
caught a glimpse of the wreaths Mattie and her sisters had made
for Christmas, the wreaths of pine and holly and mistletoe naming
the towns of Morgan's greatest victories, Lebanon and Hartsville
and Gallatin, the names starting to turn brown now after the
holiday.*

*The snow swirled around him where he stood on the front
doorstep. Snowflakes were drawn inside around the edges of the
door, the crystals sparkling momentarily before they disappeared
into vapor. "No, it's something else. The kind of change I'm talking about has been coming about for a long time. You're only an
indication of the changes in him, not the reason. In a court of
law, you'd be known only as an intervening cause."*

*"I think you should leave now, Judson. You're no longer wel-
come in this house. John and I don't want you here. . . ."*

He left the canal path near the abandoned lock, crossed the
railroad tracks, and started up through the lower end of town,
using the Lyles' ivy-covered house on the distant hillside as his
lodestar. He was wearing out fast, he had pushed himself too
much to come so far.

Close to the river were icehouses, small factories and mills,
brick- and coal and lumberyards. Along the ridged and rutted
streets were frame row houses, Irish and German churches. Families, two and three to a house, sat crowded on the front stoops
in the warm afternoon sunlight. The men, home from the mills

for one day, were dressed formally in tattered suits; the women were poor parodies of the well-dressed ladies he had seen uptown this morning going to church. In a vacant field, some boys kicked a ball back and forth; the several taverns were busy, men spilling out onto the streets in front. If anyone noticed Walker, no one said anything. Riprapped into the slope below the main street were cottages, small frame houses, shacks. Children dressed in little more than rags played in a mudhole at the community spring, hitting at the murky water with sticks; the smells of the refuse dumps and outhouses hung in the dusty air. A woman wearing only a shift stood in the doorway of a lopsided house, a baby saddled on her hip, watching him pass.

How could people live like this? These were the people who labored to fight the Southern Cause—who, if someone exposed him right now as a Southern spy, would probably run from their houses and beat him to death, tear him limb from limb for being a traitor—these were the people who supported the war, to free the slaves they said, and yet they lived like slaves themselves, worse because they thought they were free. It depressed him that people let themselves be reduced to these squalid conditions. It depressed him further to think that he might know some of them. He might have played with them as children when his family still lived in the area. There was the chance that he could have ended up living like this himself, working in a mill, if his family hadn't moved away. Did he hate them? No, but he didn't want to live like them. And he didn't want them telling him how to live either. He walked on.

He avoided the main street, following a path up behind the rows of buildings until it gave out into an open field. Burrs stuck to his trouser legs; with each step grasshoppers arced away in front of him. A stray white dog joined him for a while along a dusty lane, loping beside him, a fellow traveler, before plunging into the tall grass again after a rabbit; the waving grass marked the progress of the chase over a ridge. In a stand of oak trees two crows watched Walker pass without comment. He took off the suit coat and draped it over his shoulder; he had sweated through the back of his shirt and the damp cloth was cool against his skin despite the heat. From this height he could again see the layout of the town, the steamworks along the river; he wondered if Reid and Lyle were still chugging around in circles but the buildings surrounding the compound blocked his view. As he got closer, the Lyles' house rose from behind a knoll. The peak of the central pitched roof cut into the sky like the bow of a ship above the ivy-choked walls; on the second-floor balcony below the gable, the French doors were open to catch whatever breeze was about— the doors to Libby's and Colin's bedroom. George stood at the side of the house, examining a rosebush, but turned away and headed toward the back as soon as he saw Walker.

As Walker crossed the front lawn, Sally appeared in the shadows inside the open front door. She stepped out onto the porch as he mounted the stairs.

"You hurt your side again," she said.

"No, it's okay. I just wore myself out."

"You shouldn't be walking around like this in the heat of the day. You're still not well."

"So I found out," Walker said, trying to make a joke.

Sally wasn't unfriendly, she just wasn't friendly; her broad pretty face remained unsmiling. She tilted her head as she talked to him, as if trying to see around him to something on the other side, and her large brown eyes seemed distant. She kept her hands rolled in her apron.

"There's fresh lemonade, you better come get you some. And I made a large pot of beans and ham. The way people are coming and going in this house, people can just help themselves whenever they're hungry."

"And cornbread?" Walker asked.

"Yes, and cornbread," Sally said and turned and swept back inside the door.

As soon as she was inside the house, Sally seemed to become part of the shadows of the house. Walker followed her as she floated through the vestibule into the hall.

"Is Mrs. Lyle at home?" he said after her.

Sally stopped and turned around quickly; her wide hoopskirt tilted and twisted back and forth as if it were trying to unscrew itself from around her waist. Under her apron she was wearing a ball gown of blue gauze, the top cut low across her shoulders. She swayed from side to side to keep the hoop swinging.

"My Miss Elizabeth is upstairs in her room. The doctor gave her something to make her headache worse."

"You mean better, don't you?"

Sally swung her skirt back and forth, her hands rolled in her apron as if in a muff. "I don't know. My Miss Elizabeth, she always says she has a headache before the doctor gives her the medicine. But it's only after she takes the medicine that she gets sick. There's times I wish the doctor would keep his medicine to himself. There's times I think my Miss Elizabeth is better off without it." She looked at him suddenly pop-eyed, as if to say What do you make of that?

"Does she get these headaches often?"

"She usually gets them about the same time that Mr. Colin starts working real hard on one of his steam engines and stays down there at the steamworks to do his sleeping and eating. But I've never figured out if he stays down there because she's starting to get one of her headaches, or if she gets one of her headaches because he's starting to stay down there." She pumped her shoulders, a mystery.

"Doesn't the doctor know the medicine makes her sick? I thought the two of them were close friends."

Sally's eyes got a faraway look again, her skirt swaying back and forth as if she were dancing to a distant tune. "Not too many Northern folk talk to a lonely Southern lady when she first gets here. Not too many people that a Southern lady wants to talk to in an unfriendly Northern town. You know, when we first came here, my Miss Elizabeth had a big dog that she liked a lot. Then when her dog got run over by a buggy, she started to like Dr. McArtle." She thought a minute. "Now my Miss Elizabeth seems to like you too."

"The way you say that, it doesn't sound very complimentary," Walker laughed.

Sally stopped swaying and looked at him disdainfully. "I didn't say I liked you. I said my Miss Elizabeth does."

"You don't have to be afraid of me, Sally."

"There's nothing that says I have to like anything or anybody that pretends to be something it's not."

Walker felt a pit in his stomach. She knows who I am. She knows.

"You say you're this Captain Walker," Sally went on, "but I know you're somebody else."

"Who do you think I am?"

She was standing in the shadows beside the stairs. In the dim light the whites of her eyes were the color of old parchment. "You're from the dead. You're one of the death men. You're the Rider on the Red Horse, the horseman who's come to take our peace away. I've heard all about you. You've come to make us part of your terrible harvest."

"What are you talking about, dead? Who told you about me?"

She turned and started back down the hallway toward the kitchen. Walker thought to go after her but decided it was better not to; whatever she was talking about, she apparently didn't suspect them of being Rebels. Does she see me as dead? Does she think I'm about to die? At the end of the hall she stopped and looked back at him. She took her hands from beneath the folds of her apron; in one hand she held a large kitchen knife.

The house grew still around him. Walker listened, but he couldn't hear anything from the kitchen; Sally seemed to have stepped through the doorway and disappeared. He looked up the long dark stairway to the second floor. Nothing. There were no sounds from Libby's room, no indication that there was anyone left in the house. He felt suddenly alone, and chided himself for it. Why start feeling lonesome now? You're no more alone than you have been. Don't start getting crazy on me. He took a few wandering steps toward the front door, shaking each foot in turn as he lifted it, as if trying to shake loose something he had stepped in. The wood of the house creaked around him, from the dining room came the tinkling of glassware on a shelf. Christ, I barely move and the place sounds like it's ready to fall apart, as if if I stamped my foot the walls would come tumbling down around my ears. Walker stood in the darkness of the hall looking through the vestibule to the outside.

Through the open doorway was a glimpse of another, brighter world, the ivy-covered pillars beside the front steps, the front lawn and the hills on the other side of the valley. Did Libby share Sally's suspicions of him? How much did either one of them know or guess? Reid was wrong, it was more important than ever that he stay here in the house where he could keep an eye on these two women. There was more going on with this household than he would have ever imagined, secrets; that was the only reason he continued to stay here. Lord knew he didn't feel safe or at ease in the house. At this point he was ready to get his bedroll from the stable and sleep out under the sycamores. Maids with knives in their aprons, mysterious headaches and closed doors. Walker touched the gun at his side, just to feel its presence. There was always trouble indoors, he had found. The troubles he had trouble handling.

He was tired and needed to rest. Across the hall he stuck his head into Lyle's study; he wanted a book to read, it was a long time since he had had such a luxury, and decided there was nothing wrong if he borrowed one for the evening. The room looked different in the shadows of day from in the shadows of night; the night they arrived, the study appeared comfortable and warm, a man's room, civilized, the kind of room Walker wanted for his own study someday, when this war was over. Now the room seemed stuffy, hollow, lifeless. The fireplace was a gaping hole, the windows shrouded as if in a room for laying out the dead. The book-lined walls reminded him of the life he had had before the war, the small law practice he had built up in Lexington after his political work in Washington, the small house he had just bought for himself in a nice area on the outskirts of town. The plans and dreams he had had for himself, before the war came along and he knew what he had to do. Cut that out, there isn't time for that now. You made your choice. He entered the room like a man entering a crypt.

There were books on engineering and mechanics, which he wouldn't understand and wasn't interested in anyway; there were books on philosophy, which he wasn't in the mood for; there were novels, which seemed irrelevant after what he had seen during the war over the past few years. What did he want to read? He was starting to get depressed. On the round table beside Lyle's chair were several books along with a two-chimneyed lamp, a pipe that hadn't been used in a while, a pair of reading glasses, a magnifying glass, a letter opener, and a tintype of two children dressed in white sitting side by side, a boy about eight and a girl a few years younger; the books were Emerson's *The Conduct of Life*, a collection of poems by Whittier, and the one Libby had told him about on their walk home from the cemetery, *Woman and Her Needs.* It was a slender volume, more of a pamphlet than anything else, with a *carte de visite* keeping the place, a small photograph of Colin Lyle looking uncomfortable in a long-tailed coat and black silk hat standing beside an empty high-backed chair. Walker read:

> It is often said "a woman's view of the world is in her affections, her empire is home." This is only in part true, and true only to a part of her sex. There are thousands of men, and women too, unfitted for the family relation. Men so dull and imbecile where the social affections are concerned, that they can neither minister, nor be ministered to, in this way, but who are clear, good abstract reasoners, apt at invention and capable of advancing science—though cold, selfish, and unsympathizing; women too, dogmatic, ambitious, antagonistic, who would value some intellectual triumph worth a thousand hearts, and dearer than any recognition of the affections. These have nothing in themselves to bring them into harmony with the family relation. Their attempts at tenderness look foolish. . . .

He closed the book and took it with him upstairs to his room.

He lay on the bed reading for about an hour before he fell asleep. When he woke it was late afternoon. He went downstairs but there was no one around, the house was as quiet as before. On the stove, as Sally had said, was a pot of beans and ham. He helped himself to some dinner and went back to his room.

He read until it was long after dark, absorbed and fascinated by the book, in thinking about the fact that women were different from men, that women did in fact have needs that he knew nothing about and had never considered before.

Our right to a full life—to the exercise of full life—
is the foundation of a plea—not that of the nursery and
kitchen merely—not that of the luxurious saloon, the
haunts of fashion merely—for disguise it as men and
women may, this perpetual adulation, this fostering of
our pettiness, our vanity, our love of luxury, is but the
mode of holding us in the pupilage of sex—recognizing
only our relation in one aspect of life, and ignoring all
other claims . . .

It was strong, radical stuff, like nothing he had ever heard of
before. In one sense it made him chuckle: Lyle certainly must
have his hands full with Libby. Folks think they have trouble
now with the South rising up, just wait till all the women do it
too. But it also made him think. He remembered when he first
met Mattie, in Washington, when she was little more than a
child—only seventeen, and yet a woman, or filling a woman's
role. The popular concept of a woman's role, according to Mrs.
E. Oakes Smith: a thing of beauty and fluff. He thought at the
time that it came naturally to her, that she must have been born
with it.

*. . . He was standing in Charles Ready's home in Washington,
he was there to deliver some papers and the congressman was
making a point about the Whigs, when the girls came in from an
outing, their laughter and excited voices preceding them through
the house and down the hall before they burst into the study.*

*"Oh excuse us, Daddy," they said almost in unison when they
saw Walker there, then broke into giggles all over again. Ready
tried to look stern at the interruption but he couldn't hide his
pleasure in seeing them.*

*"Girls, this is Judson Walker. He's on the staff of my distin-
guished colleague from our sister state of Kentucky. As you've*

undoubtedly guessed, Mr. Walker, this giggling gaggle of geese are my daughters. My eldest, Mary; my youngest, Alice; and this is Mattie. I call her my troublingest."

The young women curtsied in turn but it was Mattie who met his gaze and held it. She continued to look at him as she removed her bonnet, shaking out her long brown hair.

"What's that on your forehead?" Charles Ready said. Hanging down in the center of Mattie's forehead was a single curl.

"It's the latest fashion, Daddy. . . ," Mary said.

"And Mattie started it," Alice chimed in, and the sisters laughed among themselves again.

"I decided it looked distinguished," Mattie said, recovering her composure. She brushed past Walker, very close, to look at herself in the mirror, making sure that the curl was just so, then faced them again. "And now it seems that everyone in Washington society is copying me. Imagine."

"My daughters, as you might have guessed, are quite the social butterflies since we've come to Washington," Ready said to Walker. "So tell me, girls, where were you today? Promenading again?"

"We went to a fortune teller's," Alice spoke up.

"Alice!" Mary said.

"Why? We did, didn't we?" Alice said.

"What on earth were you doing at a fortune teller's?" Ready said.

Mattie adjusted her shawl regally about her shoulders. She remained across the room, apart from the others, so that she was the focus of attention, so that Walker had to look either at her or at her sisters, so there was no question that he was looking at her. They're born with it, Walker thought. . . .

"We went to see whether I should marry," Mattie said.

"You're too young to be thinking about marriage, my girl," Ready said.

"*Representative Samuel Scott Marshall is going to ask Mattie to marry him,*" *Alice said.*

Mary, the oldest sister, took off her bonnet as well. "*It's a fact, Daddy. And you know he's quite a catch. I do believe I'm a bit in love with him myself. . . .*"

"*What do you make of all this, Judson?*" *Ready said, taking off his spectacles to clean them with his handkerchief.*

"*Yes, Mr. Walker,*" *Mattie said,* "*what do you say?*"

"*I'd say that Representative Marshall is a very lucky man if he is under your serious consideration,*" *Walker said in his best oratorical style, as if he were laying down a brief in court.* "*But I would add that in this circumstance Representative Marshall is not the only one involved in this proposal who should be considered quite a catch.*"

Ready nodded approval; Mary and Alice tittered; and Mattie looked more brazen than ever. It was also obvious that she was pleased, and he went on.

"*But I would question whether a fortune teller is the best source for information in such an important decision.*"

"*We read the future in some coffee grounds, if you must know,*" *Mattie smiled.*

"*If you have to snuff out the candle twice before you go to bed,*" *Alice said,* "*it means you won't get married for two years. And you can tell the number of children you're going to have by the number of seeds in an orange.*"

"*And what did the coffee grounds tell you about your circumstance?*" *Walker asked Mattie.*

Mattie tilted her head; her Southern drawl became stronger than ever. "*Why Mr. Walker, I do believe you're expressing what you lawyers call a vested interest.*"

They're born with it, Walker thought, they know even as children how to turn us inside out, she knows already what she can do to me when she looks at me like that and she knows already

*that I think she's the most interesting and beautiful girl I've ever
seen in my life. . . .*

There were voices coming from the backyard. Walker snuffed
out the lamp, grabbed his gun from its holster on the back of the
chair, and went to the window. The backyard was glowing in
bluish light. In the moonlight under the sycamores, Libby was
walking in the garden, dressed only in her nightgown, her dark
hair loose and flowing about her shoulders. She was walking
slowly between the rows of vegetables, bending over and fingering
the different plants, her gown trailing white gossamer about her;
she was singing, but Walker couldn't make out either the words
or the tune. Sally stood nearby on the grass, holding her own
robe closed about her.

"Shame on you, Miss Elizabeth. You shouldn't be running
around like this in all this moonlight. Suppose somebody sees you
like this."

Libby straightened up, opened her arms wide, and turned
around in a circle as if inviting the whole world to see. She said
something to Sally but Walker couldn't hear what it was.

George started to come from the stables but Sally chased him
away again. When Libby got near the end of a row, Sally took
her hand and led her away from the dark garden back toward the
house. In a minute or so they came up the stairs. He listened at
the door but only heard Sally continue to scold her. He was sitting on the edge of the bed ready to light the lamp again when
he heard Libby's door close and faint footsteps come down the
hall, past the head of the stairs and stop outside his door. Walker
waited, not moving. After a few minutes, the doorknob turned
quietly and the door started to open, then closed again. In another minute, Sally tiptoed away, back downstairs. Walker kept
the light out as he got ready for bed. But he decided from now
on to keep the revolver under his pillow.

FIVE

In the morning, Walker was in the stable checking the horses when George appeared in the doorway.

"Sally says to tell you there's soldiers coming."

"Where?"

The urgency in Walker's voice made the large black man turn around, as if from what Walker said he expected to see the soldiers standing behind him. In his befuddlement, George took off his battered hat and held it in his hands. He studied the toes of his shoes; one foot lay beached on the other.

"Where, George?" Walker said, trying to be calmer so as not to scare him. "Where are the soldiers coming?"

"They coming up the valley. From the Ohio's. I didn't mean to do nothing wrong. Sally said you'd want to know."

"That was good, George. Very good." Walker grabbed his field glasses from their case on his saddle. He started past George toward the door, then stopped. "And you've done a good job taking care of the horses." Walker squeezed George's shoulder. The heat from the man's body came through the thin muslin shirt as if from a stove banked low.

"I like taking care of the horses best. Even though your horses made more work for George."

"I appreciate it, George. The horses appreciate it."

George beamed happily. Walker ran on across the backyard and around to the front of the house. Sally stood at the fence at the end of the front yard. She was wearing a crimson walking dress, the high collar buttoned at her neck like a shackle; the hem of the full skirt was the color of dried blood from dew on the grass. Around her shoulders was a summer shawl the same color as the dress. Walker wondered if she had the bread knife with her this time—and just in case kept a respectful distance away. She pointed to a cloud of dust making its way through the streets of the lower end of town close to the river.

"I happened to notice from the upstairs window. Funny how a person can pick out something like that, isn't it?"

Walker trained the glasses in that direction. There were four wagons with a dozen riders in Yankee uniforms riding escort; from this distance he couldn't make out the faces or insignias, he couldn't tell whether they were his men or not. If they were his men, they must have had trouble, there were fewer than when he left them in Cincinnati. The little column appeared headed toward the steamworks.

"It looks like whatever you been afraid of or waiting for has come," Sally said. "I wonder which one 'tis." She blinked lazy-eyed at him, almost as if she were flirting.

Walker hurried back to the stable. George had the roan saddled and ready for him; he was standing in the bay inside the door, holding the bridle and patting the big horse, a proud grin on his face. As soon as Walker gathered the reins and swung up into the saddle, George ran behind the feed bin and hid.

It was a different world he entered as he started down the trails and roads, a different town—different than he had seen it at any time before, either the night they arrived or from the seclusion of the Lyles' house on the hill or yesterday on a sleepy Sunday morning. The main street was crowded with wagons hauling coal and wood and finished goods; there were the crack of whips and the jingle of the harnesses, the creak and rumble of the wagons, the whistles and calls of the draymen. Women hurried along the sidewalks, in and out of the stores, their hoopskirts and crinolines swaying like silent bells, while at the hitching posts and watering troughs, men stood in groups talking, workmen waiting for their shifts to begin or local merchants discussing possibilities. But the greatest difference was in the presence of the mills themselves; now, in full operation, they seemed somehow overwhelming, beyond comprehension, threatening. From the main street he looked across at the rows of smokestacks churning forth clouds of steam and black and yellow smoke, almost a wall of smoke; as he continued down the hill, the smoke and steam rose above him as if he descended into a lower region, the smoke filling the sky and spreading high above the valley, above the hills, as if it would cover the entire world, turning the day hazy though still bright. The sounds of the mills were no longer an undercurrent, they were part of the life of the town—the slapping belts of the machines, the throbbing of dozens of steam engines, the pounding hammers and the ringing of metal against metal. He felt as though he were entering into a great machine itself, full of gears and levers and things he didn't understand, a place where he should never be and where he could be caught up and crushed. His horse balked as they got closer.

Come on girl, I don't want to be here either. If I can do it, you can too.

Before there had been catches of smells, but now the smells of oil and sulfur and coke were all-pervasive, they were the air he breathed, the air itself was something heavy and could be seen. Farther up the river, the blast furnaces at the Buchanan Works were spewing flame and red smoke; on the hillside beyond the town, coke fires smoldered. He urged the roan across the tracks of the sidings and rode through the gates of the steamworks, unbuttoning the suit coat and pulling his holster forward in case he needed to get at it quickly. In case they weren't his men he had seen from the house and he was riding into a trap. The clatter of the horse's hooves on the cobblestones between the buildings became lost to the noise of the mill even before he entered the yard.

The wagons had come to a stop a little ways inside the compound and the men had dismounted. Some of the men had wandered over to look at one of the road engines sitting outside the doors of the shops. Lyle stood in the window of the main office, watching. At the head of the column, Reid was talking to Sergeant Grady. The sergeant turned and eyed Walker suspiciously as he rode up and dismounted, then grinned. Reid broke off what he was saying and went to have a look at the wagons.

"I didn't recognize you right off in them purty city duds," Grady twanged, speaking loudly, almost a shout, to be heard above the din. He looked at Walker edgewise as he came over to him, squinting with one eye as if there were a glare. "Do I still salute you or are you a civilian now?"

"You still salute, just like any other good Union sergeant," Walker said and grinned. After exchanging salutes, they shook hands.

"I didn't know. 'Tweren't no way of telling if you converted or something."

Walker was relieved to see them, relieved that they had made it and were back in his charge again. The hardest part of the last week or so had been not knowing what his men were going through, not being with them to tell them what to do if there was trouble. And he was glad to see Grady. The sergeant was another one of Morgan's men from the early Green River days, though Grady wasn't from Lexington or that part of Kentucky, he was from the hill country and spoke with a mountain accent. He was a small, compact man with salt-and-pepper hair, a large droopy mustache with pointy ends that turned inward like pinchers, and gray eyes barreled into his skull. His face was weathered the color of his saddle. Grady was always a bit edgy, but he seemed jumpier than usual, as if exhaustion had pushed him to some limit.

"Where are the rest of the men?" Walker asked.

"We got half a dozen sick with the green shits or something. They're in the last wagon. And Vance got bucked off and bunged his head, he's in there too. Otherwise, 'tweren't no trouble. We seen a couple Yankee patrols but they kept on going." Grady looked around quickly, as if they might still be in the neighborhood. "What about you? Reid said you took one under your arm."

Walker filled him in on what had happened since they left Cincinnati and what the situation was here.

"Any word from Morgan?" Grady asked. "When's he going to join the party?"

"Nothing so far. Have Sparky tap into the telegraph lines right away to see if he can make contact. We need to know what the story is."

"Sparky's as tired as the rest of us, Capt'n. I don't know how much good he can do without some rest."

"He'll have to do what he can. Get him on it right away. And get those men away from the buildings and those steam engines. I want them to stay with the column."

Grady chuckled without humor. He looked about the yard as if there were too many things to watch at one time. "We come a long way on account of those engines, Capt'n, the men just want to have a look at—"

"None of this is open for discussion, Sergeant. It's what has to be done. While you take care of those things, I'm going to have a look at the wagons."

Grady hobbled off bowlegged, still stiff from the long ride, a dangerous gnome, muttering to himself. Walker wondered how it happened: here he was, glad to see Grady and the others, and he ended up chewing on them, or at least that's the way the men would probably see it. It's what has to be done, damn it, it doesn't matter what they think, why do they always have to make it more difficult than it is? Bastards. Walker turned his thoughts to something else.

The mules and horses were nervous from the noise of the machines coming from the shops. On the lead wagon, a corporal known as the Parson had climbed back into the saddle on the near-pole mule, trying to quiet the team.

"We better be moving to someplace else pretty quick, Captain," the Parson called to him as his mule appeared to try to sidestep out of its harness. "These mules is going to find themselves a hundred new ways to get tangled up."

Walker nodded as he climbed up on the toolbox to peer inside the wagon. "How was the ride here?"

"Not bad, if you like pain. Me, I ain't 'specially fond of it, so I'd rather sit the next dance card out, if you-all don't mind. The Lord giveth, and the Lord taketh away, as the Book says. On this trip, howsomever, the Lord giveth a lot of dust and flies and bumpy roads, but He didn't do so good on the taketh away part. Whoa, mule! Damn it, you make a holy man swear, that's what you do."

Walker pulled back the canvas. The crates inside the wagon seemed in good shape, things didn't appear to be jostled around too badly. But only Reid would know for sure if the material was damaged or not. Walker closed the flap and dropped to the ground again. Reid was in the second wagon, rooting through the crates. Walker went on to the last wagon. Even with the tailgate down, the stench inside the wagon was hard to stomach. The half dozen sick men had soiled themselves and were lying in pools of their own and each other's urine and shit. Vance was kneeling over one of the men, trying to arrange a makeshift pillow.

"How are they?" Walker asked him, trying not to gag.

"Poorly, Captain. Right poorly. I don't know what got into 'em, but it's making everything inside of 'em come out, both ends at once. It sure would be a help if we could find a place to stretch 'em out. A body needs some room to breathe, and that includes the body taking care of 'em."

"I hear you got bucked."

The boy's face broke into a large grin; he touched the bandage wrapped around his skull, almost proudly. "Right on my head, Captain Walker. Sergeant Grady said it was the safest place for me to land." He laughed in a kind of whinny.

One of the men lying there noticed Walker and lifted a hand as if to say something, then let it fall again. Walker gave a half-hearted wave and stepped away from the wagon, gulping a lung-ful of the sulfurous air that hung in the yard.

Around the other side of the wagon, Spider and Fern squatted on their haunches against the wheel. When they saw Walker they rose quickly and dusted themselves off.

"Hey Captain," Spider said. "When can we go up to town and get us a couple of horns?"

"Yeah, and try us out some of them Northern women," Fern said. "It's up to Morgan's men to spread the seed of rebellion, right?"

The two men guffawed and folded into each other. When Walker kept on going, they straightened up. Behind him he heard, "I told you not to say nothing about that."

"Ow, that hurt! You son of a bitch!"

Reid was climbing down from his inspection of the second wagon. Flecks of the sawdust used for packing were in his beard and his derby hat was askew. He looked ecstatic.

"Everything all right?"

"Everything's fine, fine. There doesn't seem to be any damage at all." Reid rubbed his hands together. "They came through better than I ever hoped."

"How soon are you going to be ready for this stuff?"

"I won't be ready for 'this stuff' for a day or so. But I need it close by where I can get at it. I may have to check some dimensions as we do the modifications to the road engines."

As Grady came shuffling back again, Walker said, "Sergeant, take the wagons and set up camp over there at the far end of the yard, close to the river. You'll be out of the way but still near enough if Reid needs to see something in the wagons."

Grady looked puzzled. "Mr. Reid said we could sleep in the dormitory. We won't have to set up camp a'tall."

Walker looked at Reid.

Reid shrugged. "It just makes sense. There's lots of space in the dormitories. And after all these men have been through, I think they deserve to have a comfortable bed to sleep in—"

"This is a military operation, don't you understand that?" Walker exploded. "These men are under my command, they will follow my orders, not yours."

"I certainly don't see what harm it would do to let them have a decent place to sleep—"

They were interrupted by a piercing hiss as a boiler in one of the shops vented steam; the cloud roiled low across the yard, engulfing men and horses and wagons in an oily mist, a warm fog in which everything around them disappeared momentarily, Reid and the sergeant only vague gray figures in front of him. The men ran to steady the horses and mules; the only thing that could be heard above the hiss of the steam were the cries of the terrified animals. After a minute or so, the hissing stopped and the air cleared and the animals settled down again. When Walker spoke again his voice was low and intense, barely audible above the sounds of the machines around them, but with the same insistence.

"You still don't understand, do you? You're going to put these men in that dormitory, where they're going to have daily contact with Yankee workmen. Never mind the fact that you've got a whole troop of soldiers here and every man jack of them has a Southern accent that could be spotted a mile away. What happens when some of those workmen start asking questions about what we're doing here? What happens when some Yankee makes a derogatory comment about the South? What happens if a Yankee provost marshal gets wind that there's a bunch of soldiers down here that nobody knows anything about and sends a patrol to investigate? What happens if we have to defend your dumb ass and your goddamn machines and you've got men spread out all over this place?"

The soldiers stopped what they were doing to watch. Reid had stiffened and turned his face aside, as if caught in a sudden wind; his cheeks were flushed and he looked as if he might cry. Walker turned away.

"Sergeant, you will take your men and the wagons and set up camp where I told you. Set up the tents, make it appear like a regular army bivouac. Post guards on the camp and the wagons. The men are to stay in camp until I say differently, no exceptions. There is to be no contact between the men and the workmen at this place, and if any of the workmen come around they are to be turned away. I'll arrange for fresh supplies to be sent down, and I'm going now to get a doctor for those sick men. You've got your orders."

Grady gave a salute that was more like flicking something off the brim of his Yankee forage cap, spat into the dirt, and turned to the men. "You-all heard the capt'n."

"No, no, careful! Be careful!" Reid shouted. He ran across the floor of the shop to the scaffold beside the road engine. Two smiths had laid a metal strap on the side of the engine and one was beating on the strap with a hammer, trying to fit it to the curve of the boiler. The two workmen looked blankly at Reid as he joined them on the temporary scaffold.

"We need to be very careful not to damage the boiler in fitting these straps," Reid said, leaning close to the men to be heard above the noise of the shop. He tempered his voice to hide his impatience, so that only his enthusiasm would come across. "And we've got to be careful of these chains for the steering mechanism too. Did either of you happen to work on this engine when it was built?"

"I did, he didn't," said one of the smiths, a large droopy man whose heavy jowls seemed ready to slide off his face from their own weight. Both men's faces were smudged with soot and grease; their eyes stared out at him from the grime as if from within masks.

"Well, we don't want to weaken the boiler and destroy all your good work, do we?" Reid laughed good-naturedly. He lifted the strap from the boiler and eyeballed the half-formed curve. "It's critical that the straps bear on the boiler along this whole circumference. Hmm . . . Tell you what. You need to go up to the carpenter shop and get a large adjustable template so we can determine the exact curve of the boiler at this point. If they give you any trouble about taking it, tell them to see Colin Lyle. Then . . . if you heat the strap in this area here, you'll be able to bend the curve fairly easily around a number eighteen pin. At least it looks that way to me, what do you think?"

The two smiths looked at the strap, looked at each other, and nodded.

"An eighteen or a twenty-four," said the smaller of the two men. Reid noticed for the first time that most of the fingers on the smaller man's left hand were mangled like a rolled-up glove. He made a point not to look at the hand again.

"I'll leave that to you men. You're the experts. But we need to get this done as soon as possible so we can start hanging the iron plates."

The two smiths climbed down from the scaffold with new purpose to get the job done. Reid smiled to himself. Like children. Like brute animals. Throw them a bone, give them a little something, and they're as happy as can be. It had been easy to deal with the workmen, to get them set on the right track; it was always easy to handle underlings, he had no respect for someone who made a big deal out of it. Like Walker and his anger about his men in the yard. Totally uncalled for. It only proved what Reid had suspected all along, that Walker didn't know what he was doing, that the mission would be better off without him. That Reid should take command himself. All workmen are the same, North and South, the same as the masses anywhere. You have to lead them by the hand, you have to do their thinking for them. Idiots.

As he stood on the low scaffold he looked around the shop. It was a long, narrow building, this floor several stories tall, with additional floors above for storage and light assembly. The noise inside the hollow structure was continuous and deafening. A row of monstrous steam-driven hammers banged away on sheets of iron, forming the struts and platforms, while steam-driven punches punched holes for rivets and smiths worked at anvils on the smaller supports. Overhead cranes clattered by, lifting sheets of iron from one part of the shop to another; the sheets warped back and forth in the slings with an otherworldly twang. There was the clunk of enormous gears and the slap of drive belts and the hiss of escaping steam. Flames leapt from the doors of the forges and heating furnaces, and periodically thick acrid smoke rolled through the aisles and bays. A scene from hell for some, perhaps, but Reid loved it. He wouldn't have stayed at the Lyles' house now for anything, not with the chance to be here night and day amid the excitement of the work going on. These sights and sounds and smells meant everything to him, they were his life. This is what I've waited for, he thought, this is what I've worked and planned and wanted for so long, and now it's really happening, I'm really here, this isn't just a dream, I'm the happiest I've ever been and no one is going to take it away from me, no one.

Now that he was up on the scaffold, he took the opportunity to see how the work was coming along. Lyle had been surprised at some of the modifications Reid wanted to make to each road engine—including the addition of a platform across the front and the extension of the rear platform. Though Reid didn't explain what the new platforms were for, Lyle agreed to go along with them as part of the contract to sell the engines. He would show Lyle that he knew what he was doing, he would show them all.

He had found in his life that too many people did not take his ideas seriously. The problem as he saw it was his background: he came from a poor family, he hadn't had the formal education or training that other engineers had, he hadn't had the connections to go to West Point or Annapolis. Reid's lack of formal education would always hold him back in the hierarchy of government positions, he was aware of that; it was actually a wonder that he had come as far as he had. Reid started as a teenage apprentice at Tredegar Iron Works in Richmond; because he was smart and learned quickly, he made his way through the ranks of puddlers and heaters and rollers to become a foreman before he was barely twenty. The turning point of his life happened early in the war when he was chosen to work with John M. Brooke on a special project at the Gosport Naval Shipyards. It was while he was working with Brooke to convert the steam frigate *Merrimac* into a seagoing ironclad that the idea for a land vehicle came to him. But he had learned something else from working with Brooke, something more than how thick and at what angle an iron plate has to be in order to deflect a cannonball; he learned that you have to look out for your own interests, because there are plenty of people ready to strip you of your accomplishments for their own gain. Brooke was an all-but-forgotten man now, the glory for the development of the *Merrimac* going to Stephen Mallory, Confederate secretary of the navy. Reid would make sure that the same thing didn't happen to him with this project, he had worked too long and too hard, he had risked too much, to see the glory for this idea go to somebody else. Whether it was Lyle or Walker or even the great man himself, Morgan. Reid would show them all, the world would know his name by the time he was through.

He was standing on tiptoe on the scaffold, checking the layout for a roof support to be fitted on top of the firebox, when he happened to look out the grimy window across the shop. Parked on the other side of the compound, near where Sergeant Grady had moved the wagons and was setting up camp, was a buggy that looked like the one Dr. McArtle drove to the Lyles' the other evening. Walker must be out of his mind, sending a fool like that doctor down here where he can snoop around. I've got to stop him before he ruins everything. Reid hurried down from the scaffold, brushing past the two smiths who proudly held the reworked metal strap for his inspection, and out the door of the shop.

The sick men had been taken from the wagon and laid on the ground while the tents were being erected. Dr. McArtle worked among them, attended by another soldier with his head wrapped in bandages. When he saw Reid approaching, McArtle left the sick men and came over to him.

"It appears as though I've been drawn into your secret project," McArtle said, shifting his medicine case under his arm in order to shake hands. He adjusted his waistcoat over his protruding stomach and looked around the compound. "I hope I don't need a password or something to be here, heh heh."

"How are the men?" Reid said brusquely, ignoring the man's attempts at humor.

"Hmm, yes. Well, you've got some pretty severe cases of dysentery on your hands. A disease that the men themselves aptly call 'The Shits.' That, and I noticed that all of them seem to have Southern accents. At first I was afraid they were afflicted with some other rare disease, 'Confederatitus' or some such thing, but I remembered Mrs. Lyle did say that Captain Walker and his men were Kentucky cavalry, didn't she?"

Was McArtle really suspicious or just being facetious? Reid decided it was best to let it pass. "How sick are they? Will they be able to travel in a few days?"

The doctor shrugged. "One or two of the men may be starting to recover. For the rest, it's too soon to tell. Even to tell if they'll recover at all."

"You mean they could die?"

"It's been known to happen, Mr. Reid," McArtle said, making little attempt to hide a smile. On his broad, fleshy face, haloed by his pale sideburns, his lips curled like mating slugs. "Fatal diseases have a peculiar way of living up to their name."

Reid felt himself color, not from embarrassment but from anger. "I didn't know it was that serious."

"Actually, I suppose you're right. Something known as the 'Virginia Quick Steps' or the 'Tennessee Trots' shouldn't really be classified as a fatal disease. And the fact is, it doesn't necessarily have to be fatal. It's just that it normally is. Evidently, no one has told the disease." McArtle smiled smugly.

"I trust you're doing everything you can for them."

"Of course. But the truth of the matter is we can't do very much for them at all. Make them as comfortable as we can, that's about the extent of it. Or the extent that I'm willing to do."

"You mean to say that with all the advances of the modern world, there's nothing you can do to cure a common disease like dysentery?"

"As we discovered the other evening, Mr. Reid, of the two of us, I'm afraid you are the one with faith in the advances of the modern world. Not I. The most common so-called modern remedy for dysentery, as advocated by the medical profession today, is to administer large doses of what is known as 'the salts,' followed by, if that doesn't work, even larger doses of castor oil. My own personal experience is that such practices only make the disease worse, not better, but so far such observations have done nothing to convince the majority of my colleagues otherwise. As for myself, I've found that the best thing to do is to do nothing. We try to keep the patients comfortable. We try to keep them clean, if we can. I instructed Sergeant Grady that as soon as the tents are up, the sick men should be carried down to the river and bathed; if they're too weak to wash themselves, then somebody else should do it for them. That and we'll get them into clean clothes and off the ground and into cots as soon as we can. Otherwise"—McArtle paused to rub viciously at the end of his nose, then twitched it back and forth like a rabbit—"it's pretty much a case of wait and see."

"You have a curious attitude for a man of science."

"You're disappointed, aren't you? I suspected that the other evening at dinner. I suppose you thought that as fellow 'men of science,' we could sit around and have enlightened conversations about the coming of 'the modern world' or some such thing. I'm afraid that would be more in Colin's line, not mine."

"I'm beginning to suspect that Colin Lyle is more of a dilettante than anything else," Reid said, surprised himself that he said it out loud.

"You're very hard on people, young man," McArtle said.

"I'm very hard on myself."

"I suppose you are. Though perhaps not in the right ways. In the short time that you've been here, you've made your dislike or disdain for most of us readily apparent. You might be surprised to learn, though I doubt that you will be able to grasp it, that many of us are not fond of you either. Myself, in particular. Now if you will excuse me, this 'man of science' has some sick farmers to go see. One of whom may very well ask me to help deliver a farrow of pigs. I'll stop here again later, unless you or Captain Walker decide that your sick men are better off without me. In which case, you'll have to shoot me to keep me away. I may not be able to do very much for your sick men, Mr. Reid, but I do care about them. And I will do everything to my own satisfaction to see that they are properly taken care of. That isn't being a man of science, or even modern; that is what's known as being a doctor. Good day."

As soon as McArtle was in his buggy and heading out of the compound, Reid, his cheeks stinging as if he had just been slapped, his cold blue eyes narrowed to slits, went in search of Sergeant Grady.

The campsite was beyond the crisscross tracks for the works' donkey engines, the stockpiles of scrap iron and slag, coal and firebrick and wood, beside the tracks of the mainline heading up the valley. On the other side of the mainline, a small embankment led down to a strip of bank along the river where some of the men were stripping off their clothes to go swimming. It seemed remarkably peaceful and open here, away from the encirclement of buildings, the sounds and smells of the works; there was a breeze coming from the river, the sound and smell of the water. Across the river, the curving bluffs of the valley formed a solid green wall. Grady was watching the last of the half dozen cone-shaped tents go up.

"Sure be nice tents, ain't they sir?" Grady said, squinting against the smoke of a cigar sticking out of one side of his mouth. "Found them in the wagons we commandeered outside Cincinnati. I figured we better save them, they just might come in handy, and damned if they didn't. Makes us look like an official U.S. of A. Army detachment, don't they? I got to say this, these Yanks sure do have nice equipment—"

"Sergeant, I want you to keep a sharp eye on that doctor if and when he comes back again."

Grady took the cigar from his mouth. It was a short stub of a cigar, one that he had obviously saved and been working on for some time, the shape and color of a dried turd.

"The doc? What's wrong with him?"

"I'm afraid of his snooping around too much. He was asking me a lot of suspicious questions, such as why all you boys have Southern accents."

"I'm surprised to hear that. He seemed all right to me, and I figured, seeing as how Capt'n Walker sent him. . . ."

Reid laughed without meaning to. Grady squinted at him. "Something wrong about the capt'n?"

"Why do you ask?" Reid said.

"I don't know. He didn't quite seem like himself, if you 'twere to ask me. You know something I should know?"

"You mean, because of his blowup a little while ago? Because he wants you to sleep out here in these tents, while he's staying in the comfort of the Lyles' home?"

"Is that where he is? I was a-wondering. . . ."

"Sure, you can see the place from here." Over the rooftops of the steamworks, Reid pointed out the big house on the hillside above the town. "I'm surprised he didn't tell you himself. Of course, maybe he was feeling a little sheepish about it."

Grady shook his head and laughed, a kind of cackle. "Well, it's probably a good thing for him, I'd say, what with his being wounded and all."

"Yes, and a pretty lady, Mrs. Lyle, to help nurse him."

Grady took the cigar from his mouth and studied it; a string of saliva hung from the moist end, elongating down, then dropped off into the dust near his square-toed boot. "'Tweren't no denying the capt'n sure does seem different. . . ."

"Sergeant, let's take a little walk, you and me."

Reid led them away from the camp, across the tracks of the mainline to the embankment overlooking the river. In the shallow water, half a dozen of the men were splashing around naked, their bodies pale as grubs; Reid looked away. The sergeant watched him closely through the haze of his cigar smoke, his deep-set eyes restless. Be careful, be very careful. Do it right.

"Sergeant, I may need—I definitely will need your help in the future. There are a few things regarding this mission that you probably don't know about—"

"'Twere a whole lot of things I don't know about. For starters, what in the hell are we doing here, anyway?"

Reid contained his smile. "You'll find out about that too, soon enough. What I want to say is that you and Captain Walker and your men were assigned to make sure that I got here safely."

"Yep," Grady said. He removed the cigar from between his mandible-like mustache and spit. "And here you be."

"Yes. What you probably don't know is that General Morgan gave me the authority to take command of this mission, if I felt it was necessary once we arrived here."

"Now hold on a minute, you're telling me—"

"I wouldn't expect you to believe me on something as important as this. But I have a letter from General Morgan that will verify it."

Reid took a letter from inside his coat pocket and handed it to Grady. The sergeant opened it carefully and read it and handed it back to Reid. His eyes darted around, looking at the river, the hills on the other side, the grass on the embankment, as if he might find some answers somewhere about him.

"'Tweren't no reason to believe that Morgan would do a thing like that to Capt'n Walker . . ."

"Morgan only gave me this authority in case I felt it was absolutely necessary, in case some sort of dispute arose between myself and the captain that I felt jeopardized the purpose of the mission or put the safety of the road engines in question."

"And you think that's what's happening now? You think the capt'n 'twere doing something that could hurt the reason why we're here? Whatever the hell that reason is."

"No, I didn't mean to imply that. I only meant that it may become necessary in the future, if the captain continues to act strangely as you noticed. We have to keep in mind that the captain was wounded, and that it could be clouding his judgment. This mission is bigger and more important than any one person, I hope you realize that."

"I don't realize anything of the kind, because I still don't know what the hell your goddamn mission is about. But if you're a-asking me whether or not I'll go along with it if you take over command, I don't know what choice I have, do I? Seeing as how you have that there letter from Morgan."

"That's all I'm asking you, Sergeant. I'm hoping that such an extreme measure doesn't come about. But in case it does, I wanted you to be aware of the situation."

"Yeah, 'twere a situation, all right," Grady said, and headed back across the tracks, the bowlegged man stepping simian-like over the rails.

In the river, two of the men were dunking a third, the victim thrashing wildly as if he were afraid his companions were trying to drown him in the shallow water. What did Grady think of what Reid had told him? Did Grady believe him? Could Reid trust him if he tried to take over the command from Walker? Reid couldn't tell. He realized he still held the letter from Morgan in his hand; he hurriedly put it away for safekeeping inside his coat. It's a risk I had to take, the die is cast now, but that's a leader's role, isn't it, to gather his men around him, to determine who he can trust and who he can't, I guess I better get used to it, being a leader of men, being important, when these road engines are unveiled I'll be famous, I'll be the one who is looked to for answers not somebody else, I've waited so long for that. He started back across the tracks when there was shouting behind him. In the river several men were carrying the man who had been dunked toward shore, while Grady and others ran toward them. They laid the lifeless form of the dunked man on the narrow bank, but no one seemed to know what to do next. When Grady reached them he knelt quickly beside the man, listening for a heartbeat, then punched him once in the stomach. A stream of water shot from the man's mouth, spraying those standing around; the man rolled on his side coughing, trying to catch his breath. The men cheered.

Idiots.

Reid continued back across the compound.

Inside the shops it was deathly quiet: the steam hammers stood idle, the cranes hung frozen in place, the stationery engines barely coughed and hissed. Everyone had disappeared. For a moment he panicked. What happened? What's wrong? He found the men sitting on the floor along the wall, a long line of them, shoulder to shoulder, knees drawn up or feet stretched out, eating. Reid was furious. How can they think of eating at a time like this, Jesus Christ, I've barely eaten in days, don't they know what's at stake here, don't they know . . . then he got ahold of himself again.

Poor souls. Poor dumb souls. Let them have a little time, they deserved it; there were long hours ahead of them in the next few days, for all of them. He wandered along the aisle that ran the length of the shop. From the tall windows, sunlight slanted down through the dusty air, angled between the rows of supporting pillars as if in a great cathedral. In the center of the shop, in the transept of the cruciform-shaped building, the two road engines stood encased in their scaffolding, penned in like two great beasts upon an altar. He loved these engines. Loved them more than anything else he had ever known in his life. As he walked around them, admiring them, he was aware that the men along the wall were watching him, no doubt talking about him among themselves. Let them. They would remember him when this work was over, they would tell their children and their children's children of the time they worked with Jonathan Reid, the man who developed the War Engine. He was a man of vision, he knew that, and he knew that such men always stood apart. What he didn't understand was why, now that everything he had worked for was coming true, he felt empty, alone.

Six

The inside of the tent was luminous, gray, as if she were inside a pearl. A cone-shaped pearl. She thought of being underwater, living underwater. She thought of being drowned, her limbs moving not from themselves but from the tide.

She thought of the tent. Of a tepee, the Great Plains, Indians. She thought of herself as a squaw, a white woman captured by Indians. A slave. What will they do to me? They're coming.

She smiled to herself. She stepped outside for a moment and tied back the flap of the tent, to let more light, more fresh air, inside. The sunlight fell across the feet of the men in their cots.

The inside of the tent smelled of dust, musty canvas, men. She thought of the drawings she had seen of army camps. Row upon row of tents. She thought of all the brave young men who needed her help. Someone to love them.

There are rows upon rows of men, they are marching toward me, their bayonets pointing toward me, they are coming for me, that look in their eyes.

She smiled to herself. The medicine for her headaches seemed to be lingering more than usual this time. She mustn't act silly, she must get ahold of herself.

She stood in the center of the tent, beside the pole. The men in the cots radiated out from her. Their feet in the sunlight from the open flap, their heads in the shadows. The luminous gray shadows. Watching her.

I must be like a vision to them. Like a mother to them, no, like the girl they left behind. All grace and loveliness. All the sweet brave young men.

She had heard yesterday afternoon from the doctor that the sick men were down here. He said they didn't need anything, that it was better that she stayed away. That the men were half-crazed from fever and riding in the wagons. From their long journey.

But she hadn't listened. She knew the men needed a woman's touch. McArtle was just trying to shield her. Like a caged bird. His caged bird.

The men watched her as she wrung out the washcloth in the basin of water. Watched her as she went from one to another, wiping off their brows. What would Mr. Lyle say if he saw her doing this?

What would Captain Walker? Now he wouldn't think of her as the weak little flower who faints at the sight of blood. She smiled to herself.

Corporal Vance ducked into the tent, carrying the slop bucket he had emptied for her.

"Here you go, ma'am."

"Thank you, Corporal. But I could have gotten it."

"My pleasure, ma'am." He touched the bandage around his head as if he were going to tip it like a hat. "Well, I don't mean it's a pleasure, exactly. But I'm glad to help out. A lady shouldn't have to go around emptying slop pails for a bunch of soldiers."

"Now you sound just like my husband. And Captain Walker."

"I don't know about your husband, ma'am. But if that's what Captain Walker said, then you shouldn't be here. And I shouldn't be helping you."

"You can relax, Corporal. I meant it only figuratively. Captain Walker didn't say anything of the sort."

"I just don't want no trouble with the captain."

As she wiped the forehead of one of the men, he reached up and grabbed her wrist. He lifted up from the cot, looking at her wild-eyed.

"Tell Captain Walker there's hundreds of 'em right ahead in the brush. Tell the captain."

"I will, I will," Libby said, easing the man back on the cot. He still had hold of her wrist.

Vance hurried over to come to her assistance. Libby warned him away with a look.

"You tell the captain." The man looked at her, looked past her at something only he could see.

"I'll make sure he knows." She gently loosened the man's grip, laid his arm back on his chest again.

"He'll know what to do. He'll get us out of this." The man closed his eyes again, went to sleep.

Libby motioned with her head for Vance to follow her outside.

There were several men standing beside the wagons parked nearby. When she appeared from the tent, the men looked embarrassed, looked away. They're waiting for me, they want to see me. She walked over to them.

"Would one of you kind gentlemen be so good as to fetch me another pail of water?"

The men blushed, stepped all over themselves to be the one to get her the pail. She smiled to herself. As she walked toward the other tent, she heard them still squabbling behind her.

Silly men. Such brave soldiers. I just looked at them and they became like little boys. There's nothing to fear here.

She ducked inside the second tent of sick men. It had been her idea to have two tents; when she arrived she found them all crowded into one. Sergeant Grady looked at her when she told him her idea, cocked his head.

"You be Mrs. Lyle?"

"Why yes, how did you know?"

"Call it a hunch," he said, and sauntered off to get some men to move the cots.

Even with the flaps open, the air inside the tents was stifling, close. The day was cloudy but still bright; the dampness hung in the air, clung to her. She pushed her sleeves up past her elbows.

The men watched her. She smiled to them. To herself. My beautiful milk-like skin. What would the town think? What would Captain . . . As she moved about the tent, wringing out the washcloths, placing them fresh and cool on the men's brows, she set her hoopskirt to swinging. A kind of dance. Stirring a little breeze about her. The men watched her. I haven't had so many men watch me since I was a girl on the front porch of our home among the willows and the breeze would stir in the early evening and the fireflies would be out and the whippoorwills would sing from the orchard and all the beaus would come to call, all my pretty young men, How do you do, kind sir.

She reached for a slop pan beside one of the cots. Vance tried to reach it before her but she brushed him aside with a look that said I can get it and picked it up.

And then wished she hadn't. Watery, stinking, greenish-brown gruel. The contents of her stomach came to her throat but she choked it back. I've done this for my children and worse, I can do this, don't let them see you. She carried the pan over and emptied it into the bucket and placed the pan back beside the man's bed.

"Your Captain Walker," she said, fighting the nausea, fighting to keep her voice steady, "he sounds like something of a tyrant."

"Oh no, ma'am. He's not a tyrant at all. He's very fair. You just don't want to cross him, that's all."

"Do the men like him?"

"They don't have to like him, ma'am. He's an officer."

"Yes, of course." She was feeling a little lightheaded. "Let's go outside."

Two of the men she had asked to help her earlier were coming up from the river, carrying a pail of water between them. Rather than helping each other, each appeared to be trying to wrest the handle from the other. A third man trailed along behind, trying to help too. Libby told them to put the bucket in the tent and thanked them.

She felt better as soon as she was in the open. But her clothes still felt damp and heavy, not from perspiring but from the air itself. Hot, pearly, close day. She walked between the tents and headed toward the river. As she walked she rubbed the bare underside of her wrists together, scratching one with the other.

"It sure is peaceable here," Vance said, following her across the railroad tracks. He joined her on the low embankment overlooking the river. "It's a purty place."

"Is it?" Libby said. "I guess I never think about it."

"Oh yes, ma'am. It's about as purty a place as I've ever seen. All these trees and all. What's the country like on up the valley?"

"Isolated. Much of the state is isolated to the north. A few farms here and there, once in a while a town, that's about all. I haven't been north myself very much."

"Sounds like heaven to me. This is the kind of country I'd like to settle in someday. Hide away in one of these valleys. Get me a little piece of land, couple of cows, be off by myself. Nobody telling a body what to do. And no wars."

"You don't like the war?"

The young man lowered his head. He touched his bandage, as if to check that it was still there. "No ma'am. I don't. I've seen the war, and I've seen enough. I feel bad because of the other men but I can't change it. I just want to be away from it."

She thought of what Walker had told her of war. Of the chaos and horror of battle, of missing body parts and half-filled caskets. She had her dreams and fantasies of war and soldiers, she knew that, but this was different. She knew this was real.

Her heart went out to this young man, his moral dilemma. She thought of all the young men caught up in the senseless slaughter. She thought of how she would feel if this was her own son. She thought of Captain Walker, how she would feel now, after knowing him this little time. Such a little time if he was going into battle again.

Why would I care about Captain Walker? I hardly know him. Now you're being silly again.

And she certainly knew what it was like to want to be away from people. From people telling you what to do. People who tried to make you bow to their will.

She looked at the young man. So young, so young. He had a broad, eager face, polished-apple cheeks. A wisp of hair peeked down from the edge of the bandage across his forehead. She looked at the river again, the water rushing past.

And on some level of her mind she thought Walker would be proud of her. Proud if he knew what she was thinking. The man, in such a little time, had had an influence upon her, on the way she thought. On the way she viewed the world.

Why would I care what Captain Walker thinks? He said his name is Judson.

Along the bank of the river, dragonflies flitted back and forth above the rocks. A cloud of midges danced out over the water. A pesky fly was attracted to her lilac-scented powder. She brushed the fly away from in front of her face with a slow toss of her hand.

"You shouldn't feel bad about wanting to be away from the war."

"It's not right for a soldier to feel that way."

"Not everybody was meant to be a soldier. Not everybody was meant to be brave. You're helping me take care of these sick men. That seems to me better than being brave."

"That's nothing. They was sick, that's all."

"You can't live your life thinking of what other people think of you. It will eat you up inside. If you know what you want to do, then you should do it. And not let anyone stand in your way. You can be a coward and go to war. You can be a brave man and want peace."

"You really think so, ma'am?"

Before she could reply, Captain Walker came from between the tents toward them.

"Uh-oh," Vance said, and moved away from her, along the embankment to circle back to the camp.

"What are you doing here?" Walker said, crossing the railroad tracks.

"Good day yourself, Captain Walker. It's a pleasure to see you too."

Walker stood in front of her, looking as though he couldn't believe his eyes.

"What are you doing here? I asked Sally where you were and she said you were visiting your children."

"I admit I was naughty and told Sally to tell you that. I knew you wouldn't want me to bother myself with your sick soldiers. But it's really no bother at all. Come, let me show you what I've done so far—"

"That isn't the point. The point is you shouldn't be here at all, for any reason. You shouldn't be around these men. I mean, these men have been . . . you just can't come here and. . . ." Walker gestured helplessly.

My, my, the good captain is lost for words. I never thought I could.

"My, my, Captain, you seem lost for words. But you really needn't worry, I'm in no danger from these good Southern boys."

The color was suddenly gone from Walker's face.

"Captain, you are the one who told me y'all are from Kentucky. And these boys' sweet Southern accents still come a-rolling through those Yankee uniforms."

For a brief moment Walker looked as if he didn't know what to do. Then he looked as if he knew exactly; his voice was low, measured.

"There are dangers here that you know nothing about."

This man could kill me. I read him wrong completely. This is the man who could really hurt me. He is the one to be afraid of. This is the one I've waited for, this is the one I've been afraid would come.

And suddenly she felt cheap. Tawdry, like a whore. She hadn't come here to help these men. She had only come here to have them look at her. To flit around and get them to pay attention to her. Or was it to get Walker to pay attention to her?

The doctor had accused her of flirting with Walker. Said that she was paying too much attention to him. More than was necessary. Of course Eugene was jealous of Walker. But did he in fact have a right to be? Was she attracted to Walker, more than she was aware of? In ways that she never considered?

She was more disgusted with herself than ever. But the last thing on earth she would ever do is to let Walker see it. Any of it.

She glanced once more into his brown eyes, cold now with intensity. At the firm-set jaw, his lips beneath the dark, full mustache. And sashayed away from him. Took a few pointed steps along the rail of the track, a tightrope walker. Her hoopskirt swinging blithely about her.

"Tell me, Captain Walker. Are you ready for our Tuesday Night Entertainments?"

"What?" Walker said.

Without looking at him, she could hear the confoundment, the exasperation, in his voice. She smiled to herself, and went on. Breezily, on across the tracks, heading back toward the camp. Assuming that he would follow her. He did.

"Our Tuesday Night Entertainments. I remember telling you about them, the evening you arrived. It's a regular tradition in our household. We get together with Dr. McArtle or anyone else in town who we think would be interested to make music and maybe give a recitation or two. I hope you can attend. Better, I hope you have something to perform for us."

She either heard him pull up or sensed it. I went too far. When she turned around, he was just standing there, looking at her, a look of total bafflement on his face. Then he burst out laughing.

"I'll take that to mean yes, Captain."

"You're quite a lady, Mrs. Lyle."

"You were going to call me Libby."

"Actually, I was going to call you Elizabeth."

"That's better. But I am Libby. Mr. Lyle once knew me as Elizabeth, but she doesn't exist now. Only Libby."

"All right. You're quite a lady, Libby."

"And what do you mean by a lady?"

Walker shook his head. Either looking at the ground between himself and Libby, or at his feet as he crossed it, he came forward and stood in front of her again.

"Yes, I'll try to be at your Entertainments tonight."

"Good, we'll look forward to it."

They walked together back to the camp. Not saying anything, each lost in thought. Like old friends, it occurred to her. Comfortable together.

Like we are a couple, already, like we have always fit together, two halves of a whole, my Captain Walker, this is the way I always thought it should feel to be with someone, like I found the missing half, what a strange idea, but I'm kidding myself of course.

There was space for them to continue side by side between the tents. But he held back, letting her go first. A perfect gentleman. Thank you, kind sir. He smiled as if he read her thoughts.

As she walked ahead of him, did he watch the swing of her hoopskirt? I wore a hoop today just for him, because I knew he would be here, didn't I? Is he watching my. . . ? She scratched again the undersides of her wrists together, one against the other. She thought her hands held in front of her that way looked as if they were tied.

Where were they headed? Where did he think they were going? She didn't know, but continued beside him. As they passed the wagons the two soldiers named Spider and Fern came over to him. Walker lagged behind to speak to them. Libby walked ahead, slowly, as if paying them no mind. But she listened.

"Hey Captain, I got an idea. Why not send me and Spider up to Pittsburgh to do a little reconnoitering?"

"This weren't my idea, Captain."

"You-all would sure as hell want to go along if he said yes."

"Well, sure."

"What's your idea?" Walker said.

"I was thinking we could scout around up there in Pittsburgh, keep our ears peeled, find out what people are thinking, you know?"

"Yeah, and brothels are always good places to find out what people are thinking."

"I didn't say nothing about no brothels, did I, Captain?"

"I don't care," Walker said. "Nobody goes anywhere. Everybody stays in camp."

"See that, you dumb son of a bitch, you-all went and started talking about brothels and ruined my good idea."

"It weren't no good idea at all. And who the hell you calling a son of a bitch, you son of a bitch."

There was scuffling behind her. She turned around. The two men were rolling in the dust at Walker's feet, swinging and kicking at each other, half in fun and half for real. Other soldiers formed a half circle around them, egging them on. For a moment Walker looked bemused. When the fight became more serious, one man trying to gouge the eyes of the other, Walker waded into them. Grabbing at them, trying to pull them apart as best he could with his good arm. Sergeant Grady came running and dragged one man away while Walker held the other.

Then as quickly as it started it stopped. The two combatants, Walker, all the men standing around became suddenly quiet and grim. And all seemed to be looking at her. What did I do? No. From among the background noise of the steamworks came the sound of hooves, the creak of saddles and the jingle of tack, rattling sabers.

"What's going on here?" came a voice from behind her.

There were a dozen of them, cavalry, local militia. She had seen them, parading around, from the county seat up the valley at New Inverness. Makeshift soldiers. At the start of the war without uniforms or guns. Now they had both.

"What's going on?" the lieutenant repeated, pulling up his horse near the circle of men. He had drawn his pistol. "What's the meaning of this?"

"Everybody takes it real calm," Walker said quietly to his men.

The patrol stayed in their column of twos as they reined in. The lieutenant was the only one with his pistol drawn, and he was having trouble controlling the reins and holding on to the pistol at the same time. His horse began to back up, colliding with that of the trooper behind him carrying the guidon. Then the horse began to kick.

Sergeant Grady, still holding on to Fern, dropped him on the ground, went over and grabbed the horse's bridle, talking to the animal and patting its neck. The horse settled down.

"Thank you, Sergeant, but I've got him under control now," the lieutenant said. He tried to look stern. "A high-spirited animal."

"Yes sir," Grady said. But kept hold of the bridle.

The lieutenant was an earnest, clean-shaven young man in his early thirties. An aristocrat, Libby thought, or someone trying to be, perhaps academy trained. His men were a collection of shop clerks, out-of-work laborers, thugs. Men who wanted to be soldiers but didn't want to go to war.

"You still haven't told me what's going on here," the lieutenant demanded.

"Just a little scuffle between some of the men," Walker said easily. "A misunderstanding about furloughs."

Spider and Fern were on their feet, brushing themselves off, looking a bit sheepish.

"Some people don't know when they're well off," Spider said.

"Some people don't know when to shut up," Fern said.

"That's enough, both of you," Walker said. But he grinned.

The lieutenant leaned forward, his pistol resting across the pommel of his saddle. "I want to know what a civilian is doing giving orders and breaking up fights among enlisted men."

"Because I'm a captain in the U.S.—"

"No, I want to hear it from one of these men in uniform. Sergeant?"

Grady, still holding the horse's bridle, looked up at the lieutenant. For a moment he didn't say anything; it appeared as if he wasn't going to say anything at all. Finally, he drawled, "That there's Captain Walker. Sir. First Kentucky Cavalry, United

States Army. You be a-thinking I'd take orders from just anyone? Sir?"

"I didn't hear anything about a new unit being detailed to my region. Now I come down here and find a troop of cavalry supposedly under the command of a captain who's in civilian clothes. You could be spies for all I know."

"It's a long story, Lieutenant," Walker said, ambling closer to him, standing beside Grady. "But I'll make it as short as possible. I'm not wearing my uniform because I was shot by Rebel scouts on the way here and my jacket's being repaired. And you didn't hear that we were going to be here because this is a top secret government mission."

The lieutenant looked dubious. Colin had come out of his office across the compound and was standing on the steps, watching.

"That's the owner of the Keystone Steam Works," Walker said, pointing him out. "Does he look like anyone is holding a gun to his head? And this is his wife, Elizabeth. The Lyles have been gracious enough to open their home to me while we're here on business. Does she look as if she thought we were spies?"

Libby was about to speak up when the lieutenant looked around him. While Walker had moved forward and distracted him, Walker's men had unholstered their own pistols or picked up their carbines and were holding the weapons down at their sides. Casually, but ready. The lieutenant's eyes became worried.

"What the sergeant here didn't tell you is that these men are part of Frank Wolford's First Kentucky Cavalry. That means they've spent the better part of this war chasing John Hunt Morgan up and down the hills of Kentucky and Tennessee, and they're in no mood to be trifled with now. Especially if it means calling into question their ability to protect this special mission. You can see for yourself these men are veterans. If we were spies, you all would be dead by now. We would have shot you down the minute you came prancing in here."

The lieutenant looked around. At the armed men circled in front of him, at his own troop behind him. Walker took the bridle from Grady and moved closer to the lieutenant. Speaking up to him quietly.

"Son, I'm trying to save you from making a terrible mistake here. If I were you I'd just turn your troop of home soldiers around and go your own way. You'll find out what was going on here soon enough. Till then I'd forget that you ever even saw us. Believe me, it'll be better for everybody in the long run. I don't want to see anyone get hurt here foolishly."

The young lieutenant stared down at Walker, as if weighing his options. As if Walker were his worst nightmare, and even blinking repeatedly in broad daylight wouldn't make him go away. Finally, he holstered his pistol, snapped the reins to free the bridle from Walker's grasp, and wheeled his horse around. Rigid in the saddle, backbone straight, he led his troop back across the yard. He did not look at Lyle as they passed the steps to the office, and he did not look back.

Walker's men watched silently as the troop disappeared between the buildings. Then they hooted and dissolved in laughter. One man pulled out a fife and began to toodle a song, a couple of the men linked arms and pulled each other around in circles. Walker grinned.

"You have delivered us once again from out of the lion's den, Captain," said the Parson. "Even if this time the lion was only a cub."

Grady spit in the dust. "Ain't seen a bit of acting like that since the time we was outside Charleston. 'Twere a credit to the general himself."

"I didn't lie," Walker shrugged. "I didn't say why we followed Morgan all those years."

She thought he must have forgotten about her. Forgotten she was there. Or had forgotten something else. Unkind, kind sir. He spun around abruptly and looked at her. Libby stood where she had been, on the outskirts of the circle of men with their guns. The men now in the midst of their giddiness and celebration. What have I done, oh God, God, what have I done? She met his eyes and smiled.

SEVEN

As the afternoon wore on, the outside windows became leaden, full of diminishing gray light, while the inside windows flickered red and orange more intensely, reflecting the lights of the forges and heating furnaces. Colin considered lighting a lamp, then got up heavily from his desk, stretched, and went over to the windows overlooking the shop. His office was on the second floor, with a wall of windows that looked down into the long expanse of the shop area. When he built the administration building for the steamworks adjacent to the main shop, he had had these interior windows put in specially; even though many of his duties required him to be in his office, he wanted to feel part of the work going on in the shop below. At the moment, however, he didn't feel at all part of the work going on.

Three-quarters of the way down the length of the shop, in the center of the cruciform of the cross-shaped building, Reid was scrambling over the temporary scaffolding erected around the two road engines, supervising the workmen as they fitted the iron plates to the sides of the boilers. Colin listened and watched carefully; no, everything seemed to be going smoothly now, Reid apparently had settled down, his tantrums over for the time being. As work proceeded on the modifications, Reid had become increasingly short-tempered and abusive. Matters had become serious this afternoon when Colin happened into the shop after being outside and found Reid screaming at a couple of Colin's men.

"What's the problem?" Colin said, hurrying over to them. Reid was waving an iron bracket in the face of a blacksmith named Josef.

"Look at this!" Reid said, red-faced. "Just look at what this man did to this bracket!"

Colin took the bracket and examined it. "I don't see. . . ."

"It's been heated too long. It's starting to weaken here at the midpoint."

"It might be overheated slightly," Colin said, "but I certainly don't think it's to the critical stage."

"I had to overheat it because he wasn't satisfied the way I bent it the first time," Josef said. He was a large man, in a leather apron and brimless cap, with jowls like twin bellows and upper arms the size of Reid's thighs.

"Well, it wasn't right," Reid said.

"It was good enough that I didn't want to weaken it by heating it again, the way you had me do," Josef said. His small eyes were focused on Reid.

"Good enough for you isn't good enough for me," Reid said. "To allow such work is an insult."

Colin smiled a little to himself and looked at Josef. He had worked with the man for many years; if Josef said it was good enough, it was better than most. "Is this the shape it's supposed to be from the drawings?"

"It was when I finished it the first time. Now it's the shape he wants it now." Josef broke his gaze from Reid long enough to speak to Colin, then focused back on the young man with the red beard and derby hat. Colin had seen that look on his face before, once in the yard when a bully had assaulted a friend of Josef's and Josef went after him, destroying the man's face with his fists.

"The work on these engines has to be of the highest quality. The highest quality," Reid said.

"And I'm sure it is if Josef is working on it."

Reid laughed through his nose. "Work like this is an insult to my design."

"No it's not," Colin said, still keeping his good humor, trying to smooth it over.

"Yes it is," Reid said, drawn up into himself.

Colin's voice went low, quiet. "No, it's not." For a second their eyes met. Then he caught a glimpse of Josef starting to move forward. Colin stepped in front of the blacksmith, took Reid by the elbow, and nearly dragged him outside.

Why hadn't he put Reid in his place before this? For that matter, why hadn't he let Josef settle him, at least put a bit of a scare into him; but Colin knew that would have been morally wrong. Reid thought he had Colin over a barrel because he knew the Keystone Steam Works needed this job, badly. But Reid needed Colin—or at least the steamworks—as much or even more. Instead of confronting Reid, Colin had put aside his own anger, had tried to be conciliatory, with the result that he had suffered more of Reid's arrogance as soon as they were outside.

"Let go of me! How dare you treat me this way! Let go!" As soon as they were outside the doors and Colin let up on his grip, Reid pulled his arm away. "What's the meaning of this?"

"I thought if you and I have something to discuss, we should do it away from the workmen," Colin said.

Reid straightened his suit coat, brushed himself off as he tried to regain his dignity.

"Well, I agree we should keep such discussions from the work-men. It's important to present a united front. But I am incensed at some of the things that go on in there. I can't impress enough upon these men—and you, too—the importance that this project be done with the highest levels of workmanship."

"I think if you give them a chance, you'll see that these men are among the best mechanics you'll find anywhere."

"Lord help us if that's true."

Colin looked at him for an explanation, but Reid only shook his head.

"I've never had trouble getting decent work out of them," Colin said.

"Decent," Reid said. He looked as though Colin had just presented him with a bug. "I guess it all comes down to a matter of standards. The difference in what you and I will settle for. I will never settle for anything less than first-rate in this world."

"Then you're going to spend a lot of your time being disappointed. And with a lot more than just the Keystone Steam Works."

"Then I would much rather be disappointed, than to know that I settled for less. Than to know that I could be satisfied to be second-rate."

Colin looked away momentarily. "Feelings always run high on an important project like this. Maybe it would do you good to get away from it for a while. Tonight is the night my wife and I host our weekly Entertainments—"

"Entertainments? At a time like this? No, I don't believe so." Reid looked as though everything he had suspected about Colin had just been confirmed. He turned to walk away, then looked back. "I suppose Walker will be there too."

"Yes, I'm sure that Libby invited him—"

"If she invited him, he'll be there all right." Reid laughed through his nose and went back inside the shop.

In a way, Colin almost envied him. To be that sure of yourself, that sure you're right. It had been a long time since Colin had that kind of confidence in himself, though he could remember a time when he was probably just as overbearing, just as pigheaded and intolerable. Was that the way his father had seen Colin? Was that in fact the way Colin had acted toward his father? He didn't like to think so, but he was afraid it could be true.

No wonder the old man moved off into the hills, no wonder he moved back to the old Ironmaster's House above the creek where the original blast furnace had been, and didn't want to see me anymore, not because he hated me because I sold off my half of the ironworks to start the steamworks—our half I suppose, what he had left his family—but because he found he didn't have anything to say to me anymore, or rather he knew he didn't have anything to say that I'd listen to.

Colin looked around his office, picking absently at the place on his forehead where his hairline had been. There was still work that could be done this evening, but he decided that there wasn't anything that couldn't wait until tomorrow. He straightened the piles of papers and drawings so the room would look neat when he arrived in the morning, closed the safe, rolled down his shirt-sleeves and put on his suit coat and hat. For reasons he never understood, he always had an indescribable sense of loss whenever he left his office or the steamworks at the end of the day, a catch at the heart of his being as if something were being wrenched out of him. Accordingly, as soon as he started for his office door, he didn't look back.

The administration building was nearly deserted at this hour, there were only a few clerks and draftsmen left at the rows of desks. Colin, without saying good night to anyone, went down the side stairs and out the door into the passageway between the buildings. The evening was hot and muggy. He was already sweating before he left his office, but he never took his jacket off on these walks home, feeling that it was improper, even immod-est, to be seen in town without it. Crossing the tracks and starting up the hill to the main part of town, he walked briskly, leaning into the slope of the hillside the same as he always did, winter or summer, determined not to let the steepness or the weather or his desire to let up get the better of him.

It was the kind of early summer evening he thought about when he thought about early summer evenings in Furnass. Hot, sticky, the sky close overhead, a sense of it wanting to rain and being unable to as yet; the day was still bright though hazy, the smoke and the steam diffusing what was left of the sunlight, the light flat, metallic, without shadows or definition, melancholy. He thought of Reid's insinuation that he was second-rate, that he had settled for less than he should have. Harsh words, though they were nothing Colin hadn't wondered about himself at one time or another. It was ironic—but certainly within Colin's understanding of how the world worked—that the young man who brought the opportunity for Colin to break out of his circle of failure was the same young man who most reminded him of that failure.

There were a number of things about Reid that reminded Colin of himself. The determination, the drive. Yes, and the brilliance. There was no question that the young man was intelligent. It was also ironic and in keeping with Colin's understanding of the world's workings that Reid would see Colin as contemptible, something hateful to him, everything Reid was afraid of becoming. Relax, young man, there are worse things in the world than to be me. I wonder if I mean that. He could understand why Reid would feel that way about him; Colin had felt much the same way about his own father, the ironmaster himself, the man who had forged his dream for a town here into a reality but who was immalleable to any ideas from his son. When it comes right down to it I guess I don't have to worry about comparisons with my father: he was a success. Walker, on the other hand, was a different matter. There was nothing about Walker that Colin felt was like himself. Or anything about himself that was at all like Walker. That bothered him more than Reid ever could.

On the main street, people were making their way toward the Alhambra Theater; the marquee announced the appearance of a spiritualist and seer. GUARANTEED TO ANSWER ALL QUESTIONS OF THE GREAT UNKNOWN. From the saloons and taverns came the sounds of music, fiddles and pianos and concertinas, singing, the sounds of laughter and people enjoying themselves. Along the wooden sidewalks, passersby, local businessmen with their wives on their arms, and workmen from the mills standing around the curbsides, all addressed him as he passed: "Good evening, Colin." "Evenin', Mr. Lyle." "Hello, sir." He was Colin Lyle, the owner of the Keystone Steam Works. Prominent Citizen. But no one would think to stop to talk to him, nor would it ever occur to Colin to stop to talk to them. He climbed on, toward Sycamore House farther up the hillside.

And he thought about Reid's other insinuation, about Walker and Libby. Well, he could have expected that. Expected that Libby would spend as much time with Walker as she could, expected that people would think the worst. Did Colin think there was any danger that Libby would run off with her dashing cavalry officer? No, not really. He knew Libby—his version of Libby—he knew that she would be interested in Walker, but he was certain that it was no more than an infatuation, another of Libby's dreams and fantasies. Women were dreamers, you had to expect such things, but Libby was intelligent enough to know when and where the dream ended.

No, he was secure in the knowledge that Libby was true, that Libby's interest in Captain Walker wasn't serious; Libby might pack up and return to her beloved South one day, she might even take it into her head to just disappear, go away where no one would find her, but she wouldn't do it for the sake of another man, of that Colin was sure. Walker was no more to her than a diversion, a relief from boredom, something to keep her interested and her mind occupied. It would be something else next week, after Walker was gone. Colin would just have to tolerate it for now, the same way he tolerated these dreadful Tuesday Night Entertainments. The way he tolerated all these years her flirtations with McArtle.

It all sounded so admirable. So accepting. So self-reliant. Emerson would be proud of me, Ralph Waldo. Nothing can bring you peace but yourself. Yet he wasn't at peace, and he knew it. He couldn't get the image of Walker and Libby out of his mind; he had seen the two of them today across the compound from his office window, walking together on their way back from the river. She came down just to see him. She didn't come into the office to see me when she arrived, and she didn't stop to say good-bye when she left. The first time she ever came down to the steamworks when I didn't have to drag her there, when she didn't look as if she hated it the whole time and wanted to be away from it as soon as possible. The first time she ever came on her own to her husband's mill, and it wasn't to see her husband. It wasn't to see me. O Libby, all I ever wanted from you was for you to love me. Or to even just pay attention to me. I wonder if that's true.

As he crossed the front lawn toward the house there was music, the sound of the piano and violin, coming through the open windows, and he could see the glow of a lamp within the darkness of the parlor. He hung up his coat and hat in the vestibule, went around to the back of the house to wash at the pump, and returned to put his suit coat back on. In the dusky mirror of the hall stand he adjusted his tie, smoothed down his hair, and tried out his polite smile. He supposed he was ready for anything.

The music coming from the parlor he recognized as a Mozart sonata. He peeked through the crack of the double doors. The room was in darkness except for the few lamps, the fading sunlight outside already gone from the house. In the light of the lamp beside her music, Libby looked elegant at the piano, the yellowish glow softening her features. McArtle stood nearby, bowing away intently, a look of pained concentration on his boyish face. Sitting facing them was Walker, looking out of place and uncomfortable. Colin smiled to himself. Not wishing to disrupt things, he tiptoed on down the dark hallway.

The sliding double doors between the dining room and parlor were open, forming a proscenium around the scene in the front room, a tableau of the music makers and their audience of one. Laid out on the dining room table was a buffet, plates of sliced roast beef and ham, bowls of pickled beets and snap beans and potatoes with dill. Colin picked at the food as he listened. He had to admit that Libby and the doctor were getting better; when they started playing together years ago, they had been rough, to put it nicely, Libby rushing the tempo at times, McArtle concentrating so much on his fingering and bowing that what he played was lifeless, mechanical. Though they weren't concert hall quality yet, they were close. He envied McArtle that, sharing an interest in music with Libby, having something to do together; he and Libby shared very little, it seemed—dinnertimes, a few hours' conversation in the evenings, an occasional ride in the carriage, that was about all. But he supposed it was unavoidable, husbands and wives were supposed to have separate lives.

Something moved in the darkness of the corner. Sally stood in the entryway to the kitchen, a vague form in the shadows.

"I didn't see you there, Sally," Colin whispered, going over to her. She was wearing a dark blue silk evening dress, cut low across her shoulders and with a full hoopskirt, one of Libby's dresses before she started wearing only black. Over the dress she wore her apron; she kept her hands tucked away in the folds. "You don't usually see Sally, Mr. Colin."

"What do you mean?"

"I mean you're not supposed to see Sally, are you Mr. Colin? Sally is always in the shadows, Sally is the shadows to someone like you, ain't that right, Mr. Colin? You can't read Sally in one of your books."

What was she getting at? He didn't think she seemed unfriendly, but he couldn't tell; he had rarely been around Negroes before Sally and her husband arrived with Libby, and he couldn't read their expressions and moods, they were a mystery to him. Maybe that was what she referred to. He tried to go on as if nothing was out of the ordinary.

"How is Libby this evening? Is she still having her headaches?"

"No one knows how my Miss Elizabeth is. She keeps it all to herself. Not Sally, not you, not that doctor."

"That's why we need you to take good care of her. And you do take good care of her."

"Captain Walker, he knows."

"How would he know about Libby? Does he spend that much time with her?"

"He don't need to," Sally whispered, more like a hiss. "Captain Walker, he's not a walker at all."

Colin's heart sank. "What are you talking about? Who is he if he's not Walker?"

Her eyes danced and she stifled a high-pitched laugh. "He's the Rider, that's who he is. The Rider."

Before he could say anything, she turned around with a swish of crinolines and disappeared back into the darkness of the kitchen.

What is she talking about? Sometimes she acts as mad as Libby—no, I mustn't ever. For a moment he had been afraid that Sally had found out something about Walker. But he quickly put away such thoughts and turned back to the scene in front of him. As it grew darker outside, the room beyond the open double doors became more pronounced in the glow of the lamps, the shadows within the room deeper. Walker sat forward stiffly in the low platform rocker, his knees close to his chest. His dark mustache and deep-set eyes, his hair that refused to stay put and kept sliding down his forehead, added to the darkness of his face; he was staring intently at Libby, concentrating as if he were repeating each note in his mind. He looked like a man truly out of his element, an adventurer plucked from the hinterlands and stuffed into one of Colin's suits and dropped into this comfortable parlor as some sort of cruel joke, though who the joke was on was unclear. So why did he decide to come tonight? But I know the answer.

For all that, Colin could understand why Libby would be attracted to him. Beyond her romantic fantasies of the dashing cavalry officer. Beyond the realities of this tall brooding figure. To a restless woman like Libby, after living with the years of Colin's false starts and dead ends, a man like Walker must seem like everything her husband wasn't. It certainly seemed that way to Colin.

The music ended; Walker and Colin applauded. Dr. McArtle, his face flushed from his effort and obviously pleased with his performance, bowed deeply from the waist, then went over to the piano, took Libby's hand, and led her forward for another bow.

"Excellent, excellent," Colin said. He crossed into the front room and kissed Libby's hand. McArtle appeared to color even more.

Libby and McArtle took seats across the room from Walker; Colin stood off to the side, in the curve of the piano. Walker continued to watch Libby intently, but Libby seemed to be purposefully avoiding looking at him, even when she spoke to him.

"Well, Captain Walker, what is your opinion? Did we do justice to Mr. Mozart, or were we hopelessly amateurish?"

"I'm afraid my background in music is somewhat limited, so I'm not really the one to judge. But to me, it sounded beautiful."

McArtle bent over where he was seated to put his violin back in its case, struggling against his protruding stomach like a man pushing against a large balloon. "No, I don't suppose you do get much of a chance to hear good music there in the backcountry."

"Kentucky is not the wild frontier, Eugene," Libby said. "And if you are referring to the South in general, I take offense. I experienced more true beauty and culture—and good music, I might add—in the South than I ever did here in the North."

"No, no, I didn't mean anything of the sort. . . ," McArtle said, puffing from the exertion of leaning over and trying to smooth his clothes back into order again.

"It's true that I didn't have much opportunity to hear good music when I was growing up in Kentucky," Walker said. "But when I was in Washington I was fortunate enough to hear a number of very fine concerts. And I thought what I heard tonight was equally fine."

"Touché, Doctor," Libby said, still avoiding looking at Walker. "You have been complimented and bested in one stroke."

"I certainly didn't mean to offend anyone. . . ."

"Don't pout, Eugene," Libby reached over and patted his leg. "It doesn't become you. Perhaps you'll favor us by going first with a recitation."

McArtle brightened up again immediately, a little boy called upon to do his party piece. He stood, clasping his hands off center in his recitation pose.

"This is from a long poem entitled *Love in the Bowery* by F. A. Durivage. I have no idea what the 'F. A.' stands for, perhaps 'Far Afield,' but I assume it to be a male if only from the subject matter. It is the story of the unrequited love of a fire laddie in New York City, hence the reference to Number 9. You'll also notice the colorful Manhattan dialect. It carries, incidentally, this epigraph from what is called the *Bowery Edition of Shakespeare*: 'The course of true love never did run smooth.' Ahem.

"I seen her on the sidewalk,
When I run with No. 9:
My eyes spontaneous sought out hern—
And hern was fixed on mine.
She waved her pocket handkerchief,
As we went rushin' by—
No boss that ever killed in York
Was happier than I.

"Before the bridle halter,
I thought to call her mine—
The day was fixed when she to me
Her hand and heart should jine.
But bless me! if she didn't slip
Her halter on the day;
A peddler from Connecticut,
He carried her away.

"Well, let it pass—there's other gals,
As beautiful as she;
And many a butcher's lovely child
Has cast sheep's eyes at me.
I wears no crape upon my hat,
'Cause I'm a packin' sent—
I only takes an extra horn,
Observing, 'Let her went!'"

Colin watched Walker watch Libby through the doctor's recitation and the applause afterward, watched him watch her as the
doctor was seated and it was Libby's turn. She stood and cleared
her throat, adjusting the fall of her long black dress around her.

She continued to avoid looking at Walker; instead, she glanced at Colin as if to make sure he was paying attention, and began.

> "How small the choice, from cradle to the grave,
> Between the lot of Hireling and of Slave!
> To each alike applies the stern decree,
> That man shall labor; whether bond or free,
> For all that toil, the recompense we claim—
> Food, fire, a home and clothing—is the same.
> What blessing to the churl has freedom proved,
> What want supplied, what task or toil removed. . . ?"

The Hireling and the Slave, thought Colin. Which does she think she is? It had been a while since she recited it, though she did periodically, excerpts of the long poem, whenever she wanted to assail her husband about something in a polite fashion. She must have trotted it out now for Walker's benefit, though she continued to avoid looking at him. Why does she do these things? Why does she always try to hurt or humiliate me? Why does she insist on seeing love as a battleground, and me as the enemy? And then he thought Why do I put up with it?

He looked at Libby standing there in the flowing, open-necked black dress, this delicate-boned, delicate-complected, iron-willed woman, her figure crescented in the glow of the lamp. Did he love her? He wasn't sure. He wasn't sure what was meant when you said you loved someone. He had always thought that love involved a choice, a choosing of one person over another, but he had had no choice with Libby, really. The things he had felt the first time he saw her, he had no control over, he had feelings regardless how he wanted to feel. And then when she appeared here in Furnass one day uninvited, he had had no choice there, either. Even if he had wanted to (which he didn't), he was too much of a gentleman to simply send her away. She was here, she had come here to be with him, and that was that. It had been her choice, not his. And there were times it seemed as though she were bound and determined to make him pay for it ever since.

She was finished and Walker and McArtle were applauding as she sat back down again, looking satisfied that she had made a point.

"Now, Colin," McArtle said, turning in his chair to look at him, "what about your weekly dose of Emerson?"

"Shame on you, Eugene," Libby said, her face still flushed. As if she momentarily forgot herself, she looked at Walker as she started to explain—and just as quickly looked away. "The doctor is referring to the fact that my husband usually has memorized something from Mr. Emerson."

"Usually?" McArtle said, puffing out his cheeks. "My dear, there are a few certainties in this world—death being one, pestilence being another. A third, and perhaps in the same category, would be Colin quoting Emerson."

"I've heard you speak derisively of Mr. Lyle's love of Emerson several times now," Walker said, looking at the doctor. "What I can't figure out is which one is actually the subject of your derision, Emerson or Mr. Lyle."

McArtle colored and started to sputter.

"And shame on you, Captain Walker," Libby said lightly, smiling at McArtle. "You broke a cardinal rule of our little gatherings. You told the truth. Now I certainly hope you won't disappoint me by trying to apologize."

"I wouldn't want to disappoint you about anything," Walker said. "And I don't see anything to apologize for. I meant it only as an observation."

"And you, Eugene. You mustn't hold a grudge because the good captain said out loud what others might only think."

"I wouldn't think of holding a grudge," McArtle said, trying hard to keep his composure. "I tip my hat to the honesty of frontier sensibilities."

"And none of your bitter sarcasms either. They not only don't become you, but you leave yourself open for more of the captain's unblinking truthfulness. Colin?"

His selection for the evening was in fact from Emerson, a poem entitled "Give All to Love." He had known it for years, it was one of his favorites, words that he tried to live by, but it had never seemed right as a recitation before. Until now. Without introduction he started through the first verses, "Give all to love; / Obey thy heart; / Friends, kindred, days. . . ," working his way through the early arguments—that love is a stern master and requires devotion in order to follow its ups and downs, that love in due course will grant its reward—addressing Walker and McArtle. But when the logic of the piece started to turn, he looked at Libby:

> "Leave all for love;
> Yet, hear me, yet,
> One word more thy heart behoved,
> One pulse more of firm endeavor,—
> Keep thee today,
> Tomorrow, forever,
> Free as an Arab
> Of thy beloved.

> "Cling with life to the maid;
> But when the surprise,
> First vague shadow of surmise
> Flits across her bosom young,
> Of a joy apart from thee,
> Free be she, fancy-free;

Nor thou detain her vesture's hem,
Nor the palest rose she flung
From her summer diadem.

"Though thou loved her as thyself,
As a self of purer clay,
Though her parting dims the day,
Stealing grace from all alive;
Heartily know,
When half-gods go,
The gods arrive."

For a moment there was an awkward silence. Colin studied his hands, the damage done from working with the men in the shop—the torn and bruised nails, the iron filings ground irreparably into the lines and pores of his skin.

"It would seem," McArtle said finally, pausing to rub fervently at the end of his nose, "that the good captain is not the only one who can be faulted for honesty. Or barbed comments."

"I think it is we who owe you an apology, Captain Walker," Libby said. "We've said more here tonight than we ever meant to."

"Don't I also get a chance to recite something?" Walker said.

"Well, of course," Libby said, looking surprised. "I had no idea that—"

"It's not much, to be sure." Walker slowly unfolded from the chair and stood up, looking all the more uncomfortable but determined to go through with what he had started; the room seemed to reduce in size around his tall lanky figure. "It's a passage I found in a book you told me about. But I read it and it made a lot of sense to me. In fact, it changed my outlook on a few things, and I put it to memory so I wouldn't forget it. I'll give it a try, if you don't mind."

"Go ahead, please."

Walker glanced at Colin and McArtle—in the shadows of the room Colin couldn't see his eyes, only the dark slits where the eyes should be—and began in a measured voice.

"The lions have written the books, and having persisted in making that part of our character which brings us in relation to themselves the prominent subject of comment, they have ignored our other attributes, till there is a vague feeling engendered that a woman is the worse for large endowments of any kind whatever. Iago's narrow and coarse exposition of her vocation, 'To suckle fools, and chronicle small beer,' is not far from the popular estimate. Genius and beauty, God's crowning gifts, are looked upon with distrust, if not with dread. The fear that a woman may deviate the slightest from conventionalism in any way, has become a nervous disease with the public. Indeed, so little is she trusted as a creation, that one would think she were made marvelously beautiful, and endowed with gifts of thought and emotion only for the purpose of endangering her safety—a sort of spiritual locomotion with no checkwheel, a rare piece of porcelain to be handled gingerly— in fact a creature with no conservative elements within herself, but left expressly thus, that men might supply them, and lead and guide, and coerce, and cajole her as it pleased him best. She is a blind angel, neither adapted to heaven nor earth in herself, but if submitting graciously to man's guidance, capable of filling a narrow, somewhat smoky and very uncertain nook on this small planet, and possibly to win heaven through the perfection of suffering here."

Across the River

As Colin watched, Libby looked up from studying her hands folded in her lap and met Walker's eyes. She looked as happy and as pleased as he'd ever seen her.

The night air was heavy, oppressive, a physical presence around him, dank, warm. His clothes stuck to him, even here outside of the confines of the house; his skin felt bristly, his body felt weighted down. Overhead, the night sky throbbed with color. The solid layer of clouds fit across the top of the hills like a lid, gray not black, reflecting the glow of the blast furnaces along the river and the coke ovens in the hills, pulsing, flickering, by turns an entire sky of orange and yellow and red. Smoke and steam rose from the mills and furnaces, only to flatten out against the lowering sky, lowering it even more, bringing the lid closer, as if the valley would fill in from the sky down.

"Must be going to rain," the doctor said, standing on the front porch, ready to leave. "The smoke can't rise."

"I hope it does rain," Colin said, not looking at him, looking out over the front steps, the dark lawn, to the valley below. "It would break this heat."

"We need it, certainly," McArtle said. "The rain, that is."

"Yes."

The two men stood side by side on the top step, not looking at each other. Above the darkness, bats flittered across the gray and orangish sky, gone with a blink. A nighthawk whistled far away over the valley.

"You seem rather subdued," McArtle said after a moment's silence. His voice was deep, resonant, melodic—his doctor's voice, inquiring after a patient.

"Do I? I apologize, I didn't mean to be impolite."

"It's understandable, of course. I'd be subdued too, if my wife was interested in a man like that."

"I don't know what you're talking about."

McArtle laughed humorlessly. "Come now, Colin. They were looking at each other all evening. There's obviously something going on between them. And in your own home too."

Colin looked at him. In the glow of the sky, McArtle's soft boyish face fringed with sideburns was discolored, a sickly yellow, and seemed to flicker. It occurred to Colin that his own face must appear the same.

"I think you're just irritated with the captain. He challenged you on a couple of the things you said this evening and he made you look bad."

"I don't know how this man has convinced you otherwise, but I think everything about his being here in this house and this deal with you is shady."

"First of all, he is a guest in my house. And as my guest he is entitled to every consideration. That includes talking to and being friends with my wife, if she so chooses. He's the first person from the South that Libby has had to talk to in many years. I would be a very poor host indeed if I then turned around and suspected him in some way for simply responding to our hospitality. And as for the deal between Walker and Reid and myself, you know nothing about it. I'm sad to say that you're very misguided in all of this."

"I'm going to tell you something, Colin. There's too many things about this man Walker and his friend that don't add up. And I think you're being foolish in regards to the possibilities, and to the consequences. You don't know the first thing about these men, except what they've told you themselves. They're from the South, all right, the whole lot of them. It wouldn't surprise me in the least to find out they're actually Confederate spies."

Colin's heart froze. He tried hard to keep himself under control. "This project is the chance I've been waiting for. After all the years of working hard and getting nowhere, I can finally show the world what my road engines can do. And I can finally make the steamworks a success, once and for all. I would think you'd be happy for me. Happy for Libby."

"How can you talk that way if there's even a chance these men aren't who they say they are? No, I don't know what your deal is with them or what you're doing down at the works, and I don't care either. What I care about is if there's something going on here that could threaten our efforts in the war, even threaten our entire country. How could you just hand over your most important ideas to a man that you have every right to think may be a traitor or a spy?"

Colin stared at him for a moment. Now. The time is now. When he spoke, his voice was barely audible, even to himself. "How could I just hand over my wife to you all these years?"

McArtle looked suddenly drained, as if everything inside him had run out. He walked down the steps and melded into the darkness across the lawn.

EIGHT

Walker went looking for her as soon as he got up, as soon as he saw her bedroom door was open and didn't find anyone about, searching through the empty house and then outside in the yard.

It was early, before seven o'clock, though he couldn't tell without his watch; there was no sun, a gray day, but already hot, already sticky at this hour, and the air was full of the smells of the mills from the valley, there was a dinginess about the morning that pervaded even the grass and the trees on the hill. He found her in the garden, though at first he didn't know it was her. She was wearing an off-white morning dress with large red bows up the front and large billowy sleeves. As he came across the backyard from the house, he couldn't see her face; she was turned away from him and was wearing a sunbonnet despite the lack of sun, a fancy-dress bonnet, fit for an outing or a party, of white silk and decorated with ribbons and red poppies along the brim. Seeing the figure on her knees digging between the rows of flowers, Walker supposed it was Sally. But as he got closer, Libby began talking to him as if she were expecting him.

"Are there a lot of trees where you come from in Kentucky, Captain Walker?"

Walker looked around, at the tall sycamores in the yard. "Yes, some, but not like these. There's a lot of scrub oak."

"We had oak trees on our plantation in South Carolina too. Before we lost it, that is. I don't know if they're still there or not." She sat back on her knees, looking at the trees on the hillside. "There was one old oak tree that sat all alone in the middle of a field. My father's father, when he founded the plantation, directed his field hands—I guess I should say the word, shouldn't I: directed his field slaves—to plow around it, and my father directed his slaves to do likewise. Now that I think about it, it's a wonder it wasn't struck down by lightning or blown over by the wind, standing out there all alone that way. But mainly there were willow trees, lots and lots of willows. I loved to stand at the end of the drive and see them all lined up like soldiers marching toward the house."

"It sounds very colorful."

"It was. Though I doubt it was colorful when the real soldiers marched toward the house. I'm told the Yankees made a point of burning the plantations in our region, simply as a matter of course. Simply as a matter of course."

"I'm sorry," Walker said.

"That's nice of you, but you needn't be. I know you had nothing to do with it." She glanced up at him, then went back to scratching at the weeds with a dibble. "And I remember we had water lilies. We called them lotuses, at least my father did, but I'm sure they were plain old water lilies. Hundreds of them, or so it seemed at the time. They grew so thick on the pond behind the house that they eventually choked themselves out. As I think back on it now, it seems very fitting that we'd have so many water lilies in the South."

"I'm not sure I understand."

Libby continued to scratch at the dirt, as if she were considering carefully what she wanted to say, as if she thought she might uncover it there among the rows of zinnias and sunflowers around the perimeter of the vegetable garden. Then she sat back again and looked up at him, peeked at him around the rim of the sunbonnet as if around the edge of some half-opened door.

"They say that South Carolina women have the sweetest voices in the world." She lapsed momentarily into a thick Southern drawl. "You-all speak like this, and you-all just make everything sound so sweet and melodic that—don't you know?—you-all could just cut it with a knife. And then, just to make it complete, you-all end each little ol' sentence with a little ol' sigh."

She sighed. When she spoke again, she tried to drop the accent, but it continued to bob up into her speech here and there, as if, having once been allowed to surface, it refused to stay submerged.

"It makes you sound as if you're always about to expire, as if you've used your last bit of energy and strength just to get a few words out of your mouth. The result is that the woman presents herself as a weak person and in need of a good strong man to see her through the everyday trials and tribulations. Eventually, the women in such a culture choke on their own sweetness, the culture as a whole becomes tangled up in its own cloyingness. That's why I've worked so hard to lose my accent, or at least exchange it for another. No matter how fond Mr. Lyle is of hearing me talk that way. I came here to get away from such attitudes, not transplant them."

"Your husband doesn't seem like the kind of man who would subjugate or hurt you in any way."

"Perhaps not willingly. But that doesn't mean he wouldn't do it, and that the effect on me wouldn't be the same as if he intended it. A lot of things happen in marriage that nobody means to happen. But they still happen."

"I wouldn't know about that," Walker said.

"The way you deal with marriage is through make-believe. You pretend about things that happen, and things that don't, in order to survive. I would think you would know quite a lot about that, Captain Walker."

"Why would I? I told you I was never married."

"You know a lot about pretending to be a Union cavalry officer. I assume it's in order to survive."

Walker looked around the yard, the hillside, to make sure no one else could hear, to make sure this wasn't a trap. But he knew already that it wasn't.

Libby got to her feet and looked at him, not around the edge of the sunbonnet but straight on. Her voice was questioning, not angry. "Who are you? What are you doing here?"

"My name is Judson Walker. I am a captain in the Kentucky cavalry, as I said. Only it's the Second Kentucky Cavalry, Confederate States of America."

She cocked her head as she thought about something. "Then where's your sword, Captain?"

"We don't use swords much nowadays. Neither side does. They've been replaced by more expedient weapons, like carbines and pistols. I don't understand your question."

"It's nothing," Libby said with a toss of her hand. She smiled wistfully. "A foolish dream."

Walker was puzzled but went on. "I'm one of Morgan's raiders."

If she was surprised, her face didn't register it. "And why are you here to see my husband?"

"The road engines. Reid has a plan to use them in the war. My job was to get him here, and to get him and the engines out again."

"Was?" she asked, studying him. "Has that job changed?"

"A lot of things seemed to have changed." He smiled wryly. "It's like you were describing marriage. A lot of things happen in a war that you don't mean to happen."

"I assume one of the reasons you decided to stay here at the house and you were keeping an eye on me is that you were going to take me hostage if things didn't go well. Is that correct?"

"At the beginning, yes." Walker looked away, then back at her. "Please don't be frightened. Because I wouldn't—"

"No, it doesn't frighten me. I guessed or figured out most of it. I don't know how much Mr. Lyle knows. I would imagine that he suspects something, but then again he may be oblivious to it. As he is to so much. We haven't talked about it. We don't talk about very many things."

"You're not very close to him, are you?"

"What makes you say that?"

"You don't act as if you are. You don't talk about him, at least to me, as if he's someone you're close to."

She smiled to herself about something. She walked a couple steps past him, then came back, standing in front of him with her feet crossed, so that, from the tips of her shoes showing beneath the edge of her long dress, her feet seemed transposed.

"Mr. Lyle respects me. Even if he doesn't understand me. But he's absorbed with his machines. They are his passion, if you will. I knew that when I married him. Sometimes I wonder if that is the reason I married him."

Walker thought a moment about what he wanted to say. "Did you ever think of having something more? With someone else?"

"Ah. You mean love. Or 'only love,' as I think you phrased it the other day. That's an old-fashioned idea, isn't it?"

"I thought Northern women were all for free love. Showing their affections and following their hearts."

"There's bitterness in your voice, Captain. Almost anger. Are you angry with me about something? Maybe that's why you're attracted to me, is that it? Do you think I'm a believer in free love?"

Before he could think of what to say, she turned and walked on a few steps between the rows of flowers. She looked across the yard toward the house.

"Of course, we'd have to define our terms before we could get too deep in our discussion, wouldn't we? Just what does it mean, 'free love'? What's free about it? Not very much, in any context or meaning of the word that I'm familiar with."

"I didn't mean to imply. . . ."

Libby turned and came toward him again. The bottom of her skirt swept between the rows of flowers, brushing past the leaves and buds.

"The reason I love Mr. Lyle, if 'love' is the correct term, is because he gives me the freedom to be myself. I said that machines are Mr. Lyle's passion. He also tends to see people as machines. In his view of the world, people follow certain courses of action because they were made that way; if a person acts differently than the normal pattern, it is only because that person needs a bit of an adjustment, a valve needs opened or closed, a bolt needs turned one direction or the other. He's undoubtedly come to that conclusion both from his love of machines, and from watching himself. Mr. Lyle's life has been one of making continual adjustments—albeit, usually too much in the opposite direction—to what happens in the world around him. Be that as it may, I'm glad he is the way he is, I wouldn't have it any other way. It's easy to live with. It allows me to be who I am. I am not his slave, machines are his slaves."

"You make it sound as if he had to have a slave of some kind."

"I think most people do, in one form or another. Someone to do your bidding, someone or something to have dominion over. I am mistress over Sally, and Sally is mistress over her husband George. As for George, he has his horses."

"I suppose you could make a statement like that, if you see the world only in terms of power." Why was he having this discussion with her? What, or whom, was he actually talking about here? He thought of Mattie, of the changes that came over her after she married Morgan, after she had a taste of being the wife of the Great Man. *You're no longer welcome in this house, Judson, John and I don't want you here. . . .* He thought of the changes that came over Morgan when he started to believe he was the Great Man people said he was. *And suppose I order you to go to Pennsylvania, Captain Walker, what can you do about it?*

"I am not saying I like the world that way," Libby went on, spinning the dibble in her hands. "I'm not saying that's the way I want it to be. I'm only saying that's the way it is, unfortunately. The fact is I wish the world and the people in it were very, very different. How else do you see it, Captain Walker? Let's take an example. Why did you go to all the trouble of memorizing that passage from Mrs. Oakes Smith and reciting it last night? Because you knew it would give you power over me by pleasing me."

"If power is the only motivation, why didn't you expose me as a spy last night? That would have given you power over me."

"Maybe not." She turned suddenly coquettish, playful, sashaying a few steps as she had at the steamworks yesterday, a different Libby, as if she had gone too far in a serious vein, said too much. "Maybe I can hold more power over you by not exposing you."

"And maybe the reason I memorized that passage was not to have power over you, but only to please you for its own sake. Because it was important for me to please you."

He watched her as the words sunk in, to both of them. *Is that possible? Could that be true?* For a moment she seemed confused and embarrassed. She dropped the dibble and they both squatted down to retrieve it. As he reached for it between the rows of flowers, she grabbed his wrist and hissed at him, inches from his face.

"Be careful, be very very careful. You don't know what you're getting into here. You just don't know."

Someone was calling his name. Walker stood up quickly. A trooper on horseback—Walker relaxed, it was Spider—had reined in on the path leading to the stable.

"Sorry to bother you, Captain Walker, but the sergeant thought you'd want to know. Vance is gone."

Things were happening too quickly for Walker; for a moment the message didn't sink in.

"Corporal Vance?" Libby said, getting to her feet. "Isn't that the young man who helped me take care of the sick soldiers?"

"Yes ma'am," Spider said. "I guess everybody thought he was still taking care of 'em. He must've just walked away during the night. None of the horses is missing, and a teamster there at the steamworks said he saw a trooper this morning trying to hitch a ride on a freight wagon north of town."

"Good for him," Libby said and smiled happily.

"Get my horse," Walker told Spider. While the trooper headed toward the stable, Walker turned to Libby.

"Why would you be happy that Vance deserted?"

"I'm proud of him. He said he was sick and tired of the war and wanted to get away from it. In fact, I encouraged him to get away from it, if that's what he believed was right."

"What did you tell him?"

"He asked about the country to the north. I told him most of it was fairly isolated. It was the kind of country he was looking for, someplace where people would leave him alone and let him live his life in peace. If more men who thought that way followed their convictions and just walked away from it, this terrible war would be over."

She glared at him defiantly, as if daring him to argue with her. Walker started toward the stable.

"What difference does one man make to you?" she said after him. "He's not even a man, he's only a boy who wasn't much good to you anyway. Why can't you just let him go?"

Walker stopped and turned to her slowly. "Because if they catch him, he'll not only be hung for a spy, he's liable to tell them something that could put us all in jeopardy. And that includes your husband. Folks around here might not take too kindly to the fact that the Keystone Steam Works is currently building war engines for the Confederacy. They could hang your husband for a spy. They could hang you too."

The color emptied from Libby's face. "I never thought about the consequences," she said quietly.

Dear lady, I wish I hadn't. For any of us. Walker went on to the stable.

On the road north of town, beyond where he and Reid had crossed the river six days earlier to come into Furnass from this direction, beyond the large S-curve of the river that held the town, into the wilder country farther up the narrowing valley, there was a point where the smoke and smells of the mills lifted, or rather, where the two riders passed beyond them as if they cut through the line of a curtain, a point where Walker could look across the valley and see the hills on the opposite side, the mirror image of the hills on which he rode, but when he looked back in the direction from which they came, the valley and the trees and the river were gray and indistinct, faded into nothing.

Spider turned in the saddle and looked back too, trying to see what interested Walker. "What you-all think the sergeant'll do when that servant-fellow tells 'im we went after Vance?"

"He better do what I told him to. Which was to stay put." Walker turned his attention again to the road in front of them, the wooded slopes above and below them.

"When'd you-all tell 'im we'd be back?"

"By tomorrow. At the very latest. We can't afford to spend any more time chasing after Vance. He's on foot and hitching rides, so he can't get too far, and we know the general direction he's headed. If we haven't found him by then, we'll hope he got far enough away that nobody will link him to us if they catch him."

"You-all think Vance would say something if the Yankees caught 'im?"

"He wouldn't have to say much."

"Crazy kid," Spider said.

No, crazy me. This doesn't make sense, old son. You're thirty-eight years old in a war you don't believe in anymore or at least since they changed it on you, chasing after a kid who had enough sense even after being hit on the head to know he wanted out before it went and killed him. You tell me who's crazy.

Though it was clearer as they got away from the town and the furnaces, the day was still hazy and hot; the sky was overcast, the air heavy, and it felt like rain, that it had to rain soon. The road was cut across the slope of the hill, midway between the ridgeline and the river. Along the roadside he recognized pearly everlasting and cocklebur, ragweed and poison sumac, black currant and blackberry bushes. Red-winged blackbirds flitted among the brambles; deeper in the woods came the sound of crows, the grind of cicadas. The forest close to the road was second growth, with ferns and underbrush among the young trees, but the rest of the hillside was primordial forest, the beeches and oaks and red maples untouched for hundreds of years. Occasionally through the trees he caught glimpses of the river several hundred feet below, the railroad tracks alongside it.

As they rode deeper into the valley, closer to the area where his family's farm had been, there were parts of the landscape that seemed familiar to him, though strangely different from the way he remembered; it occurred to him that he had probably never seen this part of the valley head-on before, that as a child he had always ridden in the back of the wagon with his brothers and sisters and that his viewpoint had always been one of going away. He wondered, now that he thought about it, if too much of his life had been spent that way.

This is no time to be thinking thoughts like that, if they've already caught Vance and found out who you are they could be coming after you right now, you could be saving them the trouble of having to come looking for you by riding right into them. Keep your goddamn eyes on what's in goddamn front of you.

His plan was to go as far as New Inverness, the county seat ten miles up the valley; if they hadn't found any trace of Vance by then, they'd turn around and come back more slowly, trying to flush him out or head him off. The day grew hotter still, more oppressive, though the sky remained gray, without clouds or definition, just above the branches of the trees. The river, below on the valley floor, was the color of old lead. His clothes stuck to him, damp and heavy with sweat; his wound was a dull ache under his arm. They rode on, neither one speaking, scanning the dark and quiet woods on either side of the road for some sign of where the boy might be hiding, if he was hiding, some indication that he might have passed this way.

And Walker thought of the time only a year earlier, in Tennessee, when he rode with Morgan after some other missing men, though these were men and boys from the town of Gallatin, hostages the Yankees rounded up and herded off toward Nashville, threatening to kill them for collaborating with Morgan during his recent raid on the L&N Railroad. Some people said the war changed that day, at least in that part of the country; some people said Morgan did. Walker thought there were probably many such days, many such incidents, when the war gradually became more brutal, more personal in a way at the same time that it became more impersonal; and as for Morgan, Walker wondered if he actually changed at Gallatin or only showed what had been there all along.

. . . it was back in the days when Morgan still camped with his men, when he slept in a tent or in the open like everyone else, when he would sleep in a hotel or private home if one happened to be nearby but he didn't insist upon it, didn't say that he had to have a headquarters that befitted an important person such as himself, didn't choose the campsites for his men according to comfortable accommodations for himself, back in the days when any one of his men could go see him with a problem at any time, that Walker went to Morgan's tent. The tent sat by itself on the edge of the Gallatin fairgrounds, glowing intensely yellow in the darkness. Beyond a stand of willows, a creek gurgled with the same sound as a man being gutted. The tent flaps were closed despite the heat. Walker knocked on the tent pole; after a moment, Morgan said to come in. There were half a dozen lamps sitting around on the table and on boxes; the air was choking with smoke and the smell of lamp oil. Morgan was still in his boots and pants but without his jacket and shirt, his braces hanging loose against his pale skin. He sat on the edge of his cot, soaking his swollen hands in a basin of water on a camp stool between his legs. He glanced up at Walker, then looked back at his hands in the water.

"I figured you'd be coming to see me."

When Walker didn't say anything, Morgan went on. "Yes sir, I told myself on the ride back here, ol' Walker will be coming to see me tonight, you can bet on it. Look at these hands, will you? Swollen up like bread dough. My feet are the same way. I'm afraid

to take off my boots, I'd never get them back on again. Sad state
of affairs for a man, wouldn't you say?"

Morgan held his hands up to the light to examine them. His
hands were normally small and he was proud of them; it was a
joke among his men about how much time Morgan spent keeping
them clean. Now they were as he said, red and blotchy and puffy.

"Why all the lamps?" Walker said.

"Because I felt like it," Morgan shot back. Then he softened
as he put his hands back into the water. "Because I felt like it,
that's all. Anything wrong with that?"

"No, there's nothing wrong with that. Except you're about to
asphyxiate yourself. It's like a smokehouse in here."

"A smokehouse. That's a good one. I must remember that to
tell the Chartered Libertines. Sterritt and the others will get a
kick out of it. They'll also get a kick out of hearing that it came
from you."

"I didn't mean it to be funny."

Morgan looked up at him again. "What do you want from me,
Judson? What do you want me to tell you? You were there, you
saw what happened. I didn't see you do anything to stop anybody,
so you're as much at fault as anyone else. But I don't see anyone
at fault. I wouldn't have changed a thing. As a matter of fact I'm
proud of my boys and what we did today. We showed the Yankees
they can't treat us that way."

Yes, he was there, he saw what happened. He was there when
the boy rode into their camp at Hartsville in the middle of the
night with the news that after Morgan had left the area the Yankees returned to Gallatin and rounded up every male over the age
of twelve and were taking them to Nashville to be hung as spies;
he was there on the gray dawn when they reached Gallatin after
riding all night and were immediately surrounded by the entire
female population, just as they usually were when Morgan rode
into a town except that all these women were crying hysterically,

*most of them dressed only in their nightgowns with their hair
disheveled and in their bare feet on the damp streets, rushing
from their homes and grabbing at Morgan to tell him what had
happened, to entreat him to rescue their sons and husbands and
fathers. The women told how the Federals searched their homes,
tore rings from the women's fingers and earrings from their ears
and pins from their breasts. They told how a Union soldier stole
silk dresses from one house, and how another collected women's
petticoats. On a street in the center of town the women showed
Morgan where the Yankees had surprised one of the men Morgan
had left in town with Lieutenant Manly and killed him, kicking
and cuffing the body after he was dead. And Walker was there
when they found the dark stain of blood still on the planks of the
bridge outside of town where it was said that Manly had tried to
surrender and was shot down in cold blood.*

*"There's no quarter for Yankees today," someone said from
the ranks.*

*Morgan stared at the blood a long time, then turned in the
saddle to the others. "No prisoners today, boys. They can't do
this to Morgan. No prisoners. Let's go."*

*And he was there when they caught up to them on the road to
Nashville, when the first Yankee Morgan came across was driving
forward at bayonet point an exhausted old man in his eighties.
Morgan put his horse between the soldier and the old man and
forced the soldier down a railroad embankment. The soldier
dropped his rifle and pleaded for his life, but Morgan slid his
horse down the embankment after the Yankee and shot him. Then
the collective killing began. To Walker it became a dream, a
nightmare that he lived over and over: all around him his men
were killing the Yankees who had thrown down their rifles and
were trying to surrender, killing any of the blue-coated soldiers
they could get their hands on; even the civilians who moments
earlier were captives themselves turned on their captors and*

overpowered them and beat them to death with rifle butts and stones and bare fists. In the midst of the scuffling and the dust and the yelling and the screams a Yankee wearing a red silk dress over a green one dropped to his knees in front of him and begged, "Please don't kill me! They're for my wife, she's never had a fine dress!" But before Walker could do anything—he was mesmerized by the horror going on around him, he felt powerless to stop it, he sat on his horse as if transfixed—two of his men grabbed the Yankee from behind and slit his throat.

Morgan appeared out of the dust and the noise, his pistol in hand, grinning joyously.

"There's so many," Morgan shouted as his horse reared with the excitement, "we can hardly shoot them all!"

"Don't worry none, Colonel, we'll manage," a trooper shouted back and hurried on to find someone else to kill.

The Yankees who got away fled down the tracks, some on handcars, the rest on foot. The Rebels caught up with them again at Edgefield Junction, where the Yankees took refuge in one of the stockades built to protect the line. The stockade was con-structed of heavy timbers set upright in the ground, ten or twelve feet high; there were loopholes cut so the men inside could fire out, and a ditch surrounded the fortification. By the time Walker arrived, Morgan had already sent Company A in several hopeless frontal assaults against the stockade; a number of the Rebels had been killed including a couple of officers, and Morgan was getting ready to hurl the men at the stockade again. It was only with the arrival of Morgan's brother-in-law, Basil Duke, that Morgan lis-tened to reason and agreed to call off the attacks. Later, on their way back to Gallatin, they overtook a procession of buggies and wagons; the women of the town had driven out and were taking their menfolk home. When the townsfolk caught sight of Morgan they cheered wildly, calling him "The Savior of the South! Our Savior! . . ."

From the fairgrounds where the men were camped for the night came the sounds of fiddles and laughter, the stomp of dancing feet, the celebration the town hastily organized to honor the soldiers. Morgan looked up at Walker who still stood near the entrance of the tent.

"You're not at the festivities," he said.

"I don't feel much like celebrating. On the other hand, perhaps I should. We passed a number of milestones today in the history of Morgan's raiders. Now we've begun to kill our prisoners. And you've given up the strategy and tactics of partisan cavalry in favor of traditional frontal assaults on fortified positions. With disastrous results, I might add."

"I wanted those Yankee bastards," Morgan said through clenched teeth. He raised one of his swollen fists from the water and shook it in the air. "I wanted to make them pay. You saw Manly's blood there on that bridge."

"Manly and his men were killed because you left them on their own overnight here in Gallatin. And the reason you left them here alone was so they could burn the fairgrounds in the morning, so you and the rest of the men weren't around when they did it so the townspeople wouldn't blame you for it. So they wouldn't think less of you. So they wouldn't think their beloved Morgan would do such a despicable thing as burn down their fairgrounds. That way you could tell the townspeople afterward that it was all a mistake, that Manly acted against your orders or some such thing, and the town—the women—would still love you. That's another milestone we passed, another reason to celebrate: Gallatin is the first time we ever gave up our hit and run tactics and left some of our men behind."

Morgan's head was down; when he raised it, Walker could see he was weeping. "Don't you think I know that? Don't you think I carry all that with me?"

He stared into the water several moments as he fought to compose himself. When he spoke again, he didn't look at Walker.

"I did what I had to do. I did what I thought was right, what each situation warranted for the good of the command. That's what being a leader of men is. It's easy to play the role of conscience, Judson, when you're not the one making the decisions, the only one making the decisions. I hope and pray for your sake that you're never put in that position, and have to live with those decisions afterward. Things may look very different to you then."

Walker turned to leave.

"And Captain, one more thing." Walker looked back as Morgan raised his head. He was no longer crying, and there was no trace that he had been; his face was set, deadly. "Don't ever speak to me in that fashion again. Don't ever question one of my decisions, either at the time I make it or afterward. If you do, I'll court-martial you on the spot. Maybe you could get away with speaking that way to John Morgan of Lexington; maybe I let you speak to me that way when we were only the Green River Boys. But I expect to be promoted soon, and no one speaks to General Morgan that way. No one. . . ."

They overtook a number of freight wagons but none of the teamsters had seen a trooper on foot; they met a number of wagons heading toward Furnass, but no one had seen a lone trooper on the road. Then close to midday an Amish family in a buggy coming from New Inverness told them that a little ways back they had passed a militia patrol questioning a soldier with a bandage on his head. They said the militia had taken the soldier down the slope into the woods near a place called Indian Camp.

"The sons of bitches got 'im," Spider growled after the buggy rolled on.

"We'll see." Walker reset his hat and nodded them forward. In a few miles they saw columns of smoke lifting above the trees from campfires toward the river. The two men dismounted and led their horses into the woods. After taking their carbines from the saddle scabbards, they hid the horses behind some rocks and continued slowly down the hill.

There were a dozen of them, in a clearing beside a small creek, the same patrol that had come to the steamworks the day before. It appeared they used the clearing often; there were crude stone fireplaces, and the men were comfortable enough that they hadn't bothered to assign pickets. Some of the men were cooking bacon and biscuits, others were taking it easy, talking or playing cards. Their rifles were still in their scabbards with the horses, which were tied in a level area on the other side of the creek, back up the hillside closer to the road; some of the men had taken off their pistol belts along with their tunics. Vance was seated with a few of the others on a circle of logs, talking to the lieutenant and a sergeant. The bandage from his fall was still wrapped around his head.

"They got 'im prisoner, or did they just invite 'im for something to eat?" Spider whispered.

Walker shook his head. "I can't tell. But we're not going to take any chances."

The two men had a clear view down into the camp from an outcropping of rocks. After watching a few more minutes, Walker whispered, "Circle back around and get on the other side of the creek. The sound of the water will help cover any noise you make. Untie their horses, then find yourself a spot where you can get a good aim—preferably two or three different spots where you can scoot back and forth. We've got to make them think there's more of us than there are."

Spider nodded and grinned. He was ready to get started but Walker grabbed his arm and continued.

"I'll wait till you start firing. Make sure those horses take off, shoot some of them if you have to. We want those men to scatter down the hill toward the river. But your first target—get this—your first target is that sergeant talking to the lieutenant and Vance. You get him, and I'll take care of the lieutenant. Without any officers, those militiamen should take off like rabbits."

"And we can waltz ol' Fancy Vancy out of there."

"Get going," Walker said. "And be careful."

Spider crawled off through the brush. After giving him a few minutes, Walker scouted around the rocks to find a couple more vantage points of his own, then settled down to wait. On the hillside below him a woodcock scuttled through dry leaves looking for bugs. Two squirrels were chasing each other around the base of a tree; beside him a chipmunk appeared from between the rocks, scampered over the barrel of his carbine, stopped to smell the unfamiliar metal, then realized things weren't right and high-tailed it away. Walker grinned. In the branches overhead, a cardinal whistled a complicated song. Crows called from the river.

Below in the clearing, most of the men were eating. It reminded Walker that he hadn't eaten today; the coffee and bacon smelled awfully good, his stomach felt hollow. He also had to piss. From the other side of the creek the horses grew restless, one whinnied. Careful, Spider, careful. Walker held his breath. A few of the men stopped eating, looking up the hill toward the horses; one of the men put down his plate and stood up, ready to go up and see what was wrong. Shit. Walker pumped the carbine, but the others told the standing man to sit down again, jeered at him. The man picked up a stone and threw it good-naturedly at one of the others and sat down.

None of the men around Vance were eating, they were still sitting there talking. What are they asking him, what is he telling them? Come on, Spider. Walker sighted down the barrel at the lieutenant who sat hunched over, his head cocked, listening carefully to whatever Vance was telling him. A single rifle shot broke the quiet of the woods. For a second nothing happened, nothing changed, the scene below in the clearing was frozen in time, then the sergeant sitting on the other side of Vance toppled backward off the log into the brush. The lieutenant stood up quickly; as Walker squeezed the trigger he watched in the sights of the carbine as the back of the man's head exploded into a red mist. When Vance stood up, Walker thought his second shot got him in the chest but just to make sure he fired again into his body on the ground.

Walker ducked down and ran over to another position and fired two quick rounds into one of the groups of men who had stopped eating and were looking around wildly; one of the men slumped to the ground. As the men regained their wits and began scurrying for cover, Spider's shots rang out and a man running toward the trees spun off his feet. More shots followed from the other side of the creek and Walker could hear the horses whinnying and crashing off through the woods. Spider was shouting at the top of his lungs.

"Duke, take your men and hit their flank! Trigg, head 'em off before they can reach the river! Get 'em boys!"

Walker almost laughed but he was too busy. He ran to a third position and fired several rounds then ducked back to his first position as he reloaded and began firing again. A few of the militiamen had recovered their weapons and were firing blindly but most of the men were running down the hill through the trees; when the ones who were still firing realized they were being left behind they turned and ran after the others. Between himself and Spider Walker thought they were able to drop one or two more before the Yankees disappeared into the woods. Then just as quickly as it had begun, the woods were quiet again, quieter than before without the birds. Smoke from the guns drifted in the air. He caught Spider's attention across the creek and waved him back up the hill.

Walker was out of breath when he reached the horses. He untied both horses and mounted up, reloading his carbine and holding it across the saddle horn. In a few minutes Spider came running up the hill through the brush. His pants legs were soaked from the creek.

"We going after 'em?" Spider said as he swung up into the saddle.

"No, we're getting out of here as fast as we can. No telling who might've heard those shots from the road."

"Captain, those Yankee bastards shot Vance. I saw 'im go down right after the shooting started."

"There's nothing we can do about that now. Listen to me. Get up there on that road and ride as hard as you can back to town. We've got to make sure nobody happened along while it was going on and is heading to Furnass to get help. If you do catch up with anybody, try to take care of them if you can but you'll have to use your judgment. And if anybody heading this way stops you and asks you what's going on, tell them there are bushwhackers ahead. When you reach town go in nice and slow. Avoid the main part of town and get to the steamworks as soon as you can. Somebody still might have beat you there with the news."

"Where are you going?"

"I'm counting on those Yankees heading upstream to New Inverness, but I'll angle down toward the river and make sure none of them are heading that way toward Furnass. As I remember there's an old canal path running along the bank."

"What about Vance?"

"We leave him. Now ride."

Spider stared at him for a moment, then pulled his horse around and headed back up the hill toward the main road.

When he was certain that Spider was gone, Walker headed his horse slowly out of the rocks and into the trees, across the face of the slope, crossing the creek so he could approach the clearing

from that direction. The Yankees' horses had scattered as he had
hoped, none had lingered; one lay dead in the area where they
had been tied. Walker's horse nickered. Easy girl, that's not going
to happen to you, not if I can help it. He eased the roan forward,
on down the slope and back again across the creek, his carbine
cradled across his arm, ready, watching the woods for signs of
movement. The woods had returned to normal, the clearing appeared as if nothing had happened here, except for the bodies. In
a beech tree across the clearing, a blue jay argued with a squirrel.
Finches trilled nearby. The creek burbled soothingly. Along the
bank, a muskrat hurried by on muskrat business.

As if nothing had happened here at all, girl, as if it had never
happened. That's the terrible part, isn't it? No, that's only one
of the terrible parts.

He walked the horse to the bottom of the clearing, standing
at the edge of the brush.

"Hello?" he called. "Anyone here?"

He waited, but there was no response.

What would we have done if somebody answered?

The horse had no reply. Walker patted its neck and turned
the roan back across the clearing. There was no question that the
lieutenant and the sergeant were dead; two of the other men were
also dead, but a third was still breathing. The man was in his
mid- or late thirties, with a carefully trimmed Vandyke beard; he
was lying twisted about himself, one arm folded under him, his
legs askew, like a collapsed doll, lying close to one of the fireplaces, among the tin plates and cups strewn about where his
comrades left them. The side of his face was resting on the
ground, but he watched as Walker dismounted and came toward
him.

"You're one of them, aren't you?" the man said. His breathing
was labored but he sounded unafraid.

"Yes." Walker squatted down in front of him, leaning on the carbine, tilting his head so he could see the face of the man on the ground.

"I thought so. There's a light around you, like no other light I ever seen. It's very beautiful in a way, but I can tell it comes from death. Would you mind backing up a little?" He stopped to cough. There was blood starting to slobber out of the side of his mouth, stringing down to the dirt beneath his cheek. "I can't quite see you there."

Walker stood up, checked the woods around the clearing again just to make sure, then stepped back a couple paces and squatted down again.

"Yeah, that's better," the man on the ground said. "You were too close before." He was quiet for a while, his energy taken up with breathing.

"Is there anything I can get you?" Walker said.

"No, no. There's not much I could use at this point. I just wanted to see somebody, before, you know. . . ." He coughed a bit. "Was you the one that got me?"

"No, I don't think so, it all happened pretty fast."

"It would be all right if you was, I mean I wish you hadn't, but it's okay. It's funny, I never thought I could feel a thing like that."

"Why don't you take it easy now."

"Yeah." His eyes closed slightly, then opened again. "You stay here a little while?"

"Yes. I'll stay here. As long as I can."

"Thanks." The man muttered something else but Walker didn't catch it. In a few minutes his breath rattled, then grew quicker and fainter, then was gone. Walker waited another moment before he went over and closed the man's eyes. He stood up slowly and looked down at the body.

I wish there was something to say to you but there isn't. You must have known I was going to have to finish you off if you didn't die anyway. Take him, Lord. This was a good one.

Walker led his horse back to the circle of logs. After picking up Vance's haversack from where he had been sitting, Walker knelt down and went through the boy's pockets. There was a letter from a Miss Ginny Talbot of Atlanta, Georgia; a few Yankee dollars and a Confederate five-dollar bill; a stiff and encrusted blue print handkerchief; a small pocket knife. With the knife he cut off the buttons and insignias from Vance's Yankee uniform, then put all the items in the haversack, slung it over his saddle horn, and mounted up again. After checking the scene one last time, he rode through the clearing and entered the trees on the other side, heading down the slope toward the river.

The path along the abandoned canal was overgrown with grass and there were no signs that anyone had come this way. But just to make sure he put his spurs to the horse and rode hard along the river for several miles. When he didn't overtake anyone, he slowed the horse again. It was starting to rain. A few drops hit him in the face, then it grew heavier, coming in sheets. He pulled up and dismounted. In the distance there was thunder, but this seemed only the edge of the storm. He looked around. From the trees nearby came the calls of crows; he recognized Crow Island in the middle of the river, narrowing the channel at this point. But he decided it was still wide enough. He gathered a few stones and put them into Vance's haversack, then spun it around several times and sent it flying out over the water. It sank at once. Like that. Gone. Then he squatted down on the bank.

Beyond the island, the walls on the other side of the valley rose into the mist and the rain. He stayed there a long time, not thinking anything, his mind empty, watching the rain pockmark the surface of the river, letting the rain wash over him, listening to the sound of the water on the water and on the leaves of the trees and to the sound of his own breathing.

NINE

In the ladle, the molten iron shimmered with each jolt as if it were something alive. The heat from the surface of the white-hot metal lifted in waves; the two men tending the suspended ladle appeared mirage-like as they guided the heavy vessel, pulling on chains to maneuver it along the overhead track, into position over the mold. As the ladle hung there, the apprentice reached for his shovel on the floor in front of the mold, but Eckhart, the casting foreman, grabbed the boy's arm and motioned him to stay back. Heavy acrid smoke drifted through the foundry, illuminated by flare-ups of the furnaces; there was the measured gasp of the bellows, the hiss of safety valves and the throb of the steam engines that ran the other machinery, the clank and clatter of gears and pistons and pulleys. Colin, his shirtsleeves rolled and his collar removed because of the heat, his clothes and sideburns flecked with soot and ash, stood close by on the pulpit where he could watch the pour.

When the ladle was in position, the foreman went around beside it and took hold of the pouring bar. The suspension for the ladle was counterbalanced—another innovation of Colin's—so that one man by himself could control the flow of the molten iron into the mold. The ladle tilted, the white-hot metal began to flow over the lip and stream down into the gate—but what happened next Colin was helpless to prevent. The apprentice evidently grew impatient and once again reached across in front of the mold to pick up his shovel . . . at the same time that a chain holding the ladle slipped a link which startled one of the holders and he momentarily lost his grip. The ladle jumped, not badly, but enough to splatter the flow of molten iron onto a puddle of water on the floor; the white-hot metal exploded when it hit the water, sending a shower of sparks and molten fragments aimed at the apprentice.

The boy screamed and collapsed on the floor, writhing in pain, the back of his shirt on fire where the molten metal ignited the cloth. For a second the foreman looked helplessly at Colin, then at the screaming boy, knowing that if he stopped pouring the molten iron the casting would be ruined, knowing that if somebody didn't help the boy he could burn to death right before their eyes. Eckhart hesitated, but continued the pour, turning his attention back to the stream of molten metal, tilting the ladle slowly, watching the gate at the top of the mold until it filled and puddled with metal so he knew the casting was complete. The boy, still shrieking, in flames, had staggered to his feet and tried to outrun the pain but two of the other men caught him in midflight and threw him to the floor again, covering his back with leather aprons to smother the fire. He lay now in agony as somebody ran for a stretcher; his back was smoking and the smell of singed flesh carried over the other smells of the foundry.

Eckhart seemed at a loss. He stood holding his hands, looking as if he both blamed Colin for what had happened and needed Colin's reassurance that he had done the right thing.

"The casting's going to be okay, Mr. Lyle."

Colin turned away, left the pulpit and started back across the shop, heartsick. The circle of workmen who had gathered to see what happened parted to let him through.

"Get back to work, men," Colin said softly. "There's nothing you can do. They'll get the boy to the hospital right away. Give him some air."

The men turned away reluctantly, dispersing slowly down the aisles and bays of the foundry, back to their own areas, their own jobs, responsibilities, fading into the smoke and steam and darkness of the shop, fading before him like phantoms, like memories, accusations.

And he wondered: Did Eckhart choose to continue the casting because of his sense of workmanship, or was it because his boss was standing there watching him? Would he have made the same choice if I wasn't there? Does that make me somehow responsible? No, of course not, don't be a fool, you have enough reasons to feel guilty without manufacturing more. But why would Eckhart think that the casting is more important to me than the boy? Is he right? Is that the way I really am? He should talk to Libby, she'd agree with him. Colin the heartless monster.

He realized he had walked away from the scene of the accident before he actually knew that the boy was being taken care of. He looked back. Across the shop, the boy was being carried toward the door on a stretcher, Eckhart and a few of the others trailing behind.

Let them go, if it makes them feel better. You couldn't have done anything if you had stayed, you would have been in the way. That's just an excuse, and it's true too. I don't even know the boy's name.

Colin continued out of the foundry and back through the rolling mill. Here, work was going on as before, no one even knew that there had been an accident, that a boy in the next building was in agony and probably dying.

From his own stupidity or impetuousness or ignorance. But some of us will carry his smoldering body on our shoulders for the rest of our lives. No, the fact is we will and we won't. We'll learn to live with it, we'll carry it along with everything else. Climb aboard, there's always room for one more body. That's one of the sad discoveries of life: each body becomes lighter, the more you carry. I suppose if you were someone like Walker, you'd have so many with you they wouldn't weigh anything at all. Lucky man. How many angels can dance on the head of a pin? How many bodies can one man carry on his soul? Conundrums. Idle speculations. Fanciful ideas. Has nothing to do with the real suffering of the world. The pain we inflict on each other. Even those we love. Especially. Libby.

In the dark, cavernous mill, his thoughts were interrupted by the *hsssss!* of hot metal being cooled in a water trough. MacNab stood in front of the reverbatory furnace, mopping his face with his handkerchief as he took a momentary break. The puddler was a short squat man with a full beard down to his chest and a stovepipe hat that was pitted and lopsided and streaked with ash; he rested his long puddling hook on end like a bishop's crosier. As Colin approached MacNab nodded, a perfunctory greeting, but kept his attention on the open door of the furnace where his helper, MacPhail, was stirring the fire to get it hotter, preparing the next heat. MacPhail was a taller, broader version of the puddler; he wore the same full beard, the same checked gingham shirt and red suspenders, though instead of MacNab's battered stovepipe hat MacPhail wore a balmoral canted sharply to one side of his head. The helper glanced at Colin over his shoulder, but otherwise ignored him, concerned only with what was happening within the furnace.

The iron floor of the hearth had been covered with cinders and fired until the cinders melted and fused into a lining; the pigs to be worked in this heat had been broken and put into the furnace.

MacPhail stopped poking at the fire and the two men peered inside the furnace for a moment, each shielding his eyes from the heat with an outstretched hand; in the light of the fire from the open door, their faces glowed yellowish red, sweat glistened on their foreheads and cheeks, trickling down into their beards. Colin thought they looked enough alike to be brothers, twins. They've worked together so long they've begun to even look alike, like some people do when they're married. MacPhail poked at the fire one more time for good measure, then looked at MacNab to see what he thought; MacNab nodded and went around to the other door of the furnace.

With the long puddling hook, MacNab began to break up the iron, which by this time had become almost pasty, and mix it with the molten cinders. Small balls of iron the size of peas began to appear in the cinders; as MacNab continued to turn the balls and MacPhail continued to stir the fire in the grate, the balls of iron grew larger and began to stick to one another. MacNab was working furiously now to keep the lumps of iron and cinders turning so they would heat evenly. Then he removed the puddling bar from the furnace and doused it quickly in the trough of water, cooling it somewhat, before he returned it to the heat to push the smaller lumps together into several round balls, each twelve or fifteen inches in diameter. His face and beard dripping with sweat, MacNab pulled the hooking bar from the furnace and used it to slam the door shut. He nodded to MacPhail, who stopped stirring the fire and went to get the tongs and handcart.

MacNab doused the puddling bar in the water again, then removed his hat and mopped his face with his handkerchief. He grinned to Colin, his eyes twinkling.

"Aye, laddie, she's coming to her nature now. 'Twill be a good heat. Not my best perhaps, but a good one, sure enough."

Colin nodded and went on, continued through the rolling mill on his way to the steam shop. The puddling furnace was one of the things he had always wanted to show Libby—that, and the way they squeezed out the surplus slag to form blooms, and the three-high roll train that he had designed himself, the only one of its kind for sheet iron in this part of the country; for that matter he thought he would be happy if he could get Libby to even stick her head inside some of the buildings—but she had never been interested enough to take the time. He wanted her to understand why the steamworks was important to him, he wanted her to understand that to him the machinery and the work that went on here was beautiful. But Libby had her own ideas of who Colin was and what he thought important, and that was that, she had never understood him. Any more, he supposed, than he understood her.

When he got home that day, long ago it seemed now, Sally was in the dining room dressed in Libby's green velvet ball gown.

"What are you doing with one of Libby's good dresses?" Colin asked.

"Why, I'm setting the table," Sally said. "What does it look like I'm doing, Mr. Colin?" She twisted her hips a couple of times, setting the hoopskirt rotating back and forth like the hairspring of a watch, and looked at him saucily, almost flirty, though with an edge. Then she laughed and headed back to the kitchen. Colin went upstairs to find Libby.

She was in her bedroom, standing in front of the full-length mirror, trying on a black satin dress that he'd never seen before. The dress had long sleeves with black lace at the wrists, a high stand-up collar, and a tailored bodice drawn in at the waist that traced the line of her breasts; the hoopskirt was formed to accent the line of her buttocks, emphasized all the more by a large black bow in the small of her back. He remembered thinking at the time that the dress was anything but somber; it was almost as if she were mocking somberness. Lying about on the bed and the chairs were a half dozen more new black dresses.

She looked at him in the mirror and cocked her head. "What do you think?"

"What's going on? Sally's downstairs setting the table in your ball gown—"

"I know, it's cute, isn't it? I thought she might as well get some wear out of it, if she wanted to. The LBLs of this town—in this case the Low-Bred Ladies—would die for a dress like that, and here's my maid wearing it around to do chores." Libby laughed and turned in the mirror to admire her profile.

"But what are all these?" Colin said, looking around at all the black dresses.

"I decided it was time for a change."

In the corner, the baby stirred in his crib. Libby went over and cooed to him, jostling the crib a few times, and the baby settled down again. She reached down and brushed her hand over the child's hair, cupping her hand over the little boy's head, looking fondly at her baby, her first-born, though distant, as if considering something, thinking of something else. When she came back, she stood again in the mirror, looking at Colin past her own reflection.

"I'm a mother now. And pregnant already with my second child. I'm no longer somebody's little girl. I'm the wife of one of this town's most prominent citizens, and it's time I dressed like the other ladies." She ran her hands down over her waist, smoothing the material as she watched herself in the glass. "Well, something like the other ladies. No more of those flounces and bright colors."

Colin was uneasy. "I always liked those flounces and bright colors. I always liked the fact that you didn't dress like the other ladies in town. It made you . . . different."

"One can get tired of being different. Black is the fashion now. And I intend to wear nothing but black from now on."

"It seems so somber, so, I don't know . . . funereal."

"Well, funerals are in fashion too. People dying, people going away; people's lives changing, that's a kind of dying too. I suppose all that has something to do with it as well, but we're not going to think about that, are we? It will be our little secret. No one will know the real reasons, just you and me. A kind of marriage vow."

"Are you that unhappy, Libby?"

For a moment she stopped and looked at her hands; she placed the fingertips of one hand against those of the other and pressed them together, watching as they spread and compressed, spread and compressed in perfect symmetry. Then she brought them to her mouth, speaking through the web of fingers.

"I don't know. I think that's what bothers me the most. I don't know if I'm unhappy or not."

He thought she might turn and face him then, he thought she might turn and come to him to be held, the way he thought a woman should if she was troubled, the way he had always heard that women did, but she only lowered her hands from her face and continued to look at him through her reflection, the two of them, man and wife, at opposite ends of the room, standing together there in the glass. . . .

Over the years she continued to have other dresses made for her by the seamstresses in town, dresses other than her standard wardrobe now of black dresses—ball gowns and walking dresses and dresses to wear around the house, brightly colored things in the latest styles that she found in magazines—but all Libby did with them was to turn around and give them to Sally. Why did she do that? What purpose did it serve? Colin had an idea, but he wouldn't think about it now, refused to think about it any longer, there were too many other things to worry about, things that he did understand and had some control over. In the steam shop, the large double doors were standing open; the two road engines had been wheeled outside, and everyone apparently had gone with them. Colin crossed the deserted shop and stepped out into the early evening sunlight.

There were still a few wet spots around the compound from the rain that afternoon. The evening wasn't quite as hot, the air was still damp though not so oppressive, and the cloud cover had lifted; tall cumulus clouds mounted high above the valley, reds and pinks edged with gray, moving steadily eastward across the tops of the hills. The road engines were sitting outside the double doors, surrounded by a crowd of workmen who were looking over the modifications. Half-inch plate covered the sides, and heavy iron roofs extended over the cabs and boilers, leaving a foot-high space between the roof and sides so the drivers could see where they were going. The new platforms in front and the enlarged cabs at the rear were also armor-plated—the road engines looked like iron boxes on wheels. Colin understood the need for protection, but the changes didn't make sense to him; he thought the engines normally would be so far behind the lines delivering supplies that they would never be exposed to gunfire, and that the extra weight would only slow them down. But he supposed there was always the chance of ambushes and bushwhackers. There was no question that the engines were now ready for war.

One of the army wagons had been brought over close to the engines and Reid was directing the unloading of a crate. When he saw Colin, Reid called to him.

"Just in time, Mr. Lyle. I want to show you the future."

"From what you've shown me so far, I'm not sure I like the present."

Reid laughed. The crate was the size of a child's coffin. Four soldiers lifted it out of the wagon and set it down beside the front platform of the nearest engine. Reid pried open the lid with a crowbar, then motioned Colin over beside him. Nestled within the heavy oiled paper was what appeared to be a small many-barreled cannon.

"Behold the latest revolving battery gun of Dr. Richard J. Gatling," Reid said proudly.

"I've heard of Gatling guns. . . ," Colin said.

"Actually, Gatling calls it a machine gun, which is undoubtedly a better name for it. This gun bears the same relation to other firearms as McCormick's reaper does to the sickle, or Howe's sewing machine does to the needle. In terms of war, what you are looking at is the ultimate machine."

Colin knelt down for a closer look. The gun consisted of six parallel rifle barrels arranged to revolve around an axis. Behind the barrels was a short open trough; behind each barrel and the loading trough were six strikers. A hand crank rotated the entire assembly within the gun's frame. Even in its crate the gun looked deadly, but he couldn't help admiring the precision workmanship, the careful machining, the sheen of the burnished metal.

"It's one of the latest models Gatling made for the navy," Reid said over Colin's shoulder. "It fires a new metal-jacketed fifty-eight-caliber cartridge, and the loading trough is modified to eliminate the jamming that plagued the earlier models. Plus the bores on these new models have been rifled. At the navy trials a couple months ago, a gun just like this fired an average of 150 rounds a minute with an accuracy of ninety to ninety-five percent at a range of up to one mile. Can you imagine that?"

Colin stood up slowly, picking at his forehead. At the moment he was unable to imagine anything; his mind was racing, he was unable to think clearly, there were too many thoughts and images all clamoring for his attention at once.

Reid nodded to the soldiers; they lifted the gun out of the crate and carried it over to the front platform of the road engine. The red-haired young man beamed, barely able to contain his excitement; he stood with his hands in his pants pockets, his arms winged out at the sides, rocking back on his heels.

"I couldn't believe our luck in getting these new models. And they're just the right size. They're made to fit on the deck railings of gunboats."

"Just the right size for what?" Colin asked with a growing sense of dread.

But he could see the answer for himself. The corners of the front and rear platforms were rounded and protruded slightly beyond the sides of the vehicle; the iron plating was cut out to waist level around the corners as well as a similar curved area projecting out from the middle of the front platform, with a bracket placed in the center of each curve. As the soldiers hoisted the gun onto the corner of the platform and held it in place, Reid scrambled up the steps to attach the gun to the bracket. When it was secure, he swung it back and forth a couple times to make sure that it had adequate freedom of movement, raised and lowered the elevation with the jackscrew to make sure that it was in working order. Satisfied, he did a little jig on the steps of the platform.

"You never told me you were going to arm the engines," Colin said to him.

"Mr. Lyle, the firepower of two of these Gatling guns is equal to that of an entire regiment. Those two guns cost about three thousand dollars. To get a regiment ready to take the field costs fifty thousand dollars, and another hundred and fifty thousand to keep it in service for a year, providing of course that you can find that many good men to begin with. In my configuration of these engines, each one will carry five Gatlings, three forward and two aft. That's the firepower of two and a half regiments, and you don't need uniforms or have to worry about the condition of their feet. Now, you're a businessman, you tell me which is the most efficient?"

"You never intended the engines to transport supplies at all, did you?" Colin felt embarrassed even as he said it. What did you think? You fool, you fool.

"That was your idea, not mine. I'm afraid your vision was rather limited as to what these engines can do. With these Gatling guns mounted on them, your engines are the most powerful tools for war the world has ever known. Here, let me show you something."

He hurried over to the wagon, opened a box of ammunition, and carried an armful of cartridges back up onto the platform. As Reid dumped the cartridges into the hopper and readied the gun, Walker rode slowly into the compound. Walker hadn't been at the steamworks all day, and Colin had wondered what happened to him, wondered if he was still up at the house. Wondered if he was with Libby. Now that Walker was here, however, Colin didn't know whether he felt easier or not. He watched as the captain dismounted away from the circle of men gathered around the engines. Sergeant Grady hurried over to talk to him and handed him several sheets of paper, but Walker seemed uninterested. He gazed past the sergeant at the goings-on, his face drawn, hollow eyed, then noticed Colin. For a moment the two men looked at each other across the compound, before Walker lowered his eyes and looked away. He knew all along what the engines were for, he knew all along that I didn't know and that I couldn't see what was right in front of my face. No, it wasn't that at all, he knew all along that I wouldn't look at it, that I wouldn't admit to myself what was going on because I wanted it to be different, I wanted it to be something else. God, how I wanted it. He must think I'm worse than a fool, he must think I'm an idiot. Colin's thoughts were interrupted by Reid calling to him from the platform.

"You don't mind a few pockmarks in your wall over there, do you?" Reid said, pointing to the warehouse across the compound.

"No, I guess not, but—"

Before Colin could say anything more, Reid sighted down the barrel of the gun, adjusted the elevation, then turned the crank at the rear of the breech several revolutions, firing off twenty rounds or so in rapid succession, the bullets pounding into the brick wall on the other side of the yard, gunsmoke filling the air. After the fusillade, the reports continued to echo around the compound for a few seconds. The men were dumbstruck. The mules attached to the army wagon were braying and kicking in their traces, terrified; for a moment the only other sound was that of the machinery in the buildings around the yard. Then the crowd broke into cheers, the soldiers shouting the loudest of all.

"What do you think, Mr. Lyle?" Reid said, looking down over the side of the gunport at him, grinning. "What do you think of your road engines now?"

Colin looked at Walker again, but Walker had turned away.

The dusk seemed to be rising about him, something that gathered up from the ground, rather than settled over the valley. Above the hills the evening sky was still luminous, purplish, with great gray clouds trailing single file beyond the ridgeline, while in the valley the darkness was beyond shadow, a grayness that carried with it the feeling of night. He finally found Walker beyond the tents, squatting on the bank beside the river.

"I was wondering where you went to," Reid said. "One minute you were there, and the next minute you were gone."

Walker looked up at him, tilting his head sideways. "You-all done with your little show?"

"Show?"

"Chewing up Lyle's wall with that Gatling."

"I thought the gun made quite an impression."

"It certainly did on the wall," Walker said.

Reid laughed, thinking Walker meant it as a joke, or even a compliment.

Walker looked away into the dusk toward the river. "That kind of stupidity is enough to get us killed."

"I wanted to show Lyle how important this project is. I wanted to make a believer out of him."

"You wanted to show off. Well, you did. Now every one of those workmen in the yard has quite a story to tell the next time he's up in town at a bar. And there's a whole wall full of evidence the next time that militia patrol, or one like it, comes snooping around."

"Evidence of what? That we have the Gatlings? That we're converting Lyle's road engines into fighting machines? As far as anyone knows we're representatives of the U.S. government on official business."

"Until somebody directs enough questions to the right levels of government and finds out that nobody in Washington ever heard of us. And there's going to be more people around here asking questions than before."

Reid looked at him. "Why? What makes you think they'll be asking more questions now?"

Walker didn't say anything, only stared ahead of him at the river. He was growing increasingly dim in the growing darkness; Reid stepped closer to see him more clearly.

"What happened?" Reid said. "Why are there going to be more questions now?" He thought a moment. "What happened with your deserter? Did you find him?"

"Yes, we found him. He's not going to say anything to anybody now."

"Well then, what's the problem? We're almost ready to leave this place, there's only a little work to be done on the engines and we can get out of here. And as soon as we can link up with Morgan—"

"I think you better have a look at these," Walker said, taking several sheets of paper from his inside coat pocket and handing them to him.

In the half-light, the handwritten messages were illegible. "I can't make them out."

Walker looked up, as if noticing for the first time that it was growing dark around him. "I'll tell you what they say. They're telegraph messages that Sparky intercepted off the wire. The first one says that Grant is tightening the siege at Vicksburg and the town isn't expected to be able to hold out for more than a few days. The second one says that Lee is engaged at a place called Gettysburg and that Meade is hurrying reinforcements to make it a major effort to stop Lee's invasion once and for all. And the third one says that Morgan has been sighted getting ready to cross the Cumberland at Burkesville."

"I don't know where Burkesville is. . . . "

"Burkesville is only a little ways across the border into Kentucky. That means Morgan is just now leaving Tennessee. That means he's barely getting started, he hasn't even crossed the Ohio yet. It will be weeks before he can get here—that is, if he ever intended to get here at all."

"But we can't stay here weeks," Reid said looking around, half-afraid that Yankee soldiers might suddenly materialize out of the evening. "You said yourself that there's going to be more people asking questions. . . . "

"I know what I said," Walker growled. "And I know we can't stay here."

In the twilight, the hills across the river loomed in front of him, a wall of darker gray towering over him. And for a brief instant he had the physical sensation that he was sinking, as if something within or without decidedly gave way. Everything he had worked for, everything for which he had planned and struggled, all of his dreams, seemed to be slipping away from him, just as they were within his grasp. He chewed on the corners of his mustache; when those were gone, he chewed on his lip. Upstream, around the bend of the river, the furnaces at the Buchanan Works flared across the dark waters, flickering against the valley wall in front of him. In the dancing reddish-yellowish light he could make out the individual trees across the river, the rock formations of the bluffs, the curve of the bank opposite him; then the light died again, the evening darker than before. He turned to Walker, suddenly elated.

"This will be even better."

Walker looked at him through the gloom but didn't say anything.

"It will be better for us without Morgan. Now we won't have to wait for him or worry about how to link up with him. Our fate is in our own hands."

"Our fate, as you call it, sounds to me as if it's sealed. Without Morgan we're stranded."

"That's just it, we're not," Reid said, gesturing with his hands in his enthusiasm. "We're in a better position now without him. Think about it. Wherever Morgan goes, he attracts attention. This telegram is proof of that. They're keeping track of him before he even crosses the Cumberland, much less the Ohio. If he was able to make it all the way here, he'd have half the Union Army trailing after him. Without him, we can go on ahead with our plans to move these engines out of here without anyone noticing."

"You don't think you're going to attract a crowd moving those engines about? And where do you think you're going to take them? From the sounds of it, we're too late to help Lee at

Gettysburg or wherever it is he's engaged, and we'd never make it to Vicksburg in time."

"I never seriously considered Vicksburg," Reid said. "That was always a last resort. We want these engines used to their best advantage, we want them where they will strike fear into the hearts of the Yankees. And that means Lee. Whatever the outcome of Gettysburg, with the war engines he'll be invincible."

"Morgan's grand idea of a linkup with Lee," Walker said.

Reid paced a few steps away along the bank and came back, thinking carefully what he wanted to say. It had never occurred to him before that Walker might see Morgan as less than a hero, that there might be more to Walker than just one of Morgan's men dutifully following orders.

"Morgan is a charlatan and a fool. The only reason he wanted to link up with Lee is to regain some of the spotlight for himself. He's begun to believe all the wonderful things people have said about him—that he originated a new use of cavalry, that he invented his own brand of hit and run tactics—and he's jealous that Jeb Stuart and Mosby and Forrest are getting more attention in the papers lately than he is. So he came up with the idea of a 'Great Raid' to go deeper into Northern territory than any other commanders have gone. A totally unauthorized plan, I might add. As far as I know, Richmond never approved such a raid, much less for Morgan to join Lee in Pennsylvania. Can you imagine what the War Department would say when they found out that one of their commanders is not only traipsing through the enemy countryside but is changing his theater of operations without telling them?"

"If that's what you think of Morgan, why did you get mixed up with him in the first place?"

"Because without him I could never get these engines made. And I figured that when our government sees what my engines can do, their only concern will be how to get more of them, not how we got these."

"The truth is that nobody in Richmond knows you're here or what you're doing, do they? This isn't a Confederate project, it's a project for you."

"I'm doing it for the Confederacy."

"And the reason you went to Morgan is that nobody else would listen to you. That's it, isn't it? Only Morgan was crazy enough to go along with the idea."

"I knew Morgan wanted to go on a raid here in the North. I thought my engines would give him some real purpose for the raid, I thought we could help each other."

Walker shook his head, looked at the ground in front of where he was squatting, the shallow bank falling away in the grayness toward the river. Reid was surprised: he expected Walker to be angry, but instead he seemed only bemused, abstracted. Maybe I can still trust him, maybe he'll still help me, oh please, please. Walker picked up a few stones from between his legs and flipped them half-heartedly into the dark water.

"You didn't figure on Mattie."

"I don't understand," Reid said.

Walker thought a moment. "His wife. You didn't figure on Morgan sticking around until she had her baby. Or maybe just wanting to be with her a little while longer."

"Is that what you think delayed him?"

"I don't know it for a fact, but I know Morgan. And I know he's late. Too late, now."

"It doesn't matter now," Reid said, squatting down to get closer to him. "We don't need him, we're better off without him. That's my point. Look, you and I have had our differences, I know that. But basically we want the same thing: we want the South to win this war, we want the Yankees to leave us alone. And these engines can be the very thing to turn the tide. The

North doesn't have the heart for a prolonged war, they want it over as soon as possible. The war engines will help even the odds so we can prolong it, and they'll give the South hope again that we can win, that we can outlast the Yankees. I'm convinced it's possible to get these engines to Lee, and that they'll make the difference in his campaign. But I can't get them to Lee without you. I need your help."

Walker's face seemed to be receding into the nightfall right before his eyes, gray within the gray. Reid wondered if he had read him wrong; maybe Walker was a lot weaker than Reid realized, maybe his wound had drained him more than Walker would admit. Maybe there wasn't that much fight left in him. No, please, not now, not when I need your strength, not when I'm so close now to finally doing it, I'm so close. When Walker finally spoke, his voice sounded far away, remote.

"How are you going to get them around Pittsburgh? When the garrisons there see you come chugging down the road, they're going to want to know who you are and what you're doing. Yankee uniforms and playing Union can only go so far."

"I've thought of that," Reid said, getting excited again, encouraged that Walker was asking questions. "The rain today should raise the rivers enough that we can use flatboats. We don't have to go that far, only past the city and down the Monongahela. Of course the closer we can get to Gettysburg or wherever Lee is, the better. But we won't have much time. The rivers will be down again in a couple of days."

"And you don't think the garrisons in Pittsburgh will be watching the rivers?"

Reid smiled. "Saturday is the Fourth of July. We can cover the engines with tarps or bales of wheat or whatever and take them upstream in broad daylight. If Pittsburgh is like most towns on the Fourth of July, the garrison will be too drunk to care about a couple of ordinary-looking flatboats. It's risky, of course. But anything we do at this point is risky. Even just sitting here."

"We won't be able to do that much longer."

"You keep saying that. This is a way for us to get out of here and accomplish what we set out to do. We can do it if we work together, I know we can. We've come this far."

Please, don't give up on me now, don't let me down. You have to do it, you have to. Walker didn't say anything; he sat there on his haunches, gaunt and distant, rolling a couple of small stones in his palm like dice. Reid decided it was best not to push him further.

"Tomorrow I'll go to Pittsburgh to look things over and try to line up the flatboats. You get the wagons loaded and the men ready and anything else that needs to be taken care of. If I can arrange for the boats, we'll pull out the first thing the day after tomorrow. That will give us time to get the boats loaded and ready to take by Pittsburgh on Saturday. Lyle knows what still needs to be done on the Scylla and Charybdis."

"The what?"

Reid stood up again. "That's what Lyle decided to name the engines."

"It's appropriate," Walker said.

"I guess it's the least we can do for him. You should get yourself back up to the house. You look like you could use some rest."

Walker tossed the remaining stones in his hand into the river and stood up slowly, brushing his hands on his pants. "Yeah, you're right. I do."

He said that the way one friend would to another. We've been through a lot together, he's a valuable man. Maybe we can be friends yet. Maybe he doesn't think I'm stupid after all.

"We're going to do this, Walker," Reid said, overcome suddenly with emotion. He grabbed Walker's hand and shook it. "We're going to show the world."

Walker only looked at him in the gloom.

This is where we walked together, was that only yesterday? It seems like a year, a lifetime. This is where we talked, she walked on the rail like a ballerina and then started to lose her balance and reached out and I took her hand to steady her, she held my hand longer than she needed to and looked at me that way, was that only yesterday?

Walker looked around for Reid. Where did he go? What were they talking about? Did they cover everything that had to be discussed? In the twilight he caught a glimpse of Reid walking between the tents, heading back across the compound toward the steamworks. What was happening to him? He was fine until a little bit ago, in the middle of talking to Reid, when all his energy seemed to drain out of him at once; he felt more exhausted now than after he was shot, exhausted beyond tiredness, emptied. What was he talking to Reid about?

I wonder if Vance had family, I never heard, I don't even know where he was from, I never asked. No. You've killed men before, this wasn't any different, he would've got you all killed if you hadn't, it doesn't matter now. I cut off his buttons and the insignias, they weren't even his that's the strange part and they could've come back to haunt you, made him look like a deserter from the wrong army, when the Indians kill a man he's lucky if they only take the scalp, sometimes they cut off the balls for a medicine pouch, no. I'm not going to think about this, that's all done now.

On the hillside above the steamworks, the lights were starting to come on in the town, the gaslights along the main street, the windows of the little houses. Sycamore House was indistinguishable among the dark trees on the slope. The sky above him was black, starless; the tops of the hills above the town were outlined by the red glow as if the next valley were on fire. Swifts darted back and forth across the glow.

He didn't want to talk to anyone else. He didn't want to risk being incoherent or saying something that would indicate how weak he felt. Walker went along the tracks, beyond the line of tents to where the horses were tied. A sentry started to challenge him, then saluted.

"Oh, it's you, Captain. I had her fed and rubbed down when you brought her in. I didn't know you might be leaving again."

"Thank you, Private."

"I'll get someone to saddle her for you—"

"No, remain at your post." He said it sharper than he meant to. "I can get it myself. It's more important for you to keep your eyes open."

"You expecting trouble, Captain?" the trooper said, holding his carbine a little tighter, looking around in the darkness.

"Just keep your eyes open."

When he went to saddle his horse, he regretted not taking the sentry's offer; he could barely lift the saddle, and when he did manage to hoist it onto the roan's back he pulled his side, setting the pain to throbbing again. Serves you right, you dumb son of a bitch, thinking you always have to do everything yourself. When you going to learn, old son? He was adjusting the bit when Grady appeared out of the darkness.

"You leaving again, Capt'n?"

"That all right with you, Sergeant?"

Grady shrugged. "'Tweren't mine to say, one way or t'other. I just thought, if you were leaving, you might have some orders you wanted to tell me. Then again, maybe not."

Walker rested against the side of the horse a moment, his arm hooked at the wrist over the roan's neck. Easy, easy. His eyes were burning, they felt as if they were ready to drop out of his head. What's wrong with me? You've got to get ahold of yourself, he can't see you this way, nobody can, you have to do it now. He finished adjusting the bridle, checked the cinch strap.

"You okay?" Grady said.

Walker straightened up. "It looks as though we'll be leaving day after tomorrow. I'll be here tomorrow morning to help make final preparations. In the meantime, make sure the men you've chosen as gun crews know what they're doing with the Gatlings. Who's going to be the drivers?"

"Spider and Fern. They volunteered the loudest. Actually, I'm not sure which one had the idea first, but then neither one could back out 'cause both 'twere afraid of t'other."

"At least it'll keep those two occupied for a while," Walker said.

Walker was ready to mount up when Grady said, "When Spider got back here this afternoon he told me about Vance."

"I figured he would."

"Sounds like you-all had yourself a purty good fight out there. Sorry I missed it. The bastards. Too bad about the boy."

Walker nodded and pulled himself up into the saddle. Grady reset the Yankee forage cap on his head, spit into the straw at the horse's feet.

"Southern boys should be buried in Southern soil."

"Now that Lee is invading the North," Walker said, "there will be a lot of Southern boys who won't see home again."

Grady sucked on his lips several times, his teeth bared below his pincer-like mustache. "Mebbe so. Still, too bad you couldn't bring him back with you. T'weren't like us to leave the boy to be handled by strangers. And 'specially by no Yankee bastards."

"He left us, Sergeant. Remember that. Vance made the choice to go over the hill. It was a choice that was bound to be deadly for somebody."

"'Twas surely that."

Walker glared down at the sergeant to make sure he got his message. Grady turned away and saluted into the darkness.

The windows of the steamworks were lit with the furnaces inside, flickering and dancing against the smudged glass, and the lanterns of the crews working late. In front of the open shop doors, more lanterns illuminated the two war engines, where the men continued to unload the wagons and fit the Gatlings to the gun mounts. One of the men stood at a mounted Gatling and aimed it back and forth across the compound, making repeating gun noises, *Tat-a-tat-a-tat-a-tat-a*, while a companion hooted encouragement.

"The sounds of Armageddon, Parson," Walker said to the corporal tending a team of mules.

"Begging your pardon, Captain," the Parson said, rubbing the nose of the lead mule, "but to me it's the sound of Rachel crying for her children. Only the children haven't gone yet."

"We'll be leaving soon enough, Parson. Soon enough."

"Like the children of Abraham, looking for the promised land," the Parson said after him.

Which Abraham, Parson? Lincoln? And which promised land? There seem to be several, none of which I've seen. Crazy bastard. He rode on slowly to the passageway and out between the buildings into the evening.

He was feeling better, stronger, now that he was on the move again. Away from the noise and confusion of the steamworks, away from his men. It had been a long day, a lot had happened. When I bent down to cut off your buttons and insignias, what would I have done if you looked up at me, if you weren't dead yet. Probably slit your throat. No choice. But he couldn't dwell on any of that now. There were too many other things to consider. Such as the word about Morgan. He's abandoned us, tossed us away. How can you do that to your own men? I guess I'm a fine one to talk, I kill mine. But Morgan made his choice a long time ago. And now on top of everything else, Reid wanted to be his friend. What was Reid up to? Besides needing Walker and his men to get him to where he wanted to go. It was depressing to think that he might need Reid as well. But his thoughts kept returning to Morgan.

. . . It was New Year's Eve when he finally reached Murfrees-boro, after riding hard for two days through snow and freezing rain and Yankee patrols to get there from Bardstown. The house sat in the snow and ice like a confectionery house, all sugar and marzipan, frost like sugar crystals eclipsing the windows, the light from the windows spilling out over the frozen bushes. In the night, the horizon flickered and there was a not-too-distant rumble, the batteries of Bragg's and Rosecrans' armies exchanging volleys a few miles northwest of town. As he knocked at the front door and heard the stirrings inside, recognized her voice calling from some-where that she would get it, he thought of all the other times, all the other doors she had opened for him. But this time the woman who opened the door was a Mattie he barely knew.

"Judson, it's you. You're supposed to be on the raid, aren't you? Oh no, don't tell me!"

The color drained from her face and for a moment she looked as though she might faint.

"No, there's nothing wrong. Don't worry. He just sent me with a note for you."

She fanned herself with her hand, then made sure her curls were in place. "For a second you gave me quite a fright. I should be angry with you, Judson, for scaring me that way."

Light snow swirled around him where he stood on the front doorstep. Snowflakes were drawn inside around the edges of the door, the crystals sparkling momentarily before they disappeared into vapor. In the hallway behind her were the Christmas wreaths Mattie and her sisters had made for her and Morgan's wedding earlier in the month, the wreaths of pine and holly and mistletoe naming the towns of Morgan's greatest victories—Lebanon, Hartsville, Gallatin—the names starting to turn brown now after the holiday.

"Well, I suppose I should ask you in," she said, looking at his wet clothes. "Would you like something hot to drink?"

"Thank you, but I can't stay. I need to get back. I don't think Morgan knows that Rosecrans is this close to Murfreesboro and that there's a major battle going on."

"At least step inside so we don't cool off the entire house." As Walker tried to scrape the worst of the mud and slush from his boots and stepped into the vestibule, Mattie prattled on. "Yes, the armies have been at it all day. Everyone says that Bragg has won the field and is only waiting to mop up the Yankees tomorrow. Isn't it exciting? It's all going on just a little ways up the Stones River. Another glorious victory for the South! I'm very happy for General Bragg, he's such an old dear. Do you remember the imitation Dr. Yandell did of him at the wedding? Like a big scowly bear pacing back and forth. Oh, that's right, you weren't here then, were you?"

She was dressed in a blue velvet ball gown, cut low across her fine broad shoulders, with a cameo on a velvet ribbon around her neck. He wondered if she had company, but he didn't hear anyone else in the house. In the warmth of the vestibule, steam began to rise from his half-frozen overcoat. Mattie stood well back from him, as if he were more than just dirty and wet. Now that he was inside, he wished she would renew the offer of something warm to drink, and maybe something to eat.

"So, General Morgan chose you to deliver a message to me. He's been sending me letters every day, the dear, but up till now the couriers have always been boys. It must be important if he entrusted it with a captain."

Across the River

He had had plenty of time on the long ride here to think about why Morgan had ordered him away from Bardstown, away from his command in the midst of a major raid, just to deliver a love letter. Perhaps it was Morgan's idea of a bizarre joke. Or a chance to impress upon Walker that Mattie was Morgan's wife now, that Walker was in effect only a lackey where she was concerned. Or maybe it was something else. Basil Duke, Morgan's second-in-command, had been wounded in a rear-guard skirmish as they crossed the Rolling Fork River; Duke was the conscience of Morgan's men, and that night at Bardstown, with Duke gone, discipline had broken down completely. Maybe Morgan didn't want Walker around to witness any further breakdowns. . . .

"Don't keep me waiting, Judson," Mattie said impatiently, stamping her foot. "Let me see John's letter."

He dug the letter from his inside pocket and stood awkwardly beside the hall stand as she tore open the envelope and read it. Her eagerness turned to smiles.

"Oh listen, Judson. 'Our success far exceeded my expectations and if our generals will or have done their part of the work, then our common foe will be driven out of our state, Tennessee . . . the greatest pleasure my expedition has afforded is the knowledge that our great success will gratify and delight you.'"

She clasped the letter to her breast; Walker thought she might swoon.

"Oh my darling hero! Isn't he wonderful? He's my own Robin Hood!"

Walker felt the stinging in his cheeks; he hoped she thought it was only because he had come in from the cold.

"What's the matter, Judson?" she said, her eyes narrowing. "Is there something here that displeases you?"

"No. Maybe I'm a little surprised to hear him refer to Tennessee as our state. Morgan used to pride himself on being a Kentuckian."

"*That was in his old life. Haven't you noticed the changes in him?*"

"*Yes indeed.*"

"*What is that supposed to mean?*" *she said, studying him.* "*John has become a very different man lately, everyone says so, and I'm proud to think that it's our relationship together that has changed him. He's given up his gambling and all his running around. And he's even becoming interested in religion. For the first time in his life, he's started going to church, and some evenings we read the Bible or kneel down together to pray.*"

Walker's laugh erupted like a burp.

"*Judson, I will not tolerate you being disrespectful to General Morgan. I understand that you may be jealous because John and I have reached an intimacy in our love that you and I could never attain. But that does not give you the right to criticize or be disrespectful to my husband. John Morgan is a hero of the Confederacy and deserves to be treated as such, even by disappointed suitors, and most especially by his subordinates.*"

"*The last time I saw your hero of the Confederacy, he had just stolen a dress for you. A magnificent dress to be sure, red silk with black lace sleeves, very pretty. . . .*"

"*I'm sure if John got me a new dress, he paid for it.*"

"*Oh, he went through the motions of paying for it, all right. The thing is, he paid with Confederate money, knowing as well as the store owner that Confederate money is worthless in Kentucky. When the store owner protested, your Robin Hood just laughed.*"

"*I have no doubt that John thought he was paying for the dress in good faith. Besides, store owners in your Kentucky and everywhere else better get used to Confederate money, they'll all be using it soon enough. Especially when John Morgan gets through with them.*"

"In Bardstown, the night I left, no one was pretending to pay with Confederate money anymore. Morgan's men became Morgan's mob. The stores in town were looted, the post office was broken into and mail scattered all over the streets, the town was cleaned out. And Morgan didn't do a thing to stop it. I saw one trooper coming out of a store carrying a dozen pairs of shoes, with eight or ten hats stacked up on his head. It would have been comical, except that he also carried an axe, in case somebody got in his way. Morgan has become just another plunderer of the South, as bad as the Yankees he's supposedly trying to defend against."

"After Gallatin last summer, John warned Union sympathizers that he would retaliate against the private property of anyone who stood against our cause. I think it's about time he forced those people to pay for their actions."

"And I think it's a very sad war when you can no longer tell the difference between their side and ours. You're right, Morgan has changed from the man I rode with at the beginning of the war. He's a different person now."

"If you're attacking the changes in John, then you're attacking me," Mattie said, drawing herself up, outlined by the lamplight in the hall behind her. "Because John and I have joined our spirits. We have become one person."

"No, it's something else. The changes I'm talking about have been coming about for a long time, before he ever met you. And they're the kind of changes that have to do with the fundamental character of the man. You're only an indication of how far the changes in him have gone, not the reason behind them. In a court of law, you'd be known only as an intervening cause."

"I think you should leave now, Judson. You're no longer welcome in this house. John and I don't want you here. . . ."

The roan climbed at a walk up the hill, past the lights and the sounds of the taverns along the main street, and into the darkness beyond. Firecrackers erupted in the front yard of a house; a sparkler cut figure eights in the air, the night closing around the afterimage like a wound. Out of the evening came the sound of children running, chasing one another, a child's voice calling, "Bang-bang, I got you! You're dead!" The road up the hillside was illuminated only occasionally by flashes and flickers from the mills back down the slope along the river. Walker continued on, sighting a course for the clump of trees that marked the Lyles' house.

He thought of Libby. It seemed too much to hope that she might still be awake. He thought of their conversation this morning in the garden. Was it only this morning? A lifetime ago. His lifetime. In many ways their talk had raised more questions than it answered. Are you angry with me about something, Captain? Maybe that's why you're attracted to me, is that it? Do you think I believe in free love? . . . Maybe I can hold more power over you by not exposing you. . . . Why did she say that about him being attracted to her? Was he attracted to her? He didn't think he was. . . .

Maybe the reason I memorized that passage was because it was important for me to please you. . . .

Be careful, be very very careful. You don't know what you're getting into here. You just don't know.

There seemed to be more and more things he didn't know. He did know that he had to be more and more careful, now there was no question that she knew who he was and why he was there. But from their talk this morning he felt close to her—two exiles in a strange land, fellow travelers, sharers of secrets—and after all that had happened today he wished he could talk to someone as a friend, someone who understood something about him.

That didn't seem possible tonight. The large ivy-covered house sat dark and foreboding among the darker sycamores, the windows lifeless; Libby was probably asleep already, if she was here at all. In the stable behind the house, Walker fed and watered the roan, then rubbed her down with a gunny sack and brushed her, not because she needed it but because he was reluctant to leave her just yet. *What're you going to do with me, huh girl? I was anxious to get here to the house, and now that I'm here I don't want to go in. Crazy, isn't it? This whole business is crazy. You did great today. It's you and me, girl. We're going to be leaving here soon, I told you I'd get you out of here okay and I will. It'll be high times in ol' Kentucky before you know it. A bellyful of bluegrass for the lady. . . .* When his weariness finally got too much for him, he patted the horse on the rump one last time and blew out the lantern.

He left the stable and was headed toward the house when he saw Libby across the yard. She was standing beside the pump at the rear of the house, dressed only in a nightgown with her hair down, the same as she was the night he saw her from the window wandering in the garden. *She's doing her moondance again.* He thought to avoid her by heading around the side of the house but she hurried toward him, her gown luminous about her.

"Oh Judson, I was so worried. Did you find that young soldier?"

"What are you doing out here dressed like that at this time of night?"

"I couldn't sleep. And I couldn't stop thinking and worrying. I didn't know what had happened, I hadn't heard anything all day, and I kept thinking that this whole thing was my fault, if I hadn't said all those things to him and encouraged him he might not have run off and you wouldn't have had to go after him. If something bad had happened today because of my foolishness I don't know what I would have done. That's the trouble with me,

I'm up here in this house all day, Mr. Lyle goes away and leaves me alone much too much, and sometimes my thoughts just get the better of me. Mr. Lyle thinks the doctor's company helps make up for the fact that he's not here more, I know Mr. Lyle does it out of the goodness of his heart, that silly man, I mean the doctor not Mr. Lyle—that silly man standing in his patch of light, I'm a woman who needs more than specters and voyeurs. And what do you mean, 'dressed like that,' I don't think I'm dressed so badly, do you?"

She stepped away from him and did a pirouette on the dark grass, her arms outstretched. Then she laughed. "Judson, I'm not embarrassing you, am I? Don't worry. I often come out here in the garden at night when I can't sleep. Or when I just need a breath of fresh air. It's so beautiful out here. And it's so comfortable tonight."

She turned toward the hillside and the trees and opened her arms as if she wanted to embrace the night. Or maybe fly away.

Walker looked around in the darkness. He supposed she probably was safe enough out here. Unless there was someone hiding in the woods. That possibility made him uneasy all over again.

"You still haven't told me what happened today and put my mind at ease," she said, her back to him, looking off into the night. Her long loose hair fell in dark waves about her shoulders.

"You don't have to worry. Vance is safe now."

She turned to him, at first as if surprised. Then she looked up into his face intently and took his hand in both of hers. "I wasn't worried about him. I was worried about you. You're the one I care about."

He enfolded her in his arms and he kissed her, at first gently; then she curled to him, with a strength that surprised him, one leg trying to hook his, her face twisting around the pivot of his mouth as if she were trying to find some way inside him. Then she broke away from him just as abruptly, pulled away and stepped back but still held on to his hand as if she were tethered. She looked at him in the darkness for a moment, tilting her head from one side to the other as if to see him from different angles, her face in a sad smile.

"Come upstairs with me. Now. There's no one here, just you and me, my darling."

Don't you do this. Don't even think it. You'll regret this.

He started to pull his hand away but she held it tighter and he felt her weight against his sore arm and he pulled her to him again and kissed her again, his strength this time meeting and surpassing hers. As they walked toward the house, each with an arm around the other, he thought he saw someone standing at an upstairs window, thought he saw Sally watching them, but as they made their way through the dark house and up the stairs to Libby's room there was no sign of the maid, no sign of anyone.

TEN

Walker tapped on the door, softly at first, then, when there was no response, harder, louder.

"Libby. Elizabeth."

A floorboard creaked behind him. Walker turned quickly, reaching for his gun before remembering that he had left it back in his room. Sally stepped out of the shadows of the hallway, came toward him.

"My Miss Elizabeth isn't there. She's gone already this morning."

He felt a momentary panic, a tangle of loss within him, but he knew he couldn't let himself feel such things now. Not with what lay ahead of him.

"Where is she? Where did she go?"

"The Rider is strong this morning. That's good. He's going to need it."

"I haven't got time for any of that nonsense now, Sally."

"No, you are right," Sally said. She was standing half in, half out of a patch of light coming from an open bedroom door across the hall. The light was musty and obscure here in the hallway, barely able to penetrate the shadows; it dimly illuminated the side of her face, then disintegrated and fell in slivers down the ruffles of her dress. "There's no time for the Rider now. Now that the Rider's time has come."

Oh for shit's sake. He tried the knob, ready to knock the door down if he had to, but it was unlocked. Morning sunlight flooded the room from the open windows, the curtains belled inward then settled into place again. Lying on the floor around the bed were her nightgown, her underthings, where they had tossed them the night before. He could only glance at the unmade bed, the scattering of pillows, the impression of their bodies left in the wrinkles of the sheets, shaped like a vulva, like an eye. Sally floated in the doorway behind him. Outside in the trees a crow was calling.

"Where's your mistress, Sally?"

She sang in a soft, husky voice, clapping her hands lightly as if for a spiritual.

> "One crow is for bad news,
> Two crows are for mirth,
> Three crows are for a wedding,
> Four crows for a birth. . . ."

She laughed lustily, then tilted her head at him. "My Miss Elizabeth had my George hitch up the team and take her down into town. She said she had some things to buy. Maybe she's getting things for her going away."

"Why would she be going away? Where is she going?" I can't care where she is going, this doesn't concern me, I can't.

Sally did a little two-step in place, keeping the beat of her song, her hoopskirt bobbing up and down like a mechanical toy. "Won't she be going away with you now? Isn't that why you've come, to take her away?"

"What are you talking about?"

Sally hummed to herself, her eyes closed, swaying to the rhythm. "This morning, my Miss Elizabeth was the happiest I seen her for a long time. Not since we left Willow. Not since she met Mr. Colin and she made us come to this place." She opened her eyes and looked at him. "My Miss Elizabeth has entered your soul. She's yours now. You're going to take us back to Willow, aren't you, the Rider on the Red Horse. I thought you came bringing death, but it's not for us, is it? I can see it all around you, how you glow. You've come for retribution, and to take your children home.

"Nine crows are for a secret,
Ten crows are for sorrow,
Eleven crows are for love,
Twelve crows—joy tomorrow."

Sally raised back her head and laughed again, clapping her hands with delight. Outside in the trees, the crow sounded as if it were laughing with her. Walker brushed by her and went back to his room for his gun and coat and hat. Then he hurried downstairs, left the house and got his horse from the stable and rode down the hill into the town.

He wanted to find Libby, he wanted to talk to her about what happened last night, though he didn't know what he wanted to say to her. Didn't know what he could say to her. All he knew was that he had to see her. That he wanted to see her more than anything else right now. I told myself not to do it and then went on ahead and did it anyway. So much for character and resolve. Oh love, love, love, she chanted over and over in my ear, like some litany to a private God . . . but oh she felt so wonderful, it's been so long, finding her soft flesh among all those folds of cloth, Oh love, love, she smelled so good, like lilacs everywhere and all those woman smells, I peeled her out of her clothes like the ripest fruit. . . .

He found George sitting in the carriage parked on the main street. When Walker asked where Libby was, the black man pointed with the whip to a crowd of people gathered down the street.

"Miss Elizabeth, she's with those dead folks."

"Who's dead, George?" Walker asked, wondering if he meant Northerners in general.

"Miss Elizabeth, she said she wanted to do some shopping. She said she wanted to get you a gift, Captain Walker, that's you. She said she wanted to get you something special, but then we came to town and she saw those dead folks and now she just stands there. I don't know what I'm s'posed to do, Captain Walker. Sally, she'll skin me alive if I can't bring Miss Elizabeth home. She won't let me drive Miss Elizabeth no more. I didn't mean to do nothing wrong."

"You didn't do anything wrong, George. I'll go get Miss Elizabeth."

"Good. Then I can take her home, like I'm s'posed to. Like Sally said."

Walker tied his horse to a hitching post and approached the crowd, a feeling of dread building within him. Several dozen people stood gathered around three open wagons that were drawn up in front of the newspaper office. Propped up in the back of each wagon were two open pine coffins; in one wagon were the bodies of the lieutenant and the sergeant of the militia, in another were the bodies of the soldier Walker had watched die, and Vance. A hand-lettered sign was placed at the foot of the lieutenant's coffin:

CITIZENS!
THESE BRAVE SOLDIERS OF THE REPUBLIC

WERE KILLED IN COWARDLY AMBUSH
ON THE ROAD FROM FURNASS
TO NEW INVERNESS
ON THE AFTERNOON OF JULY 1!
ANYONE SEEING ANYTHING SUSPICIOUS
PLEASE REPORT IT IMMEDIATELY!
THE REBELS ARE EVERYWHERE!
BEWARE!

A sign at the foot of Vance's coffin said,

DOES ANYONE KNOW THIS MAN?

Two militiamen as escorts stood at attention with fixed bayonets on the board sidewalk, looking appropriately solemn. Libby stood nearby, on the edge of the crowd—Walker almost didn't recognize her. She was wearing a white and gold carriage dress, a white summer shawl around her shoulders, with a matching flowered bonnet and a white parasol; her clothes were festive, almost virginal, compared to those of the townspeople, but she was staring dumbstruck at the coffins, staring at Vance, her hand covering her mouth, her teeth locked on to the knuckle of her gloved finger. When she noticed Walker coming toward her, she turned and hurried down the sidewalk in the opposite direction.

"Libby, don't run away from me," Walker said as he caught up to her. He took her elbow to stop her but she pulled her arm away.

"Is this what you meant when you said Vance was safe now? He certainly wasn't safe from you."

She started to walk away again, then stopped and turned back to him again. "What kind of man are you? You're not a man at all, you're an animal. Some kind of animal that I don't even know."

"Libby, I can't talk to you about this here, there's too many people. Let's go back to the house. . . ."

"Why? So you can kill me too?"

He took a step toward her but she hissed, "Don't you come near me. You stay away from me. You come any closer and I'll tell all those people who you are, I'll tell them who Vance is and who killed him and what you're doing here. I'll make sure you don't hurt me or anybody else ever again."

"How could you think I could ever hurt you after what happened last night?"

She straightened up, looked at him quizzically. "Last night? What happened last night?"

"Between us, you and me."

"Nothing happened between you and me last night," she said and laughed. "What are you talking about?"

"Libby. . . ."

"Why would anything happen between you and me? I'm a married woman, you know that. You must be out of your mind."

She laughed again, and then it was as if the laugh took on a life of its own; she began laughing hysterically, looking at him wide-eyed, her face otherwise immobile. Walker took her by the arm and half carried her across the street to her carriage. When she tried to resist getting in, Walker lifted her up into the seat beside George.

"You take your mistress home now, don't stop for anything. And when you get there you tell Sally to keep an eye on her until I can get there later. Do you understand me?"

"Yes sir, Captain Walker."

Libby suddenly stopped laughing and leaned toward him, grabbing Walker's hand where it rested on top of the wheel. "Come with me. If you care about me, come with me now. Don't leave me alone. Not now. I want to understand. I want to know what happens."

"I can't come now. With the militia showing those bodies around there's bound to be trouble. I have to get down to the steamworks."

"The steamworks," Libby said, letting go of his hand and sitting upright again. "It's always to the steamworks."

"My men are down there. And your husband."

"Yes. My husband. Funny that you'd be concerned about him now, of all people. But go on ahead. Do what you have to."

"I'll come as soon as I can. I want to talk to you. That's why I came looking for you, because I want to talk to you."

She didn't say anything; she only smiled sadly, knowingly, looking at him briefly with her sunken eyes, then nodded for George to drive on.

When he was sure they were safely on their way, Walker mounted his horse and took the nearest side street down the hill, riding slowly so as not to call attention to himself. He was already making checklists in his mind of things that had to be done to get ready to leave tomorrow, things to be aware of in case the militia came looking for them today. At the steamworks, the morning's activities were going on as if nothing were out of the ordinary. As if nothing has changed or ever could. He had a fleeting image of Libby lying naked in his arms, felt a tug at his crotch. No. That's gone now. It doesn't matter now. That's not what matters now. A donkey engine shunted several coal cars toward the powerhouse, the sounds of the machinery from inside the buildings echoed around the compound; overhead, in the warm dry air, smoke from the stacks lifted straight up to the heavens. One of the war engines chugged by with Spider and Fern at the controls.

"Hey Captain!" Spider yelled as they trundled past, leaning out over the rear platform. "We're the mechanized cavalry now!"

Behind him on the platform, Fern waved and tooted the whistle.

"Don't do that, you'll scare the horses!" Spider turned around and swatted him.

Fern swatted him in return and the two men grappled over the controls as the war engine rumbled on, almost running over a pile of wood and a couple workmen.

Lord help us, Walker thought. Somebody better.

The other war engine was parked close to the shops; the two-man gun crews were cleaning the Gatlings and storing ammunition in the metal lockers on the front and rear platforms. As Walker rode by, the Parson, helping to unload a crate of ammunition from the rear of a wagon, called to him, "You're just in time, Captain."

"Where's Sergeant Grady?"

"That's what I mean. He was here a little while ago talking to one of the teamsters from the steamworks, and then the next minute he got this sort of crazed look in his eye and lit out toward the camp muttering something about Vance. He was acting like a devil got ahold of him. . . ."

Walker dug his spurs into the roan's sides and hurried across the yard to the row of tents close to the river. Grady had saddled his horse and was ready to mount up but the sentry was trying to stop him, standing in his way, blocking him with his carbine. Grady grabbed the carbine and the two of them were struggling when Walker rode up and dismounted.

"What's going on here, Sergeant?"

"'Tweren't nothing going on," Grady said, letting go of the sentry's gun and stepping back. The small wiry man was wild-eyed, sweat was running from his forehead as if a fever had broken. "That's the whole trouble. T'weren't nothing going on here a'tall. We done set on our dead asses for a whole week now, and we ain't done one thing to let those Yankee bastards know we're here. This ain't what Morgan's men do, Capt'n, this sneaking around and playing nursemaid ain't what none of us signed on for. It's driving the men crazy, it's driving me crazy. . . ."

"Settle down, Sergeant—"

"I'm through settling down. I've settled down too much as it is. 'Twere time somebody got worked up around here. 'Twere time we did what we're supposed to do, and that's to raise hell with the Yankees. Maybe we can't win no war, here or anywhere else, but we sure as hell can show these Yankee bastards who the hell they're messing with."

The young sentry was as wild-eyed as the sergeant, except his was from anxiety, trying to figure out what he was supposed to do. Walker had no heart for a confrontation like this now, particularly not with Grady—beside the fact that they had been through so much together, Grady was his second-in-command, Walker needed to be able to depend on him—and he tried to reason with him.

"What about our mission? Morgan himself was the one who sent us here. You just going to throw that all away?"

"This whole idea is crazy, Capt'n, crazy. You know that." Grady took off the Yankee forage cap and threw it in the dust at his feet. For a moment he wandered around in a small circle as if dazed; when he looked at Walker again his eyes were pleading. "What am I supposed to do, Capt'n? Tell me, what am I supposed to do? What good am I? What am I doing here? What good am I to the men? We done messed around here long enough that we went and got Vance killed, and for nothing. And now those Yankee bastards are up there parading his body around in the back end of a wagon. Yankee bastards." The pleading was gone; whatever had taken hold of him earlier took hold of him again. "I can't tolerate it no more, I'm taking some of the men and we're going up there and get that boy's body and then we're burning this Yankee bastard town to the ground."

This time when Grady reached for his horse the sentry stood back, uncertain what to do. But Walker's voice stopped him.

"You're not going anywhere, Sergeant."

Grady looked at him, one hand reaching for the pommel of the saddle, ready to pull himself up. "And what are you going to do to stop me? Shoot me?"

Walker drew his pistol and pointed it at him. "If that's what it takes. Yes."

"Captain. . . ," the sentry said.

Grady met Walker's eyes. For a moment the two men stared at each other. Slowly, Grady took his hand down from the saddle.

"'Twere a convincing argument. Thing is about the capt'n, he means what he says," he said to the sentry. Grady picked up the Yankee cap from the dirt, beat it against his leg a couple of times to dust it off, and angled it back on his head. "He'll shoot you too, if you interfere."

"Sentry, take his horse and unsaddle it," Walker said. He lowered the gun to his side, but he didn't put it away just yet. "And if the sergeant comes back for it again without my orders, shoot him."

The sentry looked from Walker to Grady and back again. Grady was calmer now, the wildness gone from his eyes, but it was replaced with a sullenness that in some ways seemed even more dangerous.

"Don't be worried, son, 'tweren't something that's open for discussion," Grady said. He patted the nose of his horse; the horse nuzzled him in return. "You got your orders. Shoot me or anybody else that tries to take a horse without the capt'n's orders. And if you don't, I'll shoot you myself. That's what this whole shebang is about, ain't it, Capt'n? Shooting people."

"I was looking for you all afternoon," Colin said. "When I saw you with your men out there in the yard, I thought I better call you while I had the chance."

"I've been pretty busy today," Walker said.

"I can see that. It looks like you're getting ready to leave."

"Reid didn't say anything to you?"

"No. Only that he wanted me to teach a couple of the men how to drive the road engines. The war engines, as they're called now. I'm not sure that my teaching had much effect. The two men you've chosen as drivers have more enthusiasm than skill. Or good sense, if you don't mind my saying so."

A flicker of a smile passed across Walker's mouth, but that was all. Walker seemed edgier and more withdrawn than usual. He stood near the windows, not venturing deeper into Colin's office, keeping an eye on his men at work in the compound. Seen in profile, his high cheekbones, the planes and angles of his roughed-out features, were accented all the more by the afternoon sunlight. He looked at Colin only occasionally; when he did so, his tunneled eyes studied Colin, like a man looking for an ambush.

"I'm surprised Reid didn't say anything, you definitely should know what's going on. Yes, we're leaving here tomorrow."

"And taking the war engines with you."

Walker nodded. "Reid's up in Pittsburgh today, trying to arrange for a couple of flatboats. It would be better if you didn't talk about this to anyone."

"No, of course not," Colin said. He stood with his back against the plan table; the edge across the base of his spine felt strangely comforting. As he talked he held a drafting pen, turning it slowly, end over end, in his hands. "My workmen will undoubtedly put two and two together and may say something up in town, but there's little we can do about that. I'll try to discourage any talk if I hear it." He watched his fingertips slide down the length of the pen until the upright pen toppled over from its own weight and his fingertips began their journey again. "The reason I asked is that there may be a couple of things you'll need for the engines that you haven't thought of. Such as enough coal to get you to where you're going. I'm assuming you won't be taking them on the flatboats the whole way."

Walker washed his hand down over his face. He turned away from the windows and sat down in a chair near Colin's desk. "No, I hadn't thought of that. Reid undoubtedly would have when he got back, but it would have delayed us. I've been too busy thinking about food for the men and horses."

"You'll need a couple more wagons than you've got, coal wagons. You can burn wood that you find along the way, of course, but you probably won't want to spend the time cutting up trees. I can let you have a couple of my wagons, if you agree to send them back."

"Thank you. We'll pay you for the use of them."

Colin shrugged. "That would be appreciated if you could, but you don't have to. I want to make sure my engines do well, whatever they're assigned to do."

"No, we'll pay you, of course."

Walker seemed to be wrestling with something in his mind. Colin didn't push him; there was a plan taking shape in his own mind, a course of action for himself that was falling into place like the tumblers of a lock, even though he couldn't yet see the final configuration. After a moment, Walker went on.

"Look, there's something you should know about all of this."

"Such as, that you're actually Confederates?"

Walker studied him again. "How long have you known?"

"I think from the night you rode up here. It was too improbable that the U.S. government would reverse itself to such a degree, there was too much opposition to my ideas, even though the engines did well at the performance trials. Opposition: they thought I was mad." Colin laughed a little at himself. "Why it's taken me so long to admit to myself that you're Confederates is a different matter. But if you're worried that I'll tell the authorities who you are, you can put your mind at ease. I would have done so before now if I was so inclined."

"I think I understand why you wouldn't want to admit who we are. Why you wouldn't want to turn us in."

Colin put the pen on the drafting table behind him and sat in the chair at his desk, his hands folded judge-like before him. "I was flattered that anyone—even Confederates—would be interested in my ideas, in my work. And I guess I wanted to prove something. To the town. To Libby."

Walker looked uncomfortable at the mention of her name. It made Colin want to talk about her all the more.

"It's been hard for Libby, all these years, I know that. She's been very disappointed, both because of me, and for me. She knew how much I wanted success. When she couldn't stand to see me hurt or disappointed anymore, she removed herself from it, in her own fashion. And I've made some terrible mistakes with Libby. The truth is I ran away from her, I didn't deal with her head on, and that's what Libby demands more than anything. Love to her is a confrontation. Libby needs a wall to run up against, so she can bounce back into herself and know that it's her. Perhaps if I had stood up to her more and given her more attention, she wouldn't need so much now from other people."

Walker looked away. Colin felt as pleased with himself as if he had struck him. Walker took off his hat, examined it, pinched his fingers around the circle of the brim, then placed it over his knee.

"I think Libby understands that machines are your passion. I'm sure she knew what she was getting into when she married you."

"Why do you say that?"

"She told me, for one thing."

"You seem to have talked about a lot of things with Libby."

"Yes." Walker met Colin's eyes, and this time he didn't look away.

"I suppose my 'passion' for engines is something else I haven't wanted to look at too closely. I know I've become more preoccupied with my work over the years. It's become my refuge. You see, I've known from the beginning that Libby's coming here had very little to do with me. I was only an idea to her, some picture she had in her mind of who she thought I was. That was what she loved, not the actual person. Not me."

Colin got up from his desk and went to the window overlooking the interior of the shop. He believed everything he had said about Libby, he had suspected her reasons for coming here to Furnass from the day she arrived. But how could he blame her for anything that she had done or felt, when in his heart he was afraid that his own motives were just as suspect? Maybe he had never really loved her at all. Maybe the only reason he married her was to have somebody, anybody. Maybe he had accepted her into his life because at the time hers was the only attention he could get. And how could he blame her now if she spent time with this man? That was no worse than his own desire lately, which was simply to be left alone. He had begun to wish on some level of his mind that she would pack her sea trunks and leave, go wherever she wanted to, just let him work in peace. It would be lonely without her, but it would be easier to bear than the loneliness with her.

The window flickered and danced with the glow of the furnaces in the shop below; he spoke to Walker's reflection in the glass.

"I want to ask you something. I hope you give me an honest answer." In the glass, Walker moved uneasily in his chair. Colin smiled a little to himself. *He thinks I'm going to ask him about Libby. About him and Libby.* "What is your opinion of the war engines?"

Walker looked relieved but still puzzled. "I don't know what you mean."

"I want to know what you think of them. I guess I want to know if you think they'll work, if they'll do the job they're supposed to."

"I don't know. Nothing like this has ever been tried before, at least that I know of. Reid thinks they'll revolutionize warfare, but. . . ."

Colin turned around to face him again. "I guess I'm actually asking you several things at once. Among them, whether or not you think my engines themselves will do all right, and of course you can't answer that and I have no right to ask. But I'm also wondering what you think of the moral aspect of these machines."

Walker shook his head. "I'm the last person in the world that you should be asking about the moral aspect of anything."

"I don't believe that. I couldn't be standing here talking to you right now if I believed that. What bothers me is if a machine such as the war engine takes away the individual's chance for honor and singularity in battle. The idea that one can crank a lever or push a button over here and over there a dozen men die as a result seems to take away anything that's noble or definitive about combat. It becomes totally impersonal."

"There's nothing noble or personal about war as it is. Even if you only have two men fighting each other, it's the most impersonal thing in the world. There's only the killing, and that's as impersonal as it gets. It has to be, or you couldn't do it."

"And yet honor does exist in combat. Men risk their lives for other men, men do heroic deeds."

"I'm not sure. Sometimes I think it's just the fear of being embarrassed. A man would much rather face trooping out into a hail of bullets than stand up in front of other people and say I don't want to do that. Sometimes I think it's the strongest motivator there is. Even animals can't stand to be embarrassed."

Colin went back to his desk and sat down. "I still believe the individual can have an effect, that the individual's role is important. Perhaps in the midst of the raging battle, the real battle is going on within each person just to be there. But whatever, I still believe the individual can make a decision that can change what's going on around him."

"If I recall, when you said something similar to that the other evening at dinner, Dr. McArtle accused you of reading too much Emerson."

"You wanted me to know that you're Confederates, so let me return the favor. You don't have to worry about me saying anything to the authorities. But I'm not so sure about the doctor. I don't want any harm to come to him, McArtle is a friend, regardless of his shortcomings. But you should be aware that he's very suspicious of you and what you're doing here. And I'm not sure what he'll do about it."

"Why are you telling me this?"

"Frankly, I don't know. I don't know why I would tell you any of what I have. Perhaps in spite of everything, I feel I can trust you."

"Well, don't. Because I'm still your enemy. And we're a long ways away from the end of all this." Walker put his hat back on and got up and went to the windows again. He stood looking out into the compound several moments as he thought about something. "I appreciate everything you've done for us here. And there's something else you should know about what we're doing. Reid hasn't said anything definite, but he'll probably want you to come with us. Both to help with any problems or breakdowns along the way, and to be available later on to build more of the war engines in the South. I don't mean to make it sound as if there will be a choice involved. He'll force you along with us. At gunpoint, if need be."

"Thank you, Captain. I thought there might be something of the sort. Knowing it for sure will help me make my own choices."

"You know, don't you, that after we leave and people find out what's gone on here, you'll probably be labeled a traitor."

"Yes, I'm aware of that." Colin thought a moment. "A man will do strange things to keep the love of his wife, won't he?"

Walker headed toward the door.

"One more favor, Captain."

Walker stopped in the doorway to listen to him, his head bent, looking at Colin up under the brim of his hat. He thinks I'm going to ask him not to take Libby, he doesn't know that she wouldn't go with him anyway, he doesn't suspect me in the least.

"You said that Reid is arranging for flatboats to carry the war engines. That means you'll have to load them on the Ohio River, probably up at Taylor's Landing. The Allehela still isn't deep enough for a boat that size."

"If you say so," Walker said. "You or Reid would know more about that than I would."

"I don't see any other way, given the weight of the engines and the shallowness of the rivers at this time of year. Which means you'll have to drive the engines to where you're going to load the boats. My request is that when you drive them out of here, you take them up through town. Right down the main street, a kind of parade. Make it seem a grand patriotic display, decorate the engines with bunting and all, part of an early Fourth of July celebration. It well help me head off the accusations of being a traitor after you're gone."

A wry smile flickered along the edge of Walker's mouth.

"It would help you too," Colin added. "The best way to hide something is to flaunt it right under people's noses."

Walker thought a moment. "You're probably right. People will be less suspicious if we make something of a show out of it.

The bunting is a good idea, even if I'm liable to have a rebellion on my hands trying to get my men to do it."

"It would mean a lot to me," Colin said. "And to Libby."

Their eyes met one last time before Walker closed the door behind him. Colin went to the windows and watched the tall, lanky figure walking down the outside steps and across the compound toward the encampment.

I couldn't resist one last poke at him, I almost ruined it, but it's all right, he doesn't suspect a thing, he doesn't suspect me of anything. I've made my choice, I know what I have to do, what I want to do, I feel clearer in my mind than I can ever remember. Libby, Libby. I'll make you see I'm somebody yet.

The house sat in the darkness of the hillside, a black hole the exact size and shape of a house. As Walker dismounted, he looked once more down the slope, past the lights of the town strung along the main street, down through the darkness of the evening to the glow of the furnaces along the river, the few remaining lights that defined the buildings of the steamworks. As if I'm going to be able to see something from all the way up here, as if I could tell from here that everything's still okay, that everything's the way I left it. Wonder if Reid got back yet. Did I tell Grady about that extra salt? Got to stop this, we're as ready as we're going to be, I can't do any more. In the warm evening air, the underside of the smoke and steam pouring from the stacks pulsed with the flare-ups of the furnaces. The tops of the clouds disappeared into the black sky. Isn't that right, girl? He patted the roan's neck and started across the dark lawn toward the house.

Their house is always dark. Every time I've come here at night the house is dark, haven't these people ever heard of keeping a light in the window for welcome? It's dark in the daylight too, all that ivy, a dark leafy thing, like living in a bower. They must like it this way, Libby must. They live in the dark.

As he stepped up onto the front porch, he remembered the first night he came here, when Libby appeared out of the shadows, carrying the lamp in one hand, the front of her dress awash with lamplight, her face lit from below, a pistol in her other hand. You can't be too careful these days, what with all the talk of spies and invasion. Sweet lady, you weren't careful enough. Or in the right ways. The darkness closed about him in the vestibule. He stopped, hoping his eyes would get used to the darkness of the house. Listened. To the heavy tock of the clock in the hallway, the small grindings of the mechanism. To the stillness of the house. The soft thump of his own blood in his temples. I wonder if she still has the gun. She must. You don't suppose she would . . . Hell hath no fury like a . . . Let's go back to the house. Why, so you can shoot me too? Come with me now, if you care about me, I want to know what happens. Happens what? What makes people kill each other, or what will happen to us? I can't think this. At the end of the hallway was a faint glow coming from the kitchen. He eased himself through the darkness, his hand on his gun in its holster. I can't think this.

A single candle burned on the kitchen table. Sally sat at the edge of the circle of candlelight, dressed in one of Libby's black dresses. She was clutching herself, rocking back and forth, chanting softly and staring at the flame as if she were singing to it. When Walker entered the room, she stopped singing and looked at him. Her eyes were moist as if she had been crying.

"You're too late, Rider. My Miss Elizabeth, she's gone."

"Gone where?"

She looked back at the candle and rocked a couple times. "Into the fire. Into the flame."

"Where is she, Sally?"

"I thought maybe you could keep her from it. I thought maybe the Rider had come and would take her away so she could stay away from the flame. But it's too late, Rider. You're too late. She waited for you and you didn't come and my Miss Elizabeth went without you."

"Where, Sally?"

"You didn't come, and now she's where no one can ever touch her."

She's dead. Oh my God. Walker spun around and started for the door.

"Wait, Rider!"

It was a different voice from Sally, low, raspy, almost a man's voice, almost as if someone else had spoken through her. Sally got up and took the candle from the table. Her voice was normal again.

"I'll take you to my Miss Elizabeth. But you won't find her now. Not now, Rider, you waited too long. She's far away from you now. From everybody. My Miss Elizabeth. I'll take you."

Ahead of him in the dark hallway, her figure was haloed by the candlelight, shifting, dancing with the movements of the flame. Her elongated shadow climbed the stairs on the wall behind her. Walker thought his lungs, his heart would burst, he could barely catch his breath, it came in short, shallow gasps. Sally led him down the upstairs hall to Libby's room and opened the door, then stepped back, disappearing behind the candlelight as if absorbed by it.

Inside the bedroom was another candle, this one sitting on the nightstand. Libby lay on the bed in her nightgown, curled into herself on top of the spread, her legs drawn up and her hands tucked under her chin. Her eyes were open, glazed, staring blankly at the flame. He touched her cheek, expecting her to be cold, but she was warm; he felt her pulse in her neck. She was alive.

"Libby?"

She didn't stir, didn't act as if she heard him at all. Sally floated into the room behind him. In the added light he noticed a bottle on the nightstand. He unstoppered it and took a whiff. Laudanum.

"Is this one of her headaches?"

Sally stood at the foot of the bed, gazing sadly at Libby. She hummed a lullaby to herself.

This is why she was out in the garden that night, she acted out of her mind because she was. What else has she done lately because she was out of her mind, because she was living in this bottle? How much has been Libby and how much the opium?

"Is she like this often?" he asked Sally.

"It's only the man in the window."

"What man?" Walker looked around quickly. The rest of the room was lost in the shadows beyond the candlelight. "What man in the window?"

"It's the man in the window that does it to her. My Miss Elizabeth, she'd be okay I think, but then she sees the man and that reminds her of everything and she gets another one of her headaches from the bottle."

"What man are you talking about?" Walker said, angry now.

Sally turned and seemed to be carried along on an unseen current deeper into the room, the darkness washing away in front of her. Walker followed her to the windows.

In the warm night air, the lights of the town, of the mills, glimmered below in the valley. There was no man here, he didn't know what she was talking about. He looked at her, standing beside the drapes. Sally didn't say anything; she nodded, encouraging him. Walker looked again into the night. There was only the darkness of the hills and the sky, the chain of lights along the main street, a few windows aglow . . . and then he saw it, on the edge of town, in the house closest to them down the slope, a tall lighted window, perhaps a French door, and the figure of a man, standing motionless, a dark silhouette facing their direction.

"The doctor, he stands there night after night. And during the daytime too, whenever he gets the chance. Whenever he's not here staring at my Miss Elizabeth. My Miss Elizabeth, she acts like she don't know he's there, but I knows she knows. She can only take it so long and then he gets the better of her and she has to go get another bottle from him for her headaches."

"He's the one that gives her these bottles? The doctor?"

That silly man standing in his patch of light, I'm a woman who needs more than specters and voyeurs. If you care for me, come with me now.

"How long has this been going on?"

"For years and years. Ever since he had that house built down there so he could stand there and look up at my Miss Elizabeth." She turned and looked at Libby on the bed. "My poor Miss Elizabeth. There's nobody in the world to look after her but poor Sally."

Walker started toward the door but Sally grabbed his arm. She held up the candle and searched his face. Then she burst out laughing.

Eugene McArtle was having trouble getting the fingering right. Standing in the music room—there was little to differentiate this room from any other in the house, except for the music stand in the center of the oriental rug and a stack of scores on the hassock, but he liked to name the various rooms in his house, the breakfast room, his study, the sunroom, because he thought the names gave a homey touch, the rooms didn't seem so all alike, that is, barren, lonely—he took up his violin and worked his way again through the legato section of the Schubert. He had to get it right before their next Tuesday Night Entertainments. In his mind's eye he could already see Libby look up from the piano at him if he stumbled over it, an eyebrow cocked, that look of bemusement and disdain that always seemed to go right through him. In his mind's ear he could already hear her say, My, Eugene, I thought you said you had been practicing. . . .

He had been thinking a lot about Libby this evening, more so than usual, though he was always thinking about her it seemed, on some level of his mind, she was always there. A few minutes earlier he had gone back upstairs, up to his bedroom, and stood on the little balcony again, looking at the house in the darkness farther up the slope, looking for some sign of her, some indication of what she might be doing or what was going on. But Sycamore House remained dark, there was only a trace of light in Libby's window. He thought he knew what that meant, and he didn't like it. She had told him once that when she took the laudanum, she would lie on her bed staring into the flame of a candle, watching the colors, the dance of light and shadow, enchanted and lost in the beauty of it. She told him that at such moments she seemed to fly away from herself, that they were the only times when she didn't think, that her mind was at peace. McArtle was pleased to be part of something that meant that much to her, pleased to be the one who could provide it for her; but lately he was afraid that she was taking too much laudanum, and taking it too often. Afraid that she was flying too far away. He wanted to hitch up his buggy and go up there to see for himself that she was all right . . . but it would undoubtedly be a wasted trip. When he stopped by that afternoon to see Libby, Sally met him at the front door and wouldn't let him in. He decided not to force the issue—besides, her husband George loomed in the shadows behind her—he wanted to stay on the good side of Sally as much as he could, he would need her over the years. McArtle planned to be around the household for a long time.

One and two-e-and-e deedaladat da dee. His fingers still wouldn't do what he wanted them to. He stared at the score several minutes, tapping the side of the bow against his leg, a soft flagellation, then took a run at the troublesome passage again.

I thought you had been practicing. I am I am.

He had been in town only a few years when Libby arrived. Prior to that, he and Colin had become fairly close friends in a short amount of time. McArtle came from the eastern part of the state, Lancaster County, and was used to gently rolling farm country, gentle hills. When he heard that Furnass, in the western part of the state, was looking for a doctor, it sounded like the ideal location for a young man a few years out of school—a small town with growing industry, a place to settle down and make his mark. But he wasn't ready for the sharply valleyed landscape, the dirt and noise of a mill town, the people as hard-edged as the iron and steel they made. Nor was the town ready to accept this boyish-faced, slightly puffy young man with the melodious voice who called himself a doctor. They resented his cynical nature and facetious sense of humor, they rebuffed his attempts at friendship and preferred to nurse their own ailments, the way they had always done; after several months of practice, his only patient was a farmer with a colicky horse—it didn't help matters that the horse died after McArtle looked at it.

It had come to the point where he was ready to pack up and return to Lancaster County. Then late one night Colin appeared at his door and insisted that McArtle come with him to his father's house. The old man lived with a housekeeper in what was known as the Ironmaster's House, a small two-story brick house sitting by itself in the hills beyond the main part of town. When they got there, Colin wouldn't come inside, but said he'd wait for him. McArtle found the old man lying in bed with a fever. A couple of hours later when he was climbing back into Colin's buggy ready to be driven home again, the old man, wearing only his nightshirt, came to the door of the house and called after him,

"And I want to see you tomorrow with some more of that goddamned medicine!" The old man slammed the door.

"What was that about medicine?" Colin said as they rolled through the middle of the night, back toward town. "The message his housekeeper sent me said the old man wanted to be bled. That's why I got you."

"That's what he told me too, that he wanted to be bled. But I told him I wouldn't do it."

"You told Malcolm Lyle you weren't going to bleed him, when he specifically told you that's what he wanted? It's a wonder he didn't throw you out."

"He did, but I didn't go."

"You're a braver man than I am."

McArtle shrugged. "It wasn't really bravery. He was so weak there didn't seem to be much he could do about it." McArtle chuckled. "But I'll admit I was afraid he was going to hemorrhage there for a moment, the way he sputtered."

Colin laughed in the darkness. McArtle was beginning to feel friendly to this man; on the way from town, they had barely spoken, but now there was an easiness between them as if they had known each other a long time—or known something separately a long time.

"So what did you do to him? He didn't look very sick standing there at the door. The way the housekeeper put it, I thought he was dying."

"He's still plenty sick, but I think he's on the mend. I told him I wasn't going to bleed him because I'm convinced it only makes people sicker, no matter what the prevailing medical theory is nowadays. I told him I'd seen dozen of cases of pneumonia or diphtheria where the patient was bled, and in each case the patient died. I may have exaggerated the number slightly, but I've still seen enough to convince me."

"Another man's conviction is not usually enough to sway Malcolm Lyle. He must have been sicker than I realized."

"Actually, I told him that it was like a machine. As far as we know the pumping of the blood has something to do with making the human engine run, though we're not yet smart enough to know exactly how it's accomplished. At any rate, when the fluid heats up in a mechanical pump, you don't drain it out of the system, because all you'll end up doing is make the machine weaker. And I figure the human machine is no different. I told him he needed all the blood he had in order to get better."

"And that made him change his mind?"

"Well, it helped that I gave him some of that medicine he liked."

"Which is?"

"Try some for yourself." McArtle opened his doctor's bag on his lap and handed Colin a small vial. Colin sniffed it, and took a sip. Then he took a swallow.

"Apricot brandy," McArtle said. "I'm not sure why it makes people feel better. But it always does. Your father will probably sleep well tonight, and that's usually the best thing for a fever."

"If Malcolm Lyle, a founder of the First Congregational Presbyterian Church in this town, knew that you gave him apricot brandy, he would have you run out of town on a rail."

"Don't you think he knows?"

The two men looked at each other in the dark of the buggy and laughed.

McArtle returned to the Ironmaster's House the following day, and for many days following, until the old man was on his feet again, as cantankerous as ever. It proved to be McArtle's passport to acceptance in the town. Word got around, and people figured if Malcolm Lyle would trust him, the doctor must be all right. It was also the start of the friendship between McArtle and Colin. At the time Colin lived in a small house at the edge of the steamworks, and the doctor had a couple of rooms at the back of his storefront office. The town was of the opinion that Colin, being Malcolm Lyle's son, was a teetotaler, and Colin, in deference to his father's feelings (and perhaps fear of his wrath), had been careful to uphold the image. But after that ride to his father's house in the middle of the night, Colin began to stop by the doctor's several evenings a week for a glass of sherry or two and a couple hours of spirited conversation. Colin's friendship helped make Furnass a little more tolerable to McArtle, but the town still seemed to him the end of the world.

Or rather, hell incarnate. There were days the smoke was so thick that he could barely see his horse in front of his buggy; the air perpetually carried the smells of sulfur and oil and coke; and the nights flickered red and yellow from the glow of the furnaces. The people who lived here, the Scotch and Scotch-Irish who originally settled the town, and the Germans and Welsh and English who came here later to work in the mills and the mines, were decent enough people, he supposed, but their view of the world tended to be as narrow and limited as the valley they lived in. Even the landscape itself was no consolation to him, those days when the smoke was light enough that he could see it; the town to him wasn't in a valley, it was in a crevice, and he couldn't lose the feeling that someday the hills on either side would start to close in and bury him, bury the town and everyone in it, without a trace. There were days when it seemed the best thing that could happen to it.

Into this world of fire and smoke and closed-minded people came Libby. For McArtle, it wasn't exactly a case of love at first sight. It was more as if he had always loved her, had always known she was there, somewhere deep inside him. McArtle understood her twists and turns by instinct, rather than Colin's futile attempts to do so with reason; the traits of her personality that drove Colin batty made perfectly good sense to him. When troubles developed between Colin and Libby, almost from the time she arrived, McArtle could sympathize with his friend, but such troubles seemed inevitable, seeing as how she had married the wrong man. He felt it was just the sort of bad joke the world would play on him, that the love of his life would be married to a silly, uneducated failure of a man whom he befriended mainly out of desperation. That was why Colin's remark the other evening struck McArtle so deeply. Colin had said that he had handed Libby over to him all these years, but McArtle didn't see it that way at all. McArtle had been proud of himself all these years, had congratulated himself on his restraint, because he hadn't taken Libby away from him. Because he thought, if he ever wanted to, he could.

A tonic third. Who on earth would put a tonic third right there? Who, besides Schubert? He must be trying to break somebody's fingers. Clamping the violin under his chin, the instrument sticking out in front of him like a shelf, McArtle took his fingers from the fingerboard and wriggled them in the air, trying to work the kinks out of them. He gave the piece another try as his thoughts ran on about Libby, as he remembered times they had spent together.

She had only been there a short time, it was only a year or so after Libby arrived and she and Colin were married, the three of them went on a picnic in the hills north of town. McArtle remembered they left his buggy by the roadside and hiked up the hill through fields of wildflowers—it must have been at this time of year, no, maybe a little earlier, the year they had an early spring—till they came to a knoll overlooking a bend in the river, Colin said he used to play there as a child. Libby had packed a hamper for the occasion, McArtle playing the gallant and offering to carry it and then wishing he hadn't, damn thing weighed a ton; Colin offered to spell him but of course the doctor couldn't let him, even though Colin always was in better physical condition, strong as an ox and just as stubborn. They spread a blanket on the grass and she knelt on the edge and unpacked the lunch and there was a bottle of champagne—where did she get champagne in a town like Furnass?—they sat on the ground and ate fried chicken and strawberries dipped in sugar and made a toast to friendship and long life though he noticed as the afternoon went on that Colin stopped drinking, it was he and Libby who finished the bottle. The two of them. What did they talk about, the two of them, he couldn't remember now, he only remembered that Colin lay across the blanket from them, stretched out crosswise, on the downward slope, his back to them, looking over his shoulder at them from time to time but mostly looking away at the view, listening as he and Libby had a spirited conversation about something—Furnass, that's what it was, they were talking about the town and the people, they were laughing about things Libby had observed, the funny traits and all the things people did here that were unlike what she was used to in the South— that was probably why Colin kept his back to them, Colin never liked to hear such things and they could feel his disapproval radiating from him like heat but it only made him and Libby all the more catty and cutting. That's right, she was comparing the people in town to different vegetables, potatoes and cabbages and a few string beans, he and Libby becoming quite hilarious as the afternoon went on.

"And what am I, Libby?"

"You, Doctor? Let me think a moment . . . I have it, a sweet potato."

"I told you you were putting on weight lately," Colin said over his shoulder.

"Most of the people in Furnass are plain old potatoes, but you are different, that's why I say a sweet potato. I would call you a yam, but I'm not sure you have them up here in the North."

"A yam I am," McArtle said, and Libby laughed. He always loved it when she laughed. When he could make her laugh. "What about Colin?"

"Ah, that's difficult," she said. Libby was wearing a white ruffled dress and a bonnet with lace along the brim and the sunlight filtered down across her face, softening her complexion even more. He thought that day she was the most beautiful woman in the world, and even if she wasn't, it didn't matter, she was to him. "You see, Colin is my husband. . . ."

"Such are the rumors," McArtle said.

". . . he is my husband," she repeated, reprimanding him with her eyes, "so it is hard to judge." She thought a moment, striking a pretty pose, a finger underneath her chin. Then her sad eyes lit up. "But I would say a carrot. No, a parsnip."

"I would have said a rhubarb," McArtle said, trying to be funny, feeling awkward that they were talking about Colin, about how Libby felt about her husband. Was that when he first suspected? When he first knew? Knew what?

"I'm afraid to think," Colin said, looking over his shoulder, "why you would think me a carrot or a parsnip."

Libby looked at her hands, smoothing the wrinkles from her lap. "I said a carrot, because on the surface you seem leafy and green and friendly, that's all that most people ever see. But under the surface, hidden underground is the real Colin, long and thin and hard like a projectile aimed at the depths. Then I changed my mind and said a parsnip, because you're more bitter than a carrot. You can even be poisonous, in the wild."

McArtle laughed, it was more like a guffaw, thinking that they were still having fun. But no one said very much after that, they just sat watching the hills and the river and the clouds above the valley.

When it was time to start back, Libby almost toppled over when she tried to stand up and McArtle had to help her.

"Oh, I'm so lightheaded," she giggled, steadying herself against him.

"That's what happens when one drinks to excess," Colin said. He looked at them standing there, Libby leaning against McArtle, her head on his chest, the doctor's arm around her shoulders, she was so frail, and Colin picked up the hamper and the blanket and started down the hill ahead of them.

As they followed, McArtle put his arm around Libby's waist and almost had to carry her. She covered her mouth and giggled.

"He's going to be mad at me."

"Why? For drinking a little too much?"

"Oh, he won't say anything. But I know what he thinks." She stopped and pulled away from him and for a moment he thought she was angry at him, but she struck an orator's pose and raised a finger, lowering her voice to sound more like Colin's. "As Mr. Emerson says, moderation in all things." Then she dissolved in giggles and almost fell over again and McArtle had to steady her again. She leaned against him again and he held her tighter than he needed to. "Emerson, Schmemerson, what do I care about some moldy old Transcendentalist? Oh, but don't tell Mr. Lyle I said that, it would break his heart."

As they continued down the slope, he could feel her body, her narrow waist, through her clothes, he wanted her against him more than anything, but the mention of Colin's name made him self-conscious even though her husband was far ahead of them by now, only a distant figure across the fields, and McArtle started to take his hand away. But she clasped his hand and pressed it hard against herself again, only this time lower, he could feel the bone of her pelvis, the movement of her hips.

"Please keep it there."

"I was afraid I was being improper."

"You're not doing anything I don't want you to. I'll tell you if you ever do. Until then I need you close to me."

McArtle's own head was spinning then, but it wasn't because of the champagne. He hoped this time with her would never end, he prayed that the fields of wildflowers would go on forever. Since that day he had had occasion to explore every curve and crevice of her body, he had delivered her children—he looked forward to her office visits as a man would to visits from his lover because that's what they were to him, they were the moments when he could be close to her body; he had feelings about her that a doctor should never have for a patient because she could never be just a patient to him—and yet that day, wending their way down the slope through the fields of columbine and larkspur and buttercup, Libby tipsy and pressed against him, his arm around her waist, is the day he would remember most, the day he would remember always, because it was the day he felt closest to her, because she wanted him with her that day not because he was a doctor but because he was something else to her that day, a friend certainly, but something more too. That was the day he knew there would always be a spot for him in her heart no matter whom else she was with, and the day he knew that he could be content with that. Treasure it.

When they reached the buggy, Colin was already sitting in the rear seat, the hamper and blanket on his lap. McArtle lifted Libby up to her seat but she stood for a moment, her arms outstretched to the day.

"My two brave heroes," she announced, looking in turn at Colin and McArtle. "One, the captain of my mind; the other, the captain of my body."

"The problem is," Colin said, "knowing which one is which."

"Oh, that's no problem for me," she said, sitting down beside the doctor and making herself comfortable. "I'm very clear as to the difference. And keeping them separate means that neither one of you can say that you own the whole of me."

"I didn't mean it in regard to you. I've never doubted that you're very clear in your mind, about everything you do. The problem may be for your two brave heroes."

"Speak for yourself," McArtle said, flicking the reins to set the horse in motion. And at the time he thought he did know the difference, which one of them she wanted for her mind and which one for her body. At the time he was sure of so many things. Perhaps that was why she continued the conversation as she did.

"Are you familiar with what Mr. Emerson says about sexuality, Doctor?"

McArtle sputtered, taken aback.

"I've embarrassed you, Doctor. I thought you would be one person I could talk to about such a thing. After all, you are a medical man. Mr. Lyle won't talk to me about it either, and yet Mr. Lyle's views on the subject affect me as much as they do him. I don't think that's quite fair, do you?"

"I don't believe I'm in a position to comment," McArtle said, even though he was curious to hear more of what was on her mind, to learn more of what it might tell him about her and Colin's personal relations. He glanced behind him but Colin maintained a stony silence, staring at the landscape rolling by, only the slightest indication of his displeasure around his eyes.

Libby talked on, also looking at the landscape, addressing her comments to the day or to the hills or to some imagined listener, as if Colin and McArtle were meant only to overhear what she said.

"Mr. Emerson apparently feels that the sexual experience takes too much energy from a man—I notice that he never talks about women in these matters—as if the sexual experience somehow depletes a man and takes something vital away from him. Of course, I am no expert, nor am I a famous sage, but my own observation is that men aren't depleted at all after the sexual experience, in fact they generally seem a good deal stronger and freer and happier for it. What would you say, Doctor?"

Colin stirred in the seat behind him. "Libby, I don't think we should—"

"I know you don't, my dear. But I would genuinely like to hear what the doctor thinks about the matter."

Colin's growing discomfort spurred him on; it was as if she and McArtle shared a secret that her husband wasn't privy to. "I can't deny that I've noticed men generally seem happier with it than without."

"If the sexual experience depletes a man," she went on, "then I'd say whatever was lost was something worth losing. The only thing I've noticed it takes away from a man is some of his stiff-ness."

She realized the double meaning of what she had just said and giggled.

"Emerson doesn't say that a man should refrain from sexual experiences altogether," Colin said. "He only says that a man should be well advised before he goes around spending himself."

"If you ask me, Mr. Emerson sounds like a man who doesn't like women very much. Or at least doesn't like his wife very much. It sounds to me as if he would prefer some idealized saintly version of a woman rather than a creature of flesh and blood."

"Libby, I really think you should watch what you say," Colin said.

"What? Flesh and blood? Are those indecencies now? That's funny, I thought that's all we knew of each other, flesh and blood."

"There is more to humankind than base instincts and animal nature. Wouldn't you agree, Doctor?"

"There may be. But in this case I'm afraid I have to agree with Libby. The flesh and blood are all we know. . . ."

There was a noise behind him. A figure stood in the doorway, in the shadows of the hall, watching him. Like Death.

"Captain Walker. How long have you been standing there? I didn't hear you come in."

Walker didn't say anything, didn't move. McArtle realized his heart was pounding, his breath came in catches. Standing there like Death itself. Scared the bejesus out of. Get ahold of. He laughed.

"You caught me at an awkward moment," he said, putting the violin back in its case lying open on the settee. "One does not like to get caught red-handed butchering a fine composer like Schubert. Though in this instance, it seems more that Schubert is butchering me. Very strange composer. At times I get the feeling that he's being difficult purely for the sake of being difficult. All that sweetness on the surface, but underneath is the heart of a killer, particularly to anyone who tries to play him. Heh heh. You'll have to come again to Libby's Tuesday Night Entertainments to hear if I'm making any progress."

I'm prattling on, he must think me an idiot. McArtle rubbed his hands together, clasped them, smiled to the figure in the doorway. Walker hadn't moved, hadn't said a thing. Why am I like this? He's the trespasser. Easy now, dangerous.

"Well, what can I do for you? I'm surprised I didn't hear you come in. I was probably sawing away and didn't hear you knock. Heh heh. Good thing you found your own way in from the front door."

"I came in through the back."

The figure moved and McArtle jumped. Walker came into the room, into the light. McArtle started to turn around, realized he didn't know where he was going, and turned back. In the glow of the several lamps in the room Walker's horsey face looked more drawn than ever, gaunt, though not weak. He was watching McArtle closely from eyes barreled deep into his skull. Jesus, he really does look like Death. A skeleton with a mustache. A thrill of danger ran through McArtle, a chill of excitement. Careful. Really could be dangerous. No.

"As a matter of fact, I'm glad you stopped by. I was wondering how your wound is healing up. I'd be glad to take a look at it again for you."

"No, it's fine."

"If you'll take off your coat and shirt—"

"It's fine."

"Suit yourself. Care for some sherry?" McArtle went over to the cupboard and poured himself a glass. "You're probably right. Better to leave things alone and let them heal by themselves. There's so little we know about wounds of any kind. We don't even know the purpose of something as basic as suppuration. Most doctors think it essential to the healing process—'laudable pus,' as the expression goes. I can't prove it, of course, but sometimes I wonder if the discharge isn't actually a sign of infection and should be cleaned away from the wound, maybe it's even harmful. Who's to say? As a medical man, I'm supposed to have all the answers, yet I know little more than anyone else."

"That hasn't stopped you from practicing."

"No, I've continued to work with what I do know. Providing small comforts where I can."

McArtle was drinking too fast—he was already three-quarters of the way through the glass of sherry and was thinking about having another—but he couldn't seem to help himself. He was nervous because of Walker, but it wasn't fear; it was excitement, there was something churning in him, rising toward the surface, that he couldn't fully recognize. Why is he here? No, I know that,

I wonder what his reason is. Across the room, the tall lanky figure wandered a few steps away from the lamplight. Walker stared for a few moments at a glassed-in bookcase, ran his finger around the rim of an empty bowl sitting on top. Then he came forward again as if he had made up his mind about something. Under the brim of his hat, there was only a black space where his eyes should be.

"Providing small comforts. Such as providing opium to Libby."

Ah. Of course. McArtle took another sip of sherry and put the glass down on the end table; he decided against having any more, he wanted to be clear-headed for what was going to happen. "She asked me for it for her headaches."

"Perhaps. Initially."

"And I've continued to give it to her."

"After you've seen what it does to her. What she does with it."

"Pain is a difficult thing to define or assess, especially when you're not the one suffering it. Libby is in more pain of one kind or another than most people are aware of. Her life in many ways is built on pain."

"And you think that justifies giving laudanum to her. You think that absolves you of responsibility for turning her into an opium eater. All you're doing is tying her to you, making her more dependent on that bottle, and on you."

"Excuse me, Captain, but I find this all rather hypocritical, coming from a man whose sole purpose these days is to inflict as much pain and suffering and, ideally, death, on as many young men as he possibly can. As a doctor I am increasingly aware of how unsuccessful I am in my attempts to help people, but at least I am in the profession of healing, or trying to heal. You are a soldier, Captain Walker, assuming your name is in fact Walker and that you're a captain in one army or the other. The truth is it doesn't matter which side you happen to be on in this war. Your profession is death, killing."

"There's a difference," Walker said.

"What?" Have I pushed him too far? Far enough?

Walker was silent for a moment. "All death is the same. But there are different kinds of killing."

It is here. McArtle was elated, almost giddy. All the years of waiting, terrified, all the years of cowering, and now that it had arrived it was a liberation, a joy. Face-to-face with it, he wasn't afraid after all. Now. "And that's why you've come here tonight, isn't it Captain? To kill me?"

For several moments Walker didn't move, there was no glimmer of movement or recognition from the dark place where his eyes should be. Then he turned and left the room.

ELEVEN

The two war engines were parked in front of the shop buildings. Sentries kept watch nearby, their carbines cradled in their arms; otherwise the compound of the steamworks was deserted for the night. Draped in U.S. flags, the two engines looked like twin speakers' platforms, though in the darkness of the yard, the red bunting appeared purplish, the blue appeared black. Reid stood on the front gun platform of one of the engines, lost in thought. When he saw Walker approaching on his horse, he swung down from the platform and hurried to meet him. Reid looked pleased with himself.

"I've got the flatboats! Two of them. Cost an arm and a leg but they can do the job. I left them up the Ohio at—"

"Taylor's Landing," Walker said, climbing down from his horse.

"That's right. How did you know?"

"Lyle said that's what you'd have to do. He said a flatboat large enough to carry one of the engines would never make it up the Allehela at this time of year."

"Oh." Reid seemed momentarily deflated, but recovered quickly. "The old man's pretty smart. What else did he tell you?"

"He wants us to make a parade out of it when we take the engines out of here, like it was a celebration. Drive them up through the main part of town so everybody can get a look at them. I guess he wants the town to see what he's accomplished. That's why all the bunting."

"'What *he's* accomplished,'" Reid said dryly, rolling his eyes. "Actually, the bunting is a good idea. A nice patriotic touch. Sure, I guess we can do that for him, show off *his* war engines for him. Where is he, do you know?"

"I just got back. I've been gone for a while."

"I can't decide whether to tell him that we want him to go with us, or if we should just grab him and take him along when the time comes. I'm leaning toward the idea of just grabbing him. He seems content with the life he has here, I'm not sure he'll want to go with us." Reid looked around the darkness of the compound as if he found the idea hard to believe.

"If you take him against his will, how do you know you can trust him?"

In the darkness, Reid's eyes narrowed with intensity. "I have to make sure he's available when I need him. There are things about these engines that only he knows. We can't take a chance with the nicety of an invitation at this point."

Walker flipped the ends of the reins into his other hand, catching them. Son, you wouldn't know a nicety if it sat up and bit you.

"What about up at the house?" Reid went on. "Maybe he's there."

"I was just up there. Lyle hasn't been home all day."

The steamworks seemed unnaturally quiet because of the late hour. A few oil lamps marked the outline of the buildings, there were lights in the dormitory windows, the remains of the fires on the other side of the compound where his men were camped; otherwise, the collection of buildings was dark, still. But above the rooftops the burning sky silhouetted the black columns of the smokestacks, black pillars supporting the black canopy that covered the world. In the darkness Reid was studying Walker's face.

"What about you?"

"What about me?"

"You still coming with me? Without Morgan?"

"I'm coming with you."

Reid was elated. He walked away a few steps, came back. "I thought I could sense a change in your attitude. You seem more like your old self, before we got to this godforsaken part of the country. You must be getting your strength back."

I'm going to have to be strong now. There's no other way. But Walker didn't say anything.

"What made you change your mind? No, don't tell me. I'm just glad you're going to be with me and that I can count on you."

"You can count on me."

"I didn't want to have to order you to come along." Reid laughed.

"What makes you think you could give me an order like that? Or that I'd follow it even if you did?"

"Actually, I have that authority. I didn't want to say anything—and now I don't have to because you're going to do what I want you to do anyway—but Morgan gave me a letter before we left. It authorizes me to take command if I think our mission is in jeopardy. I'll admit I thought I was going to have to use it a couple times, some of the scrapes you got us into on our way here, but I held off. And now I'm glad I did. This will work so much better, with you and me in command together."

And suppose I order you to go to Pennsylvania, Captain Walker, what can you do about it? Walker looked across the dark expanse of the compound, past the piles of scrap iron and coal and discarded machine parts, to the few cookfires of his men, burning down now after the evening meal. A small stick figure appeared in front of one of the fires, bending over to get something, probably one more cup of coffee before turning in, then melded into the shadows again. "No, you won't have to use your letter."

"The boats should be able to transport the engines fifteen miles or so up the Monongahela. That will put them well past Pittsburgh, then you can link up with us with the wagons and the rest of the men. The news in town is that the skirmish at Gettysburg turned into a real battle but that Lee is in control of the field and will finish off Meade, if he hasn't already then tomorrow. That means that Lee might be headed our direction afterwards. Or if he heads north or east, he'll probably be able to send us an escort as soon as we contact him and tell him what we're bringing him. Wouldn't that be the final irony if he sent Jeb Stuart? Morgan would die when he heard about it."

Morgan said Everybody makes such a fuss about Jeb Stuart's raid around McClellan's army—that only lasted five days. I'm talking about a raid that could last five weeks, maybe several months, across the Ohio. . . . Walker's playing with the ends of the reins was making the roan nervous. He patted the horse's neck, rubbed its nose. "You're right, girl, I'll stop."

"It's all falling into place, Walker. We're almost there."

"Don't kid yourself. We've got a long way to go. A long way."

"You don't understand. These engines aren't just the future of war, they're the future of the modern world. In years to come engines like these will be used for hundreds of different things, in all phases of everyday life. It doesn't matter if we make it to Lee or not. It doesn't even matter if the South wins the war or not. When we drive these engines out of here, the world changes forever. And we're the ones who are making it happen. We are the future. You mark my words, tomorrow will be a day people remember. I've devoted my life to this, Walker. What we're fighting for is of a higher order."

No, you don't understand. I'm fighting because evidently it's all I know how to do now. If something gets in my way, all I know is to kill it. For the briefest moment he again saw McArtle standing in his music room. Felt again ready to draw his pistol and shoot him. Why? Because of Libby. And why didn't he? Only because it would have caused more trouble. No other reason. No right or wrong. No should or shouldn't. And that's why you've come here tonight, isn't it Captain? To kill me? The only reason he didn't kill him was because it would have raised more opportunity for someone to ask questions, for someone to figure out why he and his men were here. It was more expedient to let the man live. That's how far I've come, that's where I've crossed over to. And what difference did it make to him anyway, how these people, Libby and Lyle and McArtle, lived their lives? They had their own little world here, it had nothing to do with him. He couldn't change anything. He and Libby—that was over now, it had been only a fleeting moment. Best to just leave them to their own devices.

The roan was getting restless, pulled on the reins. He had to go see his men. He turned away and started toward the camp.

"Walker?"

Reid was watching him apprehensively.

"You okay?"

"I'm going to be."

"You seemed to fade out on me there for a minute." Reid laughed.

"I'm going to check on my men. Make sure everything's ready for tomorrow."

"Yes. Good idea." For a moment Reid didn't know what to do with his hands. "Well, see you in the morning."

Walker nodded and led the horse on across the dark compound.

He would see them riding together in the afternoons, the two of them, Morgan and Mattie, as soon as the roads were passable again after the winter thaw, riding together in the springtime air out into the countryside, Mattie in her fine black riding habit with a hat and veil, and Morgan in a new roundabout jacket with brass buttons, his sky-blue pants tucked into tall cavalry boots and his black felt hat clipped up at the side, the correspondents from Richmond and Charleston would come to see the elegant couple ride by. They were handsome together, almost too beautiful to be believed, and Morgan's men stared at the couple as if they were witnessing a vision, as indeed they were, proud at least that the couple was their vision, belonged to them in some way, their general and his new bride, though there were other feelings too, they were aware that their general, who when he was just plain Morgan used to camp with them and share their hardships, had spent the coldest winter in memory locked up snug each night in the arms of his bride in a comfortable house while they huddled in makeshift shelters in the hills with barely enough to eat, the men waking up each morning to the cracking of the ice on their frozen blankets and rising from their frost-covered mounds like some unholy resurrection, the smell of dead horses in the air, the cries of the starving animals attending them through the days and there was nothing they could do for them. What was he thinking of? Walker wondered. Morgan, Morgan. Love blinded the man until he no longer thought of anything except hurrying home each day to Mattie. He became so blind that he didn't see or didn't want to see as the men became sloppier and looser in their discipline each passing day, he couldn't see that what they needed from him wasn't for Morgan to turn his back on their transgressions or his passing attempts to invoke the old camaraderie, what they needed from their general was leadership and rules and to know that he cared enough to be strong enough to tell them what and what not to do. The men waited for Morgan to come and save them from themselves but he only rode by in his elegant new clothes with his new wife by his side. Morgan became a general that springtime but less of a leader. . . .

There were the smells of honeysuckle and clover in the air and bees hummed in the morning glory vines twisted up the pillars of the plantation house; a dozen sentries lounged on the front steps, twice the number that used to be at their headquarters: a month earlier Yankee cavalry broke through their lines and stormed eight abreast down the main street of McMinnville, which up to then had always been considered impregnable and Morgan's private sanctuary; the Yankees would have caught him that day except Morgan was already mounted on his horse when they attacked and he was able to make a run for it, though now from the attitude of his headquarters guard one would have never known that debacle ever happened: their weapons were stacked on the lawn and the men appeared like a club of well-fed privileged fellows who knew they had it soft and were proud of it, which in many ways was exactly what they had become; on the front porch Sterritt and Trigg and Ballard, Morgan's "chartered libertines," were sitting in the shadows hunched over a wicker table playing cards, a woman who looked like she belonged to the plantation, or vice versa, sitting on the arm of Sterritt's chair twining an idle finger through his hair.

"Well, well, look who's come a-calling," Trigg said, looking up from his hand.

Ballard nodded. "Hullo, Walker." The woman looked at the newcomer and began to make evaluations.

"Want a drink, Walker?" Ballard said. He hoisted a tumbler and took a drink himself to show that they had whiskey.

Walker shook his head. "Too early for this child."

"*Walker don't approve, do you, Walker?*" Sterritt said, still looking at his cards, not looking at him yet.

"*I think you know, Jeff, that I like a drink as well as the next man. You and me have hoisted a number of horns together in our time.*"

"*I don't mean just about that.*" Sterritt studied the cards on the table before he added one to them. He reached up and removed the woman's hand from his hair before he looked at him. "*I mean about the whole setup. Us playing cards and being here at all.*"

"*I think you know I like cards once in a while too. I'll admit I am surprised to see you playing here, though. I thought Morgan put an end to it a while back.*"

"*You mean when the provost guard caught us at that faro game in McMinnville? The general asked me afterwards what I was doing there when I got arrested.*" Sterritt laughed and looked around at his companions, obviously rehashing a story he'd told a dozen times. "*'What was I doing?' says I. 'General, as best as I can recollect, I was getting ready to bet against the ace.'*"

Trigg and Ballard grinned and nodded agreement; the woman laughed like she thought it was the funniest story she had ever heard. Sterritt looked up at her, annoyed.

"*I don't disapprove of any of it,*" Walker said, "*as long as the men get what they need.*"

"*The regiment already has one conscience, we don't need another one,*" Sterritt said. "*You ain't nothing but an old friend.*"

"*Once upon a time that would have been enough.*"

"*Once upon a time is only good in fairy tales.*" Sterritt looked at his cards and then threw down the entire hand in disgust.

Walker went on inside the house Morgan had appropriated for his headquarters, that he had picked out because it was the kind of house Mattie liked to stay in when she came to visit. In the parlor there was a fire in the fireplace even though the spring day was warm. Morgan was sitting stretched out upon a sofa in front *of the fire, one booted leg thrown up on the cushions, the other resting on the floor, as he stared into the flames. Walker could tell already that the man was in one of his moods. Morgan barely glanced at him as he came in, nodding for Walker to sit in the chair across from him. From the coffee table Morgan took a newspaper and threw it to him.*

"Take a look at that."

It was the Nashville Daily Union, *a Yankee paper. There was a passage circled in the middle of an editorial:*

> *. . . Morgan seems to have been losing his character for enterprise and daring; many of his rivals, ladies particularly, are unkind enough to attribute his present inefficiency to the fact that he is married. The fair Delilah, they assume, has shorn him of his locks. Maybe so.*

"They have no right to talk about Mattie that way. Yankee bastards," Morgan said.

"If I'm not mistaken, they're talking more about you than Mattie."

Morgan ignored him as if he didn't hear him. But Walker knew he had. "Mattie tells me that people say we're a lovesick couple. She boasts about it, of course, as if it were something to be proud of. Dear child. It may be fine for a young woman to be referred to in such terms, but it is certainly unbefitting a military man of my stature. Have you heard anybody say such things?"

"Yes."

Morgan glared at him then. "What sort of things?"

Walker shrugged, but Morgan wouldn't let it go.

"I want to know what they say about me. I order you to tell me."

"*You're right: they say that you and Mattie are a lovesick couple. They say that love has you tied up in knots, that it has ruined you as a partisan. They say that you get your raids over with as quickly as possible, no matter how many of your men you get killed, so you can run back home again at night to see your wifey—*"

"*Who says that?*" Morgan shouted as he jumped to his feet, eyes glaring. "*I want to know!*"

"*I won't tell you.*"

"*You have to tell me! Did some of my men say that? I order you to tell me!*"

"*So you can court-martial them? Not on your life.*"

"*I'll court-martial you if you don't tell me.*"

"*Then you'll have to court-martial me.*"

Morgan stared at him for a moment before collapsing back on the sofa again, rubbing the heels of his hands into his eyes as if to clear away a film, then swept his hands back over his hair.

"*How dare you speak to me like that.*" He said it low enough to be a growl, but his tone sounded hurt.

"*Why do you ask me such things if you don't want to hear what I'm going to say? You know I won't lie to you. That's why you ask me in the first place.*"

"*Yes, and I keep hoping that just once you'll surprise me.*"

Morgan looked at him several moments, his elbows resting on his thighs, as if trying to decide what to do with him. Then his mood changed again just as quickly. Morgan sat back on the sofa, one leg drawn up as if riding sidesaddle.

"*Well, none of that matters now. What I'm going to tell you will change all that. Soon the headlines will be saying 'Morgan's Back' and 'Morgan's Done It Again' and 'Our Marion Has Returned.' What I'm going to tell you I haven't told another living soul, except Mattie of course. And she's thrilled with the idea.*"

Morgan got up and started pacing back and forth. "I've been talking to a young engineer named Reid who has some interesting ideas. I'll admit half the time I don't understand what the hell he's talking about, but the part I do understand fits into an idea I've been working on. Which is: A Great Raid into the North. Everybody makes such a fuss about Jeb Stuart's raid around McClellan's army—that only lasted five days. I'm talking about a raid that could last five weeks, maybe several months, across the Ohio. I'm talking about a raid into Indiana and Ohio, and then if everything goes well, on into Pennsylvania to link up with General Lee himself."

"You're not serious."

"I'm very serious."

"Crossing the Ohio isn't like crossing Stones River or the Cumberland. You're talking about ferrying twenty-five hundred men and half again as many horses into enemy territory. To say nothing of what could be waiting for us on the other side. And what will be coming after us as soon as they know what we're doing."

"I've always been a gambler," Morgan said, his eyes glistening with excitement.

"Maybe. But you've never been a fool."

"I'm going to try to forget you said that." Morgan stopped pacing, his fists clenched at his sides for a moment, until he regained control of himself. "Reid's idea has to do with mounting some kind of special guns on steam engines that don't need rails—something of the sort. It'll require getting Reid to Cincinnati to pick up the guns, then taking him and the guns on to Western Pennsylvania where the steam engines are."

"What kind of guns? What kind of steam engines? You don't seem to know very much about any of this."

"I don't have to know. That's why I'm the general and you're the captain. That's why I'm putting you in charge of the mission,

so you can take care of it. And at the same time, you can scout out that part of the country for the main body of my Great Raid."

"I won't do it. I won't ask that of the men. You can't expect men to go that deep into enemy territory because some unknown engineer has an 'interesting' idea—it's suicide. No, it's murder."

"And suppose I order you to go to Pennsylvania, Captain Walker, what can you do about it?"

In the camp most of the fires had burned down to coals and the men were beginning to turn in for the night. The tents were luminous in the darkness with the candles and lamps inside. The flaps were open because of the warm evening; a few men sat writing letters or making notes in their journals, others cleaned their carbines or pistols, mended clothes. They know this may be the last time they have to do such things for a while, a long while. They know without anyone having to tell them. Someone was tootling a fife: "When I Saw Sweet Nellie Home." Behind a wagon Spider and Fern and several others crouched around a lamp, playing craps. When they saw Walker, they froze, guilt written on their upturned faces.

"Wrap it up soon, men. It's a big day tomorrow."

"Right, Captain."

"Yes sir."

As he continued on he heard one of them hiss, "You son of a bitch, you said the captain's never here at night."

"The captain never is here at night."

"Well, who the hell do you think that was, you flop-eared bastard? He coulda had our asses. . . ."

Now that he was here he wondered why he thought it was so urgent to check on the men; everything seemed to be in order, there was nothing he saw that needed his attention. He also realized he hadn't eaten since breakfast. At the remains of one of the fires he found a piece of leftover bacon congealed in its own grease in a skillet; he ate it on a hunk of bread as he led the roan to where the other horses were tied. A sentry offered to take care of his horse and for once Walker decided to let someone else do it. With his bedroll slung over his shoulder, he gave the roan a good-night pat and headed toward the river.

Behind the tents was an old tree stump close to the edge of the bank. Walker spread his blanket on the ground and sat for a while, his back against the stump, looking off into the darkness of the river, the dark bluffs on the other side, trying to think if he had forgotten anything for their leaving here tomorrow. Trying to forget what he would be leaving behind. Morgan, Morgan, damn your eyes. He thought of Libby. The hell of it was that on one level of his mind he could understand how Morgan could sacrifice anything to stay with the woman he loved. At one time in his life, Walker could see himself doing the same thing to be with Mattie, if things had worked out differently between them. Right now he could see himself doing the same thing, sacrificing the mission and his men and anything else that threatened to hold him back, to be with Libby. That is, if he let himself. Libby was an exceptional woman, he didn't expect to meet another like her in his lifetime. But he had seen the toll of Morgan's felicity, he wasn't going to let that happen to him, to those who were dependent on him. You were supposed to come get us and you discarded us, we loved you and you tossed us away, we trusted you and shared your dream and now you've crossed over to another dream and left us on the other side. Overhead the sky flared orange and yellow from the steelworks farther up the river. In the flickering half-light, Grady came from the direction of the river toward him.

"Surprised to see you here, Capt'n. I supposed you'd be up at the house tonight. The last night and all."

"No. I thought my place was here."

"'Twere true enough." Grady squatted down a few feet away from Walker, turned away from him toward the river.

"I was looking for you. Everything seems to be in good shape."

"A few odds and ends to take care of in the morning, 'twere all. I just took a little walk along the river. Trying to sort out a few things in my head." He was quiet for a moment, thinking about something. "You still planning to go ahead with this little show?"

"You mean with Reid and the war engines?"

Grady nodded, still looking toward the river.

"I take it you don't like the idea."

"'Tweren't fond of it. Never was."

"I don't like it either, if that's any consolation to you."

"Then a man might raise the question as to why we're a-doing it."

"Because it's the only way I can see out of this, now that Morgan's not coming. If we abandon Reid, he's liable to tell the Yankees about us to save his own skin before we can get very far. And he's liable to turn the war engines over to them as well. We don't know if those engines will work the way they're supposed to or not, but if they do, the South can't afford to have them used against us. Reid thinks they'll win the war for the Confederacy if we have them. If there's a chance of that, I don't see how we can just ride away and leave them."

Grady spit. "He's a mean-spirited little bastard."

Walker laughed a little. "Very true, Sergeant. But so far, he's a mean-spirited little bastard on our side."

The flickering sky had diminished into blackness again, with only a dull orangish glow outlining the rooftops of the buildings closest to them. Grady was quiet for a few moments, looking away into the darkness where the river should be.

"I think I figured out about Vance. Why you've been so touchy about the subject."

Walker waited for him to go on.

"I figure you're the one who must've shot him."

"Yes."

Grady's head lowered to his chest and he stared at the ground in front of him.

"We been together a long time, Capt'n. We been through a lot together. But I never thought I'd hear something like that. Shooting your own man. A boy."

"It had to be done, Sergeant. There was no choice. I couldn't trust him not to say something that would get a lot more of the men killed."

"I don't know what to think about that. I'm a simple man. I don't pretend to understand a whole lot. And I don't understand how somebody can kill another body they care about."

"It happens all the time, Sergeant. In many different ways."

"Like I say, I don't know anything about that." Grady turned slightly and looked across his shoulder toward Walker. In the darkness, Walker still couldn't see his face, couldn't see if the man had settled down from this morning when he was ready to charge up the hill to get Vance's body back and burn the town to the ground. "You say you shot Vance because you couldn't trust him. How is a body supposed to trust you after a thing like that? Shooting your own man like that. You even drew your pistol already on me today. That there poses a real question for a simple man like me."

What was he getting at? How much of a threat was in his voice? The way that Grady was hunkered down, Walker couldn't see his gun hand, couldn't see if the sergeant had drawn his pistol or not. Walker sat with his legs stretched out in front of him, his hands folded in his lap. He couldn't reach for his own pistol without being obvious.

"What's your question, Sergeant?"

"If I can't trust you, and I follow your logic to its rightful conclusion, don't that mean I should be a-thinking about shooting you? Maybe you can tell me what the difference is, before I go and do something crazy."

"The difference," came a voice behind Walker, "is that I'm standing here with a carbine."

The Parson stepped forward out of the darkness, his rifle at his hip aimed in Grady's direction.

"I admire your guts, Parson. Always have." Grady rose slowly to his feet. His gun was in his holster, his hand was nowhere near it. "But 'tweren't like that at all."

"The Good Lord must have directed me to this place for some reason. For we have made a covenant with Death, and with Hell we have an agreement."

"I ain't in agreement with nobody," Grady said, scuffling away toward the tents. "And I still ain't got me an answer."

TWELVE

In her dream, the wind, the warm gentle wind that she always remembered from the South, that she always thought of when she thought of home, came to her over the fields, bringing with it the smell of lilacs, the sweet smell overwhelming her momentarily, and then the smells of violets and roses and orange blossoms, and magnolias, of course always magnolias, as overhead the branches of the willow trees along the lane leading to the house stirred in the wind, flecking the sunlight across her face. At the end of the lane she could see the tall white pillars of the house and there were horses running in the fields and everywhere it was sunny, so sunny and bright and warm, and she was standing in the middle of the lane dressed in a long white gown with her shoulders bare, waiting for her father to come to her to explain what happened to the young corporal known as Vance. Her father came toward her along the lane, in the dazzling shifting sunlight among the willows, and then it wasn't her father at all, it was Captain Walker, and he came over to the bed, closer to the candlelight, and looked down at her—would he take her now she wondered, would he rip the clothes from her body and would she roll again naked in his arms, or would he scoop her up in his arms and take her away from here once and for all, take her far away where she would never be lonely and frightened again; but he only looked at her—his face showing his concern as he picked up the bottle of medicine from the nightstand and held it to the candlelight, took out the stopper and smelled it. Then his face no longer belonged to him, it became a separate entity, hovering over her like the moon, like the sun, as he said something to Sally though she couldn't quite make out the words, she could only hear the worry tones, the anger. Somewhere deep inside her she giggled; she hoped that neither he nor Sally heard her. His face ascended slowly into the dark heavens and joined his body again and Walker and Sally moved away from her, across the room to the window, and Libby floated after them, floated out of her body and trailed behind them, caught up in their wake through the air, looking with them down the dark hillside to the lights of the doctor's house, to the lone figure of the man standing in the second-floor window looking back at them, and she said to herself, that silly man, I have toyed with my heart too long, too long, I played with it so long there is nothing left now that love has finally come, it is easier now to live without it.

Walker turned abruptly from the window and headed back across the room, passing through Libby as she hovered in the air behind him, and she disintegrated into a thousand particles, falling in droplets like rain back on the bed where she lay staring into the flame of the candle again, as bright as the sun, and she stood in the lane again among the willows and Walker came toward her, his arms outstretched to her, and she ran to meet him only now it was her father instead and she was a little girl and he lifted her up into his arms. He carried her on his arm along the lane toward the house and she watched the willows wheel away from her and cooed in her father's ear, You are the flame that lights my days, you are the sun around which I revolve, but he said Shush now, child, as he carried her to the house and then around behind it, into the slave quarters.

It was dusk, the hands were in from the fields, families sat in the doorways of their shacks and children played in the dusty lanes, there were the smells of wood smoke and bacon frying and sweat; a woman was singing O let my people go, and from somewhere came the sound of a fiddle and bare feet slapping time on bare boards and someone called her name, Elizabeth, Elizabeth. She walked on. She was no longer a little child in her father's arms, she walked beside him to a cabin set off by itself and he took her hand and led her inside. It was dark except for a small window that flickered like a candle but gradually her eyes became used to the darkness and she could see that there were two cells side by side though only one cell had a door, the cell beside it was open so whomever was inside could come and go. It was the cabin where they put the new slaves, the ones who had trouble adjusting to life on the plantation; the troublemaker was put into the locked cell, and through the day an old man would come and sit in the cell next door, talking to the newcomer and trying to console him, telling him that life was good on the plantation and that he needn't be locked up if only he would conform like the others, the troublemaker kept there until his spirit was broken and he realized that the only way not to be a prisoner of the cell was to become a prisoner of the plantation, realized that the only way to gain his freedom was to give up his independence.

As she stood there the cell door closed behind her and she was alone and frightened and she knelt in the darkness at the window to the open cell next door expecting to see her father's face, expecting to hear him tell her that she must try to be more like everyone else in the world, but instead it was her husband's face beyond the bars, Colin knelt beside her in the light from the candle with tears running down his cheeks. He touched her face with his fingertips and murmured, I'm sorry, Libby, so sorry for everything, but I'm going to make it better now, you'll see, I'm going to change, things are going to be different, they've turned my road engines into tools of destruction but I'm not going to let them get away with it, I'm going to stop them and then everything can get back to normal again, then you and I can be together again the way we used to be, the way we used to be when you first came here, only it will be better now between us, I'll be better now and I won't leave you alone so much, I'll be a good husband I promise you. . . . He bent down to her and kissed her forehead as she lay on the bed, then he was gone again.

She remembered the love she had for him when she first met him, or if it wasn't love, remembered the feeling she thought was love—she supposed it had been respect more than anything else, he was a kind man, a good man, intelligent; her feeling toward him then seemed so meager to her now when she thought of it, when she considered the extent to which he must have loved her—and she remembered the promise of love that the world held for her then, when she was a girl, when she was Elizabeth and not Libby, before there was a Libby. Still lying on the bed, she lifted out of herself again, floated free of her body and rose to the height of the ceiling and looked down at herself, at the middle-aged woman lying in her nightgown curled on her bed in the light of a single candle; she felt compassion for her and yet condemned her too, damned this woman for what she had allowed herself to become, for all too often taking the route of least resistance. She wanted to reach out to the woman, both to embrace her and to shake her out of her complacency, but when she tried to move she drifted across the ceiling to a far corner of the room and slipped through the walls of the house and floated up into the darkness of the night, lifting high above the town and the hills and the river, elated with the movement and the freedom of floating free of the earth and yet terrified as to what would become

of her, terrified that she would continue to lift away into the dark
heavens and join the stars, become lost forever to everything she
held dear, because at the very moment she threatened to float
away she realized that what she most held dear in her life was in
this darkened town below her, a place that she didn't love and
didn't like and where she didn't feel at home and yet was the
closest thing to home that she was going to find in her life now,
that there was love for her here among the only people now who
mattered in her life, her husband and her children and, yes, her
few friends. The hills and valleys spread below her like folds in
black cloth; the few lamps in the little town and the furnaces
along the river glowed like embers on a hearth. She wanted to go
home, home to Sycamore House, and realized there was no reason
to fear that she would float away, the truth was that her spirit
was tethered here, she could see it now that the sky was beginning
to lighten, changing from black to blue-black to blue as a band
of crimson appeared along the eastern edge and the sun cracked
above the rim of the world, there was a silver thread as fine as
spider's silk tying her to the earth, connecting her to this little
valley town below her, a thread that she was spinning from her
navel and that she could retract back into herself if she so desired,
all she had to do was will it. She began to pull herself back to
earth, digesting the silver thread into herself and lowering herself
once again to the little town, the collection of houses along the
dusty tree-lined streets where people were already beginning to
stir as they wakened with the morning, there were wagons along
the main street and workmen heading down the hillside along the
wooden sidewalks to the mills, the buildings and the yards and
the trees on the hillside growing larger as she reeled herself in like
a human kite, back toward the peaked roofs of the solitary house
poking up through the treetops on the slope above the town.
Crows danced attendant upon her in the morning air, cawing
joyously as they winged in circles around her, and someone called

her name as she descended along the silver thread back into her bedroom where Sally sat beside her on the bed holding her head in her lap and stroking her hair, crooning to her, It's all right, Miss Elizabeth, it's all right now, nothing can harm you, Sally's with you now, Sally's always with you. . . .

The sun had cleared the top of the valley rim. The ivy-covered house among the sycamores was awash in strong morning sunlight, though when he turned in the saddle to look back down the hillside, the town was still in shadow. Walker's horse continued its climb. From far below came the shriek of the war engines. As he watched, the two engines bedecked with flags crawled from between the buildings of the steamworks and started slowly up the hill toward the town. The whistles blew repeatedly to announce their coming; people hurried from their houses and stood in the streets to watch. The column of horsemen and wagons that followed the engines out of the steamworks turned along the river toward the bridge at the end of the valley. Walker urged his horse forward, there wasn't much time.

When he reached the house, he rode to the stables and quickly saddled Reid's horse. Then he led both horses around to the front of the house and left them tied to the railing beside the steps while he hurried inside. The house seemed deserted; he looked to see if Sally was in the kitchen—not that he wanted to talk to her, he didn't want to talk to anyone, that wasn't why he came back— but there was no one there. From outside the scream of the war engines below in the town was muffled and far away. The sunlight aimed at the house splintered through the heavy drapes. The clomp of his boot heels shattered the stillness of the downstairs; he didn't try to hide that he was here. He climbed the stairs two at a time and went straight to his room to gather his things. When he came back down the hall, his saddle valise slung over his shoulder, he ignored the closed door at the opposite end. He was ready to start down the stairs when her door opened.

"What's going on?" Libby said, standing in the sunlight that spilled out into the dark hallway. "There's a lot of commotion down in the town."

"It's the steam engines your husband's been working on for us. He asked us to drive them up through town to show everybody." Walker looked away. "We're leaving now."

"That certainly sounds like Colin," Libby smiled wistfully. In the patch of sunlight, her cream-colored morning dress appeared almost buttery. Her sleek black hair had been newly pulled back. "And were you going to leave without saying good-bye?"

"I thought it best. I wasn't sure you'd want to see me." As soon as he said it, he hated himself for it. Just leave it. Just go away.

"If you had left without saying good-bye, I wouldn't have had the chance to give you this."

She went back inside her room. What is she up to? She might do something crazy. In a moment she came down the dark hallway carrying something folded in her arms. She held up the Union cavalry officer's jacket.

"I told you I'd mend it for you. It seems you're going to need it now more than ever."

The bloodstains had been washed out and the cloth carefully rewoven, the bullet hole barely noticeable. She smiled, pleased with her work.

"You shouldn't have gone to so much trouble," he said.

"It was no trouble, Captain. I wanted to." She thought a moment. "I also want to apologize for the things I said to you yesterday about Corporal Vance. There are a lot of things I don't understand about this world. But I do understand that whatever happened when you went after him, you only did what you had to do. I think I know you that well."

Dear exile, you probably know me better than anyone in my life. That's what makes it hard. He looked around the upstairs hall. It was impossible to think that he would never stand here again, that this would be the last time he would see this house. See her.

"You don't have to say anything, Judson."

"No, I want to. I want to tell you that I hope you don't blame yourself for . . . the other night. I mean if you remember anything about the other night. . . ."

"Yes, I remember the other night. Why wouldn't I? I will always remember being with you, it was beautiful, and very important to me."

The image of her curled naked in his arms flashed through his mind. He wanted to hold her now. I've got to get out of here now.

"The only mistake I made," she went on, "was to confuse bodily hunger with spiritual longing. I've learned a number of things about myself from knowing you, Captain Walker. But I think that lesson will be the most lasting."

She looked up at him, her eyes searching his face for something, but it was a different Libby now, different from the Libby who could be coy and inviting, different from the Libby staring into a candle flame in an opium dream; she was the Libby he had seen when he first came here, the one he had talked to on their walk back from the cemetery, the one he had watched holding court during her Tuesday Night Entertainments. This Libby was an intelligent, willful woman with secret strengths; in many ways it was the Libby he liked best. But he knew there would always be too many Libbys for him.

"I'm glad I had the chance to see you before I left," he said. He took one long last look at her and started down the stairs.

"There's something you should know," she said.

He stopped and looked back up at her. She moved forward out of the shadows of the hall into the soft glow coming from the stairs, leaning her weight against the top of the bannister. Juliet in middle age still on her balcony. How can I leave her?

"I think Colin is going to try to stop you from taking the road engines."

"Is he here? Reid is beside himself this morning because Colin disappeared. What's he planning to do?"

"No, he's not here, not now. But he was here earlier. I didn't understand what he was talking about at the time, but I know he said he was going to stop you from taking the engines with you. He said everything would be back to normal then."

"Why are you telling me this?"

"Because I thought you'd want to know."

"No. That's not it at all, is it? You told me because you know that now I'll have to try to stop him." He started on down the steps, then stopped and looked back at her again. Which one of us are you trying to save, Libby? Which of the three of us? She leaned on the bannister, her face blank, impassive, looking down at him with her dark sunken eyes as though she had never seen him before. He felt as though he had never seen her. Walker turned and hurried on down the stairs, heading for the front door when Sally emerged from the shadows of the dining room and grabbed his arm.

"Now you have to kill him, Rider," she hissed, "You should have killed that doctor too when you had the chance but you didn't and now you don't have any choice about Mr. Colin, you have to kill him, you have to, for all he's done to my Miss Elizabeth, for all he's done to Sally."

She burst out laughing, her eyes wild, and she gripped his arm tighter with both hands, her fingers digging into his arm, trying to pull him closer to her, her face reaching up to his as if she were going to kiss or bite him. He thought he would have to hit her to make her let go but George appeared out of the shadows behind her and took hold of her, part embrace, part restraint, loosening her fingers from Walker's arm.

"You go on now, Captain Walker. I'll take care of things. She wasn't always like this, you understand, it's being ripped up from her home that's done it to her. I'll take care of Sally just like I always has, and Miss Elizabeth too. There's nothing to worry about. George is here."

It wasn't the George he knew at all. This man was no servant and no fool; his voice was resonant and strong—Walker realized it was George's voice he heard last night when he talked to Sally in the kitchen, when someone called to prevent him from running upstairs to see Libby. George must have been in the shadows then too, watching over Sally, maybe he had always been there.

I don't understand anything about this house. The distant whistles of the war engines came through the open front door. Walker hurried outside, across the porch and down the steps, to the horses. Ripping off Colin's suit coat as he went and throwing it on the grass, putting on the repaired Union jacket.

The small column of troopers and the half dozen wagons had come to a halt beside the river, on the embankment leading to the bridge. It was a wooden arch-and-truss bridge, forty feet high above the riverbed. The first war engine, with Spider and Fern at the controls, was halfway across the bridge, thick black smoke billowing from its stack; the second engine driven by Reid was a few yards behind. On the hillside people were lined up on the edge of town, still cheering and waving flags. The bunting on Reid's engine had come loose and trailed behind it, a multicolored wake. Walker had just joined Grady at the front of the column when the engines came to a stop and there seemed to be some confusion on the bridge.

"What's the trouble?" Walker said to Grady.

"Don't know, Capt'n. Everything 'twere all right a minute ago."

Walker nodded for him to follow, and the two men left the column and galloped up the rise closer to the bridge. Because of the bend in the river, the embankment was at an angle to the bridge, the deck like a stage in front of them. Reid was motioning frantically and shouting to Spider and Fern, trying to call their attention to something under the bridge deck. At first Walker didn't notice anything; then he saw a man crawling among the wooden trusswork under the deck, working his way along the arch toward the pier. When he made it to the end, Lyle leaped down onto the bank.

"Get him!" Reid shouted, able to see Lyle now as he ran out from under the bridge along the river, heading back toward the town. "Shoot him, he was trying to sabotage the bridge!"

Walker and Grady both drew their carbines but Walker reached over and grabbed Grady's arm. "Wait." Grady looked at him fiercely but Walker ignored him. He stood up in his stirrups and shouted back to the men in the column to hold their fire.

Lyle had hurt himself in the jump from the bridge pier; he stumbled along between the river and the railroad tracks, dragging his leg as he tried to run. He was almost abreast of them, coming along the base of the embankment below where Walker and Grady sat their horses. On the bridge, Reid left the controls of the war engine and unlatched the swivel of the Gatling gun on the rear platform.

"Move the engines!" Walker shouted to him. "Get the engines off the bridge!"

"Kill him! I order you!" Reid shouted back above the noise of the engine.

Reid sighted down the barrel of the Gatling and fired a burst at the figure scuttling along the bank, trying to find the range. Lyle stumbled and fell to his hands and knees in the mud; he was exhausted and stayed there a moment to catch his breath. Reid fired another burst. The reports carried over the water; the bullets thudded into the base of the embankment, plowing a trail in the dirt toward the fallen man before they stopped short. Lyle dragged himself to his feet and staggered on.

"Somebody put the bastard out of his misery," Grady muttered.

Yes. Walker raised the carbine, aimed, and fired. Reid screamed and spun away from the Gatling.

"Holy God!" Grady said, staring at Walker.

"You make your choice, Sergeant," Walker said and headed the roan down the slope toward Lyle.

Reid had pulled himself to his feet, clutching his bleeding shoulder. He leaned over the side of the platform, shouting to the other engine.

"Walker's a traitor! Kill the traitor! Kill him!"

For a moment Spider and Fern didn't know what to do. Then Spider grabbed the Gatling gun on the rear platform and fumbled with the elevation crank. Walker had reached Lyle at the edge of the river. The older man was worn out and badly shaken. Walker reached down to pull Lyle up behind him in the saddle, hoping to make it to the protection of some rocks on the slope. Behind him came a burst of gunfire from the bridge, Spider firing wildly, the bullets sending up a pattern of small fountains out in the water. Walker bent down and got his arm around Lyle's chest but the older man was too weak to help himself and when Walker tried to lift him he pulled the wound in his side, the pain excruciating. A trail of fountains marched toward them across the water as the Gatling began firing again—He's got us now—but they stopped abruptly as Grady fired from the top of the embankment and Spider fell away from the gun.

Fern ran to help Spider and then himself grabbed the crank of the Gatling and Reid had managed to prop himself against the

other gun and was ready to start firing again when the Parson
and the other troopers opened fire and the bridge suddenly
erupted into a column of smoke and flame as an explosion tore
through the underpinnings and the base of the trusses under the
deck. The deck and the two war engines seemed to lift a few feet
momentarily as the bridge and everything under them disappeared, then fell with a roar and the screams of the men into the
shallow river below. Both engines exploded on impact sending
more clouds of smoke and flame and debris billowing skyward,
into the terrible empty space where seconds before there had been
a bridge.

Bits of wood began to fall like rain and the air was full of a
kind of soot. A boot with part of a leg landed in a stand of cattails
at the edge of the water. For several minutes the men were busy
trying to get the horses and mules under control. Lyle stared at
the tangle of machinery and bridge parts lying in the river.

"You okay?" Walker said to him when his horse settled down
again.

"Oh yes. I'm much better now." Lyle blinked and shook his
head like a man waking from a dream. He looked up at Walker;
he seemed giddy with newfound defiance. "And you didn't get
my engines, did you? You didn't get anything here you wanted."

Walker looked at him a moment. "No," he said finally and
spurred the roan back up the embankment.

The men were unnerved; they watched the captain warily as
he regained the top of the slope. Grady rode toward him slowly,
his carbine resting upright against his leg. His face was drawn
and hollow-eyed, as if he had finally seen too much. I know that
look, I see it looking back at me from mirrors. Walker wanted to
say something to him, to thank him and to tell him that he understood, he wanted to say something to all the men, but he knew
it wouldn't do any good and that that wasn't what they needed
most now.

"Sergeant, unhitch those mules and get everything we'll need out of the wagons and loaded on their backs. In a hurry. Make sure every man has three days' rations on him and a hundred rounds of ammunition. And get any of the sick and wounded who want to come with us mounted up—tie them on if you have to."

Grady looked at him as if to say Now what the hell have you got in mind? Then a glimmer of recognition passed across his eyes. He rode back along the column giving orders.

As the men hurried to unhitch the teams and load them with supplies, Walker took a last look at the town. The buildings along the main street and the houses scattered across the hillside, the mills along the river and the green hills of the valley, all seemed strangely removed from him already, as if he had never been here before, as if it were a town he had only heard about or seen in pictures. As if I weren't leaving a part of me here. Leaving can be as final as killing, the deadly part is the other person goes on living without you. Don't kid yourself, old son. Don't make it something it wasn't. I'm not. In the bushes beside the road a mourning dove chanced its first call after the explosions and gunfire; crickets once again chirred in the tall grass of the embankment; on the bluffs across the river the crows began to discuss what had happened. He took his field glasses from their case. Townspeople were streaming down the slope to get a closer look at the remains of the bridge. McArtle's buggy churned up a cloud of dust along the river road as it raced toward Lyle. On the hillside above the town the Lyles' carriage hurried down the road from Sycamore House. Good-bye, Libby. Then, scanning the hills farther up the valley, he spotted a column of cavalry approaching the opposite end of town. He pulled the roan's head around.

"That's it, men. We got visitors coming. We go with what we have."

"I will fly on the wings of gladness, O Lord," the Parson said, tying a last bag of flour onto one of the mules. "Just deliver me out of this Yankee hellhole."

Grady jumped down from the back of a wagon and mounted his horse again. "Parson, I want you up front with me."

"You got the sudden need of religion, Sergeant?" the Parson said.

"There be enough trouble ahead of us. 'Twere no man that's aimed a gun at me going to ride behind me." Grady stopped and grinned at him, then grabbed the reins of one of the pack mules and headed forward along the column.

When the men were mounted and the pack mules all in tow, Walker galloped to the head of the column where Grady and the Parson were waiting for him.

Walker and Grady nodded to each other. No other words necessary.

"Amen, brothers," said the Parson.

Walker stood in the stirrups to check on his men one more time, then led the way on up the rise, past where the bridge used to be, past the twisted metal lying in the river, and down the other side toward the mouth of the Allehela—a few of the troopers let out Rebel yells when they realized where they were going, but Walker's face remained set in grim determination—across the railroad tracks beyond the end of the valley and down the bank to the Ohio River, water splashing up in rainbows from the horses' hooves as they began the crossing, heading south.

Acknowledgments

There are four people—friends, actually; dream catchers—without whom I could never have brought these books to publication:

Barbara Clark
Kim Francis
Dave Meek
Jack Ritchie

I also thank Eileen Chetti for struggling through my quirks of style and punctuation; Linnea Duly for writing a study guide; Aimee Downing for her patience with all my questions about self-publishing; and Bob Gelston, who is always around to answer questions and take on anything else that's needed. And then, of course, there's my wife Marty. . . .

Richard Snodgrass lives in Pittsburgh, PA with his wife Marty and two indomitable female tuxedo cats, raised from feral kittens, named Frankie and Becca.

To read more about the Furnass series, the town of Furnass, and special features for *Across the River*—including a Reader's Study Guide, author interviews, and omitted scenes—go to www.RichardSnodgrass.com.